STAR WARS®
REPUBLIC COMMANDO™
TRUE COLORS

By Karen Traviss

CITY OF PEARL
CROSSING THE LINE
THE WORLD BEFORE
MATRIARCH
ALLY

STAR WARS: REPUBLIC COMMANDO: HARD CONTACT
STAR WARS: REPUBLIC COMMANDO: TRIPLE ZERO
STAR WARS: REPUBLIC COMMANDO: TRUE COLORS

STAR WARS: LEGACY OF THE FORCE: BLOODLINES
STAR WARS: LEGACY OF THE FORCE: SACRIFICE

STAR WARS

REPUBLIC COMMANDO™
TRUE COLORS

KAREN TRAVISS

BALLANTINE BOOKS • NEW YORK

Star Wars: Republic Commando: True Colors is a work of fiction. Names, places, and incidents either are products of the author's imagination or are used fictitiously. Any resemblance to actual events, locales, or persons, living or dead, is entirely coincidental.

A Del Rey Mass Market Original

Copyright © 2007 by Lucasfilm Ltd. & ® or ™ where indicated. All rights reserved. Used under authorization.

Excerpt from *Star Wars: Death Star* copyright © 2007 by Lucasfilm Ltd. & ® or ™ where indicated. All rights reserved. Used under authorization.

Published in the United States by Del Rey Books, an imprint of The Random House Publishing Group, a division of Random House, Inc., New York.

DEL REY is a registered trademark and the Del Rey colophon is a trademark of Random House, Inc.

The story "*Star Wars:* Republic Commando: Odds" by Karen Traviss first appeared in *Star Wars Insider* Issue 87, in 2006. "*Star Wars:* Republic Commando: Odds" copyright © 2006 by Lucasfilm Ltd. & ® or ™ where indicated. All rights reserved. Used under authorization.

This book contains an excerpt from the hardcover edition of *Star Wars: Death Star* by Michael Reaves and Steve Perry. This excerpt has been set for this edition only and may not reflect the final content of the hardcover edition.

ISBN 978-0-345-49800-7

Printed in the United States of America

www.starwars.com
www.lucasarts.com
www.delreybooks.com

OPM 9 8 7 6 5 4 3 2 1

For Christian Stafford, TC 1219, 501st Legion,
who left this world aged eight, March 6, 2005,
and whose courage continues to inspire us all.
Nu kyr'adyc, shi taab'echaaj'la:
not gone, merely marching far away.

ACKNOWLEDGMENTS

My grateful thanks go to editors Keith Clayton (Del Rey) and Sue Rostoni (Lucasfilm); my agent Russ Galen; the LucasArts *Republic Commando* game team; Bryan Boult and Jim Gilmer—insightful first readers; Mike Krahulik and Jerry Holkins of Penny Arcade, for bestowing coolness and feeding me; Ray Ramirez (Co. A 2BN 108th Infantry snipers, ARNG), for technical advice and generous friendship; Officer Antony Serena, Los Angeles County Sheriff's Department, for outstanding starship procurement; Lance and Joanne, of the 501st Dune Sea Garrison, for practical and inspirational armor expertise; Wade Scrogham, for reliable intel; Sam Burns, for input of solid common sense; and all my good friends in the 501st Legion.

And in this twenty-fifth anniversary year of the Falklands war, my special thanks go to all the veterans of that conflict who've shared their experiences with me in the intervening years.

THE STAR WARS NOVELS TIMELINE

DRAMATIS PERSONAE

Republic commandos:
  Omega Squad:
    RC-1309 NINER
    RC-1136 DARMAN
    RC-8015 FI
    RC-3222 ATIN
  Delta Squad:
    RC-1138 BOSS
    RC-1262 SCORCH
    RC-1140 FIXER
    RC-1207 SEV
Clone trooper CT-5108/8843 CORR
Clone commander CC-3388/0021 LEVET
General BARDAN JUSIK, Jedi Knight (male human)
Sergeant KAL SKIRATA, Mandalorian mercenary (male human)
Sergeant WALON VAU, Mandalorian mercenary (male human)
Captain JALLER OBRIM, Coruscant Security Force (male human)
General ETAIN TUR-MUKAN, Jedi Knight (female human)
JINART, Qiiluran spy (female Gurlanin)
General ARLIGAN ZEY, Jedi Master (male human)
RAV BRALOR, Mandalorian bounty hunter (female human)
Null ARC troopers:
  N-7 MEREEL

N-10 JAING
N-11 ORDO
N-12 A'DEN
ARC trooper Captain A-26, MAZE
ARC trooper A-30, SULL
Agent BESANY WENNEN, Republic Treasury investigator
    (human female)

PROLOGUE

Mygeeto, Outer Rim, the vaults of the Dressian Kiolsh
Merchant Bank, 470 days after the Battle of Geonosis

We're running out of time.

We're running out of time, *all* of us.

"Sarge . . ." Scorch looks at the security locks on the strong-room hatch with the appraising eye of an expert at breaking the unbreakable. That's how I trained him: he's the best. "Sarge, we got what we came for. Why are we robbing a bank?"

"*You're* not robbing it. *I'm* robbing it. You're just opening a door." This is about justice. And relieving Separatists of their wealth stops them from spending it on armaments, after all. "And I'm a civilian now."

It doesn't feel like it. Delta are still my squad. I won't go as far as Kal Skirata and call them my boys, but . . . boys they are.

Scorch is about twelve years old. He's also twenty-four, measured in how far along that path to death he actually is, which is the only definition I care about. He's running out of time faster than me. The Kaminoans designed the Republic's clone commandos to age fast, and when I think of them as the tiny kids I first knew, it's heartbreaking—yes, even for me. My father didn't quite kill the last bit of feeling in me.

Scorch places circuit disrupters against the locks spaced around the door frame, one by one, to fry the systems and create a bogus signal that convinces the alarm there's nothing out of order. He freezes for a moment, head cocked, reading the display on his helmet's head-up display.

"What's in there, Sarge?"

I'm not robbing for gain. I'm not a greedy man. I just want *justice*. See? My Mandalorian armor's black—black, the traditional color of justice. *Beskar'gam* colors almost always have meaning. Every *Mando* who sees me understands my mission in life right away.

"Part of my inheritance," I say. "Father and I didn't agree on my career plans."

Justice for me; justice for the clone troops, used up and thrown away like flimsi napkins.

"The drinks are on you, then," says Boss, Delta's sergeant. "If we'd known you were loaded, we'd have hit you up earlier."

"*Was* loaded. Cut off without a tin cred."

I've never told them about my family or my title. I think the only person I told was Kal, and then I got the full blast of his class-war rhetoric.

Sev, Delta's sniper—silent, which might mean disapproval, or it might not—trains his DC-17 rifle on the deserted corridors leading from the labyrinth of vaults and storerooms that hold the wealth and secrets of the galaxy's richest and most powerful, including my family.

Fierfek, it's *quiet* down here. The corridors aren't made of ice, but they're smooth and white, and I can't shake the impression that they're carved straight out of this frozen planet itself. It makes the place feel ten degrees colder.

"In *three*," says Scorch. "But I'd *still* prefer a nice big bang. Three, two . . . one." I know he's grinning, helmet or not. *"Boom. Clatter. Tinkle."*

The locks yield silently and open in a sequence: *clack, clack, clack.* No alarms, no theft countermeasures to take our heads off, no guards rushing in with blasters. The vault doors roll back to reveal row upon row of polished durasteel deposit boxes lit by a sickly green light. Inside, two security droids stand immobile, circuits disrupted along with every lock in here, weapon arms slack at their sides.

"Well?" Fixer asks on the comlink. He's up on the surface a kilometer away, minding the snowspeeder we'll use to exfiltrate from Mygeeto. He'll get the icon views from all our helmet systems, but he's impatient. "What's in there?"

"The future," I tell him. His future, too, I hope.

When I touch the deposit box doors, they swing open and their contents glitter, or rustle, or . . . smell odd. It's quite a collection. Boss wanders in and fishes out a small giltframed portrait that hasn't seen the light of day for . . . well, who knows? The three commandos stare at it for a moment.

"What a waste of creds." Scorch, who's never expressed a desire for anything beyond a decent meal and more sleep, checks the droids, prodding them with the probe anchored to his belt. "You've got until the next patrol to clear out what you need, Sarge. Better hurry."

As I said, we're all running out of time, some of us faster than others. Time's the one thing you can't buy, bribe or steal when you need more.

"Go on, get out of here." I walk down the corridor lined with unimaginably excessive wealth: rare precious metals, untraceable credit chips, priceless jewels, antiques, industrial secrets, blackmail material. Ordinary credits aren't the only things that make the galaxy rotate. The Vau family box is in here. "I said *dismiss,* Delta."

Boss stands his ground. "You can't carry it all on your own."

"I can carry *enough.*" I can haul a fifty-kilo pack all right, maybe not as easily as young men like them, but I'm motivated, and that shaves years off my age. "Dismissed. Thin out. *Now.* This is my problem, not yours."

There's a lot of stuff in here. It's going to take longer than I thought.

Time. You just can't buy it. So you have to grab it any way you can.

I'll start by grabbing *this.*

1

*Look, all I know is this. The Seps can't have as many droids
as Intel says—we've seen that when we've sabotaged their
factories. And if they have gazillions of them somewhere,
why not overrun the whole Republic now and get it over
with? Come to that, why won't the Chancellor listen to the
generals and just smash the key Sep targets instead of
dragging this war out, spreading us thin from Core to Rim?
Add that garbage to the message Lama Su sent him griping
about the clone contract expiring in a couple of years—it
all stinks. And when it stinks that bad, we get ready to run,
because it's our* shebse *on the line here. Understand?*
—Sergeant Kal Skirata to the Null ARCs, discussing the
future in light of new intelligence gathered during their
unauthorized infiltration of Tipoca City, 462 days after
Geonosis

Republic fleet auxilliary *Core Conveyor,* en route for Mirial,
2nd Airborne (212th Battalion) and Omega Squad embarked,
470 days after Geonosis

"**N**ice of you to join us, Omega," said Sergeant Barlex, one
hand wrapped around the grab rail in the ship's hangar. "And
may I be the first to say that you look like a bunch of complete prats?"

Darman waited for Niner to tell Barlex where to shove his
opinion, but he didn't take the bait and carried on adjusting
the unfamiliar winged jet pack. It was just the usual bravado
that went with being scared and hyped up for a mission.

Okay, so the sky troopers' standard pack didn't fit comfortably on Republic commando Katarn armor, but for accuracy of insertion it still beat paragliding. Darman had vivid and painful memories of a low-opening emergency jump on Qiilura that hadn't been on target, unless you counted trees. So he was fine with a pair of white wings—even if they were the worst bolt-on goody in the history of procurement in the Grand Army of the Republic.

Fi activated his wing mechanism, and the two blades swung into horizontal position with a hiss of hydraulics, nearly smacking Barlex in the face. Fi smiled and flapped his arms. "Want to see my impression of a Geonosian?"

"What, plummeting to the ground in a spray of bug-splatter after I put a round through you?" said Barlex.

"You're so *masterful*."

"I'm so a *sergeant,* Private—"

"Couldn't you at least get us matte-black ones?" Fi asked. "I don't want to plunge to my doom with uncoordinated accessories. People will talk."

"You'll have white, and *like* it." Barlex was the senior NCO of Parjai Squad, airborne troops with a reputation for high-risk missions that Captain Ordo called "assertive outreach." The novelty of supporting special forces had clearly worn off. Barlex pushed Fi's flight blades back into the closed position and maintained a scowl. "Anyway, I thought you bunch were born-again Mandalorians. Jet packs should make you feel right at home."

"Off for caf and cakes afterward?"

Barlex was still unsmiling granite. "Orders are to drop extra matériel and other useless ballast, meaning you, and then shorten our survival odds again by popping in for a chat with the Seps on Mirial."

Fi did his wounded concern act, hands clasped under his chin. "Is it the *Mando* thing that's coming between us, dear?"

"Just my appreciation of the irony that we're fighting *Mando* mercenaries in some places."

"I'd better keep you away from Sergeant Kal, then . . ."

"Yeah, you do that," said Barlex. "I lost ten brothers thanks to them."

Clone troopers might have been able to sing "Vode An," but it was clear that the proud Mandalorian heritage hadn't quite percolated through *all* the ranks. Darman decided not to tell Skirata. He'd be mortified. He wanted all Jango Fett's clones to have their souls saved for the *manda* by some awareness of the only fragile roots they had. Barlex's hostility would break his heart.

The compartment went quiet. Darman flexed his shoulders, wondering how Geonosians coped with wings: did they sleep on their backs, or hang like hawk-bats, or what? He'd only ever seen the bugs moving or dead, so it remained another unanswered question. He had a lot of those. Niner, ever alert to the mood of his squad, walked around each of them and checked the makeshift securing straps, yanking hard on the harness that looped between Fi's legs. Fi yelped.

Niner gave Fi that three-beat silent stare, just like Skirata. "Don't want anything falling off, do we, son?"

"No, Sarge. Not before I've had a chance to try it out, anyway."

Niner continued the stare for a little longer. "Sitrep briefing in ten, then." He indicated the hatch and inspected the interior of his helmet. "Let's not keep General Zey waiting."

Barlex stood silent as if he was working up to telling them something, then shrugged and took Niner's indication that what was to follow wasn't for his ears. Darman did what he always did before an insertion: he settled in a corner to recheck his suit calibration. Atin inspected Fi's jet pack clips with a critical frown.

"I could *knit* better attachments than these," he muttered.

"Do you think you could try cheery and upbeat sometime, *At'ika*?" Fi asked.

Niner joined in the inspection ritual. It was all displacement activity, but nobody could ever accuse Omega Squad of leaving things to chance. "All it has to do is stay attached to Fi until he lands," he said.

Fi nodded. "That would be nice."

Atin set the encrypted holoreceiver he had been holding on a bulkhead ledge and locked the compartment hatches. Darman couldn't imagine any clone trooper being a security risk, and wondered if they were offended by being shut out of Spec Ops briefings as if they were civilians. But they seemed to take it as routine, apparently uncurious and un-complaining, because that was the way they'd been trained since birth: they had their role, and the Republic commandos had theirs. That was what the Kaminoans had told them, any-way.

But it wasn't entirely true. Trooper Corr, last surviving man of his whole company, was now on SO Brigade strength and seemed to be enjoying himself charging around the galaxy with the Null ARCs. He was becoming quite a double act with Lieutenant Mereel; they shared a taste for the finer points of booby traps. They also enjoyed exploring the social scene, as Skirata put it, of every city they happened to pass through.

Corr fits in just fine. I bet they all can, given the chance and the training.

Darman slipped on his helmet and retreated into his own world, comlinks closed except for the priority override that would let the squad break into the circuit and alert him. If he let his mind drift, the scrolling light display of his HUD blurred and became the nightscape of Coruscant, and he could immerse himself in the precious memory of those brief and illicit days in the city with Etain. Sometimes he felt as if she were standing behind him, a feeling so powerful that he'd look over his shoulder to check. Now he recognized the sensation for what it was: not his imagination or longing, but a Jedi—*his* Jedi—reaching out in the Force to him.

She's General Tur-Mukan. You're well out of line, soldier.

He felt her touch now, just the fleeting awareness of some-one right next to him. He couldn't reach back: he just hoped that however the Force worked, it let her know that he knew she was thinking of him. But why did the Force speak to so few beings, if it was universal? Darman felt a pang of mild resentment. The Force was another aspect of life that was closed to him, but at least that was true for pretty well everyone. It didn't bother him anywhere near as much as the dawning realization that he didn't have what most others did: a little choice.

He'd once asked Etain what would happen to the clone troops when the war was over—when they *won*. He couldn't think about losing. Where would they go? How would they be rewarded? She didn't know. The fact that he didn't know, either, fed a growing uneasiness.

Maybe the Senate hasn't thought that far ahead.

Fi turned to pick up his helmet and started calibrating the display, the expression on his face distracted and not at all happy. This was Fi unguarded: not funny, not wisecracking, and alone with his thoughts. Darman's helmet let him observe his brother without provoking a response. Fi had changed, and it had happened during the operation on Coruscant. Darman felt Fi was preoccupied by something the rest of them couldn't see, like a hallucination you'd never tell anyone about because you thought you were going crazy. Or maybe you were afraid nobody else would admit to it. Darman had a feeling he knew what it was, so he never talked about Etain, and Atin never went on about Laseema. It wasn't fair to Fi.

The *Core Conveyor*'s drives had a very soothing frequency. Darman settled into that light doze where he was still conscious but his thoughts rambled free of his control.

Yes, Coruscant was the problem. It had given them all a glimpse into a parallel universe where people lived normal lives. Darman was smart enough to realize that his own life wasn't normal—that he'd been *bred* to fight, nothing else—but his gut said something else entirely: that it wasn't right or fair.

He'd have volunteered, he was sure of that. They wouldn't have had to force him. All he wanted at the end of it was some time with Etain. He didn't know what else life had to offer, but he knew there was a lot of it he would never live to see. He'd been alive for eleven standard years, coming up on twelve. He was twenty-three or twenty-four, the manual said. It wasn't time enough to live.

Sergeant Kal said we'd been robbed.

Fierfek, I hope Etain can't feel me getting angry.

"I wish I could sit there and just relax like you, Dar," Atin said. "How'd you get to be so calm? You didn't learn it from Kal, that's for sure."

There's just Sergeant Kal and Etain and my brothers. Oh, and Jusik. General Jusik's one of us. Nobody else really cares.

"I've got a clean conscience," Darman said. It had come as a surprise to him after years of cloistered training on Kamino to discover that many cultures in the galaxy regarded him as a killer, something immoral. "Either that, or I'm too tired to worry."

Now he was going to Gaftikar to do some more killing. The Alpha ARCs might have been sent in to train the local rebels, but Omega were being inserted to topple a government. It wasn't the first, and it probably wouldn't be the last.

"Heads up, people, here we go." Niner activated the receiver. The blue holoimage leapt from the projector and burly, bearded Jedi General Arligan Zey, Director of Special Forces, was suddenly sitting in the compartment with them.

"Good afternoon, Omega," he said. It was the middle of the night as far as they were concerned. "I've got a little good news for you."

Fi was back on the secure helmet comlink now. Darman's red HUD audio icon indicated that only he could hear him. "Which means the rest of it is bad."

"That's good, sir," said Niner, deadpan. "Have we located ARC Alpha-Thirty?"

Zey seemed to ignore the question. "Null Sergeant A'den's sent secure drop zone coordinates, and you're clear to go in."

Fi's comlink popped in Darman's ear again. "Here comes the *but.*"

"But," Zey went on, "ARC Trooper Alpha-Thirty now has to be treated as MIA. He hasn't reported in for two months, and that isn't unusual, but the local resistance told Sergeant A'den that they lost contact about the same time."

A'den was one of Skirata's Null ARCs. He'd been sent in a few standard days ago to assess the situation, and if he couldn't find the missing ARC trooper, then the man was definitely lost, as in *dead* lost. Darman wondered what could possibly have happened to an ARC. They weren't exactly easy kills. The Nulls treated their Alpha brothers as knuckle-draggers, but they were pure Jango Fett, genetically unaltered except for their rapid aging, and they'd been trained by him personally: hard, resourceful, dangerous men. Still, even the best could have bad luck. It meant that training and motivating the Gaftikari resistance was down to A'den now.

Darman hoped it didn't end up being his job. All he could think about was how long he'd be stuck there and when he might see Etain again. Smuggled letters and comlink signals weren't enough.

So what can they do to us? So what if anyone finds out?

Darman didn't really know how hard the Grand Army or the Jedi Council could make life for him or Etain. There was always the chance that he'd never see her again. He wasn't sure he could handle that. He knew she was his only taste of a real life.

"So are we starting over, General?" Niner asked.

Zey's desk wasn't visible in the holoimage but he was sitting down, and he glanced over his shoulder as if someone had come into the room. "Not entirely. The rebel militias are competent, but they still need some help in destabilizing the Gaftikari government. And they need equipment like the Deeces we're dropping." Zey paused. "Not full spec, of course."

"I see we trust them implicitly, sir . . ."

"We've had one or two aid operations backfire, Sergeant, I admit that. No point overarming them so they can turn around and use the kit on us. This does the job."

"Any general intel update on Gaftikar?"

"No. Sorry. You'll have to fill in the gaps yourself."

"Numbers?"

"A'den says around a hundred thousand *trained* rebel troops."

Darman blinked to activate his HUD database and checked the estimated population of Gaftikar. Half a billion: capital city Eyat, population five hundred thousand. He was used to odds like that now.

"Well, at least Alpha-Thirty was busy while he was there, sir," said Niner.

"The rebels are very good at cascading training. Train ten—they train ten each—and so on."

"Given our limited numbers, sir, have you ever thought about deploying the whole GAR that way? The war would be over a lot faster."

"It's a strategy, I know . . ." Zey always had that note in his voice lately that made him sound ashamed and embarrassed. Nobody had to ask if this was how he wanted to play things. It was another objective from the Chancellor on the list of take-this-planet-and-don't-give-me-excuses orders. "But all you need to do is remove the leadership of the Eyat administration, and the rest follows. So you prepare the battleground for the infantry. Enable the rebels."

Do what you can, lads, because I can't spare any more men to help you. Great . . .

"Understood," said Niner. Sometimes Darman wanted to ram his sergeant's patient acceptance down his throat. "Omega out."

Nobody needed to remind Zey how thinly spread all the GAR forces were, especially Special Operations. They were cross-training regular troopers for commando roles now: the GAR had fewer than five thousand Republic commandos. *Inadequate* didn't even come close. It was a joke. Darman waited for Niner to sign off with a surprisingly perfunctory salute and close the link, and that wasn't good old gung-ho Niner at all. It was the closest he'd ever come to showing his frustration to the squad.

Maybe the Republic would have been better off with droids after all. They don't get hacked off about what's happening to them.

And they don't fall in love.

"I'll try to look on the bright side, seeing as that's my job," said Fi. "Last time we inserted into enemy territory without any decent intel and with *totally* inadequate numbers, we made lots of interesting new friends. Maybe I'll be the one to get lucky this time."

Darman ignored the gibe about Etain. "The Gaftikari rebels aren't your type, Fi. They're lizards."

"So are Falleen."

"I mean *lizard* lizards. Luggage on legs."

"They've got a human population, too . . ."

"Optimist."

Niner changed the subject with uncharacteristic gentleness. "Come on, we always insert without enough intel." He hadn't told Fi to shut up in ages, as if he felt sorry for him now. "It's the way the world works. Okay, buckets on. We'll be over Eyat in twenty minutes."

The *Core Conveyor*'s cargo hangar was a stark void with a ramped air lock at one end. It was an armed freighter, one of many commandeered from the merchant fleet—taken up from trade, and so nicknamed TUFTies—and it was built simply to move vehicles and supplies, and sometimes men, and unload them discreetly where required. Darman wondered what its cargo had been in peacetime. Like the small traffic interdiction vessels, it masqueraded as a neutral civilian craft for covert operations. TUFTies could be deployed on planets where the arrival of an Acclamator would get the wrong sort of attention.

The hangar was packed with speeder bikes and crates. Darman picked his way through them, following Atin to the hangar doors where a loadmaster in yellow-trimmed pilot armor minus helmet steered crates on repulsors toward the ramp and lined them up.

"Deeces," said the loadmaster, not looking up from his datapad. "And a few E-Webs and one large arty piece."

"How many 'Webs?" Atin asked.

"Fifty."

"Is that the best we can do?"

"We've been arming them for a year. Just a top-up." The loadmaster seemed satisfied that he had the correct consignments and stared at the commandos with a wary eye. He reached for the rail that ran along the bulkhead and hooked his safety line to it. "If it's any comfort, you look pretty sinister in that black rig. Even with the white wings. I don't think you're a bunch of overrated Mando-loving weirdos at all . . ."

Fi gave him a bow. "May all your future deployments be with the Galactic Marines on 'fresher detail, *ner vod*."

But Atin could never pass things off with a joke. "What's your problem, pal?"

"Just wondering," said the loadmaster.

"Wondering *what*?"

"Mandos. You ever fought those guys? I have. They keep popping up in Sep forces. They kill us. And you were raised as good little *Mando* boys. Is that who you feel you are?"

"Let's put it this way," said Fi. "I don't feel like a Republic citizen, because none of us are, in case you hadn't noticed. We don't exist. No vote, no identification docs, no rights."

Niner shoved Fi in the back. "One-Five, shut it. Loadmaster, wind your neck in and don't question our loyalty, or I'll have to smack you. Now let's get to work."

It was the first time that Darman could recall the sense of brotherhood among clones—all clones, regardless of unit—faltering. The 2nd Airborne obviously had an issue with Mandalorians, and maybe the nearest they could kick were the Republic commandos—raised, trained, and educated mostly by Mandalorian sergeants like Skirata, Vau, and Bralor. He thought it was a bad omen for the mission. Yes, Sergeant Kal would be very upset to see this.

Core Conveyor was low enough now for them to see the landscape beneath from one of the viewports. Darman could see from his HUD icon of Niner's field of view that he wasn't looking at the drop zone but was engrossed in his datapad. It was just a mass of numbers. Atin, though, was reading a message, and although Darman tried not to be nosy he couldn't help but notice that it was from Laseema, his Twi'lek girlfriend, and it was . . . *educational.*

They do say it's the quiet ones that want watching . . .

Darman tried to concentrate on Gaftikar. It looked like a nice place even at night. It wasn't a red, dusty wasteland like Geonosis, or a freezing wilderness like Fest. From this height, the city of Eyat was a mosaic of illuminated parkland and busy, straight roads fringed by regularly spaced houses speckled with gold light. A river wandered through the landscape, visible as a black glittering ribbon. It looked like the kind of place where people had normal lives and enjoyed themselves. It didn't look like enemy territory at all.

Darman cut into Fi's personal circuit to speak but was instantly deafened by the volume of the glimmik music. That was how Fi dealt with things: a thick wall of noise and chatter to shut out the next moment. Darman cut out of the circuit again.

The loadmaster lowered his visor and placed his hand over the control panel. "Okay, remember—just let yourselves drop like a normal parasail jump for a few seconds, then activate the jets. Don't power out. Opening in five . . . four . . ."

"I'd rather know if the jet pack didn't work when I still had my boots on the deck," Fi said.

". . . two . . . and . . . *go.*"

The cargo doors slid back and a fierce blast of air peppered dust against Darman's visor. The charts were over thick forest now; the loadmaster had one hand on the cargo release and his head turned toward the holochart projected on the control panel. It showed open land a few kilometers ahead. When *Conveyor* overflew it, the open space turned out to be short, dry grass. It showed up clearly in Darman's night-vision filter.

"Kit away," said the loadmaster, releasing the static lines. The crates slipped off the ramp one by one and glided toward the land on extraction parasails that looked like exotic white blooms opening in the night. The last container dwindled to a speck beneath them, hitting the grass in a plume of dust.

The ship climbed a little, and the ramp raised to a flat platform. "This is your stop, Omega. Stay safe, okay?"

Darman, like all the commandos, had done plenty of freefall jumps. He couldn't even recall how many, but he still felt a brief burst of adrenaline as he watched Atin walk calmly off the end of the ramp and vanish. Darman followed him, gripping his DC-17 flat against his chest on its sling.

One, two, three, four paces, and then *five*—on five, there was nothing beneath the soles of his boots. He fell and his stomach seemed to collide with his lungs, forcing the breath out of them for a heartbeat. He hit the jet-pack power button on his harness on the count of three. The wings ejected from their housing: the motor kicked in. He wasn't falling any longer. He was flying, with the faint vibration of the jets making his sinuses itch. The green-lit image of Gaftikar's heathland spread beneath him, and when he turned his head he could see the faint heat profile from Atin's jets. *Conveyor* was gone. The crate had a lot more acceleration than he'd thought.

"Look, Ma," said Fi's disembodied voice on the secure channel. "No hands."

"You haven't got a ma," said Darman.

"Maybe a nice old lady will adopt me. I'm very lovable."

Darman couldn't see the others now, only their viewpoint icons on his helmet's HUD. The squad split up, each man following a different flight path to the RV point, dropping as low as they could and hugging the contours of the land. The plan was to hit the ground running—literally—as soon as the terrain changed to woods they could use for cover. Darman didn't make quite the clean landing he'd expected. He somersaulted on the tip of one wing, coming to rest in low scrubby bushes.

Niner must have seen his HUD icon. "Can't you ever land on your feet, Dar?"

"Osik." Darman was more embarrassed than hurt. At least he hadn't set fire to the vegetation: the jets shut off on impact. He scrambled to his feet and reoriented himself. "I'm okay."

He couldn't tell where Fi and Atin were from the view in their HUD icons. But he could see they were moving fast, and their transponders were converging on the RV coordinates, blue squares edging toward a yellow cross superimposed on a chart of the drop zone. He realized he still had fifty meters to run with the jet pack, wings spread like an insect.

"All clear." Niner grunted as if he was struggling out of his harness. "Short-range comms only from now on, Omega. Now where—"

"Y'know, on Urun Five, the locals would stick you on top of a festival tree as a decoration."

An unfamiliar voice cut into Darman's comm circuit. Now he could see a shape in his night vision, a faint outline that didn't resolve into a man until he was right on top of it. He could see who it was now, a man who looked pretty much like himself except that, like all the Nulls, he was broader and heavier. The Kaminoans had played around with the Fett genome a little too much at first. Darman wondered how many other experiments they tried before they got the mix right.

A'den, Null ARC N-12, grabbed him by the arm and beckoned him to follow. He was wearing rough working clothes: no helmet, no plates, and no distinctive kilt-like *kama*. Darman hadn't been expecting to find him in civvies.

And as he picked his way through the undergrowth, cursing the stupid wings that now wouldn't retract because he'd bent the mechanism in the fall, he also didn't expect to see small fast-moving figures with bright reflective eyes emerging with DC-15 rifles.

They were *lizard* lizards, all right.

GAR base, Teklet, Qiilura, 470 days after Geonosis, deadline for the withdrawal of human colonists

General Etain Tur-Mukan had never felt less like doing a day's duty in her life. But she *would* do it. She had to.

Outside the army headquarters building—a modest house that had once belonged to a Trandoshan slaver, now long gone with the rest of the occupying Separatist forces—a crowd of farmers stood in grim silence. She paused in front of the doors and prepared to step outside to reason with them.

You have to leave. It's the deal we did, remember?

"I don't think you should handle this, ma'am," said the garrison's commander, Levet. His yellow-trimmed helmet was tucked under one arm; a fit, clean-shaven, black-haired man in his twenties, so much like Darman that it hurt. "Let me talk to them."

He was a clone, like Dar—*exactly* like Dar, exactly like every other clone in the Grand Army of the Republic, although without Dar's permanent expression of patient good humor. He had those same dark eyes that gave Etain a pang of loneliness and yearning at the constant reminder that Dar was . . . where? At that moment, she had no idea. She could feel him in the Force, as she always could, and he was unharmed. That was all she knew. She made a mental note to contact Ordo later to check his location.

"Ma'am," said Levet, a little more loudly. "Are you all right? I said *I'll do this.*"

Etain made a conscious effort to stop seeing Darman in Levet's face. "Responsibility of rank, Commander." Behind her, she heard a faint silken rustle like an animal moving. "But thank you."

"You need to be careful," said a low, liquid voice. "Or we'll have your nasty little sergeant to answer to."

Jinart brushed past Etain's legs. The Gurlanin shapeshifter was in her true form of a sleek black carnivore, but she could just as easily have transformed herself into the exact replica of Levet—or Etain.

Nasty little sergeant. Sergeant Kal Skirata—short, ferocious, angry—had exiled her here for a few months. She'd fallen from grace with him. Now that she was several months' pregnant, she'd started to understand why.

"I'm *being* careful," Etain said.

"He holds me responsible for your safety."

"You're scared of him, aren't you?"

"And so are *you,* girl."

Etain draped her brown robes carefully to disguise the growing bulge of pregnancy and pulled another loose coat on top. Teklet was in the grip of winter, which was just as well: the excuse for voluminous clothes was welcome. But even without the top layer, she didn't look conspicuously pregnant. She just *felt* it, tired and lonely.

Nobody here would know or care who the father was anyway.

"There's no need for you to supervise the evacuation personally," said Jinart. "The fewer who see you, the better. Don't tempt fate."

Etain ignored her and the doors parted, letting a snow-speckled gust of cold air into the lobby. Jinart shot out in front of her like a sand panther and bounded through the drifts.

"Insanity," the Gurlanin hissed. She progressed in flowing leaps. "You have a *child* to worry about."

"My son," Etain said, "is fine. And I'm not ill, I'm *pregnant.*"

And she owed her troops. She owed them like she owed Darman, RC-1136, whose last letter—a real letter, written on flimsi in a precise, disciplined hand, a mix of gossip about his squad and little longings for time with her—was sueded with constant reading and refolding, and kept safe inside her tunic, not in her belt. The snow crunched under her boots as she waded to the road cut through the drifts by constant traffic. It was a brilliantly sunny day, blindingly bright, a lovely day for a walk if this had been a normal life and she had been an ordinary woman.

It's hard not to tell him. It's hard not to mention the baby when he asks how I am. His baby.

But Skirata forbade her to tell him. She almost understood why.

Jinart continued her progression of controlled leaps. She probably hunted that way, Etain thought, pouncing on small animals burrowed deep in the snow. "Skirata will be furious if you miscarry."

Maybe not. He was angry enough when he found out I was pregnant. "I'm not going risk upsetting Kal. You know the politics of this."

"I know he means what he says. He'll have a warship reduce Qiilura to molten slag if I cross him."

Yes, he would. Etain believed him, too. Skirata would rip a hole in the galaxy if it improved the lot of the clone troops in his care. "Just under three months, and then I won't be your problem any longer."

"Local months or Galactic Standard months?"

Etain still felt queasy each morning. "Who cares? Does it matter?"

"What *would* your Jedi Masters do to you for consorting with a soldier?"

"Kick me out of the Order, probably."

"You fear such trivial things. *Let* them."

"If they kick me out," Etain whispered, "I have to surrender my command. But I have to stay with my troops. I can't sit out this war while they fight, Jinart. Don't you understand that?"

The Gurlanin snorted, leaving little clouds of breath on the icy air. "To deliberately bring a child into this galaxy during a war, to have to keep it hidden and then hand it over to that—"

Etain held up her hand for silence. "Oh, so you and Kal have been talking, have you? I know. I was mad and selfish and irresponsible. I shouldn't have taken advantage of Dar's naïveté. Go ahead. You won't be saying anything that Kal didn't, just minus the *Mando'a* abuse."

"How can he possibly raise the child for you? That mercenary? That *killer*?"

"He's raised his own, and he raised the Nulls." *I don't want that, believe me.* "He's a good father. An *experienced* father."

Etain was too far ahead of Levet for him to overhear, but she had the feeling that he would be conveniently deaf to gossip anyway. Now she could see the crowd of farmers massed at the gates in the perimeter fence, silent and grim, hands thrust into pockets. As soon as they spotted her, the rumbling chorus of complaint began. She knew why.

We armed them.

Me and General Zey . . . we turned them into a resistance army, trained them to fight Seps, made them guerrillas when it suited us, and now . . . it doesn't suit us anymore. Throw 'em away.

That was why she had to face them. She'd used them, maybe not knowingly, but they wouldn't care about that academic point.

"Commander Levet," she said. "Only open fire if you feel your men are in danger."

"Hoping to avoid that, ma'am."

"They've got DC-fifteens, remember. We armed them."

"Not full spec, though."

A cordon of clone troopers stood between Etain and the crowd, as white and glossy as the snow around them. In the distance, she could hear the grinding of gears as an AT-TE armored vehicle thudded around the perimeter of the temporary camp set up to oversee the human evacuation. The clone troopers, each man with Darman's sweetly familiar face, had their orders: the farmers had to leave.

They handled humanitarian missions surprisingly well for men who'd been bred solely to fight and had no idea of what normal family life was like. *Well, not much different from me, then.* As she came up behind them, they parted without even turning their heads. It was one of those things you could do with 360-degree helmet sensors.

In the front of the crowd, she recognized a face. She knew nearly all of them, inevitably, but Hefrar Birhan's eyes were the most difficult to meet.

"You proud of yerself, girl?"

Birhan stared at her, hostile and betrayed. He'd given her shelter when she'd been on the run from the local militia. She owed him more than kicking him out by force, tearing him away from the only home he'd ever known.

"I'd rather do my own dirty work than get someone else to do it," said Etain. "But you can start over, and the Gurlanins can't."

"Oh-ah. That's the government line all of a sudden, since we served our purpose and cleared the planet for you."

The farmers had weapons, as farmers always did, most of which were old rifles for dealing with the gdans that attacked grazing merlie herds, but some also had their Republic-issue Deeces. They held them casually, some just gripped in their hands, others resting in the crooks of their arms or slung across their backs, but Etain could feel the tension rising among both them and the line of troopers. She wondered if her unborn child could sense these things in the Force yet. She hoped not. He had enough of a war waiting for him.

"I preferred you to hear it from me than from a stranger." Not true: she was here to hide her pregnancy. She couldn't help thinking that the awful duty served her right for deceiving Darman. "You have to leave, you know that. You're being given financial aid to start over. There are established farms waiting for you on Kebolar. It's a better prospect than Qiilura."

"It's not *home*," said a man standing a little behind Birhan. "And we're not going."

"Everyone else left weeks ago."

" 'Cept two thousand of us that *haven't*, girl." Birhan folded his arms: the sound of the AT-TE had stopped, and every wild noise carried on the still, cold air. Qiilura was so very, very quiet compared with the places she'd been. "And you can't move us if we don't want to be going."

It took Etain a moment to realize he meant violence rather than Force persuasion, and she felt a little ripple of anxiety in some of the troops. She and Levet had been authorized—*ordered*—to use force if necessary. Jinart slipped forward between the troops and sat on her haunches, and some of the farmers stared at her as if she were some exotic pet or hunting animal. Of course: they'd probably never seen a Gurlanin, or at least hadn't realized they had. There were so few of them left. And they could take any form they pleased.

"The Republic will remove you, farmer, because they fear us," Jinart said. "In this war, you now count for *nothing*. We use the power we have. So go while you can."

Birhan blinked at the Gurlanin for a few moments. The only four-legged species the farmers saw were their animals, and none of them talked back. "This is a big planet. There's plenty of room for all of us."

"Not enough for you. You wiped out our prey. We've starved. You're destroying us by wiping out our food chain, and now it's our turn—"

"No more killing," Etain snapped. Levet eased through the line of troops and stood a little in front of her to her left: she could sense his readiness to intervene. Gurlanins didn't have weapons, but nature had made them efficient killers. They'd all seen plenty of evidence. "These are difficult times, Birhan, and nobody gets a happy ending. You'll be far safer where you're going. Do you understand me?"

His gaze fixed on hers. He was frail and worn out, his eyes watery and red-rimmed from age and the biting, cold air. He might have been only the same age as Kal Skirata, but agriculture here was a brutal existence that took its toll. "You'd never shoot us. You're a Jedi. You're all full of peace and pity and stuff."

"Try thinking of me as an army officer," she said softly, "and you might get a different picture. Last chance."

There were only so many ultimata she could give them, and that was the last. The compound gates opened with a metallic scrape, and Levet moved the troops forward to edge the crowd away. It was cold; they'd get fed up and wander home sooner or later. For a moment the sense of hatred and resentment in the Force was so strong that Etain thought the Qiilurans might start a riot, but it seemed to be just a staring contest, which was unwinnable against troops whose eyes they couldn't see. There was also the small matter of penetrating a wall of plastoid-alloy armor.

Levet's voice boomed from the voice projector in his helmet. Etain could have sworn that nearby branches shivered.

"Go back to your farms and get ready to leave, all of you.

Report to the landing strip in seventy-two hours. Don't make this any harder than it is."

"For you, or for us?" someone yelled from the crowd. "Would *you* abandon everything you had and start again?"

"I'd willingly trade places with you," Levet said. "But I don't have the option."

Etain couldn't help but be more interested in the clone commander for a moment. It was an odd comment, but she felt that he meant it, and that unsettled her. She was used to seeing Darman and the other commandos as comrades with needs and aspirations that nobody else expected them to have, but she'd never heard a regular trooper openly express a wish for something beyond the GAR. It was uniquely poignant.

They'd all rather be somewhere else even if they're not sure what it is. All of them, like Dar, like me, like anyone.

She felt Levet's brief embarrassment at his own frankness. But there was no gesture or head movement to indicate to anyone else that he was being literal.

I can't think of the whole galaxy any longer. My thoughts are with these slave soldiers, and that's as much caring as I can manage right now. I want them *to live. Sorry, Birhan, I'm a bad Jedi, aren't I?*

Etain had made that mental deal a long while ago. It wasn't the Jedi way, but then no Jedi had ever been faced with leading a conventional army and making brutally pragmatic combat decisions on a daily basis. No Jedi *should* have, as far as she was concerned, but she was in it now, and she'd make what difference she could to the men around her.

"I'll give you three more days to report to the landing area with your families, Birhan." Etain wanted to look a little more commanding, but she was small, skinny, and uncomfortably pregnant: the hands-on-hips stance wasn't going to work. She put one hand casually on her lightsaber hilt instead, and summoned up a little Force help to press insistently on a few minds around Birhan. *I mean this. I won't back down.* "If you don't comply, I *will* order my troops to remove you by any means necessary."

Etain stood waiting for the crowd to break up. They'd argue, complain, wait until the last moment, and then cave in. Two thousand of them: they knew they couldn't resist several dozen well-trained, well-armed troopers, let alone a whole company of them. That was the remnant of the garrison. They were keen to finish the job and rejoin their battalion, the 35th Infantry. It was one of those things Etain found most touching about these soldiers: they didn't want to be doing what they called a "cushy" job while their brothers were fighting on the front line.

She knew the feeling all too well.

Birhan and the rest of the farmers paused for a few moments, meters from the line of troopers, and then turned and trudged away in the direction of Imbraani, silent and sullen. Jinart sat watching them like one of those black marble statues on the Shir Bank building in Coruscant.

Levet cocked his head. "I don't think they're going to go quietly, ma'am. It might get unpleasant."

"It's easier to charge battle droids than civilians. If it does, we disarm them and remove them bodily."

"*Disarming* can be the rough bit."

Yes, it was quicker and simpler to kill. Etain didn't enjoy the amoral pragmatism that always overtook her lately. As she lost her focus in the unbroken carpet of snow ahead of her, she thought the black specks that began to appear in her field of vision were her eyes playing the usual tricks, just cells floating in the fluid. Then they grew larger. The white blanket bulged and suddenly shapes began forming, moving, resolving into a dozen or so glossy black creatures exactly like Jinart.

They were Gurlanins, proving that they could be *anywhere,* undetected. Etain shuddered. They trotted after the farmers, who seemed oblivious to them until someone turned around and let out a shout of surprise. Then the whole crowd turned, panicking as if they were being stalked. The Gurlanins seemed to melt into the snow again, flattening instantly into gleaming black pools that looked like voids and then merging perfectly with the white landscape. They'd vanished from sight. Several farmers were clutching their rifles, aiming randomly, but they didn't open fire. They didn't have a target.

It was a clear threat. *You can't see us, and we'll come for you in the end.* Jinart had once shown what that meant when she'd taken revenge on a family of informers. Gurlanins were predators, intelligent and powerful.

"You can't feel them in the Force, can you, ma'am?" Levet whispered. One of the clone troopers seemed to be checking his rifle's optics, clearly annoyed that he hadn't spotted the Gurlanins with the wide range of sensors in both the weapon and his helmet. "At least we're working with the same limitations for a change."

"No, I can't detect them unless they let me." Etain had once mistaken the telepathic creatures for Force-users, feeling their presence tingling in her veins, but they could vanish completely to every sense when they chose—silent, invisible, without thermal profile, beyond the reach of sonar . . . and the Force. It still alarmed her. "Perfect spies."

Levet gestured to one of the troopers, and the platoon fanned out beyond the perimeter fence. "Perfect saboteurs."

General Zey thought so, too. So did the Senate Security Council. Gurlanins were on Coruscant, in the heart of the Republic's intelligence machine, maybe in a hundred or even a thousand places where they couldn't be seen, and where they could do immense damage. If the Republic didn't honor its deal with them sooner rather than later, they could—and would—throw a huge hydrospanner in the works, and nobody would see it coming.

"I'm new to this," Etain said. "Why do we seem to create enemies for ourselves? Recruiting spies and then alienating them? Isn't that like handing someone your rifle and turning your back on them?"

"I suppose I'm new to this, too," said Levet. They headed back to the headquarters building. Poor man: he'd only seen a dozen years of life, and all he'd ever known was combat. "I stay away from policy. All I can do is handle what comes down the pike at us."

Etain had to ask. "Would you really swap places with a farmer?"

Levet shrugged. But his casual gesture didn't fool her Jedi senses. "Farming looks quite challenging. I like the open spaces."

They often said that, these men gestated in glass vats. Dar's brother Fi loved negotiating the dizzying canyons of buildings on Coruscant; the Null ARC troopers like Ordo didn't care for confined spaces. Etain let Levet go on ahead and slowed down to concentrate on the child within her, wondering if he might turn out a little claustrophobic, too.

It's not genetic. Is it?

But will he die before his time? Will he inherit Dar's accelerated aging?

She'd been worried first for Darman, and then for herself, but her anxieties were now largely taken up by the baby and all the things she didn't know. Kal Skirata was right. She hadn't *thought.* She'd been so set on giving Darman a son that—Force-guided or not—there were too many things she hadn't considered carefully enough.

Accelerating the pregnancy is convenient for me—but what about him?

She no longer had a choice. She'd agreed to hand over the baby to *Kal'buir,* Papa Kal. He must have been a good father; his clones clearly adored him, and he treated them all as if they were his own flesh and blood. Her son—and it took all her strength not to name him—would be fine with him. He *had* to be. Her Force-awareness told her that her son would touch and shape many lives.

Kal won't even let me give him a name.

She could make a run for it, but she knew Kal Skirata would find her wherever she hid.

I want this baby so badly. It's only temporary. When the war's over, I'll get him back, and . . . will he even know me?

Jinart brushed past her legs, reminding her suddenly of Walon Vau's hunting animal, a half-wild strill called Lord Mirdalan.

The Gurlanin glanced back at her with vivid orange eyes.

"The last of the farmers will leave in a few days, girl, and after that—you concentrate on producing a healthy baby. Nothing else."

There was plenty more to worry about, but Jinart was right—that was enough to be going on with. Etain went back into the house, settled into meditation, and couldn't resist reaching out in the Force to touch Darman.

He'd feel it. She knew he would.

Mygeeto, Outer Rim, vaults of the Dressian Kiolsh Merchant Bank, 470 days after Geonosis

Walon Vau enjoyed irony, and there was none more profound than seizing—as a soldier—the inheritance his father had denied him for wanting to join the army.

On the metal door of the deposit box, a cupboard with a set of sliding shelves, was an engraved plate that read VAU, COUNT OF GESL.

"When the old *chakaar* dies, that'll be me," Vau said. "In theory, anyway. It'll pass to my cousin." He looked over his shoulder, even though the sensors in his Mandalorian helmet gave him wraparound vision. "Didn't I say thin out, Delta? Move it."

Vau wasn't used to anything other than instant obedience from his squads. He'd drummed it into them on Kamino, the hard way when necessary. Skirata thought you built special forces soldiers by treats and pats on the head, but it just produced weaklings; Vau's squads had the lowest casualty rates because he reinforced the animal will to survive in every man. He was proud of it.

"You did," Boss said, "but you look like you need a hand. Anyway—you're not our sergeant any longer. Technically speaking. No disrespect . . . *Citizen* Vau."

I was hard on them because I cared. Because they had to be hard to survive. Kal never understood that, the fool.

Vau still had trouble breathing some days thanks to the

broken nose Skirata had given him. The crazy little *chakaar* didn't understand training at all.

The next droid patrol wouldn't come this way for a few hours. Security droids trundled constantly through the labyrinth of corridors deep under the Mygeetan ice, a banking stronghold the Muuns claimed could never be breached. It still made sense to get out sooner rather than later. And Delta should have banged out by now; they'd called in air strikes and sabotaged ground defenses, and Bacara's Marines were moving in again. They'd achieved their mission, and it was extraction time.

"I should have thrashed more sense into you, then," Vau said. He unfolded a plastoid bivouac sheet and knotted the corners. It was always a bad idea not to plan for the most extreme situation: he'd been certain he would only take what was rightfully his, but this was too good to pass up. "Okay, you and Scorch hold this between you while I fill it."

"We can empty the—"

"*I* steal. You don't."

It was a fine point but it mattered to Vau. Skirata might have raised a pack of hooligans, but Vau's squads were *disciplined*. Even Sev . . . Sev was psychotic and lacked even the most basic social graces, but he wasn't a criminal.

As Vau tipped the first likely-looking box into the makeshift container—cash credits and bonds, which would do very nicely indeed—the whiff of oily musk announced the arrival of his strill, Lord Mirdalan. Fixer stepped back to let the animal pass.

"Mird, I told you to wait by the exit," said Vau. All strills were intelligent, but Mird was especially smart. The animal padded down the narrow passage in velvet silence and looked up expectantly, somehow managing not to drool on the floor for once. It fixed Vau with an intense, knowing gold stare, making any anger impossible: who *couldn't* love a face like that? That strill had stood by him since boyhood, and anyone who didn't see its miraculous spirit had no common decency or heart. They said strills stank, but Vau didn't care. A little natural musk never hurt anyone. "You want to help, *Mird'ika*? Here." He slipped his flamethrower off his webbing. "Carry this. Good Mird!"

The strill took the barrel of the weapon in its massive jaws and sat back on its haunches. Drool ran down to the trigger guard and pooled on the floor.

"Cute," Sev muttered.

"And clever." Vau signaled to Mird to watch the door, and slid the drawers of the Vau deposit box from their runners. "Anyone who doesn't like my friend Mird can *slana'pi*."

"Sarge, it's the ugliest thing in the galaxy," Scorch said. "And we've seen plenty of ugly."

"Yeah, you've got a mirror," said Sev.

"Ugliness is an illusion, gentlemen." Vau began sorting through his disputed inheritance. "Like beauty. Like color. All depends on the light." The first thing that caught his eye in the family box was his mother's flawless square-cut shoroni sapphire, the size of a human thumbprint, set on a pin and flanked by two smaller matching stones. In some kinds of light, they were a vibrant cobalt blue, while in others they turned forest green. Beautiful: but real forests had been destroyed to find them, and slaves died mining them. "The only reality is action."

Sev grunted deep in his throat. He didn't like wasting time and wasn't good at hiding it. His HUD icon showed he was watching Mird carefully. "Whatever you say, Sergeant."

The strongroom held a treasure trove of portable, easily hidden, and untraceable things that could be converted to credits anywhere in the galaxy. Vau stumbled on only one deposit box whose contents were inexplicably worthless: a bundle of love letters tied with green ribbon. He read the opening line of the first three and threw them back. Apart from that one box, the rest were a rich man's emergency belt, the equivalent of the soldier's survival kit of a fishing line, blade, and a dozen compact essentials for staying alive behind enemy lines.

Vau's hundred-liter backpack had room enough for a few extras. Everything—gems, wads of flimsi bonds, cash credits, metal coins, small lacquered jewel boxes he didn't pause to open—was tipped in unceremoniously. Delta stood around fidgeting, unused to idleness while the chrono was counting down.

"I *told* you to leave me here." Vau could still manage the voice of menace. "Don't disobey me. You know what happens."

Boss hung manfully to his end of the plastoid sheet, but his voice was shaky. "You can't give us an order, *Citizen Vau.*"

They were the best special forces troops in the galaxy, and here Vau was, still unable to manage the *thank you* or *well done* that they deserved. But much as he wanted to, the cold black heart of his father, his true legacy, choked off all attempts to express it. Nothing was ever good enough for his father, especially him. Maybe the old man just couldn't bring himself to say it, and he meant to all along.

No, he didn't. Don't make excuses for him. But my boys know me. I don't have to spell it out for them.

"I ought to shoot you," Vau said. "You're getting sloppy."

Vau checked the chrono on his forearm plate. Anytime now, Bacara's Galactic Marines would start pounding the city of Jygat with glacier-busters. He was sure he'd feel it like a seismic shock.

"Looking for anything in particular?" Sev asked.

"No. Random opportunism." Vau didn't need to cover his tracks: his father didn't know or care if he was alive or dead. *Your disappointment of a son came back, Papa. You didn't even know I disappeared to Kamino for ten years, did you?* There was nothing the senile *hut'uun* could do about it anyway. Vau was the one better able to swing a crippling punch these days. "Just a smokescreen. And make it worth the trip."

He knew what their next question would have been, if they'd asked it. They never asked what they knew they didn't need to be told. *What was he going to do with it all?*

He couldn't tell them. It was too much, too soon. He was going to hand it all over to a man who'd kill him for a bet—all except what was rightfully his.

"I'm not planning to live in luxurious exile," Vau said.

Scorch stepped over Mird and stood at the door, Deece ready. "Donating it to the Treasury, then?"

"It'll be used *responsibly.*"

Vau's backpack was now stuffed solid, and heavy enough to make him wince when he heaved it up on his shoulders. He tied the plastoid sheet into a bundle—a bundle worth millions, maybe—and slung it across his chest. He hoped he didn't fall or he'd never get up again.

"Oya," he said, nodding toward the doors. "Let's go."

Mird braced visibly and then shot out into the corridor. It always responded to the word *oya* with wild, noisy enthusiasm because that meant they were going hunting, but it was intelligent enough to know when to stay silent. *Mirdala Mird:* clever Mird. It was the right name for the strill. Delta advanced down the corridor toward the ducts and environmental control room that kept the underground bank from freezing solid, following Mird's wake, which—even Vau had to admit it—was marked by a trail of saliva. Strills dribbled. It was part of their bizarre charm, like flight, six legs, and jaws that could crunch clean through bone.

Sev skidded on a patch of strill-spit. "Fierfek . . ."

"Could be worse," Scorch said. *"Much* worse."

Vau followed up the rear, his helmet's panoramic sensor showing him the view at his back. There was an art to moving forward with that image in front of you on the HUD, an image that sent the unwary stumbling. Like the men he'd trained, Vau could see past the disorienting things the visor displayed.

They were fifty meters from the vents that would take them back to the surface and Fixer's waiting snowspeeder when the watery green lighting flickered and Mird skidded to a halt, ears pricked. Vau judged by the animal's reaction, but Sev confirmed his worst fears.

"Ultrasonic spike," he said. "I don't know how, but I think we tripped an alarm."

Fixer's voice filled their helmets. "Drive's running. I'm bringing the snowie as close to the vent as I can."

Boss turned to face Vau and held his hand out for the bundle. "Come on, Sergeant."

"I can manage. Get going."

"You first."

"I said *get going,* Three-Eight."

No nicknames: that told Boss that Vau meant business. Sev and Scorch sprinted down the final stretch to the compartment doors and forced them apart again. The machine voice of rotors and pumps flooded the silent corridor. Everyone stopped dead for a split second. They could hear the clatter of approaching droid and organic guards, the noise magnified by the acoustics of the corridors. Vau estimated the minutes and seconds. It wasn't good.

"Get your *shebse* up that vent before I vape the lot of you," Vau snapped. Osik, *I put them in danger, all for this stupid jaunt, all for lousy credits.* "Now!" He shoved Boss hard in the back, and the three commandos did what they always did when he yelled at them and used a bit of force: they obeyed. "Shift it, Delta."

The vent was a steep vertical shaft. The service ladder inside was designed for maintenance droids, with small recessed footholds and a central rail. Boss looked up, assessing it.

"Let's cheat," he said, and fired his rappel line high into the shaft. The grappling hook clattered against the metal, and he tugged to check the line was secure. "Stand by . . ."

The shaft could only take one line at a time. Boss shot up the shaft with his hoist drive squealing, bouncing the soles of his boots against the wall in what looked like dramatic leaps until he vanished.

The hoist stopped whining. There was a moment of quiet punctuated by the clacking of armor plates.

"Clear," his voice echoed. Sev shot his line vertically; it made a whiffling sound like an arrow in flight as it paid out. Metal clanged, and the fibercord went tight. "Line secure, Sev."

Sev winched himself up the shaft with an ungainly skidding technique. Scorch waited for the all-clear and then followed him. Vau was left standing at the bottom of the shaft with Mird, facing a long climb. Mird could fly, but not in such a confined space. Vau fired his line, waited for one of the commandos to secure it, and then attached the bundle of valuables to it. Then he held out his hands to Mird to take the flamethrower from its mouth.

"Good Mird," he whispered. "Now, *oya.* Off you go. Up, *Mird'ika.*" The strill could hang on to the line by its jaws alone if necessary. But Mird just whined in dissent, and sat down with all the sulky determination of a human child. "Mird! *Go! Does no shabuir ever listen to me? Go!*"

Mird stayed put. *It'll never leave me. Not until the day I die.* Vau gave up and tugged the line as a signal to the commandos to haul away. He didn't have time to argue with a strill.

"If I'm not out of here in two minutes," he said, "get all this stuff to Captain Ordo. Understood?"

There was a brief silence on Vau's helmet comlink. "Understood," said Boss.

The next few moments felt stretched into forever. The staccato clatter of approaching droid guards grew louder. Mird rumbled ominously and stared toward the doors, poised on its haunches as if to spring at the first droid to appear.

It would defend Vau to the last. It always had.

Eventually the length of thin fibercord snaked back down the shaft and slapped against the floor. Boss sounded a little breathless. "Up you come, Sergeant."

Vau reattached the line to his belt and scooped Mird up in both arms, hoping his winch would handle the extra weight. As he rose, kicking away from the shaft wall, the machinery groaned and spat. He could see the cold gray light above him and a helmet not unlike his own Mandalorian T-shaped visor peering down at him, picked out in an eerie blue glow.

Now he could hear the throb of the snowspeeder's drive. Fixer was right above them. As Vau squeezed his shoulders through the top of the vent, Mird leapt clear. Scorch and Sev dropped to the rock-hard snow with their DC-17s trained on something Vau couldn't yet see. When he hauled himself out, a blaster bolt seared past his head and he found himself in the middle of a firefight. A ferocious wind roared in his throat-mike.

Vau slammed the vent's grille shut and seared it with his custom Merr-Sonn blaster, welding the metal tight to the coaming. Then he dropped a small proton grenade down the shaft through a gap. The snow shook with the explosion below. Nobody was going to be coming up behind them.

But everyone and his pet akk now knew the Dressian Ki-olsh bank had intruders—Republic troops.

A distant boom followed by the *whomp-whomp-whomp* of artillery almost drowned out the blasterfire and howling wind. The Galactic Marines were right on time.

"Okay, Bacara's started," Scorch said. "Nice of him to stage a diversion."

Mygeeto's relentlessly white landscape gave no clue that it housed cities deep below. Only a few were visible on the surface. The packed snow of eons was pierced by jagged mountains that formed glass canyons like extravagant ice sculptures. A surface patrol—six droids on snowshoe-like feet, ten organics who were probably Muuns under the cold-weather gear—had cut them off from the snowspeeder just meters away. Rounds zapped and steamed off the vessel's fuselage; Fixer, kneeling beside it, returned a hail of blue Deece fire that kept the security patrol pinned down.

If that snowie gets damaged, we're never getting off this rock.

Vau checked his panoramic vision. Mird was close at his side, pressing against him. He could see only the patrol; nothing else showed up on his sensors. That didn't mean there weren't more closing in on them, though.

The big bundle of plunder lay on the snow where Delta had dropped it. Right then, it was simply convenient cover. Vau crawled behind his oversized multimillion-credit sand-bag and took aim. The *bdapp-bdapp-bdapp* of blasters and ragged breathing filled his helmet—his, Delta's?—but there was no chatter. Delta Squad exchanged few words during engagements lately. They'd been born together, raised together, and they'd come as close to knowing one another's thoughts as any normal humans could. Now they were laying down fire exactly as he'd trained them while Fixer defended their getaway vessel, all without a word.

How the Muuns would explain away a Mandalorian fighting with Republic forces Vau wasn't sure, but then everyone knew that Mandos would fight for anyone for the right price.

Scorch clipped a grenade launcher on his Deece.

"Not good," he said. "More droids."

Vau now saw what Scorch could. His HUD picked up shapes moving in rigid formation, almost invisible to infrared but definitely showing up in the electromagnetic spectrum. Then he saw them rounding an outcrop of glittering crystal, clanking ludicrous things with long snouts, a platoon of them. Scorch fired the grenade, smashing into the front rank of four. An eruption of snow and metal fragments fanned into the air and were whipped away by the wind. The rank behind was caught by the shrapnel from their comrades; and two toppled over, decapitated by buckled chunks of metal.

But the rest kept coming. Vau checked the topography on his HUD. They were approaching down an ice wadi almost opposite the first patrol's location, about to cut across the path between Fixer and the rest of them, and that meant the only way to the speeder now was to run the enemy gauntlet.

Sev and Boss began working their way to the snowspeeder on their bellies, pausing to fire grenades high over the ice boulders and then scrambling a few more meters while the droids paused and the Muuns took brief cover. Shots hissed around the commandos as blaster bolts shaved paint off their plates and hit the snow, vaporizing it. One round deflected off Vau's helmet with an audible sizzle. He felt the impact like being slapped around the head.

All he felt at that moment was . . . foolish: not afraid, not in fear for his life, just stupid, stupid for getting it wrong. It was worse than physical terror. He'd overplayed his hand. He'd put Delta in this spot. He had to get them out.

"You're *conspicuous* in that black armor, Sarge," Scorch

said kindly. "It's worse than having Omega alongside. What say you back out of here and leave me to hold them?"

If anyone was going to do any holding, it was Vau. "Humor an old man." He fumbled in his belt for an EMP grenade. "I stop the droids, you pick off the wets." *Wets*. Organics. He was talking like Omega now. "Then we *all* run for it. Deal?"

Scorch twisted the grenade launcher to one side and switched his Deece to automatic, forcing the Muun guards to scatter. Two dropped behind a frozen outcrop. He fired again, shattering the ice, which turned out to be a brittle crystalline rock that sent shards flying like arrows. There was a shriek of agony that turned into a panting scream. It echoed off the walls of the canyon.

He grunted, apparently satisfied. "Sounds like nine wets left in play."

"Eight, if one's taking care of him," Vau said.

"Muuns aren't that nice."

"Fixer, you okay?" Vau waited for a reply. The world had suddenly gone silent except for that screaming Muun. The droids seemed to be regrouping behind a ten-meter chunk of dark gray ice. "Fixer?"

"Fine, Sarge."

"Okay, here goes."

Vau fired. This EMP grenade had enough explosive power to make a mess of a small room, but its pulse was what really did the damage over a much larger area. It fried droid circuits. The small explosion echoed and scattered chunks of ice, and then there was a long silence punctuated only by the distant pounding of cannon as the Galactic Marines smashed their way into Jygat.

Vau refocused on the EM image in his HUD. He crawled to the bundle, dragging it into cover and strapping it back on his chest. It was way too much to carry, and he couldn't move properly. He knelt on all fours like a heavily pregnant woman trying to get up. "I don't see movement."

"It's okay, Sarge, they're zapped."

"Okay, just the wets to finish off, then." He switched back

to infrared. The Muun guards would show up like beacons. "I'll warm them up while you make a move."

Vau pulled out the flamethrower, eased himself into a kneeling position, and opened the valve. Mird cocked its head, eyes fixed on the weapon.

"Where'd you get that, Sarge?" Scorch asked.

"Borrowed it from a flame trooper."

"Does he know?"

"He won't mind."

"That thing could melt droids."

"I was saving the fuel for a tight spot." There was still no movement; Vau estimated that the patrol was still in the canyon, maybe looking for a way around behind them. The Muun·who'd been injured was now silent—unconscious, or dead. "Like this. I should have a full minute's fuel, so once I start—run. You too, Mird." He gestured Mird toward the snowspeeder and pointed to the flamethrower. "Go, Mird. Follow Boss."

It was just a case of taking a blind run at it. *I'm not as fast as I used to be. And I'm carrying too much.* But a wall of flame was a blunt and terrifying instrument against almost any life-form. Vau struggled to his feet and ignited the flame.

The roaring jet spat ahead of him as he drew level with the small pass where the Muun patrol was holed up; then the sheet of flame blinded him to what lay beyond it. He only heard the screams and saw the flash on icons across his HUD as Delta Squad sprinted for the idling snowspeeder. Vau backed away, counting down the seconds left of his fuel supply, ready to switch to his blaster when it ran out.

Nobody was expecting a flamethrower on an ice patrol. Surprise was half the battle.

Vau turned and ran, gasping for breath. Not a bad turn of speed for his age, not bad at all on ice and so heavily laden, and there was Mird ahead of him, having *listened* for once, and the speeder was coming about—

And the ice opened up beneath him.

It took him a moment to realize he was falling down a sloping tunnel and not just sinking into unexpected soft snow. Fixer called out, but even though the sound filled Vau's helmet he didn't catch what was said. The two bags of booty took him down.

"Get clear!" Vau yelled, even though he had no need to with a helmet comlink. "That's an order—"

"Sarge, we can't."

"Shut *up*. Go. If you come back for me—if *anyone* comes back—I'll shoot you on sight."

"Sarge! We could—"

"I raised you to *survive*. Don't humiliate me by going soft."

I can't believe I said that.

Delta didn't argue again. Vau was in semidarkness now, his HUD scrolling with the icons of Delta's view of the ice field beneath the speeder as it lifted clear.

". . . party . . ." said a voice in his helmet, but he lost the rest of the sentence, and the link faded into raw static.

The last thing I'll ever say to them is—shut up. *Noble exit, Vau.*

Mortal danger was a funny thing. He was sure he was going to die but he wasn't terrified, and he wasn't worried about more patrols. He was more preoccupied by what he'd fallen into: a vague memory came back to him. As he slid down a few more meters, trying to stop his fall with his heels more out of instinct than intent, a detached sense of curiosity prevailed: so this was what dying was actually like. Then he remembered.

Mygeeto's ice was honeycombed by tunnels—tunnels made by giant carnivorous worms. He came to rest with a *thud* on what felt like a ledge.

"Osik," he said. Well, if he wasn't dead, he soon would be. "Mird? *Mird!* Where are you, *verd'ika*?"

There was no answer but the crunching and groaning of shifting ice. But he still had the proceeds of the robbery strapped to him, both his goal and his fate.

Vau wasn't planning on dying just yet. He was now too rich to let go of life.

2

Clone subjects in the study showed a more marked variation in biological age and genetic mutation than seen in naturally occurring zygotic twins. In the group of 100 cloned men aged 24 chronological years, and who could reasonably be expected to present as the equivalent of a 48-year-old uncloned human, key biomarkers showed a range from 34 to 65 years with a median of 53 years. Further research is needed, but exposure to battlefield contaminants and high levels of sustained stress appear to accelerate normal genetic mutation in men already designed to age at twice the normal rate. By the time Kamino clones reach the equivalent of their mid-40s, those mutations are very apparent and—like natural zygotics—they grow apart.
—Dr. Bura Veujarij, Imperial Institute of Military Medicine, "Aging and Tissue Degeneration in Kaminoan-cloned Troops," *Imperial Medical Review* 1675

Republic Administration Block, Senate District, Coruscant, 470 days after Geonosis

"**C**an't the cops shift them?" said the security guard on the main doors of the Republic Treasury offices. He stared past Treasury agent Besany Wennen—not something that many males managed—with an expression on his face that said he felt the protesters were messing up his nice tidy forecourt. "I mean, they're Sep sympathizers, aren't they? And the cops are just standing there, doing nothing."

Besany hadn't missed the protesters. She'd taken a keen

but discreet interest in them, in fact, because the war with the Separatists had become an intensely personal one for her. These were expatriate Krantians, protesting about the pounding that their neutral planet had taken in a recent battle.

They'd taken up a position opposite what they saw as one of the centers of the war effort, the Defense Department administration building, where they seemed to think they might have some impact. Several government offices ringed the pedestrian concourse. Office workers had appeared at the windows to watch for a while, then returned to their desks because it wasn't their war, not yet. They had an army to protect them.

"They're neutrals, actually," Besany said. "So how would they protest to the Separatists?"

The guard looked at her, visibly puzzled. Holoscreens dotted the wall behind him, giving him a view of every floor and corridor in the building. "What do you mean?"

"They're here because they're allowed to be. Where would they go if they wanted to lobby the CIS?"

The question seemed to have stumped the guard. He shrugged. "Want me to see you safely past them, ma'am?"

"I don't think they're a threat, but thanks." Besany wondered how she was going to spend the evening, but she knew what would occupy her: worrying about a Null ARC trooper captain called Ordo, a man she was too scared to contact because she had no idea if he was on a mission at any given moment, and if a message on his comlink would compromise his safety. "I'll risk it."

She stepped out into Coruscant's temperate, climate-controlled early-evening air and gave the small protest a wide berth. A couple of CSF officers in dark blue fatigues were watching the protest from a doorway; one acknowledged her with a nod. She couldn't recognize him because the white riot helmet obscured too much of his face, but she'd had occasional contact with the Coruscant Security Force during investigations and they obviously found it easy to recognize her. She nodded back and clasped her bag more firmly under one arm.

Life went on in Coruscant despite the war. The protest here was a small rock in a river of normality, and the current of office workers and shoppers parted around it on the concourse and merged again downstream as if nothing had ever interrupted their routine. Besany wondered if they would flow around her in the same oblivious way; she was another isolated outcrop of the war. Eighty-three days ago—she was an audit officer, and exact detail was her job—a Jedi general had shot her with a nonlethal round, and she'd been plunged into a small, close-knit community of special forces troops. It was a window on a world of war without rules, of anonymous heroism, and an extraordinary and totally unexpected *affection.*

And it was her secret. Not even the Treasury knew about it.

She'd done things that her Treasury bosses wouldn't have taken at all well. Like giving critical data—passcodes, Treasury security overrides—to a commando sergeant; like falsifying her reports to cover the fact that she'd let special forces move in on her investigation.

It's too late to worry about that now.

Besany worried anyway. She walked briskly, anxious to get home and close the apartment doors behind her, another day when she hadn't been arrested that she could check off on the calendar.

It's not like me at all. Taking a flier on trust.

She wasn't even aware of someone walking behind her. But a hand touched her shoulder, and she gasped. Guilt made her spin around to find she was staring into the reflective riot visor of one of the CSF cops.

Her stomach churned. *Oh no no no—*

"Agent Wennen," he said. The accent was familiar. "Long time no see."

But she didn't know *him,* she was sure.

"You have the advantage, Officer." Men hit on her a lot less than most people imagined. She knew she was striking, but she also knew that she was a daunting prospect because of it. Even Ordo—hugely confident, recklessly unafraid—treated her warily. Her good looks were a curse most of the time. "What can I do for you?"

The cop stood with his fists on his hips. He didn't look like he was going to draw his weapon. "Well, I know I'm not quite as unforgettable as my brother, but I thought you'd at least say, *Hi, Mereel, how are things?*"

"Oh. *Oh.*" Mereel: one of Ordo's five Null ARC brothers, *Lieutenant* Mereel. Besany's gut lurched in a different way, and she didn't bother to hide her relief. "I'm sorry, Mereel. Out of context . . ."

"So you didn't recognize me with my clothes on, then?" A couple of passersby turned to stare. He chuckled to himself. "I mean, the armor. Makes a guy look different. Anyway, what kind of covert operator would I be if I was that easy to spot? Come on, can't stand here getting funny looks all night. Walk this way and I'll make it worth your while."

"Okay." And there she was again, just dropping everything and wandering off to do the bidding of a black ops unit. This wasn't how the Treasury investigation team worked. She had *rules*. "Can I ask—"

"Ordo's fine and sends his best wishes. He's doing a little job with *Kal'buir* at the moment." Mereel might have been a clone, but he was as individual as any man. He didn't walk like Ordo, and he didn't talk like him. "I'll try to teach him some social graces when he gets back. He's got no idea how to treat a lady."

Besany strode along beside him, working on the basis that looking as if this was routine was the best way to avoid attracting attention. "I just want to know he's safe."

"We're soldiers. We're never safe."

"Mereel . . ."

"Look at it this way." He headed for a CSF patrol speeder sitting on the public landing platform overlooking the skylane. "The other side's in a *lot* more danger than we are."

Besany slid into the passenger's seat and didn't ask how he'd acquired the speeder and the uniform. CSF liked the Special Operations clones. Their anti-terrorism chief, Jaller

Obrim, was very chummy with Sergeant Skirata, *Kal'buir*—
Papa Kal. Favors were done and questions weren't asked.
Besany envied them that wonderful conspiratorial closeness.
Kal'buir seemed to get away with murder.

"Are you allowed to tell me how everyone is?" she asked.

"You really do worry about us, don't you?" Mereel steered
the speeder toward her apartment block. She didn't recall
telling him where she lived. "Okay, Omega's been deployed
to the Outer Rim where someone needs a hand with regime
change. Delta are helping out the Marines. Did I miss anyone?"

Besany felt a pang of guilt. She had to ask about the first
clone she'd ever met, the patient bomb disposal trooper
who'd ended up with a temporary desk job after losing both
hands. "How's Trooper Corr coping with life as a commando?"

"Oh, he's fine. He's learning a few saucy tricks from my
brother Kom'rk. Good man, Corr."

"And the two Jedi officers?"

"Etain's evacuating colonists from Qiilura, and *Bard'ika*—
sorry, *General* Jusik is due back this week." There were huge
gaps in Mereel's explanation: places and times vanished. He
seemed to edit the sensitive detail smoothly as he went
along. "Want to know about Vau? He's with Delta. Nobody
dead. Baffled, fed up, tired, lonely, bored, hungry, scared witless, even having fun, but not dead. Which is a plus." The
speeder climbed and darted between skylanes to veer around
the front of her apartment block. Yes, Mereel definitely knew
exactly where she lived: he set the speeder down on the right
platform, on her balcony, and opened the hatches. "So, are
you still up for doing us a few favors? Without your bosses
finding out?"

Mereel was the front line of a war that most Coruscanti
never saw and weren't fighting. Besany asked herself, as she
had on that first night, whether her tidy little rules mattered
more than a man's life. Mereel slipped his helmet off and sat
looking at her expectantly—Ordo, and yet not Ordo, and
Corr, too. Corr's existence—she had no other word for it,

and it summed up so many aspects of a clone's life—had up-
ended her, left her feeling upset, angry, betrayed, and, yes,
guilty. Her government might have let her down as a citizen
and an employee, but it had totally betrayed this slave army.

*I'm letting emotion get in the way. But isn't emotion the
way we can tell what's really right and wrong?*

"Let's talk," she said.

Mereel walked around her apartment with a comm scan,
checking for surveillance devices. "Can't be too careful. But
then you know all about this game, being a Treasury spook."

"You'd be amazed how seriously people try to avoid financial regulation."

"I would." He hesitated by her sofa as if he might sit
down, but stayed standing as if he remembered he wasn't allowed on the furniture. He looked her over. "And you're still
not armed. You need to do something about that."

"Well—"

"Simple question. Are you willing to do some investigation for us?"

"What kind of investigation?"

"Defense expenditure and budget forecasts."

It couldn't be that simple. "Those are public documents
anyway."

"I don't think all the details I need are in them."

"Ah."

"It's very sensitive stuff. Might involve the Chancellor's
office."

Besany felt her scalp tighten as adrenaline flooded her
bloodstream. She didn't feel she could sit down, either, not
now. "Can you narrow down what I might be looking for?
Procurement fraud? Bribes?"

"You might well find that," said Mereel, "but I'm more interested in transactions involving Kamino, and the payment
schedules."

Besany couldn't imagine anything that would turn up except fraud—or maybe the Republic was arming someone it
claimed it wasn't. The investigator in her told her to ask more

questions, but the public servant within asked if she really needed or wanted to know more this time.

"I can drill right down to the individual credit transfers," she said at last. "Which might give you so much information that it takes you nowhere."

"Don't worry. I'm good at collation."

She took a breath. She was in it up to her neck now. A few more centimeters wouldn't make much difference. "Why are you trusting me with this?"

"Well, for a start, I know where you live." Mereel smiled with genuine humor, but she'd also seen how fast earnest, polite Ordo could snap into being an assassin without a second thought. "And we don't take prisoners. But our lives could depend on that information, which is what really makes the difference to you. Isn't it?"

It was an ethical choice between rules or lives, and rules didn't always translate into what was right. "You know it is."

"Then we'd be especially interested in any evidence of planned payments to Kamino for more clones beyond, say, the end of the next financial year. Or not."

Besany guessed that this was the point at which she ought to have decided she had no need to know more. "Okay. What aren't you telling me?"

Mereel shrugged. "That I took a big risk getting the information that led me to ask you for *more* information."

"What's Kal's view on this?" She didn't even have to ask if Kal Skirata knew. The Nulls didn't seem to take a breath without asking him first. Their allegiance was to him, not the Republic; but while she could understand the power of his aggressive charisma, she wasn't sure if it was a good idea. "And what happens if I get caught?"

"One—he trusts you," Mereel said, deadpan. "Two? They'll probably shoot you."

He wasn't joking now. She knew it.

"Okay," she said. "I'll make a start in the morning. How do I contact you?"

"Comlink." He held out his hand, and she dropped her comlink into his palm. Then he cracked open the case, frowned at the device's entrails, and took out a tiny tool kit that looked like a toy in his palm. "Once I've made it secure . . . dear oh *dear* . . . ma'am, tell me you haven't called Ordo on this."

"No, I haven't." She felt useless and naïve. "I thought it might compromise his safety."

Mereel looked up for a moment, eyebrows raised. "Right answer. *That's* why we trust you." He prodded and poked inside the comlink for a while and then snapped the case shut again. "Totally secure now, at least once you use the prefix I'm going to give you. You can even call Ordo."

"He might be defusing a bomb or something when I call." Besany always thought things through in meticulous sequence, which made her all the more horrified to see how easily she took this dangerous leap of faith. "I'll wait for him to call me, thanks."

"See? *Kal'buir* said you had the right stuff."

"Common sense."

"Got a sister?"

"No."

"Shame." He replaced his helmet and suddenly became just another Galactic City cop. "Anyway, got to go. Any message for Ordo?"

Should have thought ahead. Stang. What can I say? She and Ordo weren't exactly a romantic role model. They'd just had a drink in the CSF bar and then a string of awkward, embarrassed conversations when everything was implied and not much said. But the bond was strong, and so was her duty to do the right thing for his brothers. "Tell him I miss him. Ask him what his favorite meal is and tell him I'll cook it for him when he comes back."

"It's roba sausage with gravy, and he's fussy about the pepper oil."

"Hang on." Besany looked around for something to send him, but there was nothing in a woman's apartment that would be of any use or amusement to a soldier. There *was* food, though. Clones were always peckish, all of them. She rummaged in the conservator and hauled out a family-sized cheffa cake whose top was paved with glittering candied nuts, something she'd kept just in case unexpected guests showed up, but they never did. "Have you got room for something small?"

"How small?"

She was nothing if not exact. "Okay, twenty-five-centimeter diameter."

"I'll warn him not to swallow it whole." Mereel tucked the container under one arm, then reached inside his jacket. He withdrew a small blaster. *"Kal'buir* insisted I make you carry this. Go careful, ma'am."

Besany took it, numb, while a voice at the back of her mind asked if she'd lost her senses. He stepped out onto the platform, and a few moments later the police speeder lifted into the evening sky, vanishing in a blur of taillights.

She locked the balcony doors and drew the blinds, the blaster still gripped in her hand. She felt *observed.* There was no other word for it. But that was her conscience nagging. When she looked at her fingers curled around the weapon, it seemed like someone else's hand, and nothing to do with her at all.

So he thinks I might need to use this.

Better work out how I'm going to cover my tracks.

She was a forensic auditor. She knew how to uncover the hidden tracks of others, all the places they hid data or salted away credits or blew smoke across the audit trail. It was just a matter of reversing the process to cover her own.

The only complication was that the trail might lead to the very highest level of government.

She'd never been so scared—and alone—in her life.

She could only begin to imagine what Ordo and the rest of the commando forces faced on a daily basis.

Calna Muun, Agamar, Outer Rim, 471 days after Geonosis

"So, *Mando,* you like her?"

A gently curved transparisteel bubble bobbed on the surface of the water, looking like one of those little transparent

submersibles that showed tourists the wonders of the Bil
Da'Gari ocean floor. But then it lifted slowly to reveal something much, much larger, and not very leisure-oriented at all.

Sergeant Kal Skirata watched the water stream off the rising hull and wondered if he'd lost his *mirshe,* coming all this
way to buy a submersible. The price was more than he'd bud-
geted for. But if you hunted Kaminoans, you needed aquatic
capability, however much it cost. And he was hunting an elu-
sive one: Chief Scientist Ko Sai.

"Not to your taste?" asked the Rodian merchant.

Skirata grunted behind the impenetrable mask of his sand-
gold helmet. The handy thing about being a Mandalorian
doing business was that you didn't need to keep a straight
face, and only the terminally stupid ever tried to dupe you.
They only tried it once, too.

" 'S'okay, I suppose."

"It's a *beast,*" the Rodian said, bouncing around on the
quayside like a demented acrobat. Rodians always struck
Skirata as looking comically harmless, totally at odds with
their true nature, which was why he had an extra blade ready
in his sleeve—just in case. "Every one unique and hand-
crafted, Mon Cal's finest. Won't take much work to make
this a—"

"It's a *freighter.* I asked for a fighter."

"I can throw in a few extra cannons."

"How long's *that* going to take?"

"Is this for the war effort?"

Skirata could see the Rodian mentally hiking the price in
the expectation that the bill would be met by one government
or another. Profiteering and war went hand in hand.

"No," said Skirata. "I'm a pacifist."

The Rodian eyed the custom Verpine sniper rifle slung
across his shoulder. "You're a Mandalorian . . ."

Skirata let his three-sided knife drop from his right forearm plate, point first, and caught the hilt in his hand. "Would
you start a fight with me?"

"No . . ."

"See? I'm a force for peace." He spun the knife and slid it

back into the housing mounted above his wrist. "What's her maximum range, then?"

"Depth, a kilometer. Atmos speed—thousand klicks. Goes like a greased ronto." The freighter was above the waterline now, forty-five meters of smooth dark green curves with four hemispherical drive housings protruding above her stern like a knuckle-duster. It was a Mon Calamari *DeepWater*-class. "Packs ninety tons of cargo, eight crew. It's got a decent defensive cannon. Hyperdrive is—"

The Rodian stopped and looked to one side of Skirata. Ordo came ambling along the quayside and paused beside the freighter, left thumb hooked in his belt. Except for his gait—always the ARC trooper captain, back slightly arched as if he had both GAR-issue pistols holstered—he was just another *Mando* in battle-scarred armor. The Rodian fidgeted as Ordo inspected the drive housings from a distance and then jumped with a hollow *thud* from the quayside onto the casing.

"I don't like the color," Ordo muttered. He prodded his toecap into the manual override of the port hatch and popped the seals. "I'll just inspect the upholstery."

Skirata turned to the Rodian. "My boy's a picky lad, I'm afraid. I've lost count of the crates we've looked at this week."

"I could get you a Hydrosphere Explorer if you're prepared to wait a few weeks." The merchant dropped his voice. "An Ubrikkian repulsorsub. A V-Fin. A Trade Federation submarine, even."

"Yeah, I'd really love the Trade boys to come after me when they find a bit of their navy missing."

"You're so suspicious, you Mandalorians."

"You're not wrong there. How much?"

"One hundred and fifty thousand."

"I don't want to buy the whole fleet, son. Just one hull."

"Hard to find, these DeepWaters."

"Y'know, that TradeFed idea wasn't bad. Maybe I ought to go see their procurement people, because if I bought a real sub, direct from the manufacturer, instead of this day-tripper . . ."

Skirata heard Ordo's voice in his earpiece. "*Kal'buir,* I think Prudii can get this cannoned up nicely . . ."

He didn't want a regular submarine anyway. He needed a multipurpose vessel—like the Mon Cal tub here. The Rodian had no idea what he wanted or how badly he wanted it, or even if he could afford it. Skirata jangled his credit chips in his belt pouch, giving the alluring sound a little longer to soften up the Rodian's resistance, walking slowly up and down the quay as if he was thinking about something else.

"Come on, *ad'ika,*" he said to Ordo, letting the merchant hear. "Got another five vessels to look at yet. Haven't got all day."

"Just checking the hull integrity . . . ," Ordo said.

Good things, helmets: nobody could hear what was being said on the comlink outside the *buy'ce* unless you let them. Ordo was using all his state-of-the-art armor sensors to check for metal fatigue, leaks, and other mechanical faults. Skirata noted the readouts being relayed to his spanking-new HUD display, a small and necessary extravagance paid for by dead terrorists. They were at their nicest when dead, he thought.

Ordo let out a long breath. "It looks a little . . . *stained* inside, but otherwise this is a sound vessel. I'd take it if I were you."

I'll still knock the price down. "Oh. Is the leak bad?" Skirata asked, theatrically loud.

"What leak?" the Rodian demanded. "There's no kriffing leak."

"My boy says there's water damage." Skirata paused for effect. "*Ord'ika,* come up and tell him."

Ordo emerged from the hatch and stood on the hull with his hands on his hips, head slightly to one side. "The decking and the upholstery. Water stains."

"It's a submarine," the Rodian snapped. "Of *course* it's got water stains. What do you want, a sail barge or something? I thought you Mandos were supposed to be hard, and here you are whining on like Neimies about *water stains.*"

"Now, that's not very customer-focused," Skirata said. He reached slowly into his belt pouch and pulled out a handful of cash credits, all big denominations with their values tantalizingly visible. Not many ship merchants could resist the lure of a ready wedge of creds, and deferred gratification didn't look like the Rodian's strong suit. "I think I'll take my custom elsewhere."

The Rodian might have been mouthy but he wasn't mathematically challenged. His beady little eyes darted over the chips. "You'd have a problem getting one of these anywhere else. The Mon Cals aren't selling them to the Seps."

If the Rodian wanted to think they were working for the Separatists, that was fine. Nobody expected to see a Mandalorian working for the Republic, and the Rodian hadn't asked. Skirata crooked his finger to beckon Ordo, and the Null strode behind, boots crunching on the sanded boards of the jetty. The trick was to walk away briskly and purposefully. They were both very good at that, even if Skirata's leg was playing up and he was limping more than usual. There was a moment, a critical second, when one or the other side would crack. If they kept on walking, it would be the Rodian.

And Jedi thought they were the only ones who could exert a little mind influence, did they?

"One hundred and twenty," the Rodian called after him.

Skirata didn't break his stride. Neither did Ordo. "Eighty," he called back.

"A hundred and ten."

"They only cost a hundred new."

"It's got extras."

"It'd need to be gold-plated to be worth that."

They were still walking. Ordo made a little grunt, but it was hard to tell if he was annoyed or amused.

"Okay, ninety," the Rodian called.

"Eighty, cash credits," Skirata said, not turning around. In fact, he speeded up. He counted to ten, and got as far as eight.

"Okay," the Rodian said at last. "I hope you'll be happy with it."

Skirata slowed and then turned around to amble back, casually counting out his credits. Ordo jumped onto the hull and disappeared down the open hatch.

"Oh, I'll be back pretty fast if I'm not," Skirata said. "That's why I don't need a warranty."

The DeepWater's drives roared into life, sending white foam churning across the harbor. The jetty trembled.

"Does he know how to drive that thing?" the Rodian asked.

"My boy knows how to do just about anything. Fast learner."

Skirata skidded across the wet hull and sealed the hatch behind him. Ordo was already in the pilot's position in the narrow cockpit, helmet on the console, looking as if he was talking to himself as he touched each of the controls in sequence. He had an eidetic memory, like all the Nulls: just one quick canter through the manual before they set out, and Ordo had the theory down pat. Skirata was ferociously proud of him, as he was all his boys, but he resented the damage the Kaminoans had done to them in the creation of what they were sure would be the perfect soldier. Their brilliance came at a price. They were all troubled souls, unpredictable and violent, the product of too much genetic tampering and a brutal infancy. Skirata would punch any fool who dared call them *nutters,* but they were a handful even for him sometimes.

But they were his life. He'd raised them as his sons. The Kaminoans had wanted to terminate them as a failed experiment, and just thinking about that still made Skirata long for revenge. All Kaminoans were sadistic vermin as far as he was concerned, and he counted their lives as cheaply as they counted the clones they bred. Ko Sai would be one of the lucky ones: he needed her alive—for a while, at least.

So my boys were surplus to requirements, were they? So will you be, sweetheart.

Ordo slid open the throttle and the DeepWater was under

way, churning foam. The Rodian dwindled to a doll, then a speck on a receding jetty, and they were in open sea beyond the harbor limits.

"Let's go catch some aiwha-bait, then." Skirata wondered why he was worried about diving in a sub when he was perfectly happy to fly in cold hard space. He'd done enough maritime exercises on Kamino, after all. "Heard from Mereel yet?"

"Yes, he's on his way, yes, he got Agent Wennen to do the job, and yes, he gave her the blaster."

Agent Wennen? Come on, son. You've got a short enough life as it is. Go for it. "She's a tough one. *Or'atin'la.*"

Ordo didn't take the bait. "*Mer'ika* says she's sent me a cheffa cake."

Ordo was touchingly clueless about women. Skirata knew he'd failed him on the emotional education front. "You're well in there, son. Smart, *tough* girl." She was a striking leggy blonde, too, but that was farther down the list for Mandalorians, after capability and endurance. She was actually too beautiful for people to feel comfortable around her, and so Skirata counted the poor kid among his growing collection of outsiders and social rejects. "You deserve the best."

"If only there were a manual for females, *Kal'buir.*"

"If there is, I never got my copy."

Ordo turned his head and gave Skirata a look that said it was no comfort to hear that. Ordo now knew what Skirata had kept from the clones for so long: that his marriage had foundered, and his two sons had eventually declared him *dar'buir,* no longer a father—the divorce of a parent, possibly the greatest shame in Mandalorian society. It was the only thing he'd ever kept from the Nulls, apart from Etain Tur-Mukan's pregnancy.

Does that worry Ordo? Does he believe me? I had to disappear. We all had to, to train our clones in secret. My kids were grown men. I left them every last credit I had, didn't I? Shab, my clones needed me more than they did. They needed me just to stay alive.

He had a daughter, too, and her name hadn't been on the

edict. He hadn't heard from her in years. One day . . . one day, he might find the courage to go and look for her. But now he had more pressing business.

"It'll be okay, son," Skirata said. "If it's the last thing I do, you'll have a full life span. Even if I have to beat that information out of Ko Sai a line at a time."

Especially if I have to.

Ordo seemed to take a sudden and intense interest in the throttle controls. "The only reason we're alive at all is because you stopped the *gihaal* from putting us down like animals." For a moment Skirata thought he was working up to saying something else, but he changed tack. "Okay, let's see if I can at least follow the manual for this one . . ."

Ordo pushed the throttle lever hard forward. The DeepWater's nose lifted slightly, and the acceleration as she burned across the surface of the waves slapped Skirata back in the seat. In the aft view from the hull-mounted safety cam, a wake of white spray and foam churned like a blizzard. The red status bar on the console showed that the speed was moving steadily closer to the flashing blue cursor labeled OPTIMUM THRUST. The airframe vibrated, the drives screamed, and then Skirata's gut plummeted as the DeepWater parted company with the surface of the sea.

"Oya!" Ordo grinned. The ship soared and he was suddenly as excited as a little boy. Novelty always delighted him. *"Kandosii!"*

Behind them, the blizzard on the monitor gave way to gray-blue sea. Skirata admitted mild relief to himself and watched Ordo laying in a course for the RV point, marveling at his instant proficiency.

"You put a lot of trust in me, *Kal'buir,*" he said. "I've never piloted a hybrid like this before."

"I look at it this way, son. If you can't do it, *nobody* can." He patted Ordo's hand, which was still gripping the throttle lever. "I name this ship . . . okay, any ideas?"

Ordo paused, staring ahead. *"Aay'han."*

"Okay . . . *Aay'han* it is." It was a telling choice: there was no Basic translation of the word, because it was a peculiarly

Mandalorian concept. *Aay'han* was that peaceful, perfect moment surrounded by family and friends and remembering dead loved ones, missing them to the point of pain, a state of mind that *bittersweet* could hardly begin to cover. It was about the intensity of love. Skirata doubted if *aruetiise,* non-Mandalorians, would believe that such a depth of feeling existed in a people they saw as a bunch of mercenary thugs. He swallowed to clear his throat and grant the name the respect it deserved. He found he was thinking of his adoptive father, Munin, and a teenage clone commando called Dov whose death in training was Skirata's fault, a pain that made his *aay'han* especially poignant. "This ship shall be known as *Aay'han,* and remembered forever."

"Gai be'bic me'sen Aay'han, meg ade partayli darasuum," Ordo repeated.

"Oya manda."

I'm sorry, Dov. There'd better be a manda *for you, some kind of immortality, or there won't be enough revenge in the galaxy for me.*

Skirata turned his attention to the living again. This wasn't a bad ship at all, and she only had to complete one mission— the most critical one, to find Ko Sai and seize her technology to halt the clones' accelerated aging. He went aft through the double doors into the crew lounge to check out the cosmetic detail. A smell of cleaning fluid, stale food, and mold hit him.

The refreshers and medbay were on the starboard side, stores and galley to port, and the galley lockers were completely empty. He made a note of supplies they'd need to lay in at the first stopover, scribbling reminders on his forearm plate with a stylus. It really didn't matter what the accommodation was like as long as *Aay'han* flew—or dived—in one piece, but he checked the cabins anyway: same gray-and-yellow trim as the rest of the interior, and not much cosmetic water damage. Not bad, not bad at all.

He prodded the mattresses on the bunks, calculating. *Eighty thousand creds—but we've got four million from scamming the terrorists, and nobody will ever miss it.* Sixteen berths, then, and if they needed it there was plenty of cargo space that could be used for crew, maybe enough for thirty people. *So if we need to bang out in a hurry, that's ample room for my boys, Corr, Omega Squad, and any of the ladies, with places to spare.* And then there were all the other Republic commando squads he'd trained, still more than eighty men out there in the field, *his* boys and *his* responsibility every bit as much as Omega, and he was *neglecting* them. They needed a refuge when this war was over, too, maybe even before then.

Did I do enough?

I can make the difference now, lads. Shab Tsad Droten— *curse the Republic.*

Skirata was still refitting *Aay'han* in his mind's eye when Ordo loomed in the hatchway.

"I think we need to change course," he said.

"Go ahead, then, son."

"I mean we need to divert to do an extraction."

Skirata sighed. Okay, they were on Republic time, and he was on Republic pay even if the clones weren't. *It had better be our lads. I hate every second I spend on civilians.* He trusted Ordo's assessment of necessity, and turned to go back to the cockpit. Ordo simply held out a crackling comlink.

"It's Delta," Ordo said. "They had to bang out of Mygeeto in a hurry, and Vau got left behind."

Skirata grabbed the comlink, all the bad blood between him and Vau forgotten. He motioned Ordo back to the cockpit, mouthing *do it* at him.

"RC one-one-three-eight here, Sergeant." It was Boss. "Apologies for the interruption."

Skirata slid into the copilot's seat, trying not to imagine how badly things had gone if Vau had been stranded behind enemy lines. He was an escape artist. "Where are you?"

"We rejoined the fleet on station. We wanted to retrieve him, but General Jusik says—"

"—we're on our way. Sitrep?"

"About twenty kilometers from Jygat. We were leaving the Dressian Kiolsh bank when we met some resistance and he fell down a crevasse."

"Bank?" They'd been there to locate communications nodes for the Marines. "Run out of creds, did he? Needed some small change?"

"It's a long story, Sergeant, and that's why General Jusik thought you'd be . . . a wiser choice."

"Than who?"

"Than telling General Zey."

"I won't waste time asking what the *shab* you were doing in a bank." Jusik: he was a smart lad, *Bard'ika*. Whatever it was, the Jedi had decided that the extraction needed to be kept quiet. "Is Vau alive?"

"Unconfirmed. We lost his signal. He had kit with him that General Jusik felt you would want to recover."

"What *kit?*"

"He cleaned out a bank vault. Credits, jewelry, bonds, the works. Two bags."

Vau robbed a bank? Skirata was taken aback. The miserable old *di'kut* was game for breaking any law, but plain theft—never. This was Skirata's style, not Vau's. "Last known position?"

"Sending you the coordinates now, with our last good ground radar scan of the terrain."

"The strill's still with him, of course."

"Yes. We didn't see it fall."

That was something. Skirata would never trust the animal, but it would lead them to Vau, if it hadn't already located his body and hauled him out. If he found the strill, he found Vau.

"Tell General Jusik we'll sort it out, Delta," he said, and closed the link.

Ordo looked totally unmoved, hand hovering over the hyperspace drive controls. "No point asking Commander Bacara to steer clear of us, is there?"

No, there wasn't. The fewer people who knew they were coming, the better. It would be hard to explain why two men in Mandalorian armor were blundering around a Separatist planet on the Republic's tab without authorization, but the fewer the records of conversations, the easier it was to make events vanish. And Bacara wasn't the kind to ask for ID first.

Skirata didn't want his useless Jedi general Ki-Adi-Mundi in the loop, either. *Jedi hypocrites. It's okay for Conehead to have a family, but they'll bust Etain down to the Agricorps for it.* Skirata would take his chances.

"No, just save Walon's *shebs* and get out of there," Skirata said. *If he's still alive.* "Jump."

Aay'han lurched into star-streaked space. She was holding together just fine.

Gaftikar, Outer Rim, rebel base, 471 days after Geonosis

Darman decided that Null sergeant A'den was a man after his own heart.

"Can't think straight on an empty stomach." A'den fired his blaster into a nest of twig shavings to get the campfire going. The sun was coming up—they'd lost a night's sleep, then—and the lizard-like Gaftikari were still trotting back and forth in neat lines ferrying the weapons they'd collected from the drop. "Got some stew left over from last night. Don't ask what's in it, 'cos I didn't."

Omega Squad sat cross-legged around the fire in their black undersuits, armor plates stacked to one side. Atin held Darman's jet pack on his lap and bent the wing hinge assembly back into shape with a pair of blunt-nosed grips. He hated letting mechanical things get the better of him. "So what happened to the ARC?"

"MIA," A'den said. His tone was totally neutral, and his expression blank: it wasn't his usual demeanor, either, because Darman could see the white lines in the deeply tanned skin around his eyes and mouth. A'den usually smiled a lot, but he wasn't smiling now. "So I've done a recce of Eyat and I've put together as complete a plan of the government buildings as I can."

"Sep force strength?" Niner asked.

"Apart from the locals, minimal."

"I thought this was a hotbed of Sep activity that had to be neutralized pronto."

"Oh dear, *ner vod,* you've been taking intel at face value again, haven't you?" A'den built the fire with meticulous care, stacking branches and dry grasses on the mound and watching the flames grow. "We better cure you of that."

Fi peered into the pot of stew. "It's okay, I've been teaching him sarcasm. He'll be ready for comic exaggeration soon."

"Looks quite a nice peaceful place," Atin said. "Not exactly strategic."

"Eyat?" A'den stirred the pot with a stick. It really did smell good. "Lovely city. Clean, pretty buildings, lots of harmless fun to enjoy. And of no military use to us whatsoever."

Darman kept an eye on the Gaftikari. Now that the sun was coming up, he could see that their light beige scales were slightly iridescent. They had sharp muzzles and small black eyes with disturbing red slit-like pupils. And he'd never seen so many varied weapons strung on one belt: they were more tooled up than Sergeant Kal in a bad mood. Their blades, blasters, and metal bars jingled like wind chimes. One tall lizard provided his own musical accompaniment as he walked, swinging his tail to balance under a load of E-Web parts.

"I see you taught them all about stealth, then," Atin said.

A'den stared at him. "Prudii warned me that you were an awkward customer."

"Funny, Ordo warned Prudii I was argumentative."

"Your reputation precedes you, then," said A'den. "They're good fighters. Trust me."

"I hear a *but* coming," said Niner. "We're specially trained to hear that coming at a hundred klicks."

"But." A'den slopped the stew into their waiting mess tins. When Darman was this hungry, he'd eat flimsi packing cases. "Yes, the *but* is that this is going to end in tears. Eyat—human city. All the cities are human settlements. But . . . scruffy little villages—lizard land."

"So who are the Gaftikari?"

"They all are. Neither species is native. The human colonists brought in the lizard lads to build the place, and now the lizards want to run the show, on account of their numbers. Actually, the lizards are Marits."

"Why are the Seps supporting the humans, then?"

"Because the Republic wants the kelerium and norax deposits here, or at least Shenio Mining does, and the humans are happier without Shenio moving in."

"I'm lost," said Niner.

"The Seps have offered to save Gaftikar from us."

"So we're going to give them something to object to?"

"I don't make the policy. I just train guerrillas and slot bad guys."

They lapsed into silence and ate the stew, which was actually remarkably tasty. The rebels—the Marits—had started assembling an E-Web without the manual, and the way a group of them clustered around the heavy blaster and handled the components gave Darman the impression that they swarmed over their enemies. There was something about the rapid and coordinated movements that reminded him of insects and unnerved him.

"Why are you a sergeant and the rest of the Nulls are officers?" Fi asked. "Didn't you pass your promotion board?"

A'den didn't seem offended. It was hard to tell what would provoke a Null; sometimes it took nothing at all. "I preferred to be an NCO. If it's good enough for *Kal'buir,* it's good enough for me."

Fi seemed satisfied with the explanation. Atin was concentrating on his stew, and Niner was watching the Marits getting to grips with the large artillery piece.

"They're good at assembling things," A'den said. "Good visuospatial ability."

It was the first time any of them had met A'den, and Darman was always keen to get the measure of another of Skirata's Nulls. How had he managed to keep them apart from the commandos during training for so many years? The young Nulls terrified the Kaminoans by running wild around Tipoca City, and that was about the only time the commando squads saw them: stealing equipment, sabotaging systems, and—Darman had never forgotten this—even scaling the supports of the huge domed ceilings, swinging around hundreds of meters above the floor and placing blasterfire to within centimeters of the Kaminoan technicians. The Nulls never cared, never seemed afraid: even then, they answered only to Kal Skirata, and the Kaminoans wouldn't dare cross *Kal'buir.*

Kal'buir said the Kaminoans had messed up the Nulls, and so they deserved what they got. If the Kaminoans complained, he said, he'd *sort them.* Skirata used *sort* as a euphemism for any form of violence, his specialist subject.

A Marit trotted over and peered into the stew, head jerking slightly like a droid. "You like it?"

Atin, kneeling down to help himself to another portion, looked up innocently. The scar across his face—the one that Vau had given him—was a thin white line now. "It's very tasty."

"My great-grandmother!" the Marit beamed. It was weird to watch a lizard smile like a human. They seemed to have a double row of small triangular teeth. "She'll be happy."

Darman noticed A'den slide forward a little and try to interrupt the exchange. "Atin—"

But Atin was off, being polite to the locals and taking his hearts-and-minds role seriously. "Is it her recipe, then?"

"Atin—"

"It's her," said the Marit, and wandered off.

Atin stared into the bowl. There was a moment of complete silence, and A'den sighed. Fi put his knuckles to his mouth to stifle nervous laughter, but it didn't work. Niner chewed to a halt. Darman tried to be culturally sensitive and all that, but he was hungry, and the Marit seemed pleased they were enjoying the meal.

"Oh fierfek . . ." Atin put his mess tin down on the ground and sat back on his heels. He screwed his eyes shut tight, and judging by the way his lips compressed he was in serious *digestive crisis,* as Ordo called it. Then he rocked back on his heels, stood up, and bolted for the nearest bushes.

"He's throwing up," Niner said, and went on eating. The faint sound of retching confirmed his diagnosis.

A'den shrugged. "It's not like they *killed* her to eat her. It's how they dispose of their dead. They like to think they do their families some good after they're gone. It's rude not to tuck in."

"Cultural diversity's a wonderful thing," Fi observed, but he looked quite pale. "What do they do for desserts?"

Niner fished out a chunk of lean meat and gazed at it, then popped it into his mouth and chewed thoughtfully. Darman didn't know he could be so daring. "I never thought I'd resort to cannibalism."

"It's not cannibalism for us, Niner," A'den said. "Just for *them.*"

"That's the Grand Army for you." Fi's face seemed back to its normal color again. "See the galaxy, meet fascinating new species, and snack on them."

"Well, we wouldn't be alone." A'den looked up, all concern, as Atin walked back unsteadily from the bushes, wiping his mouth. "You okay?"

"You did that deliberately. You could have told me before I started eating."

"I said *don't ask,* and I said I hadn't."

Atin—quiet, methodical Atin—had been one of Vau's training company, not Skirata's. It showed. A'den stared at Atin, and Atin stared back. Niner rolled his eyes as if he was shaping up to separate them, and it wouldn't have been the first time that Atin needed hauling out of a confrontation. There was something about the way Vau trained his men that gave them a core of wildness, a complete inability to see sense and back down when pushed too far.

A'den almost broke into a grin. "You tried to vibroblade Vau, didn't you? We all heard about that."

Atin gave him the silent routine. Darman waited for A'den to run out of patience and give Atin a good slap, as Fi liked to call it, but he just shrugged and rummaged in his pockets.

"Okay," said A'den. He found what he was looking for and tossed a ration bar across to Atin, who caught it. "First, you can grow a *shabla* beard. Because you're going to have to infiltrate Eyat, and they're not used to seeing quads. Mix yourselves up a bit and choose who gets to stay looking normal."

Fi perked up immediately. "I'll dress up as a lizard if I can have a trip into town."

"Done," A'den said. "But scrub the scaly look, because Marits don't go into the cities now, except to shoot the locals. That's why a human's best suited to do assassinations. Once you've got your bearings, I want two of you to recce Eyat again and get a few spycams planted. The Marits can't go in unnoticed, and whatever intel Sull put together went with him."

"Sull?" said Fi.

"Alpha-Thirty," A'den said. "That was his name. Sull."

Darman finished his stew and watched A'den. He wasn't pleased, that much was obvious. Maybe it was having to follow up on an Alpha ARC when he thought he had more important business. Maybe it was just normal irritation at being tasked to carry out a mission that looked pointless and wasn't resourced. He worked alone, and that had to take its toll on any man's will.

Niner scraped out his mess tin and rinsed it clean with water from his bottle. "I think we should be concentrating our forces on kicking the *osik* out of the main Sep homeworlds," he said suddenly. "Because if we keep this up, we'll be down to one clone per planet, showing the locals a field manual on how to throw stones."

A'den turned his head slowly and parted his lips as if to speak. He paused. He seemed to be measuring his words.

"You're in good company," he said. "Lots of us do, including General Zey. But the Chancellor wants to avoid too much collateral damage. No pounding, no surging, no offending the civvies."

"No resources."

"Enough resources not to lose, but not enough to win," A'den said. "He's just feeding a stalemate, the moron."

Darman thought it was time they got on with making friends with the Marits. He stood up and ambled over to the lizards, wondering if there might be anything in Eyat that he could *acquire* for Etain. It was hard to think of anything that a Jedi might want. They avoided possessions.

"You know what's been bothering me?" Fi's voice drifted across the center of the camp. The Marits had finished calibrating the artillery piece and were admiring it. "What if the war had broken out when we were *five* years into our training instead of eight, nine . . . ten?"

"What?" A'den asked.

"Nobody knows when a war's going to start, not years ahead, anyway. It's not like you can book one in advance. So there we are, fully trained, and then it all kicks off. Very lucky. What if it had all gone to poodoo years before? What if we'd been half trained, still just kids?"

"Then we'd have been fighting in diapers," Atin muttered. "Because the Republic didn't have any other army worth a mott's backside."

Fi raised an eyebrow. "*Shabla* lucky, if you ask me."

"Time to move it," A'den said sharply, and Darman suspected he was breaking up the speculation for a reason. Judging by the expression on Fi's face, he felt that, too. "I'll bring you up to speed with the local situation, and you can spend the rest of the day getting to know our allies."

The longer the war went on, the less sense it made to Darman. After years of clear certainty in training—knowing what he had to do, and why he would have to do it, because there had never been any doubt in anyone's mind that they would one day be deployed—the reality of the war didn't match any of it. Shambolic organization, indecisive leadership from the top, and . . . too many gray areas. The more places he was sent, the more things Darman saw that made him ask why they didn't just let planets cede from the Republic. Life would go on.

Fi's thinking was getting to him. Every thought now started with a *why*.

Stay busy. There was nothing he could about it now except get on with his job. He smiled at the Marits. "I'm Darman," he said, holding out his hand for shaking. "Want me to show you how to make shrapnel out of a droid?"

3

*No, General Zey—finding Chief Scientist Ko Sai is as much
a priority as locating General Grievous. Our survival
depends on a strong army, and that means the highest-
quality clones—conscription of ordinary citizens is a poor
second and would be politically unacceptable. Find her, if
only to deny the Separatists her expertise. You have the best
intelligence assets the Republic has ever known. So I'll
accept no excuses.*
—Chancellor Palpatine, to Jedi general Arligan Zey,
Director of Special Forces, Grand Army of the Republic

DeepWater-class ship *Aay'han*, Mygeeto space, 471 days after
Geonosis

"Fierfek." Skirata sighed, watching the transponders
mapped on the cockpit holochart. The picket of ships around
Mygeeto made it look as if it were ringed by its own constel-
lation. "I know Bacara's keeping them busy down there, but
that's still quite a gauntlet to run."

"And we're a forty-five-meter cargo ship," Ordo said.
"Just a laser cannon by way of armament. Mandalorian crew
in full *beskar'gam*. Definitely not a Republic vessel."

"What d'you think, just walk in?"

"Could do. Nothing links us to the Republic. And I always
carry a range of current transponder codes, so that's an easy
fix."

"Well, we won't win a battle with a warship, so that's our choice made for us."

"Of course, a submersible's sensors are perfect for getting an accurate three-dimensional scan of the site."

"In we go, then, *Ord'ika*."

Ordo studied the long-range orbital scan of the landing site. It was a vast glacier in a landscape of sheet ice and crystal rock. The penetrating scan showed few crevasses, but the sheet was honeycombed with irregular tunnels that meandered around one another like tangled yarn and occasionally crossed. The straight, uniform outlines of the ventilation shafts were easy to identify by contrast. Around the warm shafts, underground lakes of melted water had formed, capped by thinner ice sheets. Ordo copied the section of holochart to his datapad and didn't even have to do the calculations to realize that searching each tunnel in the site that Delta had pinpointed would take days.

Too long.

An idea formed immediately in his mind, as well as a theory on what had happened to Vau. He might have fallen into the warren of tunnels—or through the ice into the liquid water beneath.

It wasn't good either way.

"Crystal-worm tunnels," Ordo said. "It's fascinating how life-forms survive even in the most extreme places."

"If Vau's out in those temperatures," said Skirata, "he won't be one of them. It's been hours. Even in his *beskar'gam,* the seals won't keep out that kind of cold indefinitely."

Ordo slid his electronic tool case out of his sleeve and took out an overwrite probe. He selected a randomly generated transponder code with a Mandalore prefix, and *Aay'han* ceased to register as licensed on Mon Calamari.

"Okay, *Kal'buir,* now or never."

He maneuvered *Aay'han* into a landing trajectory and wondered whether to brazen it out by pinging Mygeeto Traffic Control and requesting permission to land. No water on board, a civilian vessel that anyone could scan to confirm its configuration—he'd sort *that* the moment they got out of here—and a couple of wandering mercs at the helm: even with a battle going on, he might get away with it.

He opened the traffic frequency. "Mygeeto TC, this is Mandalorian cargo vessel *Aay'han.* Request permission to set down for replenishment."

The pause was longer than he expected. "*Aay'han,* this is Mygeeto TC. For Mandalorians, you're remarkably slow to notice we have hostilities ongoing."

"Mygeeto, scan our tanks for water."

The next pause was even longer. "*Aay'han,* we note your tanks are zeroed. Unfortunately, our city facilities are closed. Remember the hostilities?"

If he was turned away now, he'd blown it. They'd drawn Mygeeto's attention to them. "Mygeeto, there appears to be water just under the surface west of the hostilities, and Mandalore does give assistance to the CIS. We'll refill at our own risk."

"*Aay'han,* okay, go ahead, and don't try to sue us if you sustain damage or injury. Make sure you're off the planet in two standard hours."

Ordo felt his shoulder muscles relax. He hadn't realized he'd tensed them. "Mygeeto, understood."

He closed the link. Skirata winked at him and grinned. *Kal'buir* was proud of him, and it made him feel as safe and confident now as it had when he was a small child.

"It's amazing how rarely you need to use force," he said, relieved.

Without the coordinates from Delta, Ordo knew he wouldn't have known where to start the search for Vau. Mygeeto's surface was a windswept icescape, dazzlingly pretty for a few minutes and then fatally disorienting. Ordo set *Aay'han* down between cliffs on the edge of the underground lake and sealed his armor, and as he opened the hatch the wind shrieked and howled. He slid off the hull, and Skirata dropped down beside him.

"He's been out here for four hours, *Kal'buir.*" Ordo activated his helmet's infrared filter, adjusted it to its most sensitive setting, and cast around on a square search of a twenty-meter grid. "If he's dead, I might still pick up a temperature differential, but it's unlikely."

Skirata paced the imaginary grid with slow, silent deliberation, sweeping a handheld scanner across the surface to locate holes and fissures, and then scanning for temperature changes. Ordo suddenly wondered if he'd been tactless, and that *Kal'buir* might be upset at the thought of Vau being dead. The two men had been at each other's throats ever since he could remember, but they also went back a long time, including all those years training clones on Kamino, erased from the galaxy and dead to all who knew them.

"I'm sorry, *Buir*," he said.

"Don't be." Skirata checked a readout on his forearm plate. "I'm scanning for metals. This detects twenty meters down."

Skirata might have been genuinely unmoved, interested only in the proceeds of the robbery. For once Ordo couldn't tell, but he doubted it. Skirata felt everything on raw nerves. They paced slowly, leaning against the wind, and Skirata seemed to be cycling through his comlink frequencies because Ordo was picking up spikes on his system. Vau might have left a link open. It was worth trying.

"No paw prints," Skirata said. "Wind's probably swept them away."

Ordo switched from infrared to the penetrating sensor. It was like checking in mail slots, a tedious progression from one hole to the next. A recent fall of snow was drifting, filling in the depressions. "He could be anywhere. He might even have got out and found shelter."

Skirata tilted his head down as if listening. Ordo caught a burst of audio on the shared comlink. "If he is, his helmet systems are down."

"I'm getting static."

"He might be down too deep."

Ordo was starting to feel the cold seeping through his armor joints. If this had been his GAR-issue suit, he'd have had temperature control, but his Mandalorian *beskar'gam* was more basic. He'd fix that as soon as he got the chance, just like he'd upgraded his helmet. It wasn't as if he spent a lot of time working in it. He'd never thought to check how Vau's suit was configured: it was just matte black, an image he dreaded as a kid, and now unsettlingly like Omega's Katarn rig. Black was the color of justice. *Kal'buir*'s armor was sand gold, the color of vengeance. Ordo had opted for deep red plates simply because he liked the color.

But black or gold, if Vau didn't have coldproofing or some other protection, he'd be dead now.

"Don't laugh, son," Skirata said, "but I'm going to try something old-fashioned. Just like you talked your way past the picket."

He stood with his arms at his sides and yelled.

"Mird! Mird, you dribbling heap, can you hear me?" The wind was drowning out his voice. He clenched his fists and tried again. *"Mird!"*

Ordo joined in calling the strill's name. He almost expected to see a patrol closing in on them, but his helmet sensors showed nothing.

"Strills can stand cold," Skirata said, pausing to get his breath. "And they've got better hearing than humans. It was worth a try." He tapped his forearm controls, adjusting his helmet's voice projector to maximum. *"Mird!"*

How would they even hear the animal if it responded to their calls? Ordo was about to go back and start using the ship's sensor systems to probe deeper into the ice, but he heard Skirata say *"Osi'kyr!"* in surprise and when he turned, the snow was shaking. The thin crust broke. A gold-furred head pushed through like a hideously ugly seedling, a thick layer of white frost on its muzzle.

"Mird, I'll never curse you again," Skirata said, and knelt down to scoop away the chunks of ice. The animal whined pitifully. "Is he down there, Mird? Is Vau down there?" He hesitated and then rubbed the folds of loose skin on its muzzle. "Map the tunnel for me, *Ord'ika*."

The holochart hung in the air, a 3-D model of the ice beneath them. The tunnel that Mird had struggled out of ran down at a thirty-degree angle and curved close to the margin of the lake before snaking away again and disappearing off the chart in the direction of Jygat.

"It's about sixty meters down to the bend, and the diameter there is only a meter," Ordo said. "If he fell, chances are he came to rest at the bend."

"Long way down." Skirata had his arms around Mird, and Ordo wasn't sure if he was hugging the animal or trying to shelter it. It was a marked change of attitude, given that he'd thrown his knife at it more than once in the past. "Mird, find Vau. Good Mird. Here." He took out a length of fibercord from his belt and knotted it around Mird's neck. "Go find him. You couldn't drag him out, could you? Is he stuck? Find him."

Mird struggled back down the tunnel, making rasping noises with its claws like a skater, and then there was silence again.

"Mird's clever, but a strill can't tie knots," said Ordo. "So if Vau's dead or unconscious, what are you doing?"

"Measuring," said Skirata. He had a tight grip on the line, watching it intently. Eventually it went taut. "Fierfek, there's never a Jedi around when you need one, is there? *Bard'ika* could have done his Force stuff and located Vau right away." He tugged on the line. "Back, Mird. Come back." The line went slack again. "Given how much line I'm holding, minus the loop, Vau's at fifty-eight meters."

"If Mird reached him."

"It'd stay with Vau. Trust me, it stopped where Vau is when the line went taut. Now all we have to do is get to him."

The solution was obvious to Ordo. "We breach the tunnel at the thinnest point of the ice, which is where it runs next to the lake, and that's less than eight meters thick."

"And flood the tunnel . . ."

"No."

"Or flush him into the lake and lose him. Either way, he's dead."

"Either way," Ordo said, utterly relieved that he recalled

every line of the DeepWater manual, "I line the ship up, star-
board-side-to, and work through the ice with the boarding
tube from the air lock. Dry entry."

Skirata looked up at him for a moment. Ordo didn't need
to see his face to know what he was thinking.

"You still manage to amaze me, son. You really do."

"Just hope we don't hit rock."

Mird crawled out of the tunnel and flopped at Skirata's
feet, panting. It was a struggle to get the strill into *Aay'han,*
probably because it thought they were leaving Vau behind,
but it was weak and frozen, and that meant Skirata and Ordo
could subdue it between them.

Ordo set the ship down on the frozen surface of the lake.
If the ice cracked and they fell through, that was fine, because it would save him the trouble of smashing through. But
it didn't.

*Shields. What did it say about shields when diving? Re-
configure.* He tapped in the commands and waited. Amber
indicators changed one by one to green. *Okay, now avoid
any serious impacts . . .*

Ordo lifted *Aay'han* clear of the surface, climbed steeply,
and fired a laser round at the lake at what he hoped was a safe
distance from the ice wall. Steam plumed up beneath him
like a geyser. A chunk of ice lifted vertically and bobbed for
a second before sliding back again.

The lake would freeze over fast. "Brace for dive," he said,
and took her in a slow nosedive.

"Osik."

"Oh yes—"

*Do other people live their lives like this? Do they take
these kinds of risks?*

It wasn't the time to worry about that. Ordo hadn't yet met
a problem he couldn't solve or a situation he couldn't survive. *Aay'han* pushed through the shattered surface, and
even at low speed it seemed like crashing into solid rock.
For a moment Ordo thought he'd got it badly wrong, but
the slow ice impact wasn't anywhere near as violent as
weapons fire, and the shield held. Chunks scraped and

screeched as she passed through the slush layer, and then everything went quiet in clear twilight water. They were in the lake itself. Now he had to align the air lock with Vau's position.

"You knew the hull would take that, right, *Ord'ika*?" Skirata jumped out of the copilot's seat and pulled off his helmet. He looked shaken.

"Of course I did. Well, ninety percent sure."

"Okay, close enough. Let's do some scanning."

The air lock was nearly two meters in diameter. Ordo aligned it at Vau's rough position and used the penetrating sensors to look for a dense mass. Skirata went into the starboard cargo bay with his metal scanner and opened the inner air lock hatch. The warning light lit up on the console, and Skirata's voice crackled over the ship's intercom.

"Big immobile lump of durasteel and *beskar* about six meters in," he said. "Good old Mandalorian iron. You can't beat the stuff. That's Vau all right."

Six meters: that was a pretty thin wall between the tunnel and the water. At least there was no worm activity, but there was no way of knowing if the shock wave from the laser round would attract them. "Let me reposition. I'm a meter off."

"I can't tell if he's alive."

"Okay, we've got to cut through that ice now."

"Heat it," Skirata said.

"We can vent the meltwater through the tanks."

"About eighty cubic meters. Maybe less."

"Okay." Ordo hiked the thermostat on the environmental controls: they needed to raise the temperature of the exposed ice on the other side of the air lock any way they could. "Maybe a combination of heat and cutting."

"And Mygeeto TC wants us out of here in . . . about an hour and a half."

Ordo extended the outer docking ring until he felt it embed in the lake wall. "Come out of the air lock, *Kal'buir.* I need to test for leaks. Clear?"

"Clear. I'm going to see what we've got in the tool locker."

"Okay, closing inner air lock." The status light changed to green again. He put *Aay'han* on autohelm to hold her steady against the ice wall. "Opening outer hatch."

The sensors showed no leaks. When Ordo maneuvered the safety cam inside the air lock chamber, he saw a smooth glassy disc of dirty ice. A few meters on the other side of that lay Walon Vau. If they got it wrong while they tried to cut through the wall, the water would flood in and sink *Aay'han*. It was a lot of trouble to go to for a few credits and a man both of them disliked.

On too many occasions, Ordo had wished Vau dead. Now he found himself willing the *chakaar* to stay alive.

Special Operations Brigade HQ, Coruscant, General Arligan Zey's office, 471 days after Geonosis

Sev thought it was just as well he had a reputation for being uncommunicative. General Zey walked up and down the short line of four commandos as if he was doing an inspection, pausing occasionally to stare at a detail of their armor or look into their eyes.

If the Jedi thought that would psych out Delta Squad, he'd have a long, long walk ahead of him.

Sev stared straight ahead, hands clasped behind his back, boots planted firmly at shoulder width. In his peripheral vision, General Jusik sat on a table swinging his legs. His disheveled Padawan image didn't fool anyone. Sev had been on enough operations with him to know that he could make Scorch look overcautious. Zey's ARC trooper aide, Captain Maze, prowled the room as if he wasn't listening to the debriefing. On balance, Sev preferred the Null ARCs. They *understood* in a way that the men trained by Fett simply didn't.

Zey came to a halt in front of Boss and stood with his nose almost touching his. "I'm not stupid," he said quietly. "Am I, Sergeant?"

"Sir, no *sir*!" Boss barked.

"Want to tell me what went wrong with your exfiltration?"

"Sir, we encountered some resistance and were forced to exit the complex via an unreconnoitered passage, sir."

Sev felt for Boss. They'd all made the decision to stick with Vau, but Boss was . . . the boss. So he got it in the neck. Sev found the occasional trips back to HQ unsettling. He wanted to be back out in the field with just his brothers for company, because Coruscant wasn't their world, and he'd already had enough of it.

Zey was still in Boss's face. "This wouldn't have anything to do with Skirata, would it, Three-Eight?"

"Sir, *no* sir!"

Well, that much was true. Nobody had actually lied to Zey yet, because Jedi had a way of telling if someone was lying. Zey took a pace back, seemed to be suppressing a smile, and then shook his head.

"Well," he said at last, sitting down behind his fancy lapiz-inlaid desk. "Good result on Mygeeto. General Ki-Adi-Mundi has sent his commendation."

Don't care. What's happened to Sergeant Vau?

"Can we eat it, sir?" Scorch asked, straight-faced.

"I realize you returned with indecent haste, Delta." Zey turned to Maze. "Captain, once I'm through with this briefing, take Delta straight to the mess and stand over them while they eat the recommended daily intake."

Maze, looking less than thrilled by his nursemaid duties, grunted, "Sir." Jusik, who'd been staring out the window, suddenly flinched as if someone unseen had walked up behind him. Jedi were weird.

"But before you eat, gentlemen, here's your new brief." Zey flicked a holochart into life, and the familiar planet-studded grid settled in the air over the briefing table. "And this comes straight from the Chancellor—a direct personal order. Find Chief Scientist Ko Sai."

Boss was still doing the talking, which suited Sev just fine, because he was far more interested in Vau's fate and was now watching Jusik carefully. The kid was like a holoreceiver. He picked up all kinds of stuff from distant events. Maybe he'd detected something now. He certainly looked distracted.

"And when we find her, sir?"

"Bring her back in one piece."

"Bummer," Fixer muttered. *"Sir."*

Zey managed a smile. "I know you have little to love the Kaminoans for, gentlemen, but I don't make the rules. Lama Su is adamant that Ko Sai defected and that she didn't die. He won't give his reasons, but that probably doesn't matter because the Chancellor wants a tame Kaminoan scientist for our own use so we aren't beholden to Tipoca, should they ever change their minds about our favored-customer status." The general shook his head as if he was arguing with himself. "So haul her back here. Top priority. He ordered me to put the best team on it."

Sev accepted that it was true. They were better than Omega because they didn't go soft and get diverted by personal issues. They had Vau to thank for that.

"She's been gone a year, sir. Why make the move so late in the day?" Boss asked.

"I'm not privy to that information, Sergeant," Zey said carefully. "But the intel we do have, via the Kaminoans, suggests that she's passed through Vaynai within the last six months."

Sev didn't know the Kaminoans had any kind of intelligence, seeing as they almost never left their homeworld, but they could clearly buy it in from outside. He chalked Ko Sai up to the long list of objectives that Delta had been set and tried to come to terms with his fears about Vau.

Boss broke position and wandered over to the holochart to locate Vaynai. "Who's tracking her, sir?"

"You."

"Understood."

"The report came from Ryn who do occasional work for the Republic. She's probably long gone, but this is the first positive lead we've had."

Sev sneaked a look at Jusik. Something had definitely distracted him, and it wasn't what was happening on the parade ground. The Jedi looked at him and gave him a discreet thumbs-up.

What does that mean? Cheer up? His grav-ball team won? Vau's okay?

Boss, Scorch, and Fixer were engrossed in the discussion on the significance of Vaynai—plenty of ocean, and she wasn't likely to be hiding out on Tatooine—and Sev just stood there, eyes pointing in the appropriate direction to look like he was following the debate.

Fear. Yes, it *was* fear. Everyone got scared, but this was different: a gnawing, hollow void in his stomach. He'd let Vau down when it mattered. If Vau survived, he'd beat Sev within a breath of his life. If he didn't—he'd haunt him. *Try harder, Sev. You let your brothers down, you let me down, you let the whole* shabla *army down. Try harder, you lazy little* chakaar, *or next time it really* will *hurt.*

Sev had tried so hard that he'd collapsed on his bunk most nights without even getting his fatigues off, and then had to catch up on his laundry in the early hours when reveille made his heart nearly leap out of his chest and he got up with his head still buzzing with lack of sleep.

He was five years old. He hadn't forgotten.

Sev was now the best sniper in the Grand Army because he didn't want to let anyone down.

". . . and this stays within this room, gentlemen, because this is the Chancellor's pet peeve." Zey's tone jerked Sev back to the present. "Nobody else in Special Operations knows about this, and I really don't want Skirata to know, because . . . fine man though he might be, he does have an issue with Kaminoans. Any man who refers to them as *tatsushi* and actually boasts of recipes is probably best kept out of the loop. Dismissed."

Scorch chuckled approvingly as they clunked their way down the corridor toward the mess with Maze at their heels. "You think Skirata would really eat a Kaminoan?"

Fixer managed a sentence, which was good going for him. "Only if he had hot sauce."

"What do you think they serve us? That isn't rollerfish on the menu." Scorch half turned as he walked, trying to drag Sev into the conversation. "You okay, Sev?"

"Terrific." They couldn't mention Vau in front of Maze. As far as Zey was concerned, Vau had done the Mygeeto recce and banged out. He certainly hadn't robbed a bank and plunged down some ice hole to freeze to death, if he hadn't already broken his neck. "Never better."

The sound of boots walking briskly down the corridor behind them broke into a clatter. Jusik caught up, looking flushed and almost pleased with himself. "I'll keep this lot in line, Captain," he said to Maze. "I'm sure you've got better things to do than make them finish their greens."

Maze turned on his heel immediately and began walking back to the command center. "Whatever it is you're doing," he said, "thank you for not involving me in it—sir."

Maze wasn't stupid. He didn't want to stand between two Jedi generals playing a game. Nobody in their right mind would. Boss stood back to let Jusik enter the mess first.

"Well, General?"

"I feel that Vau is alive."

"And we left him behind," Sev said. "We don't do that."

Jusik took Sev's arm discreetly and applied a little pressure. "And you were out of options, Private. If he'd wanted extracting, he'd have asked."

Scorch grabbed a plate of seedbreads and slapped them on a table to mark his territory. Few of the other commandos sat near Delta at mealtimes because they were one of the last complete squads who'd been decanted together in Tipoca City and stayed together this far. Heavy casualties in the early days of the war—Sev hated himself for believing all that guff about Jedi being invincible military geniuses— meant that most commando squads had been re-formed at least once and just didn't have that extra cohesion that Delta did, Sev was sure. All but one of Vau's squads had stayed in one piece; he might have been a savage instructor, but it was all for their own good. He said so. It was *true*.

"So what now, sir?" Boss asked. "How do we make this disappear? The voice traffic with Skirata?"

"Don't kid yourself that Zey doesn't know something went on." Jusik could switch from being a goofy kid to a hard man in an instant. He seemed to be learning a lot from Skirata. "He has to at least *pretend* to stick to the rules. Leave it to me. Those comlink records will vanish before anyone knows they exist."

"Thank you, sir."

"You made the right call to pass the problem to me instead of Zey," Jusik said. "You might feel disloyal, but what he doesn't officially know can't get him in trouble."

"Will you let us know when they find him?"

" 'Course I will. If anyone can extract him, *Kal'buir* and *Ord'ika* can." Jusik grabbed a seedbread from Scorch's plate and got up to leave. "The Force tells me things will work out."

Sev watched him go. If the Force was that chatty, it should have been telling the Jedi about useful strategic stuff, not vague fortune-telling.

"Kal'buir," Fixer mocked.

Boss didn't seem too upset about Vau to eat. "Wow, he's got it bad, little Jusik, hasn't he?"

"Regular little *Mando'ad*—"

"Hey, our sarge is *missing*." Sev clenched his teeth to keep his voice as low as he could. "Vau could be *dead,* and you can eat and joke? We *abandoned* him. We left him to die. We *never* leave a man behind, guys."

The other three stared at him like he was telling them something they didn't know. "Take it easy, Sev. We're all worried."

"Best thing we can do," Scorch said, "is do our job and let everyone else do theirs."

"You get that gem of wisdom off a ration pack label?" Sev snapped.

"Shut up and eat. You'll think straighter on a full stomach and a few hours' sleep." Scorch grabbed a passing server droid. "Full Corrie breakfast for the young psychopath here, tinnie."

Sev ate too fast to taste the food, but at least it filled a hole, as Fi would have said if the annoying little jerk had been here. Sev wasn't sure if he missed Omega or not. On balance, he did.

And it was all for a few credits. There weren't enough credits in the galaxy to make it worth leaving a comrade behind. Sev could imagine nothing worse.

If he ever saw Vau alive again, he wondered if he'd have the guts to apologize to him.

Mygeeto, DeepWater submersible *Aay'han*, depth fifty-eight meters, 471 days after Geonosis

Skirata wasn't sure if the fluid dripping off his nose and chin was spray from the melting ice or his own sweat.

They'd been hacking at the ice face for an hour now, and the space was too confined for both of them to work at the same time. They took turns. Skirata found he needed it: it was hot, damp, and numbing labor. Melting was useless. It seemed to be freezing again as fast as it thawed. He put his full weight against an inadequate hydrocutter and took another chunk of ice out of what he saw as a six-meter tunnel. His hands were numb and tingling from the vibration.

I'm getting too old for this.

Vau, why the shab *are we even bothering? I put my boy at risk for this?*

Ordo tapped him on the shoulder. "Break, *Kal'buir.*"

Skirata put the cutter on standby and found he could hardly move his legs. Ordo, with that perfect silent understanding, grabbed him by his boots and hauled him out of the air lock tube. Skirata leaned against the bulkhead and then slid down it in exhaustion. His hands felt lifeless. He shook them hard to stop the tingling.

It wasn't the time to say that they could have left Vau. They were both at the stage where they couldn't think of much beyond the next minute and the next chunk of ice pulled free and pushed out onto the deck. The cargo bay deck was scattered with wet gravel freed by the melt: the pristine white landscape disguised how much debris there was in the compressed snow.

There was another *thunk* from the air lock like a brick falling off a wall. Skirata struggled to his feet and stepped in to clear the ice out of Ordo's way. Even the noise of the cutting disc couldn't drown out Mird's whining and yelping, and he wondered if the strill would claw clean through the hatch to get out of the locked storage compartment. Even if nobody else loved Vau, that animal certainly did.

The good thing about repetitive and desperate physical labor was that it stopped you from speculating too much on things like the ice that had refrozen across the lake, the possibility that the lake wall would collapse under the weight of the water anyway, and that, working now without their sealed armor, they'd drown if the boarding tube gave way.

Clunk.

Ordo was young, strong, and fit. He was removing the ice a lot faster than Skirata could.

"Rewarming," Ordo yelled. Skirata was partially deaf from too much time spent around loud explosions without a helmet, but he could hear him. "When we get Vau out, he's bound to have hypothermia, however good his armor is. Got to get him thawed."

"What?"

"Rescue breathing. Warm air in the lungs. Mouth-to-mouth."

Skirata wasn't thinking fast enough. *"Osik."*

"Maybe Mird can do it . . ."

The one thing they had plenty of now was hot water. The tanks were full. Vau could at least have warm compresses.

"Warm sugar water." Ordo grunted with effort, and there was another *clunk*. He was going well. "It's all about raising core temperature."

Skirata broke out his ration pack. He never imagined he'd give Walon Vau his last energy blocks. Here he was, worrying about a *chakaar* who'd beat his men badly enough to put them in a medcenter, when he had his boys, Jusik, a pregnant

Etain, and now Besany Wennen to fret over, and they all deserved his efforts a lot more than Vau.

"Chakaar," he said to himself.

"A cryodroid might be a good investment."

"What?"

"I said, *I think a cryodroid might be a good investment.* Icebreaking." The drill drowned Ordo's voice for a while. "Should be able to melt ice faster than this."

It was a long half hour. The brief spells at the ice face were getting harder each time, and they needed to save their energy blocks for Vau. Skirata felt his strength ebbing faster. The gravel released from the ice dug into the palms of his hands when he crawled into the tube, but they were so numb now he could hardly feel it. Eventually he resorted to his blaster, and the steam made the compartment feel like a sanisteamer.

Ordo checked the thickness of the ice. "Nearly there. At least it's warm in here."

"I'm sorry, son. Getting you into this."

"Good training. Never done this before."

"You should be out on the town with your girl at your age, not—"

"I don't feel right about using Besany to spy for us."

It was right out of the blue. Ordo did that from time to time, revealing what was on his mind and making Skirata realize he didn't know everything about him, not even now. He must have been chewing it over while he slogged away at the ice.

"Mereel didn't force her, son. She knows the score."

"I meant that I wasn't expecting to feel bad about it."

So again, Skirata knew even less about Ordo than he thought. He decided not to comment and just let the lad ramble on, but Ordo went quiet again and more lumps of dirty, gritty ice fell out onto the deck as the cutter whined. He'd had his say.

The Republic uses you, son, but now we're using the Republic. Can't let an asset like Besany Wennen go to waste.

A breath of burning cold air on his face and a shout from

Ordo snapped Skirata out of an exhausted trance, and somehow his adrenaline got him back on his feet.

"We're through. I see him." There wasn't enough room for both of them in the tube. Ordo hacked frantically at the rapidly enlarging hole. When he leaned back to reach for a fibercord line, Skirata could see a black shape that didn't look like a man for a moment, but then he could make out part of the T-shaped visor of Vau's helmet. "I'm cutting his packs free."

The operation was now more like delivering a nerf calf. After much swearing and panting, Ordo backed out of the boarding tube, hauling Vau by a line around one shoulder. It sounded like he was dragging a coffin. Vau plopped onto the cargo bay deck in a heap, his armor so cold that it burned Skirata's fingers as he eased off the man's helmet.

Vau's hard, gaunt face was almost blue. Skirata pushed his eyelids back to check his pupils: they reacted to the light. Humans survived low temperatures even when they looked dead, and Vau *was definitely alive.* Skirata mentally listed all the procedures he had to follow, like looking for a pulse, counting breaths, not rubbing extremities, and diverting warmer blood from the core. "*Osik,* Walon, you *shabuir,* don't you dare go and die on me now—"

Vau's head rolled and he mumbled back at Skirata. "Mird," he said. "Mird . . ."

Skirata had gone after Vau at least twice in his life fully intending to kill him. His instinct, funny thing that it was, now focused him totally on saving the man. Ordo slithered backward out of the tube again, dragging Vau's *birgaan* and a large bundle of plastoid sheeting that chinked and clacked.

"Rescue breathing, *Kal'buir,*" he panted. The effort had even taken its toll on Ordo. He grabbed Vau and half dragged, half carried him into the medbay, heaving him onto the bunk. Skirata trailed behind with the bags. "I know your cussing can generate a few kilowatts of heat, but it's not reaching his lungs."

"He's conscious and breathing. No CPR."

"Okay. Dry. He's dry." Wet clothing leached the heat fast. "The suit held up."

Skirata pulled off Vau's armor and grabbed whatever he could find from the locker to wrap him up. His fingers showed no signs of frostbite: corpse-cold, but still soft. That was something. "Let Mird out."

Mird shot out of the store compartment and nearly knocked Skirata over. The animal was good and warm. If anyone was going to snuggle up to Vau and transfer heat, Mird was the best choice. Ordo watched the strill flop onto its master with delighted little squeals and rumbles, slobbering over his face. Ordo seemed to find it suddenly funny.

"Thanks, Mird," he said. "You saved us both from a fate worse than death. Carry on, that strill." He turned to Skirata. "It's time to seal up and get out of here."

"How are you going to break the surface ice?"

Ordo shrugged. "Torpedo."

"Well, the laser didn't attract any unwelcome attention, so go for it, son. I'll get some hot liquid into Vau."

"Secure him in the bunk, because we're going to be banging out of here at quite an angle. You might want to hold off the hot liquid until we're stable again."

Ordo never exaggerated. When he said *quite an angle,* he probably meant vertical. A few moments after the shock of an exploding torpedo bounced back at them, everything they hadn't had time to stow securely went sliding to the bulkheads and Mird howled, claws nailed deep into the bunk housing. *Aay'han* leveled out. The loose objects thudded back down on the deck.

"Drink this," Skirata said, lifting Vau's head with one hand and holding a beaker of the cube-sweetened hot water to his lips. Mird gave Skirata some grudging space but spread itself down the length of Vau's frame. "Get it in your gut, Walon, or I'll have to heat your innards by shoving a blaster down your throat."

Vau coughed, splashing a fine spray of spit in Skirata's face. "I'm going . . . to tell everyone . . . what a soft *chakaar* you are, Kal."

Well, his cognitive functions were just fine. No confused rambling there; Skirata ticked one more symptom off the first-aid list. "Can you feel any injuries?"

"Not yet . . . you look worse than me . . ."

"Come on." Skirata slopped more liquid into his mouth. He felt wrecked now. "Get this down you."

"Tell Delta?"

"Okay, yes." Vau had a few saving graces: he knew his lads would be worried sick about him, and that they needed to know he'd been extracted. "Will do. Now what the *shab* was worth nearly freezing to death for?"

"What the *shab*," Vau said hoarsely, "was worth nearly . . . killing yourself . . . to save me?"

"I wanted your armor. Better environment seals than mine, obviously. You could survive a sarlacc in that."

Vau actually smiled. He didn't do that often. He had very even, white teeth that proved he'd had a healthy and well-fed early childhood. "*Birgaan* . . . take a look inside . . ."

Ordo's voice cut into the ship's comlink system. "I'm heading for the RV point, *Kal'buir*. I've informed General Jusik that Vau's inboard."

"Good lad," said Skirata.

"Good lad," Vau chorused. "How much did this sub cost you?"

"Shut up and drink."

Skirata waited until he'd forced three beakers of diluted energy cubes down Vau's throat before giving in to an animal curiosity that overrode every weary ache and pulled muscle. He untied the bundle. As the contents spilled across the medbay deck, there was only one word he could spit out.

"Wayii!"

Vau made a coughing sound that might have been laughter. He didn't get a lot of practice at that. Skirata was transfixed by the tide of valuables, so much so that his hands were shaking when he unfastened the backpack's assortment of pouches. What spilled out stifled any further comment. He knelt down on the deck, knowing his old ankle injury was screaming for a painkiller but far too engrossed in sorting through the booty to give it any time.

There was a lot here. A *lot.* Hundreds of thousands of credits' worth. He stretched out his hand and rummaged cautiously. No—*millions.*

Skirata started making a mental inventory almost without thinking about it. Old habits died hard.

When he glanced over his shoulder, Vau was watching him, eyes half open as if he was nodding off. Mird kept guard, snuffling occasionally.

"Except for the inside pocket," he said, "you can keep the lot."

"What do you mean, *keep the lot?*"

"I'm not a thief. I took what was rightfully mine. The rest is . . . a donation to your clone welfare fund."

"Walon," Skirata said quietly, "this is something like *forty million creds,* at least." Stunned or not, he could always compose himself enough to carry out a blisteringly accurate valuation. "You nearly died to get it. You *sure* about this? You're still in shock. You—"

"Sure."

"Sure?"

"Sure."

"You liberated it for the lads? Walon, that's—"

"I liberated it to cover my *shebs,*" Vau said.

Skirata nodded, suddenly unable to meet Vau's eyes any longer. "Of course you did."

"If the only items missing . . . are from the Vau deposit box, then it narrows down the suspects." Vau reached out for the beaker and managed to get it to his lips. He spilled a lot of it, but that was okay. He was recovering fast. "Just made it look like good old-fashioned random thieving."

"Your dad couldn't touch you even if he did work out that you'd come back."

It was clearly one admission too far for Vau. He was definitely embarrassed, not angry. "Look, Kal, when you were surviving on dead borrats and gravel and playing the working-class martyr, did nobody teach you how to steal like a professional?"

Vau usually didn't have to do much to get Skirata fighting mad: breathing was normally enough. This time Skirata simply knelt there with his chin lowered, struggling to find the right words to tell Vau he was moved by his generosity.

"Thanks," he said, fidgeting with a spectacular aurodium ingot. "Thanks, *ner vod.*"

Ner vod. He'd never called Vau *brother* without a good dose of sarcasm. Forty million creds went a long way with Skirata.

"But remember my men, too, Kal. If they need help when the time comes . . . I expect it to be given."

"Walon, this is for every clone who needs help. Not just my lads. I'd buy out all three million of them if I could."

"As long as we understand each other."

"I'll get Ordo to inventory this. He's good at that."

They didn't have a crumb of food on board *Aay'han* but they were . . . *rich.* Or at least Skirata's rapidly expanding plans to secure the future for clones—his clones, Vau's clones, *any shabla* clone he could get out of the GAR in the end—were well funded. Ordo sat at the treatment table in the medbay with Skirata and worked his way through the haul with a datapad and a distracted frown.

"Is this some Mandalorian renaissance you're planning, Kal?" Vau asked.

It was starting to feel like it. He hadn't really thought that far ahead. "If I set up a place for them all, then it might as well be Mandalore."

"Yeah," Vau said. "It might as well."

Mird, draped over Vau like a badly made fur coat, watched Ordo with one red-rimmed eye. The other was shut tight. Ordo had never forgotten that Vau had set Mird on him as a kid, and it seemed that Mird hadn't forgotten that Ordo had aimed a blaster between its eyes. It rumbled deep in its throat, apparently reassured that both Ordo's hands were occupied with the proceeds of the robbery.

Ordo took a spectral analyzer from his belt tool kit and ran the beam over the gems, diligently noting the composition and weight of each piece in his datapad with a little frown of concentration like some heavily armed accountant. Skirata held his breath.

Some of the items in the bag were priceless antiques. "Be-shavo ancestral icon," Ordo said, and held up a time-stained square of gilded parchment. Collectors would happily shoot their mothers for it. They certainly shot each other. "I hope you know a reliable fence in the fine art world, *Kal'buir,* because we're going to need one."

"The fine arts," Skirata said, fighting a hysterical urge to giggle, "are my natural territory."

"You're an uncultured savage," said Vau. "But you did save my *shebs.* Here, Ordo, help me with my belt."

Ordo raised an eyebrow. "You ought to be taking it easy, Sergeant."

"Open this pouch. Come on."

Skirata did it for him. Vau fumbled and pulled out a piece of jewelry, a gold pin with three square-cut, vivid blue stones of extravagant size set along its length. He could have swapped it for a penthouse apartment in the Republica. Skirata had never seen anything like it.

"My mother's bauble," Vau said. He tossed it to Ordo, who caught it one-handed. "Give it to that pretty girl of yours, Captain. She'll do it justice."

Ordo, always an odd mix of naïveté and precocious experience, stared at it with visible dismay. He had no idea how to accept a gift like that: but then neither did Skirata. It was a showstopper. The only people who'd given him assets even remotely like it had done so at the point of his knife. Vau seemed utterly unmoved by wealth, but maybe if you started life that rich then it ceased to have meaning.

Ordo scanned the stones—dimensions, clarity, refraction, density—and tapped the datapad.

"Approximately one hundred and forty-three carats." His gaze was still fixed on the sapphires as if they were going to explode. "Current market value of the unset gems is ten million. But it's your inheritance." He sounded like a little boy again, and the fact that it was stolen property didn't enter into the objection. "It's too valuable, I'm afraid."

"Take it, Ordo. It gives me great pleasure to know that Ma Vau no longer has it, and that a better woman does."

It might simply have been embarrassed bluster, but Skirata felt that depriving his loathed parents of something was exactly what Vau wanted. He was a volunteer orphan. It was in stark contrast with Skirata, an orphan who valued family more than anything. He tried to be the best possible father to men who'd been created without the comfort of any mother at all, good or bad.

Ordo, as ever, educated Skirata again. The lad was full of surprises.

"It's very gracious of you, Sergeant Vau," he said, and put the pin carefully in his undershirt pocket. He could be quite the gentleman, just as Skirata had taught him. "Thank you. I assure you it'll be treasured."

It took another hour to tally all the items, and some still defied valuation: even so, Skirata was now looking at fifty-three and a half million credits, if he didn't count Ordo's shoroni sapphires, half of it in unregistered secured bonds that could be converted to credits anywhere. While Vau slept and Ordo piloted the ship, Skirata admired the haul for a while, imagining all the safehouses, escape routes, and new beginnings it could buy for clones who decided they'd completed their service to the Republic.

He wasn't encouraging desertion. He was liberating slaves. Men who didn't sign up had no oath or contract to honor as far as he was concerned.

Eventually he left Vau to his sleep, curled in a fetal ball with Mird still keeping vigil over him, and wandered off to the cockpit to sit with Ordo.

Ordo held out the jeweled pin. "Look. They turn green in this light." He seemed more fascinated by the chemistry of them. "What am I going to do with them, *Kal'buir*?"

Skirata shrugged. "Like Vau says, give them to Besany."

"They're stolen. That compromises her."

"Let me think of something."

"They'd buy a lot of land and a secure base. Will Vau be offended?"

"Not as long as Ma Vau doesn't get to wear them again."

"How terrible to hate your parents so much. But then parents do appalling things to their children, don't they? Like poor Etain. Given away to total strangers." Ordo pitied Jedi. It was becoming a recurring theme in his conversation. "I'm lucky to find a father who wanted me. We all are."

Does he think I was a bad father to my own kids? He never says.

"I'd kill for you, son," Skirata said. "It's that simple."

Ordo was a good lad. A *wonderful* lad. He could pilot a totally unfamiliar ship—even stage a staggering *rescue*—just on intuition and one skim of the manual, then sit down and balance the accounts. Skirata, choked silent by pride and overwhelming paternal love, leaned over the pilot's seat and gave him a hug. Ordo winked, clearly pleased with himself, and gripped Skirata's arm.

Fatherhood was a blessing. It would be a blessing for Darman, when the time came for him to find out, and now Skirata had both wealth and the prospect of Ko Sai's technology to guarantee a decent future for all of them.

But the future was a fragile concept for Mandalorians. Tomorrow was never taken for granted by soldiers, and the *Mando'a* word for it—*vencuyot*—conveyed optimism rather than a timescale. *Venku* was a good, positive Mandalorian name for any son. It would fit Darman and Etain's baby very well indeed.

Yes, Venku. That's it: Venku.

"I never adopted you formally," Skirata said. It had been bothering him in recent days, ever since he began to think of the war as having a definite timescale. "Any of you."

"Does that matter?"

Skirata now felt that it did. No *Mando'ad* would nitpick over the bond between him and his boys, and as far as the Republic was concerned clones didn't even qualify as people, but his plans to give them a decent future had now become very, very specific. That discovery of Lama Su's terse message to Palpatine just over a week ago had fast-forwarded everything.

"Yes," he said. He reached to grasp Ordo's hand and recited the short, no-frills *gai bal manda*—"name and soul," all it took to unpick history and give a child a new parentage. Mandalorians were habitual adopters. Bloodlines were just medical detail. "*Ni kyr'tayl gai sa'ad,* Ordo."

Ordo stared at their clasped hands for a moment. He had a crushing grip. "I've been your son since the day you first saved my life, *Buir.*"

"I think you boys did the saving," Skirata said. "I don't want to imagine where I'd be without you."

Skirata was now busy hating himself for not doing this before, not making the ultimate commitment, and he fretted about his five other Nulls scattered around the galaxy. Sometimes he saw them again as two-year-olds waiting to be culled—killed—because they didn't meet the spec the Kaminoans wanted. *Uncommandable. Disturbed. Defective.*

And *aruetiise* thought Mandalorians were savages, did they?

The galaxy was full of hypocrites.

4

Gaftikar, the road to Eyat, 473 days after Geonosis

"So what's your strategy?" Darman asked the lizard, trying
to build relationships. "How are you going to take over?"

Sergeant Kal said that you had to work with the locals and
use their social structures to get the job done, not try to get
them to work the Republic's way. Atin ambled along beside
Darman and the Marit, hands in his pockets, no telltale signs
of his lightweight body armor under the workman's clothes
A'den had given him. It was raining and the path through the
trees was muddy and puddled, but at least they had an excuse
to cover their heads with hoods. Atin had a visor and two
days' growth of dark beard. On a cursory glance, few would
spot that they were identical.

"We crush Eyat," the lizard said. Her name was Cebz and she had a frill of scarlet skin under her chin, apparently a sign that she was dominant and wouldn't take any backtalk from lesser lizards. She smelled of crushed leaves and carried a formidable SoroSuub blaster slung across her chest. "We concentrate our efforts on the capital, and when that falls, the regional governments can't hold out, and we take the next tier of cities, and then the next smaller ones, and so on. We have numbers on our side."

"I think our Chancellor could do with listening to you," Atin said, more to himself than to her. "He likes to start everywhere at once, so nobody feels left out of the war."

"That's how we build, by cascade process," said Cebz. "We can also *un*build the same way."

Her tail swished from side to side to keep her balance as she walked. The *whush-whush-whush* and the current of air were noticeable. "Can you sneak up on people?" Darman asked.

Cebz stopped swinging her tail and her gait became slightly more lateral, but she was now moving silently. "Yes."

"So you built the cities here."

"Yes. The hired help."

"But you don't get a say in government."

"We didn't get paid as much as humans. We can't live in the nice homes we built. If *having a say* means changing that, then yes, we want a say in government. Your other comrade in the skirt was very vexed about that, before he disappeared."

"The first ARC? Yes, I can see how that would get Alpha-Thirty annoyed . . ."

"You *understand*. You don't have any rights, either. If you ask me, it's crazy to train an army and not keep it happy. It'll turn on you in the end."

Atin coughed discreetly. "You speak very good Basic."

"Always pays to speak the customer's language."

She came to a sudden halt, motionless. Darman's instinct was to crouch and draw his sidearm. Atin did the same. Cebz stared down at them, baffled.

"What's up?"

"You stopped dead," Darman whispered, missing his helmet's sensors. "Enemy contact?"

"No, but this is as far as I go. Too close to the city. Marits stand out. Heads we can cover, but the tails are a problem." She swung around and began walking back toward the camp. "Good luck."

Reptilian species had that tendency to freeze and then burst into movement again, the GAR manual said. Knowing that didn't stop Darman from reacting every time. Atin watched Cebz go and turned to Darman again with a shrug. "Just an initial recce and maybe vehicle acquisition, all right?" he said. "Just assess the place. Just look around."

"I swear," Darman said. He had fake ID, credits, and the Marits' excellent plans of the city on his datapad. "Make sure nothing's changed since the last time the data was updated. See how far into the government complex we can get *legitimately*."

The first thing that struck him about the city was that it was clearly defined—no gradual thickening of suburbs, no ribbon development—and if he hadn't been able to see the shapes of the perimeter buildings, he'd have thought it was a walled bastion. There was little traffic entering and leaving, and it was almost entirely made up of big vessels—repulsor trucks and shuttles. The citizens of Eyat didn't venture far afield.

"Siege in all but name," Atin said. "They're scared of the Marits."

"So how do we explain that we walked in?"

Atin tapped his blaster. "We're young, tough, and crazy."

"I'll buy that."

"And from out of town."

"A'den could have mentioned it."

"We overflew the area. We should have *thought* of it."

"It'll be easier next time, once we've got a vehicle."

"Hire or buy?"

"I thought of liberating a crate, but it's a small city, and they probably take speeder theft more seriously than on Triple Zero."

"Dar, you actually *like* thieving stuff, don't you?"

"It's not *stolen*," Darman said. "It's *differently procured*."

He didn't own anything; no clone did, because everything the Kaminoans thought they needed had been provided for them. What he knew about property was learned from Sergeant Kal, and then the world of possession exploded on him when he was let loose in a galaxy where beings didn't just *own* things, they wanted *lots* of things, more than they could ever possibly use, and their entire existence was about acquiring more by any means they could.

It was one thing to understand the theory and another to *feel* it. Darman was happy to have the best kit he could get, comfortable quarters, and as much food as he could eat, but nothing else material made him want to risk his life to get it.

"Do you ever wonder what happened to the four million creds that Sergeant Kal scammed out of the terrorists?" Atin asked. They were at the limits of the woods now. Eyat had a skirt of open land around it: they were ready for the lizards. "Do you think he handed it over to General Zey?"

"No," Darman said. "I don't wonder."

They finally broke cover and sauntered like a couple of ordinary, overconfident young men toward the main route into the city. The defenses mentioned in the intel reports were now visible, watchtowers with laser cannon emplacements. The Marits had no air assets apart from speeders. Eyat was set up to repel simple infantry assault.

It wasn't expecting the Grand Army of the Republic. If it was, evidence of its Separatist allies was nowhere to be seen.

They'd been walking in the open for a matter of minutes when a repulsor truck looped off course and drew up alongside them. The driver leaned out of the cab: male human, middle-aged, dark, bearded.

"Are you nuts?" he yelled. "You can't walk outside the city—how did you get here?"

Darman fell into the role effortlessly and shrugged. "Had to dump the speeder bike kilometers back."

"Get in." He gestured to the rear of the truck. "I'll drop you off inside the boundary. You're not local, are you?"

"No. Looking for work."

The driver opened the hatches and Atin scrambled in, giving Darman a hand up. Almost as soon as they'd found somewhere to sit among the crates of food-board, the truck lurched to a halt. A fist banged on the bulkhead. Darman leaned out of the hatch and found they were inside Eyat, at an intersection with a speeder bus station on one corner of the quadrant.

"Off you go, and make sure you get transport back home, wherever that is," said the driver, and shook his head. "Dumbest thing I ever saw . . ."

"Thanks." Darman waved. The vehicle lifted off and disappeared across the intersection. "*At'ika,* this is just a test run. Let's see how far we get today."

Atin consulted his datapad. The good thing about the rebels was that they'd built Eyat, and so they still had the plans—drainage and service channels as well as the surface infrastructure. "Speeder bus to the city center."

"And pick up a city-registered airspeeder on the way out. Easier to get back in next time."

It was, as Darman had decided from the bay of the *Core Conveyor,* an ordinary place where people got on with their lives. It was a small town by comparison with Coruscant, all low-rise buildings and modest houses: he could grasp the scale. It didn't overwhelm him. He watched from the viewport of the speeder bus, head resting on the transparisteel, and saw human beings like himself.

And I'm fighting for a different species—for lizards— against humans. Sergeant Kal says species doesn't matter to Mandalorians. Why doesn't the fact that I'm human matter to human beings on Coruscant?

Darman knew of only one community where he felt at home, and that was with his brothers and the few nonclones who had thrown in their lot with them. The rest of the galaxy was alien, regardless of species.

Now he finally understood the concept of *aruetiise.*

"Look sharp, Dar." Atin nudged him in the ribs. "This is our stop." He slipped his datapad back into his pocket. "So far, so good. Nothing's changed as far as the layout goes."

"Well, their builders haven't shown up for a while, have they? No wonder nothing's changed."

According to the plans, the government building—the Assembly House—had a public gallery. Darman and Atin stood in front of the portico, admired the colonnade with appropriate out-of-town awe, and sheltered from the rain while they read the notice next to the huge pairs of doors.

"Sessions start at fourteen hundred, then, Dar."

"It's ten forty."

"Time to kill."

It wasn't time wasted. They had time to wander around the block, plant a few bead-sized surveillance holocams outside the Assembly House, and assess the point of entry for politicians attending parliamentary sessions. They took up position in a tapcaf opposite the building and settled in to eat themselves to a standstill while watching the comings and goings of delivery vessels and official-looking speeders. Darman sat side-on to the window; Atin faced outward to the road.

"I'm never eating meat again," Atin mumbled, staring at the trickle of traffic. "Ever."

"What's that in your hand, then?"

"Fish patty. Fish doesn't count."

"Reptile meat is a lot like fish."

Atin looked down at the patty, sighed, put it back on the plate, and turned to summon a server droid. He seemed a lot happier when a pile of sweet pastries turned up.

Two hours to go.

Darman tapped a few observations on exit routes into his datapad, chewing happily on a tube of pastry packed with minced roba and spices, and wondering when he might get a comlink window to contact Etain. Skirata was right: focusing on the people you loved could keep you sane in a war or distract you, and he thought he'd found the balance point. He had something to look forward to, to live for, even if he had no idea what would happen to the army when they won the war.

"We have to get Fi sorted out, *At'ika.*"

"Get him a date, you mean?"

"Hasn't Laseema got a friend or something? I hate seeing him like this."

"Maybe Agent . . ."

Darman waited, distracted by his datapad, but Atin didn't finish. "Agent what?"

Atin was staring at the traffic again, lips slightly parted. "Don't look out the window. Just turn away slowly."

"Okay . . ." Darman shifted position. He was starting to hate plainclothes ops; he longed for his helmet sensors yet again. "What is it?"

Atin's lips barely moved. Darman strained to hear him over the noise in the tapcaf. "I thought I was looking at my own reflection for a second until I remembered I'm in disguise . . . and I have scars."

It took Darman a moment to work it out.

Atin had seen another clone, up close. He'd have recognized Fi, Niner, or A'den, and there weren't supposed to be any other troops here—except A-30, Sull.

"Sure it's not a Null?"

"Only ones I haven't met are Jaing and Kom'rk, and they're still after Grievous."

"Says Kal . . ."

"Whatever. That's not one of them. He was a meter from me. He's moving away now."

Darman held his position for a little longer. Atin put his food down and made for the doors, Darman following. It wasn't what they'd come to Eyat to do, but an ARC who'd gone AWOL was—impossible. Jango Fett had raised and trained them personally, with an emphasis on absolute loyalty to the Republic. Sergeant Kal said that Jango was an unhinged *shabuir,* but he always stuck to his contract, and that contract had included creating a loyal, totally reliable army.

Darman had heard rumors to the contrary, and the Nulls were living crazy proof that a clone soldier could be as eccentric and wayward as any random human, but nothing had ever been confirmed.

"See him, *At'ika*?"

A broad back in a black leather coat vanished into a crowd

of pedestrians, but a moment later the ARC's ultrashort black crop bobbed up a little above the heads of the crowd. Atin touched his finger to his ear, activating the miniature comlink nestled deep inside; sensors under his chin and on each side of the thyroid cartilage picked up the nerve impulses from his brain and converted silent subvocalization to audible speech.

It took a little practice to think in words and not speak aloud, but Darman now found it was just like talking to himself.

"Niner, change of plan . . . ," Atin said. "Just eyeballed our MIA."

Darman picked up Niner's voice on his earpiece. "I've got your coordinates. Need backup?"

"Let's see where he goes."

Darman cut in. "Check with Jusik. See if there's something we haven't been briefed on."

"Zey said MIA," Niner said. "Unless this is a front for another mission."

A'den's voice interrupted with that gravelly indignance that marked him out. "If it is, then *I* don't know about it, either."

Darman didn't like the sound of that. There was need-to-know, and there was denying information, and not knowing where other special forces were placed struck Darman as being the latter. And the Nulls always seemed to hear about everything, whether they were intended to or not.

"This would be easier on Triple Zero," Atin said.

"He's an ARC. It wouldn't be easy *anywhere*."

Sull, not missing and seemingly at ease in Eyat, swaggered down a tree-lined promenade and dipped down a flight of steps. The two commandos quickened their pace.

It was one thing tailing an ARC trooper. It was another thing entirely working out what to do once you caught up with him.

Rendezvous Point: Mong'tar Cantina and Brasserie, Bogg V, Bogden system, 473 days after Geonosis

"You're late," said Mereel.

"We had to pick up groceries." Ordo straddled the chair

and rested his folded arms on the back. "And Vau had to stop off at the bank to get some creds."

"Next round's on him, then." Mereel lounged in the seat, legs stretched out in front of him. It was a noisy, seedy cantina of the type that Mereel seemed to enjoy. A droid and a young human male were at the table, too, concentrating on their datapads. Nobody blinked at the presence of Mandalorians in a place like this, but the two strangers were in a world of their own anyway. "So Old Psycho's okay now? Where is he? Where's *Kal'buir*?"

"Securing the *sho'sen*." Ordo didn't want to spell out *submarine* in front of strangers. *Mando'a* was almost unknown among *aruetiise* so it was a discreet code to use. "Vau and Mird are standing guard."

"Don't get agitated, but *Bard'ika* is planning to join us later."

Ordo reserved the right to a little anxiety about General Jusik, who could swing in moments from a Jedi with ageless wisdom to a daredevil lunatic like Mereel. "Why?"

"Something major he wants to discuss that he doesn't want to commit to voice traffic."

"He's as crazy as you. Zey's going to catch him one day." Ordo wondered for a moment if it was news of Etain and her pregnancy, but there were ways of passing that on discreetly without the need to meet face-to-face. He indicated the droid with a jab of his thumb. "Thought you'd seen enough tinnies for one lifetime."

"Just having a fascinating discourse about the expansion in the leisure economy with my colleagues here, who are . . ."

"Teekay-zero," said the droid sitting to Mereel's left. He looked like a taller, armored version of an R2 astromech. "And my esteemed mechanic and agent, Gaib."

"Always a pleasure," said Gaib, not looking up from his datapad. "But remember that without me, he's just fancy scrap."

Ordo switched over to his helmet comlink. Life was so much easier with a *buy'ce*. The apparent silence that followed for outsiders looked like two Mandos waiting for a comrade to show and, in their uncommunicative Mandalorian way, not having much to discuss by way of art and phi-losophy. The unheard reality on the private comlink was something else entirely.

"Okay, *Mer'ika,* why move the RV point to here, and what are you playing at with the tourists?"

Mereel turned his head as if he was staring at the bar and ignoring his brother. "The tinnie and his sidekick specialize in stolen industrial data and kit. High-tech bounty hunters. They were asked to source . . . I love that word, don't you? . . . *source* . . . like *procure* . . . so flexible . . . anyway, they were asked to find someone who'd supply untraceable laboratory equipment to beat the cloning ban. Dry-lining supplies, vats, clean room systems, plus specialist droids to fit it all, paid in cash credits and no records."

"Ko Sai?"

"I reckon."

"Where?"

"Dorumaa, tropical pleasure palace of the Mid Rim."

Ordo consulted his planetary database as it scrolled down his HUD. "Water. Water, everywhere . . ."

"Oceans, almost all of which are pretty well unexplored. And likely to stay that way for some time, because of the lov-able marine life that was revived from the ice sheet when they terraformed the place. Tropical vacations. No other in-dustry. But that's where the illegal lab stuff was heading."

"She's setting up a new research center. Who's funding it?"

"Don't know yet. Okay, let's work through it. Battle of Kamino—Separatist forces spring her. She's already stripped her critical data off the Tipoca mainframe, some of which I could reconstruct from the copy I took the other week, so she was expecting to leave. Seps then take her to Neimoidia—she stiffs them, does a runner, and ends up on Vaynai." Mereel folded his arms and looked the other way, doing a good mime of exasperated boredom. "From Vaynai, she loops back into Sep space, last place they'd expect her to run, and heads for the Cularin system, specifically Dorumaa."

"Evidence?"

"My tinnie chum got the stuff delivered to the freight port here. Tinnie, being fond of a little insurance just in case the client skips without paying, checks out the flight plan and, with a couple of transfers en route, it all ends up on Dorumaa."

"So why is he telling you?"

"He was *sourcing* items for me. Extra firepower and go-faster stripes for the submersible."

"You've got a dozen or more lowlifes you could ask for hardware."

Mereel was smiling. Ordo could hear it in his voice. "Not ones that also show up doing business with Arkania."

Ordo had to admire Mereel's ability to sift data. The risk-taking genes had expressed themselves even more in him than the rest of them, but he had a surprising patient tenacity once he'd latched on to the scent. He could give Mird a run for its money.

"So we need to beat a location out of someone."

"Once I find the pilot who delivered the consignments. Nobody's talking. I don't care how tight-lipped folks are, somebody always talks, sooner or later. One detail, one word—something always slips."

Sooner or later was the problem, as always. Time was the enemy on every level. Ko Sai wouldn't have just the Separatists hunting her. The Kaminoans had to know she'd skipped with their data because if Mereel could see it was missing, they'd have worked that out a year ago. But they wouldn't dare tell their main customer—the Republic—that they were in trouble. They'd want to get her back quietly and without fuss. They'd have engaged bounty hunters, too, if they had any sense. Their economy depended on it.

And the Arkanians, Kamino's closest rival, knew she was missing. Everyone who mattered did; gossip in the industry was hard to control. Cloning had gone underground to beat the ban, and there were plenty of companies that'd want the top aiwha-bait on their staff, so the Nulls might be elbowing a dozen pursuers out of the way to get to her if they didn't stay ahead of the pack.

"She's on the run from at least three interested parties, then," Ordo said. "This is getting crazy. Do you think Lama Su is using the excuse about the end of the current cloning contract to cover the fact that he's lost her data and now it's crunch time? How critical is it to production?"

"I don't care," Mereel said, "as long I get my hands on her skinny gray neck and she hands over whatever it takes to give you and me and all our *vode* a full life span."

TK-0 nudged Mereel. "Are we boring you? You're very quiet . . ."

"We're meditating," Mereel said. "We're very spiritual people, we *Mando'ade*. Communing with the *manda*."

"I can feel that from here," said Gaib. "When do we get paid?"

Mereel slapped two fifty-thousand-credit chips on the table. "You can keep the change if you find me the freighter pilot who delivered the kit to Dorumaa."

"The Arkanians might pay us more."

"But not as much as the Kaminoans . . ."

"Is that who you're working for?"

"Look," said Mereel. Ordo braced: his brother had that edge in his voice that usually preceded skating on very thin ice for the sheer thrill of it. He was always the one who liked rapid-roping from the highest point in Tipoca City, and he had broken bones to show for it. "Only the Kaminoans can clone *legally*. Everyone else is a *chakaar* who threatens their business interests. Get it?"

"Not really."

Mereel managed a little puff of exasperation. Ordo got ready to shut him up with deafening high-pitched feedback on his helmet audio.

"Okay, we're Republic agents," Mereel said wearily. "Stamping out illegal cloning wherever we find it. Because *Mando'ade* care about law and order."

I'm going to slap the osik *out of you one day,* Mer'ika. *Don't do this to me.*

TK-0 bristled, which was no mean feat for a droid. "This

is hardly the time to get snotty and organicist, is it? I was only *asking.* If you have a deal with Kamino, fine."

"I think it's time you tightened his nuts," Ordo said to Gaib. "Seeing as you're his mechanic."

"Find me the pilot who did the last leg of the journey, Teekay, my little *beskar'ad,* and I'll pay them as well." Mereel took one of the credit chips from the table and flipped it between his gloved fingers like a conjuring trick before making it vanish up his sleeve. "No penalties. Not the pilot's fault. Got it? That's the Republic's problem, not ours."

"Okay. Can do."

"And I want it by the time I finish the modifications to our ship."

"Aww, hang on—" said Gaib.

"Forty-eight hours." Mereel stood the remaining fifty-thousand-credit piece on one end and flicked it over with his forefinger. Gaib grabbed it with impressive speed. "Back here. Pilot's name and location."

"Don't listen to him, we'll do it," Gaib said, checking the chip with a counterfeit scanner and batting away TK-0's extended manipulator arm. "Trust us."

"I do." Mereel patted TK-0's durasteel casing with slow emphasis, making him sound like a gong. "I'm very trusting."

Ordo switched back to internal comlinks. "Quit while you're ahead, *ner vod . . .*"

The two tech hunters got up to leave. All Ordo could think of was that time was wasting, and more interested parties seemed to have a reason for hunting down Ko Sai every day.

But who's she working for? Who's bankrolling her?

If the Tipoca hatcheries found they couldn't replace the critical tech, and the Republic hadn't paid the next installment, there were several contractors waiting to fill that gap.

"Wow!" TK-0 said, spinning his cranial section 180 degrees to train his photoreceptors on the doors. "More of you? Did someone just open a new box of Mandalorians?"

Ordo looked up just as Mereel did. Skirata was walking

across the cantina with someone dressed in his father Munin's armor.

"Yeah, it's *Bard'ika*," said Mereel. "I couldn't stop him from coming."

Jedi General Bardan Jusik hadn't just shown understanding and compassion to his special forces troops; he'd gone native. He wore the Mandalorian armor that Skirata had loaned him to masquerade as his nephew during an elaborate sting operation with a Jabiimi terror cell. Ordo knew it was smarter than swaggering into the cantina in his full Jedi rig, but it was no secret now that Jusik *liked* it.

"Vode," Jusik said, taking off his helmet. He extended his arm, and Mereel clasped it in that hand-to-elbow grip that was a common *Mando* greeting. Jusik's untidy blond hair still needed cutting, but at least he'd trimmed his beard. "We really *have* to talk."

Eyat, Gaftikar, 473 days after Geonosis

The rain had stopped and the sun had come out, which was a problem. Darman and Atin could no longer rely on their hoods for disguise as they tailed ARC trooper A-30—Sull—through the city.

The ARC was walking briskly, heading north. Twice he paused to buy food from a street stall and slipped the wrapped packages inside his coat. Then he walked into the huge transparisteel foyer of the unirail terminal, forcing them to follow.

"How far are we going to take this?" Darman whispered.

"I thought we'd just follow him and see where he goes."

"Remember Sergeant Kal giving Sev and Fi an earful for doing an unplanned tail on a suspect and nearly screwing the whole operation?"

"Skirata's light-years away."

Darman wondered why he'd ever thought Atin was the quiet, thoughtful one. "That won't stop him. He hasn't just got eyes in his backside—he's got hyperspace transceivers."

"Okay, what's the alternative? Spot a *vod* who's MIA, say *Well, who'd have thought it?* and carry on chatting?"

Darman wasn't sure where prudent improvisation ended and winging it began; special operations were a blend of tediously boring planning and moments of what he could only think of as insanity on the brink of death. But Atin was right—MIA was MIA, and Sull was neither M nor IA right then, and he had intel that they needed.

The terminal had a high domed roof that reminded Darman of Tipoca City. Sull grabbed a ticket token with the casual, unconscious ease of someone who did this journey frequently, then sat down on a bench at a distance from the ticket barriers, staring at the ever-changing timetable board as he unwrapped one of the small packages he'd bought on his walk and began eating the contents. It looked like fritters of some kind. Darman and Atin wandered around the small storefronts on the terminal concourse after they grabbed their tickets, window-shopping as far as other travelers were concerned.

"He's got five unirail lines to choose from," said Atin. "You think he's spotted us?"

"Either he's better at surveillance than we are, and he has, or he delays committing himself to a direction out of habit." It was the kind of thing an ARC would have been trained to do: to move around without drawing attention to himself or giving a pursuer any notice of a last-minute change of direction. Darman began speculating about what Sull had been doing in the last couple of months. Fierfek, the man looked as if he *lived* here. The very phrase made Darman uneasy in a way he found hard to pin down, until he realized it was a bewildered envy of a world that had more options than he knew how to handle. "So is this all part of the deep cover? That even the rebels can't find him, and don't know what he's doing, so they can't compromise him if they're caught?"

"Or if they're traitors . . ."

"This is crazy. Zey would *know.* Zey would oversee his tasking."

"Dar, I think there's loads of things Zey's never told. Maybe Sull gets his instructions directly from Palpatine."

"How can anyone run a war that way?"

Atin didn't answer. The war was messy, dirty, and chaotic, they'd learned, but this was the first time Darman had faced the possibility that brother soldiers might be doing things that cut across his own mission.

The two commandos killed a little more time standing at a store window speculating on why anyone might want a vivid purple business case, watching Sull reflected in the transparisteel window: then there was a faint clacking sound as the departures board changed, and the ARC made a move for a departure point.

"What are you carrying?" Darman asked, following Sull's path.

"Vibroblade, blaster, and garrote wire." Atin boarded the railcar and sat down several rows behind Sull. "Maybe I should have brought the E-Web . . ."

"ARCs aren't invincible. Anyway, what makes you think he's going to get violent?"

"If we've crashed into a covert op of his, he'll use us for target practice."

Darman recalled Mereel saying he'd never really trusted ARCs, because they'd been ready to kill clone kids during the Battle of Kamino rather than let them fall into Sep hands. Removing two commandos who got in his way wouldn't make Sull miss a beat, then.

The railcar was half full, and Eyat wasn't Coruscant. The population was a tiny fraction of Galactic City. This was no anonymous sea of strangers who didn't take any notice of blue skin, tusks, or any of the other distinguishing features of a vast range of resident species bustling everywhere. The people here noticed, all right. Darman and Atin got the occasional glance because—he assumed—there were small details that marked them out as not local.

Or maybe some thought they'd just passed another man who looked exactly like Darman.

Sull, sitting with his back to them, took out a holozine.

Darman read all the ads on the unirail cab's walls and made a note of a couple of speeder rental agencies and a used-speeder emporium. Outside the railcar, Eyat streaked past; well-maintained apartment buildings, vessels landing at the spaceport, rolling hills in the distance. Darman followed the unirail route on his datapad and tried to think of this city as a target he was setting up for an assault. He couldn't think of another mission he'd been on where that prospect disturbed him. This was somewhere he might . . . *live,* but the Marits who'd take over weren't like him at all.

He'd never considered if he had a side to be on beyond his brothers'. All that stuff about the Republic and freedom was just words that he hadn't started to fully understand until recently. The last thing he thought about under fire was the Republic; it was always the brother right next to him, and the hope that both of them would still be alive tomorrow.

The railcar slowed as it approached another pickup point, and Sull appeared to still be reading. But as soon as it came to a halt he jumped to his feet and shot out the nearest exit. Atin and Darman scrambled to reach the doors before the railcar moved off again.

"Yeah, he does this for a living, all right," Atin said.

"Talking of which, how *does* he eat?"

"I'll stop speculating and just ask him."

"Yeah, maybe he'll make us a cup of caf and tell us about Eyat's places of interest."

Sull's exit point brought them out in a less well-heeled neighborhood than the city center, but it was still clean and orderly. It wasn't the lower levels by a long shot. They followed the ARC to a low-rise apartment building fronted by a neat lawn, where he climbed the external stairs, walked along an access balcony, and went into a second-story apartment.

Darman and Atin walked past slowly, feigning conversation, and circled the block to check for rear exits. This was where they were at their most vulnerable. There was nowhere to hide to stake out the apartment, and this wasn't a commercial center where they could hang around with nobody asking why. Darman reached into his tunic and pulled out a sensor. Then he opened the link to Niner.

"Got our coordinates, Sarge? Transmitting now . . ."

Niner responded instantly. Darman could imagine him waiting, pacing up and down and giving Fi a hard time while he fretted. "Copy that, Dar."

"Apartment seven."

"What are you planning?"

Darman glanced at Atin. "We'll walk up to the door. We'll run a sweep to see if he's got company. If we like the odds, we'll knock. If we don't, we walk away, set a spycam opposite the building, and return to rethink and monitor. Is that okay, Sarge?"

"I'd say that's not what we came to do, Dar, but an ARC on the loose without explanation could throw the whole mission, so we might as well clear it up."

Darman had a nagging thought. He had to get it off his chest. "Ask A'den why he didn't stroll into Eyat and check it out."

The Null had only been in-theater a few days. Even if he'd done a recce, there was nothing to say that he'd have seen Sull at all. Darman regretted the question immediately and hoped A'den hadn't heard.

"Will do," said Niner. "Leave your comlink open, okay?"

Darman and Atin ambled across the road and made their way to the apartment. Darman held the sensor as inconspicuously as he could, clasping his hands in front of him as if waiting for Sull to answer the door, and swept it slowly side to side.

He kept his voice at subauditory level, letting the sensors on his throat transmit on the comlink. "I'm only picking up one body in there, At'ika."

"Shame you're not a Jedi."

"Yeah . . . maybe they should have created Force-sensitive clones, and then we could have ditched half the kit."

"Okay. Knock-knock time . . ."

Darman stood to one side of the doors, hand discreetly on his blaster, and Atin pressed the bell.

Silence.

They waited. The sensor showed someone moving to one side of the door, but there was no noise. Sull was a careful man: an ARC trooper couldn't be anything else. Then the doors parted.

Sull obviously didn't have a security holocam installed. For a split second he stood side-on to the entrance, his face all wide-eyed shock, then his arm came up and Darman spun away instinctively as a blaster bolt shaved his cheek. Atin cannoned past him with a sickening *thwack* of bone. Sull fell back with Atin on top of him and Darman hit the door controls. For the next few moments they grappled, trying to get Sull onto his stomach to pin his arms, but the ARC lived up to his reputation, bringing his knee up hard in Atin's groin and landing a fist in Darman's face. Eventually they got him facedown and Darman tried the old restraining trick of hooking two fingers into Sull's nostrils and jerking back hard. It must have hurt him plenty, but not half as much as he hurt Darman when the commando loosened his grip and Sull sank his teeth hard into his hand.

Demoralizing, painful, and causes serious infection. That was what Skirata said about human bites. Darman roared with pain and brought his fist down on the back of the ARC's head. Atin pounced again and got him in a headlock with his knee in his back.

"Right," Atin panted. He had the tip of his vibroblade pressed into the hollow at the base of Sull's skull. "Unless you want this right through your spinal cord, *ner vod,* pack it in and *listen.*"

"Do it, then," Sull said. "I'd rather die. They sent you to kill me, didn't they? Go on. Finish me off, if you've got the guts."

Darman, blood welling from his bite marks, got a plastoid tie around Sull's wrists and knelt back to nurse his throbbing hand. *Bacta. Clean the wound.* What was he going on about, *they sent you to kill me*?

"We're definitely going to have to get a speeder to move him, Dar, rent one or something," Atin said. "You okay?"

"Yeah."

Niner's voice cut in on the comlink. "Sitrep, Omega . . ."

"What do you mean, Sull?" Darman asked. "What do you mean, *they* sent us? Who's *they*?"

"Who are *you*?"

"RC one-one-three-six, Darman, Omega Squad. We thought you were MIA. You *are* Alpha-Thirty, right?"

"Get knotted," Sull said. "Just get it over with."

Atin tied the ARC's ankles with plastoid tape and got to his feet. "Well, I think you need a chat with a colleague of ours . . ."

Darman held out his datapad. "Speeder rental, *At'ika*. I made a note. You get the transport, I stay here."

"Okay, you can keep Captain Charisma quiet for a while."

"Omega . . ." Niner sounded at the limit of his patience. "What the *shab* happened?"

"Alpha-Thirty thinks we're going to kill him, Sarge. We're bringing him back to base until we get this sorted."

"Moron." Sull sounded as defiant as ever. "You've got no idea, have you?"

"What?"

"You're dead men."

He didn't say it like a threat. Sull said it like Skirata did.

That was what Skirata used to call them back in training: his dead men. It was all part of his unconvincing veneer of abuse, because the whole company knew Sergeant Kal would give them his last drop of blood, but the words now made Darman shudder.

"We all are, sooner or later," he said.

It was sooner for clones than most.

5

Order 4: In the event of the Supreme Commander (Chancellor) being incapacitated, overall GAR command shall fall to the vice chair of the Senate until a successor is appointed or alternative authority identified as outlined in Section 6 (iv).

Order 5: In the event of the Supreme Commander (Chancellor) being declared unfit to issue orders, as defined in Section 6 (ii), the chief of the defense staff shall assume GAR command and form a strategic cell of senior officers (see page 1173, para 4) until a successor is appointed or alternative authority identified.

—From *Contingency Orders for the Grand Army of the Republic: Order Initiation, Orders 1 Through 150,* GAR document CO(CL) 56–95

GAR landing strip, Teklet, Qiilura, 473 days after Geonosis

Etain stood on the deserted landing strip by the troop transporter, up to her ankles in a fresh fall of snow.

The only footprints were hers and the ridged soles of army boots, whose impressions were so much larger than hers that for a moment she felt like an insignificant child.

The farmers weren't going to show. She hadn't expected them to; now her duty was unavoidable. She'd given them two extra hours, kidding herself that they might have had difficulty passing blizzard-blocked roads, but the deadline had passed and Levet was walking toward her from the HQ building, datapad in one gloved hand. She turned and walked back to save him the journey.

"One last try, Commander," she said. "I'm heading into Imbraani to give them the now-or-never speech."

Levet handed her his datapad. "Orders just in, ma'am. Direct from Zey. The Gurlanins just gave him a little demonstration of intent."

Etain swallowed to compose herself before reading.

Zey had a terse message style. She could have spoken to him by comlink, even had a virtual face-to-face meeting, but he'd sent Levet a message—stark, to the point, and leaving no opportunity for discussion or argument.

GURLANINS CLAIMED RESPONSIBILITY FOR CLASSIFIED IN-
FORMATION ON TROOP MOVEMENTS AND READINESS STATUS
RELEASED TODAY TO CIS COMMANDERS. LEAK HAS RESULTED
IN 10,653 CASUALTIES: FLEET AUXILIARY *CORE GUARDIAN* DE-
STROYED WITH ALL HANDS WHILE DEFENSIVE CANNON WAS
OFFLINE DURING UNSCHEDULED MAINTENANCE. REMOVE QIIL-
URA CONTINGENT IMMEDIATELY. CIVILIAN CASUALTIES ACCEPT-
ABLE IF COLONISTS USE LETHAL FORCE.

Etain handed the datapad back to Levet and saw ten thousand dead troopers in her mind's eye before she saw farmers, dead or otherwise. It hit her hard. Her imagination blanked out and was replaced by a cold hard focus on the next steps to remove the remaining farmers.

"He's not a happy camper, ma'am."

"They warned they could be anywhere and pass as anyone." Etain carried on walking. *Why didn't I feel them dying in the Force? Am I that out of touch?* "So there's a little reminder of the damage they can do whenever they want. It'll escalate. Let's get this over with."

"You could have prevented the deaths," said a voice behind her.

Jinart appeared out of nowhere, loping like an arc of black oil. She could have been a mound of snow, a piece of machinery, or even one of the leafless trees on the strip perimeter before she metamorphosed into her true form. She darted a little ahead Etain and Levet, leaving featureless round paw prints behind her. Gurlanins could leave false tracks, making them impossible to hunt down. They were, as so many had said, perfect spies and saboteurs—as long as they were on your side. If they were the enemy then they seemed very different indeed.

"You didn't have to kill troopers. Don't you think they've got short enough lives as it is?" Etain tried not to lose her temper, but it was hard. She didn't want the baby sensing any of this ugliness. "We're evicting the colonists anyway. You could have *waited*."

"You don't have the stomach for killing unless you're put in a corner, girl," Jinart said. "Unlike that soldier of yours. And I know where he is."

It was a risky thing to say in front of Levet, but he didn't react. Etain took a moment to realize that Jinart was making a veiled threat. Her pulse began hammering in her throat.

"If anything happens to *him*," she said, "you know what Skirata will do to *you*."

"So now you know the stakes, and what we both stand to lose . . ."

Etain's anger welled in her throat, choking off any coherent response. She stopped dead, hand going straight to her lightsaber without any conscious thought, and a blind urge to kill swept over her. It wasn't a Jedi's reaction at all. It was a woman's—a mother's, a lover's. It took all her self-control not to draw the lightsaber.

Her dead Master, Kast Fulier, would have understood. She knew he would.

"They're leaving today." She thought of the Separatist collaborators caught by Gurlanins not far from here, throats ripped out as befitted a carnivore kill. "But you can't deal with them yourselves, can you? Just two thousand humans, and that's too many for you to take on. Which tells me how *very* few of you there really are."

Jinart slowed down and looked back over her shoulder. Two twin-pointed fangs extended almost to her chin. When she spoke, they gave her a strangely comic lisp that almost took the edge off her menace. "If we were many, there would be no farmers left for you to remove. What you need to remember, Jedi, is *where* we might be, and that like your gallant little clone army, a very small force applied intelligently can cause serious damage—"

Levet interrupted at just the right moment: Like Commander Gett, he had a knack for defusing situations. "Permission to put the men in position, General?"

"The farmers have already scattered. They won't all be in Imbraani."

"I know, but we have to make a start somewhere. We'll move on and clear stragglers area by area."

Jinart loped ahead. "We'll locate them for you."

Gurlanins were predators. Etain had no doubt that tracking humans was easy for them. She watched Jinart disappear into the distance, and then she *really* disappeared—vanished, merged into the landscape, *melted.* It was disturbing to watch. Metamorphosis was a shocking enough spectacle, but the way the creatures could simply step out of existence troubled her more than anything.

She had no idea if one was right behind her, or in her room in her most private moments.

"I know all the places the colonists used to hide out during the Sep occupation," she said to Levet. "Zey and I used them, too. I still have the charts."

The commander dipped his head and put his hand to the side of his helmet for a moment as if he was listening to his internal comlink. "So, ma'am, how are you interpreting *lethal force*? Can we shoot as soon as they *try* to kill us, or do we have to wait until they actually *do*?"

Up to a year ago, Etain would have had a clear-cut answer based on a Jedi's view of the world, where dangers were sensed in advance and intentions clearly felt: she knew who meant her harm and who didn't. Now she saw the war through the senses of ordinary human men, who were trained to react instantly and whose long-drilled movement eventually bypassed conscious thought. If someone targeted them, their defensive reflex kicked in. Sometimes they got it wrong by firing; sometimes they got it wrong by hesitating. But she had no intention of handicapping them by expecting them to be able to make the judgment calls that she could. Zey could promulgate all the rules of engagement he wanted. He wasn't here, in the line of fire.

"Once they open fire on you," Etain said, "return it. They can't be civilians *and* engage in armed conflict. Their choice."

She'd square it with Zey. If she couldn't—too bad. It was her command, and she'd take the consequences. Levet summoned a speeder bike, and she climbed onto the pillion behind him. They set off for Imbraani at the head of a column of armored speeder buses and speeder bikes while an AT-TE carrier passed overhead to deploy troops to the east of the town.

"Are you wearing any armor, ma'am?" Levet asked.

The chest plate didn't fit properly now, but she couldn't tell him that her bump got in the way. She'd leaned back a little so that he wouldn't feel it press into him. To her, it felt enormous, but nobody appeared to have noticed it yet. "Assorted plates, yes. And a comlink."

"Good. Two things I don't like—a general who can't communicate with me, and a general who's dead."

"Well, I'll be a live general who listens and takes notice of her commanders in the field."

"We *like* that kind of general."

And Etain liked clones. The only thing they all had in common was their appearance—although they were starting to age differently, she could see that now—and what the Republic had done to them. Apart from that, they were individuals with the full range of virtues and habits of random humankind, and she now felt completely at home with them.

If she had a side in this war, this was the one she chose: the disenfranchised, unreasonably loyal, heartbreakingly stoic ranks of manufactured men who deserved better.

"We're going to run out of Jedi if this war spreads to more planets, Levet," she said, not sure if the lump rising in her throat was her hormonal upheaval or pity for the clones getting the better of her. "Would you mind taking a detour down the course of the river?"

"Very good, ma'am."

Levet signaled the lead speeders in the convoy to carry on and banked left. Soon they were snaking through two lines of trees between which the Braan River formed a frozen road. She'd first met Darman here: she'd sensed a child in the dark but come face-to-face with what she thought was either a droid or the Seps' Mandalorian enforcer, Ghez Hokan. She didn't imagine she was meeting the future father of her son.

I miss you, Dar.

She found herself thinking about Hokan more often these days, and finding it ironic that her first kill was a Mandalorian, and that he'd been fighting against commandos who found solace in a tenuous Mandalorian heritage. She wondered why Mandalorians bothered to fight other worlds' wars when they could have banded together for their own sole advantage.

"Five hundred meters to the town, ma'am." Levet skimmed above the frozen water. There were no gdan eyes reflecting back at her from burrows and crannies: it was too cold for them to venture out. "Are you sensing anything?"

Oops. Etain concentrated again. "Fear. Anger. But you don't need a Jedi to tell you that."

"Ma'am, they don't call me Commander Tactful for nothing . . ."

"Okay." Some of the farmers would be in the cantina in the center of the town. It had cellars; it was fortified. The farmhouses in the area were wooden construction, and a single artillery laser round was enough to reduce one to charcoal. Those farmers who weren't in the cantina would have dispersed to the hills or headed for the next settlement, a village called Tilsat. "Let's get it over with."

Imbraani wasn't much of a town. The center was an open common where merlies grazed and local kids played chase, although it was too cold today. The common was ringed by ramshackle buildings—a few farm supply stores, a cantina, two veterinarians, and a smithy. The speeders had already set down and a platoon of troopers had disembarked, some of them kneeling in a defensive line with Deeces ready.

Etain swung off the speeder, crunching through a thin layer of ice into packed snow, and for the first time she felt a hard kick from the baby.

It was too early. She had another crazy random thought: was her son already aging as fast as Darman? Had she made things worse by using her Force powers to accelerate the pregnancy? Did all first-time mothers worry about every twinge and twitch? She almost fell back on the speeder and got a curious tilt of the head from Levet.

"Steady, ma'am."

"I slipped on the ice," she said. There was no sign of activity, but a thin thread of smoke rose from the cantina's chimney. This was a world of wood fires and low tech. The high tech the Qiilurans did have was weaponry provided by the Republic. "Oh well. We know their tactics and we know the capability of their kit, because we trained and supplied them."

Normal procedure was to carry out house clearance, property by property, but Etain needed to give the farmers one final chance for her own peace of mind, even though she now knew it was pointless. It was, she realized, her deal with her conscience so that she could open fire and not be racked by guilt later.

She stood at the doors and took out her lightsaber; Master Fulier's weapon still hung from her belt.

"This is it," she called. "You come out, you get everyone together, and we load you on the transports." She paused and listened. "You don't come out—we come in and drag you out, cuff you, and load you on the transports. Your call."

There was still silence, but she sensed danger, the preparation of dozens of weapons, and the breathless panic of people who thought this was their last day.

This would be a battle.

"I'm sorry," she shouted, looking at the tiny windows just in case she caught a glimpse of a face. "I have to do this, and it has to be now."

Etain turned to Levet and gave the signal to bring up the

rapid entry teams. The troopers stacked either side of the doors, some with dispersal gas pistols, and Etain slipped a respirator mask over her face.

She could have left it all to her men.

I'm crazy. I'm pregnant and I'm leading an assault. Do I trust the Force that much? Yes, I think I do.

Etain thumbed the controls of her lightsaber, and the blue blade sprang into life. Visualizing a ball of energy building in her chest, she exhaled and aimed a massive Force push at the doors to rip them apart. Two troopers fired gas canisters inside and stood back; the rest of the platoon stormed in. Snapping and whining of blasterfire shattered the still, frosty air, and gas billowed from the entrance.

She ran in after Levet, thinking she should have gone in first, knowing that wasn't how it was done, and looking for opportunities to use the Force to bring this to an end as fast as she could. White armor was everywhere, making that distinctive *clack-clack* sound as troopers dropped into firing position or smacked up against walls for cover. The cantina was a warren of rooms and passages.

It was when she deflected blasterfire with her lightsaber and heard someone yell that she was a traitor, a *kriffing murderer,* that reality sank in.

The noise was deafening; screams, shouts, shots. The smell of blaster-seared air, charred wood and stale yeast—ale, she thought—made her gag. Levet stuck by her, holding her down at one point with a firm hand on her head.

"You're all the same! You're all the same!"

Two troopers hauled a middle-aged man past her. He was alive and cursing, gas-induced tears pouring down his face, trying to aim kicks.

The clear-cut days of friends and enemies were gone, if they had ever existed at all. Etain longed for a simple moral struggle of good versus evil, but she could feel neither that the Republic was wholly good nor that the Separatists didn't have a case. Now she was laying siege to former allies to placate spies who'd helped kill clones.

It was too much to work out. All that mattered then was

staying alive for her unborn child and looking out for the men around her. She took out Master Fulier's lightsaber and prepared to lunge forward, a blue blade of light in each hand.

Offices of the Republic Treasury Audit Division,
Investigation, Audit, and Enforcement Section,
Coruscant, 473 days after Geonosis

The best thing was to keep busy, Besany decided, and not to build her life around HNE news bulletins on the war. If Ordo had something to tell her, he'd tell her. If anything had happened to the unusual circle of military friends she'd acquired almost instantly—then Kal Skirata would tell her. He needed to keep her sweet to get his information, and she knew it.

And she had plenty to occupy her. The gaps in the accounts and audit trails for the Grand Army staggered her forensically tidy mind. Her introduction to army accounting had been a simple procurement fraud investigation a few months ago, when Ordo crashed into her life.

She sat with her elbows propped on her desk, forehead resting on extended fingers, and found she was making involuntary huffing noises of frustration at every screen that appeared on her monitor. The Grand Army had catapulted into existence 473 days ago, and the Republic budget cycle was three years: estimates, allocation, and expenditure.

But there wasn't any indication of an expenditure budget allocated to the creation of the Grand Army.

So Ordo was born around . . . eleven or twelve years ago. She found it hard to take that in even now, and simply skimmed over it again. *That means funding would have had to be in place at least three years before then, unless there was an emergency budget . . .*

Besany skipped back further and further in the archive, but there was no financial record at all of an army of millions being ordered from the Kaminoans. Prior to the Battle of Geonosis, the Republic's minimal armed forces were a very small line budget item in a balance sheet of quadrillions—some years, even quintillions—of credits.

What, the Kaminoans gave us an army for free? And what about the ships and other equipment? Who paid for that? Who paid Rothana and KDY for the initial fleet?

It was a black hole in the books. Besany wasn't a woman who felt comfortable around black holes and unexplained omissions.

Okay, so they hid the funding. Let's not ask why *at the moment. Let's ask* how much, *because that tells me the size of the carpet it needs to be swept under.*

She sat back in her seat and tried to estimate. She didn't know how much Tipoca City billed for clones, but there were a few million of them. On top of that, warships alone cost billions. So it was at the very least a trillion creds, and probably many times that. In a single transaction, that could be found even in the Republic's annual budget. It was a big lump under the carpet.

But she hadn't found it. Either it hadn't appeared, which was fraudulent accounting on an unthinkable scale, or it had been dispersed in line items around a dozen government departments—which was still counter to financial regulations.

So what other services would a big standing army need? Well, no infrastructure for accompanying families, not for those poor clones. How about . . . health?

Spread over ten or more years before Geonosis . . .

The Grand Army had appeared literally overnight. Some details of secret defense projects had to be hidden from public eyes, she accepted that. *But not the funding.* Somewhere, someone had to get approval to buy a whole army off the shelf, and that took a lot longer than the year of wrangling about the Military Creation Act before Geonosis. There was nothing in committee records before that date even to hint at it.

It was driving her crazy.

Health. Medcenters, specialist med droids, training. The Republic had never had an instant army, nor one on quite this scale in living memory. It would have—should have—sought advice on forming a medical corps and dealing with the triage, treatment, and aftercare of large numbers of casualties. Some-one might have left that detail in the system, and then she might have a name, a date, or some other hard data to track.

Besany checked through her index for the Coruscant Health Administration and identified the policy planning office. She hadn't intended to talk to anyone else while she rifled through the records on an illicit investigation—*call it what it is,* spying, *why don't you?*—because it added one more cross-reference for someone who might be checking up on *her.* But talking to public servants across departments every day was routine, and thousands of staff did it.

"What do you mean, *did we make provision* for medical support for the Grand Army?" said the Nimbanel in policy planning. "Had we been asked, we would have. I've worked here for thirty years. I recall nothing like that."

Besany shouldn't have been surprised. If the procurement of an army had been hidden that well, so would its attendant services. She decided to start from the other end—the present day. "So what does the CHA actually provide for the army now?"

"Nothing."

"So what happens if a soldier is shipped back to Coruscant for treatment?"

"CHA doesn't deal with them. Civilians only. If they're treated anywhere, it'll be by GAR medical units."

Besany wound up the conversation and went back into the Treasury records she'd already combed on the last investigation. She could track all the routine supply and procurement transactions since Geonosis—armaments, victualing, leases on merchant vessels, maintenance contracts, refueling—but still there was nothing to point her at transactions with Kamino.

Her stomach rumbled and reminded her she'd been at this for hours. It was well past her usual lunch break. *Just one more trawl, then I'll break. Come back with a fresh eye. Do a little real work to cover my lack of output today.* She'd try another route: the Customs Bureau. There might have been duty payable on something, export licenses, anything that would give her an audit trail between Tipoca City and Galactic City.

But you got Mereel's answer already. There's nothing in

the budget estimates to pay for more clones for next year or the year after. There's no indication if or how the Kaminoans are being paid at all.

That was odd in itself. The only reason she could think of was that the costs were far more than anyone imagined. It was a very good reason indeed to make the budget disappear.

"Lunch, Bez?"

Besany jumped. Jilka Zan Zentis—Corporate Tax Enforcement, no stranger to taxpayers who wanted to cut their liability via a blaster—stuck her head around Besany's doorway. Shutting the doors looked suspicious, but nobody seemed to want to know what you were working on if they could walk in and peer over your shoulder.

"Busy . . . monitoring reports to do . . ."

"Are you okay?"

Besany tried to memorize where she was on the balance sheet. "You keep asking me that lately."

"You haven't been yourself for a while."

Just get lost. I need to drill down into this budget. It's the only thing I can do that's useful right now.

"My . . . boyfriend's serving in the Grand Army," Besany said. There: she'd said the *B* word to herself, and now to Jilka. If she called Ordo anything else, she would have proved to herself that she was ashamed of what he was, making him less than human. "And I spend my days waiting to hear that he isn't dead. Okay?"

Jilka straightened up as if Besany had slapped her. "I'm sorry—I didn't realize. We don't have that many citizens serving, do we?"

Besany's common sense grappled with her conscience. *No, I won't deny him.* "Clones don't get citizenship."

The two women stared at each other for a moment, and Jilka looked away first. It was a terrible moment: and maybe Besany had said too much, revealing that she had far too much contact with the Grand Army.

"Wow," said Jilka, ducking back out of the doorway. "You must have had more fun doing that investigation at the logistics center than I thought."

Besany waited for the sound of Jilka's shoes clattering down the corridor to fade to silence, and rested her chin on her hands. That would get around the building like wildfire.

So what? I'm not ashamed.

She'd lost her appetite now. She went back to the public accounts menu on the Treasury system and started working through the Customs section, keying in KAMINO, TIPOCA, and CLONING. And it threw up a lot more documents than she'd expected, mostly the trade ban on the supply of cloning apparatus and services under Decree E49D139.41. Kamino didn't feature a great deal, but Arkania did.

Arkanian Micro must be working all kinds of dodges to get around this. Big chunk of their exports, gone in a single amendment.

There was a big, dull section marked MEDICAL EXEMPTION LICENSES. Her natural tidy curiosity told her she should see what items did manage to bypass the cloning ban, and when she did, she couldn't help but notice the sheer volume of the transactions: trillions of credits. That was a *lot* of organs and skin grafts. *Or . . .*

Or . . .

Besany checked the codes. It was always possible that the codes were wrong or falsified, but they appeared to be licenses for imports to Coruscant itself with a destination code for Centax II—especially Centax II. It was just one of Coruscant's moons: a sterile sphere used for military staging and fleet maintenance. For a moment Besany made a mental connection and wondered if there was an army medical center there, and that was why the Coruscant Health Authority took no military patients: maybe the GAR had its own acute care facility on Centax II, and the cloned tissues were destined for that.

Okay, the government doesn't want the public to see how many troops are brought back too seriously hurt even for the Mobile Surgical Units and medcenter ships to treat. Bad for citizens' morale. Keep it all offworld.

But Kamino didn't need licenses, did it? And if anyone wanted cloned organs to restore troopers to fighting health, Kamino was the obvious source. It was what the Kaminoans did. The Republic was now their only customer thanks to the decree.

A little bell started ringing at the back of Besany's mind. She knew the sound of it: it was the finely tuned instinct familiar to anyone who'd spent time uncovering that which others wanted kept covered. She had no doubt that Captain Obrim and his CSF colleagues knew that bell only too well.

What was going on here?

Besany transferred the data to her own device, far more sections than she actually needed to disguise which information she was interested in, just in case data movement was being monitored. She needed to talk to Mereel, but this wasn't the place.

She pocketed her datapad and took a late lunch far from the Treasury building.

Landing area 76B, Bogg V, Bogden system,
473 days after Geonosis

Aay'han sat on her dampers, looking scruffy. She'd been left in the water too long at one stage in her life: there was still a definite tide mark of encrusted growth even after a few searing atmospheric reentries. Mereel laughed and slapped his gauntlet against his thigh plate. Jusik just stood and stared.

"It's a hybrid submarine, General." Skirata took a piece of ruik root from his belt pouch and chewed it thoughtfully. He didn't enjoy the perfumed taste, but the texture was soothing. "I didn't charge her to the brigade budget, if that's what's worrying Zey."

"It's when you call me *General* that I worry, *Sergeant* . . ."

Jusik really didn't look like a Jedi right then. Whatever it was about the Force that gave him an air of illuminated serenity had taken a walk. He looked grimly mundane.

"Bard'ika." Skirata offered the kid a piece of root, but he waved it aside. "You've come an awful long way for just a chat, son."

Jusik took a deep breath and trudged forward as if he knew how to get into a DeepWater. "Things are getting out of hand. I had to do something that's . . . been a difficult decision."

Skirata was a magnet for waifs and strays; if someone was looking for a sense of belonging, Skirata could make them feel they belonged like nobody else. It was the necessary skill of a sergeant, someone who could bond troops with the intensity of a family, but it was also the authority of a father, and he often couldn't tell where one began and the other ended. He wasn't sure that it mattered. Jusik—clever, lonely, and increasingly at odds with Jedi policy—radiated a need for acceptance: the result was inevitable. Skirata struggled to find the line between taking advantage of the Jedi's vulnerability and getting the best deal for his clones.

Kal followed Jusik. "You can only do what you think is right, *ad'ika*."

"Then I need you to level with me."

"Be sure you want to be burdened with the answer, then."

The port-side cargo hatch edged open, and Skirata ushered Jusik inside. Mereel tutted at an interruption from his comlink and paused to answer it.

In the crew lounge, Vau sat rubbing Mird's head as it lay across his lap, and looked a much healthier color than he'd been hours earlier. He nodded gravely. The proceeds of the robbery were nowhere to be seen. Skirata sat down on one of the low tables, and Ordo and Mereel planted themselves to either side of Jusik on one of the couches. Jusik—Skirata's height, a head shorter than any clone—was swamped by Munin Skirata's green armor. Green for duty, black for justice, gold for vengeance: Mereel had opted for dark blue and Ordo for dark red, simply a matter of taste, but when they decided they had a specific cause then they might change the livery and add sigils. The word *uniform* didn't have much meaning to Mandalorians.

Mereel was deep in conversation with his comlink pressed to his ear, and all Skirata heard was, ". . . that's useful anyway . . . don't worry . . . yes, whatever you get . . ." Then he handed the comlink to Ordo. From the way the lad's face lit up, it was clear that Mereel had been talking to Besany Wennen. Skirata caught his eye and gestured to him that he was excused and he could take the call elsewhere. Ordo got up to stand by the aft engineering hatch, looking uncharacteristically embarrassed.

Skirata dragged the attention back to the conversation. "Ask away, *Bard'ika*."

Jusik's face was all reluctance. "I can't keep covering for you unless I know what you're up to, Kal. And I know you're not telling me things."

"You mean like you didn't tell Zey about the little mishap on Mygeeto."

"There's not telling people because you don't want to compromise them, and not telling them because you don't trust them."

"I trust you to be a good, decent man," Skirata said softly. "But I don't trust events, and once you know something, it shapes everything you do even if you never breathe a word. That's hard on you at best, dangerous at worst. Fierfek, Walon doesn't know half the *osik* I get up to, and vice versa. Eh, Walon?"

Vau nodded. Mird yawned massively, looking like a miniature sarlacc pit. "And I prefer it that way."

"I told Zey I was doing a morale visit to some of Bralor's squads in the field," Jusik said. "Which is partly true."

"So what bit isn't?"

Jusik was a general, and he had his own issues back at HQ. Skirata had to remind himself of that occasionally. He wasn't always off the chart and doing as he pleased; he commanded five companies, a whole commando group, five hundred men who operated in the field without him but who still had to be given objectives, briefings, and support. There was plenty Jusik knew that he didn't share. There was just too much of it.

"That I'm going to disobey an order and give you information you shouldn't have."

"Are you certain you want to tell me, son?"

"Yes." Even so, Jusik dithered for a moment, staring down at his hands. "The Chancellor's ordered Zey to find Ko Sai, top priority."

Skirata's stomach knotted. There was always the outside chance that someone might get to her first, and he could never let that happen. "*Everyone's* been looking for Ko Sai since she went missing at the Battle of Kamino. So?"

"He's sending Delta to do it. They picked up a sighting at Vaynai." Jusik held out his datapad. "Read for yourself. That's all the voice traffic and messages between Zey and Palpatine, and Delta's briefing. Zey specifically didn't want you to know."

Skirata's stomach sank. Zey wasn't a fool, and he had a good idea what a Mandalorian with a personal grudge might do to his quarry. "You're taking a risk showing me that, *Bard'ika.*"

Sometimes Jusik had the look of an old, weary man. He was in his early twenties, all of him except his eyes. "I know. You'd never forgive me if I didn't, and I wouldn't have forgiven myself, either."

Jusik had shown his true colors, then. Skirata marveled again that most of the Republic's citizens saw clones as high-spec droids, conveniently on hand to save their *shebse,* and yet others would put everything on the line to help them. Skirata got up to take the datapad, read it without comment, and passed it to Mereel.

"Thanks, *Bard'ika.*" Skirata ruffled Jusik's hair. He wasn't sure how he would have felt if the kid had divulged his critical information to Zey, though. "So you and the boss think I'm going after Ko Sai, too."

"I know you are. You said more than once that if you could, you'd grab a Kaminoan and force them to engineer normal life spans for the clones."

"You left out *by its skinny gray neck,* I think."

"Well?"

"Yes. I intend to find her."

"Is that what you're doing now? With a submersible? And why the urgency?"

Skirata didn't blink. How could he expect Jusik *not* to work it out? They'd all fought together: they could think like each other with surprising ease. And—fierfek, Jusik was a Jedi. He could sense things.

Skirata decided to concede. Jusik would know he was holding back, and the mutual trust would corrode. "Okay, *Bard'ika,* I bought a hybrid because I intend to find Ko Sai and beat the *osik* out of her until she hands over the biotech that'll stop my boys from aging fast. Being a useless arrogant piece of aiwha-bait, Ko Sai may well bolt to a maritime environment like home sweet home. Hence the *sho'sen.* Which I will be refitting shortly with military-grade sensors and weapons systems, at my own expense, although I *might* well make it available for Republic business as a gesture of goodwill. Does that answer your question?"

Jusik looked slightly pained. "I just didn't know how . . . imminent this hunt was."

Skirata had told nobody about the message from Lama Su to Palpatine that Mereel had sliced on Kamino. It was strictly between him and the Nulls, and—inevitably—Besany Wennen, who was smart enough to work things out if she stumbled across any cutoff point for clone funding.

"I'm cracking on with it," Skirata said at last, "because my boys run out of time twice as fast as you or me."

"I don't want you running into Delta and having problems, that's all."

Vau looked up. "I'd rather like to avoid that, too."

Ordo seemed to have finished his conversation. He handed back Mereel's comlink and sat down again with a glazed expression, this time on a separate seat. His thoughts were elsewhere. Skirata wondered whether to bring Jusik up to date with the hunt for Ko Sai but decided to hang on. It really would place a burden on him, and he'd radiate guilt whenever Zey came near him. Better that he didn't know yet.

"So tell me what the robbery was all about." Jusik seemed to want to change the subject. "It's not like either of you to put your men at risk for personal gain."

"Well, that's a question for me," Vau said. "I reclaimed

something that was due to me, but the bulk of the haul is for our men when they leave the army. You might have noticed the Republic hasn't made pension provisions for them."

"It hasn't made provision for them to retire, either," Jusik said. "I think I understand."

"Vau's handed the stash over to me, *Bard'ika*." Skirata was going to have to tell Vau about the apparent end of the Kamino contract, too. He had commandos in the field who were due their chance at life as much as anyone. The more Skirata's plan took detailed shape, the more people there'd be who needed to know things, and that always sat uncomfortably with him. "What you don't know can't burden you, son. If it all goes *shu'shuk*, you can at least look Zey in the eye and say you had no idea what I was up to."

Jusik leaned back in his seat. "Tell me where you're going to be, and I'll try to stop Delta from falling over you."

"I can monitor Delta, *Bard'ika*," Skirata said. "If I see them on a collision bearing, I'll ping you. Okay?"

Jusik looked wounded. The idea that Skirata didn't trust him after all they'd been through on Coruscant must have hurt. "I was useful once . . ."

Skirata ruffled his hair again. "You're one of my boys, *Bard'ika*. I said you had a father in me if you ever wanted one, and I mean it."

Jusik stared at him for a while, and Skirata couldn't work out if he was hurt or just worried. "I think I can guess anyway," he said. "Etain . . . you know, if there's anything you need me to do . . ."

Ordo stared straight ahead, but Mereel's stare was searing a hole in the side of his face. Vau looked up, too, and Mird lifted its head in response to its master's interest.

"What *about* Etain?" Vau asked.

"I *know*, Kal," Jusik said. He looked embarrassed. "I can sense these things. Don't worry about the Jedi Council. They don't know."

"It's not them I'm worried about," Skirata said. *Shab*. Maybe he should have told all the Nulls that Etain was carrying Darman's baby, not just Ordo. "It's the Kaminoans."

"Fascinating." Vau sighed. "Who doesn't know what you know, or what Kal knows, and that I don't know, but the Kaminoans don't know, either, but if they did know, then Kal knows they'd be a problem?"

"It's not funny, Walon," Skirata said. Mereel was going to get huffy when he realized Ordo had kept something of so much importance from him. "We have a personnel issue we have to factor in to all this."

"I wish I'd never taught you all those big words."

"Okay—Etain's pregnant. Short enough for you?"

Vau made a noise in his throat that sounded remarkably like Mird's gargling objection to being moved from the sofa. "I'll start knitting," he said. "Obviously the Force wasn't with her."

Nobody asked who the father was. The romance was hardly a secret: even Delta knew.

"She's on Qiilura until she gives birth," Skirata said. "And nobody says a word to the boys."

"Not even us," Mereel muttered.

"No, *Mer'ika,* not even you. Because then you can't accidentally put your great big boot in it, like the general just did."

"Sorry." Jusik hung his head. "I thought at least the Nulls would know."

"Okay, I'll brief the rest of them," said Skirata. "But Darman doesn't know, and it stays that way until he's in a position to be able to . . . well, process the news. At the moment, all he'd do is worry instead of keeping his mind on the job."

"That's not fair on the man," Vau said. "Not if you think he *is* a man, and not some helpless kid. Or a simpleton."

"Okay, *mir'sheb,* you got a better idea?"

Vau blinked a few times. "No, I don't think any answer is the right one here, other than hindsight."

"She wanted to give him a son, some kind of future. And smart move or not, I'm doing the same, so maybe it's my fault for putting ideas in her head."

Jusik got up. "I'd better go. Got to look legit by catching up with Vevut Squad." He gave Skirata a pat on the back.

"Zey's talking about bringing Rav Bralor back to train more troopers in commando skills—if he can find her. You stayed in touch with your *Cuy'val Dar* colleagues, didn't you?"

"Some." Skirata followed Jusik to the hatch, not wanting to be seen to rush him, but they had a lot to do now. "If Zey thinks *I'm* trouble, he'll have a nasty shock if he gets Rav back. You know what *Mando* females are like."

"I don't, actually, but I can guess . . ."

"What training does he want done?"

"Covert ops."

"Try Wad'e Tay'haai or Mij Gilamar, then. They'd be a bit more tolerant of the *osik* from the top. Not much, but at least Zey won't get a vibroblade in a sensitive spot if he uses the wrong fork at dinner."

"Can you contact them?"

Skirata had already sought some assistance from Mandalore, including from some of those who'd vanished from the face of the galaxy at Jango Fett's behest to train the clone army in secret. *Cuy'val Dar: those who no longer exist.* It was ironic that those who no longer existed were now helping those who didn't exist for the Republic, not as men at least.

"Leave it with me," said Skirata.

Jusik closed the hatch behind him. Mereel gave Ordo a wary look. "So maybe I shouldn't tell you what Agent Wennen dug up, seeing as I can't be trusted to know we have a clone-impregnated Jedi . . ."

"Knock it off, *Mer'ika,*" Skirata said. "It's my fault, not Ordo's. So what did Besany turn up?"

"Something confirming that Palpatine is building alternative cloning facilities. Lama Su's message mentioned Coruscant, but she's found evidence that there's something happening on Centax Two as well. Lots of equipment, she thinks, and Arkanian Micro have had a lot of exemption licenses for 'medical' cloning."

"Palpatine wants direct control of clone production, and so he wants his own scientists like Ko Sai. He's edging the Kaminoans out of the picture."

"And if he doesn't pay for the next Tipoca contract, clone production will have to switch to a new source at that time."

Ordo had been very quiet up to then. Skirata chalked it up to some emotional issue in the conversation with Besany that he wasn't prepared for.

"So what happens to the clones on Kamino at the moment? The ones who aren't yet mature? And where's the Coruscant facility?" No, Ordo had been war-gaming in his head. Besany seemed to have been forgotten as soon as he handed back the comlink. "Is he getting the equipment from Kamino? No, because the *gihaal* would know he was getting ready to leave them high and dry. Is he having incompletely matured clones moved to Coruscant, or is he starting from scratch again? If so, he has a ten-year lead time to worry about. At the current rate of loss, he won't have an army left in five years, let alone ten."

"Unless he's not going to use Kamino technology," said Mereel. Mird made an exceptionally loud noise of escaping wind, and he stared at the creature. Vau didn't seem bothered. "You have no class, Mird, you know that?"

Vau looked at Skirata and muttered, "Microtech."

It was the one obvious alternative: Arkanian Microtech. Kaminoans did it best, but they did it slow. Arkanian cloning technology was very much faster—a year or two, maybe—though the results were nowhere near as good.

"So there should be clones reaching deployment maturity each year, but we're not seeing those numbers going into the ranks," Skirata said. "So what's the Republic planning to do with them?"

Vau shrugged. "Maybe there's a problem with the quality. They ran out of fresh Jango."

"Kamino certainly doesn't like the results of second-generation cloning," Mereel said. "I found that when I sliced their research the first time."

"Well, maybe the Republic is in financial trouble, and it's happy with second-rate troopers," said Skirata. He knew this was critical information, and that the men produced would be exploited slaves as deserving of help as his own boys. But he was impatient, imagining Delta already on Ko Sai's trail. *First things first.* "Maybe Palps will have a new military strategy then. Numbers over quality. Either way, we don't want to be around when it happens."

"Agent Wennen still hasn't found anything at all on how the Kaminoans were paid or whether there's anything in the budget in the next two years for another contract," Mereel said, standing up. "But she's going to carry on. As am I, because we now have upgrades to fit to this fine vessel inside forty-eight hours." He fixed Mird with an unsympathetic eye. "Including a heavy-duty air freshener."

"I told her not to take any risks." Ordo sounded wistful.

"What did she say to that?" Skirata asked.

"She told me she'd stop taking risks when I did."

"She's a good 'un, son. *Mandokarla.*" Yes, Besany Wennen definitely had the right stuff, a *Mando* heart. "She'll earn those sapphires."

"And who told her I liked roba sausage?"

Mereel paused in the hatchway. "That'd be me, *Ord'ika . . .*"

Vau nudged Mird onto the deck and followed Mereel to start fitting the new weapons to the ship. Skirata was left with Ordo in the crew lounge, suddenly unsure what to say to him. They stood there so long in contemplation that the sound of banging and scraping began echoing through the hull as Mereel brought the hardware inboard.

"She'll be fine, *Ord'ika.*" It was obvious he was worried about Besany getting caught. "She's used to investigating fraud without anyone noticing."

"She's close to investigating the Chancellor, *Kal'buir.* That's as dangerous as it gets in her line of work."

"We'll pull her out at the first sign of trouble, I promise."

"And do what?"

Events were overtaking Skirata at breakneck speed. Part of his mind was on whether Delta had what it took to beat them to Ko Sai—possibly, because Vau trained them—and part was worrying about Etain, whom he hadn't checked on for a day. He felt guilty for the way he'd bullied her.

And part of his attention was now on the fact that three

people had put themselves at risk for his scheme, and might need to be moved to safety or given refuge very fast indeed. His plans for a safe haven, an escape route, had to be firmed up right away. He'd have to get hold of the *Cuy'val Dar* comrades he could most rely on.

"Do we exploit people like Jusik and Etain and Besany, or do we give them something they need?" Ordo asked. "These people who gravitate to us—they so want a community, a family, and that's the one thing we have in abundance. But I don't know where to draw the line. I just feel bad for them."

"Family's about being willing to do that, *Ord'ika*," Skirata said, and steered him toward the gunwell access. "No holding back. We give all we've got, too."

"What if she doesn't want to come with us?"

"Besany?"

"Yes. We're planning to desert, aren't we? It's going to be a life on the run. What if she says, *Sorry, Ordo, I like my life on Coruscant too much*? What if she tells me to get lost?"

The two of them seemed a long way from that kind of commitment, but the Nulls had come out of the Kaminoans' genetic tinkering with a capacity for instant, unshakable devotion. If they took to you, they'd die for you. If they didn't, you were dead meat. That was what happened when the genes that influenced loyalty and bonding were overcooked. But it was an existing Mandalorian tendency that the Kaminoans had exploited, and Ordo was only making the same snap decision on which partner he wanted that Skirata and most other *Mando* males made.

Besany *had* to stand by Ordo. Kal couldn't bear to see the lad's heart broken. He wanted so much for the boy, for all of them.

"She won't let you down, son," Skirata said.

She couldn't even if she wanted to. She was now in this up to her neck. Coruscant would never be the same safe home again for Besany Wennen.

6

We have laws on how we treat sentient species. We have laws on how we treat animals and semi-sentients. We even have laws protecting plants. But we have absolutely no laws whatsoever governing the welfare of clone troops— human beings. They have no legal status, no rights, no freedoms, and no representation. Every one of you here who accepted this army without murmur should hang your head in shame. If that's the depths we as a Republic can sink to in the name of democracy, it hardly surprises me that the CIS wants to break away. The end can never justify means like this.
—Senator Den Skeenah of Chandrila, addressing the Senate eighteen months after the Battle of Geonosis, after setting up a charitable appeal to fund the only veterans' welfare facility in the Republic

Rebel camp, Gaftikar, 473 days after Geonosis

Fi stared at Darman and Atin as they hauled Sull out of the speeder and half carried him to the center of the camp. The ARC trooper was hobbled, but it hadn't stopped him from taking a good kick at Atin when they had bundled him into the vehicle. He looked ready to kill now.

Darman felt guilty. *I'd be doing the same. I wouldn't let anyone take me alive.*

Fi stood with hands on hips. "So he followed you home, and now you want to keep him?" He looked Sull up and down and tutted loudly. "I suppose you couldn't resist his big appealing eyes."

Atin peeled off Sull's gag.

"Shove it," snarled the ARC.

Darman held up his bandaged hand. It was swollen and throbbing despite bacta and a one-shot of antibiotic. "He bites, too."

"Just keep him off the furniture." Fi turned toward the camp buildings, two fingers in his mouth, and delivered a piercing whistle. "Now watch A'den lose his temper. It's very entertaining."

A'den came at a run from one of the buildings, now wearing his ARC armor with its dark green sergeant's trim, helmet clipped at the small of his back and rattling against the belt of his *kama*. Sull stared. A small circle of curious Marits started to form.

The Null skidded to a halt and wheeled around on them, face like thunder. "And you lot can clear off. This is trooper business. Get lost! *Usenye!*"

Even the dominant lizards with their red frills scattered as if he'd lobbed a grenade among them. A'den had that edge, just like Ordo and the others, the look and the tone that said he was a man who would erupt into unpredictable violence: even nonhumans picked it up and heeded the warning.

"So . . . you took a prisoner," A'den said, all the scarier for suddenly being softly spoken. "Did you think it through at all? You make a habit of this. I heard it was Fi who brought home strays last time."

"Dynamic risk assessment," Fi said.

"Making it up as you go along."

"Same thing."

"Di'kut."

But Darman had done what he had to. He didn't plan on apologizing for that. "He was *supposed* to be MIA, not AWOL."

"Well, he *was* missing, and he *is* in action. Just not for the Republic." A'den looked Sull over, and Darman wondered if he was looking for injuries or just finding a fresh spot to make a bruise. "And you can't be absent without leave if you don't *get* leave. So nobody lied to you, did they?"

Atin seemed to get it a few moments later than Darman. "You *knew* he'd gone over to the Seps?"

"Some things are best left alone," said A'den. "I worked it out."

"Sure you did." Sull seemed to latch on to A'den as a brother ARC and decided he ran the show. He turned his back on Darman. "I haven't *gone over,* as you put it. I'm just not fighting for the Republic anymore."

"Subtle legal point. You'll have to explain it."

"So now that you've got me, what are you going to do? You don't have a long list of options for a deserter."

Deserter. Darman wished A'den *had* shot him. Somehow Sull would have seemed more honorable if he'd taken up arms for the Seps rather than sitting out the war while brother clones like Sicko—he never forgot Sicko, *none* of them did—died at the front. But Sull didn't strike him as a coward. Niner jogged across the clearing in his black undersuit, towel draped around his neck, and Darman braced for a lecture on doing things by the book. Fi moved in to intercept him.

"What I do next depends on how much grief you'll create for me and my brothers," A'den said. He took a look at the ARC's bound wrists as if he was thinking of untying them and then seemed to change his mind. "So we can stand here like the cabaret at the Outlander, amusing the Marits, or discuss this in private."

Sull was unbowed. "Why not just shoot me now while I'm still trussed, spook? Because I'm not going back to the GAR. If you want to make me, one of us is going to have to kill the other."

"Fierfek, what *are* you two?" Niner said. "Hibel spiders? Cut the *osik.* Regulations are clear. He's a traitor. We take him in."

"Niner, shut it." A'den took out a vibroblade, ducked down, and sliced through the plastoid tape around Sull's ankles. "And any kicking or biting, *ner vod,* and I'll remove something you're very attached to. Civilized chat, like comrades. Got it?"

Sull paused, seemed to consider dismemberment, and then nodded.

They had an audience again. The Marit rebels had edged nearer, one lizard at a time, and were now standing in earshot with their heads cocking back and forth in curiosity. A'den turned with slow menace, and they scattered again. He hadn't said Omega couldn't follow, though, so the four of them trooped after him and sat down on the long bench in the sparsely furnished ops room to watch the conversation. It was a grand name for the place. The Marits had built their camp like they built the homes for the humans in Eyat, and the HQ building was a comfortable little house with sliding interior walls and shutters made from translucent luet bark, utterly unmilitary in every respect. It would vanish in a ball of flame if anything bigger than a stun round hit it.

Rebel camp? It was a village. The weapons and artillery pieces were real, though, and the citizens of Eyat didn't appear to venture out of their city strongholds.

A'den dragged a chair across the planked floor and sat Sull down, hands still tied behind his back, while he stalked around the room. He gave Omega a glance that told them they would be watching in silence and taking notes.

"So," he said. "Tell me when you first lost your enthusiasm for a long-term military career in the glorious Grand Army of the Republic."

"Let me see." Sull looked up theatrically at a point above and to the right. "I think it was when they blew my buddy's brains out. Yes, I do believe it was."

"Who's they?" Darman asked. "You keep saying *they.*"

A'den raised an eyebrow. "*I'm* doing the interrogation."

"He asked if *they* had sent me, Sergeant."

"Okay." A'den patted Sull's head, more like a couple of slow slaps by way of warning. "Answer the man."

"You're one of Skirata's undisciplined rabble, aren't you?"

"Proud to say so, yes."

"You've got no love for the Republic, then. Ever wondered what happens to us when we're no more use?"

"Yes. But I didn't know *you* had . . ."

Darman was sure every clone did. He thought about it almost as much as he thought about Etain, which was a lot. He held his breath, waiting for some insight. Somehow he knew it wasn't going to be good news.

"So did Alpha-zero-two," said Sull. "Remember him? Spar? First off the line."

"I've got perfect recall," A'den said. "Of course I remember. He went missing more than a year before we shipped out for Geonosis. And you lot were the *second* batch—after us."

Darman marveled at the ability of any trooper to make it off Kamino. He must have been given help, and Darman could think of at least two people who would have done just that.

Sull leaned forward slightly, unable to sit back because of his handcuffs. "Spar saw what was coming and thought he would be better off taking his chances outside. And once we knew he was gone—well, quite a few of us started thinking."

"Heard from him since?"

"No."

"He's doing a little bounty hunting and merc work now." Nulls seemed to hear about everything one way or another. Darman never asked how or why, but the comment looked designed to show Sull that A'den had better intel than he did. "The family business. He's not exactly trained to do anything else, is he?"

"The Republic sent someone after him to kill him."

"Sure?"

"Sure. They didn't get him, but my buddy Tavo decided to make a run for it a few months ago, and they caught him. Then they blew his brains out."

"They."

"Republic Intelligence agents. The Chancellor's hit men." Sull didn't seem preoccupied with escape now. His mind was on events, and he looked past A'den as if there were someone standing to one side of him. He saw ghosts; Darman and every commando who'd lost close brothers saw them, too. "We're not the only hired help in town."

He's just like us.

Darman realized he didn't know the Alpha ARCs at all. Commandos and ARC troopers led totally separate lives on Kamino during training, bar necessary contact on exercises. Despite being part of Skirata's company, Omega never spent time with the Nulls during those years, and they'd seemed every bit as scary and alien as the Alpha ARCs.

So Alpha ARCs had *buddies.* Somehow he'd seen them as solitary killing machines, incapable of forming bonds like the tight-knit commando squads, and then—

That's how everyone sees us.

Darman realized he'd done what most civvies seemed to. He'd drawn a line beyond which someone else was less than him, just as citizens thought all clones were flesh machines, *wet droids* as Skirata used to call them, things sent to die because they weren't like *real* people and so it was okay.

If that's how easy it is to think that way . . .

Niner risked a comment. "So that's the punishment for going over the wall. I'm not sure we should be surprised."

"No, chum, you've got it wrong," said A'den. "This isn't punishment. Is it, Sull?"

All the fight seemed to have drained out of the ARC. Maybe he was just waiting to die. "No, because punishment is a deterrent. And to deter anyone, they have to *know* what'll happen to them. But nobody gets told about ARCs who are executed."

"Killed because they know too much?" Atin asked.

"Killed because they're nek battle dogs." A'den ran the tip of his vibroblade under his nails and inspected the manicure. "Once they're too old to fight, they can't be tamed as house pets. Dangerous, savage things. They have to be put down. Don't they, *Sull'ika*?"

"You can shove your *Mando* camaraderie," Sull said, "but you've got it about right. And they'll come for you, too, when you can't—or won't—fight any longer, Null boy. Nobody leaves the Grand Army. What do you think they had in mind for us when we weren't any more use, putting us out to stud?"

"Well, I was sort of hoping . . . ," Fi said wistfully.

"We're not even any special use as a DNA bank. We're second-generation Jango. They might as well get fresh material from troopers. They're less trouble."

Darman didn't want to look at his squad comrades. He knew what was going through their minds. It had to be the same dread: that this limited life was all there would ever be for them.

It hadn't seemed to matter back in Tipoca City. None of them had seen the world outside. Now they'd lived in cities, and met nice girls, and seen how other beings lived their lives. And they knew what they were missing.

Not me. I'm not going to end up like that.

Niner clicked his teeth in annoyance. "He *ran*. Most of the ARC troopers are still doing their duty. You'll forgive me if I don't get sentimental about his inner turmoil."

"Yeah, whatever, Niner." A'den spun the blade and gazed at the tip. "Welcome to the complex world of morality." He paused, then bent over to face Sull almost nose-to-nose. Darman expected to hear a crack of bone as the ARC head-butted him, but the two men just stared. "So what were you doing in Eyat?"

"I got a job. An apartment."

"Military sort of job? Advising the enemy?"

"Driving repulsor cabs. And Eyat's not the enemy. They're just more ordinary folks who are going to get creamed in another war."

"But if you wanted to stay there, you'd have made sure they didn't lose, wouldn't you?"

"I've been there a few months. I'm not going to walk straight in, tell them I'm defecting, and show them the plans, am I?"

"Sooner or later, Sull, you'll have to take sides, before the Marit coup happens. The attack you were training the lizards to carry out."

"So?"

"You want out?"

"I'll draw you a picture, shall I?"

"You can't stay here. I can't risk you on the outside, giving the Eyati the codes and overrides, and getting more clones killed. And you aren't coming back inside. So . . ."

A'den straightened up with the vibroblade, and for a moment Darman thought he was going to kill Sull on the spot. But he cut the plastoid cuffs and then held the point of the blade just under Sull's chin, pressing into the flesh.

The ARC rubbed his wrists. "You waiting for something?"

"Get off the planet," A'den said. He took some cash credits out of his belt pouch. "This is plenty to set you up again. I'll fix you transport to get a long way from Gaftikar, on condition that you don't compromise another clone's safety."

Sull shrugged. A'den's offer seemed to have caught him off guard. "This brotherly solidarity is touching, but we each have to look out for ourselves."

A'den glanced at his chrono. "Put it another way," he said. "You get off this rock and stay out of the war, or I put you out of circulation the permanent way."

"I *like* it here."

A'den looked up and jerked his thumb in the direction of the doors. "Omega, thin out. We're going to have a little ARC-to-ARC chat. About *kama* fashions or some such *osik*."

Niner got up without protest and made a *follow-me* gesture. The squad trooped out behind him and sat down, backs propped against the wall of the HQ building.

"He's still a traitor," Niner said at last.

Darman stared ahead in defocus. The Marits had built a mock-up of a house and seemed to be rehearsing rapid entry, minus ordnance. They paused to stare back, then returned to their drill, but Sull's arrival had grabbed their attention. Did they know who he was? Darman wondered if they could tell one clone from another except by uniform.

"He just doesn't trust the Republic," Darman said.

"I don't trust the Republic, either." Atin picked a blade of grass and studied it intently. "But that doesn't mean I'd join the Seps."

"So what's not to trust?" asked Fi. "Apart from the fact they bred us to die and treat us like dirt? Aww, anyone can make a mistake . . ."

"All that *osik* about the droid threat, for a start. I went on that sabotage mission with Prudii. I *saw* the factory. I saw the production count. They're missing quite a few decimal places. It's bogus, but I still don't know where Intelligence got it."

"*At'ika,* everyone lies like a hairy egg about troop strengths and kit and stuff," Darman said. He knew Skirata never told them the whole story—he said so—but the more the war ground on, the more Darman realized that it was all lie upon lie, on both sides. Nothing ever added up. There were too few droids around to support the kind of numbers coming out of Republic Intel. The CIS's claims were *unsubstantiated.* "Propaganda. All part of the armory."

And handy for getting the Senate to blindly approve spending. Yes, Darman could understand the politics now.

The day you know what's actually going on in a war, son, you'll know you're watching a holovid. That's what Skirata said. Wars ran as much on lies and propaganda as they did on munitions. All you could ever *really* know was what was right in front of your own eyes, and even then it was open to interpretation.

Even so, the Nulls seemed . . . *different* in the last week or so. It was right after Atin came back grumbling that Kal and Ordo had sent him home after the sabotage mission. Atin didn't need to know what they were doing, they said. They denied it was connected to the hunt for General Grievous.

Darman thought Skirata sailed too close to the wind these days. It was part of what made him a beloved *buir* but it also kept Darman awake some nights.

I don't mind being shot at. It's having a government that lies to me that I hate.

The clump-clump-clump of boots vibrated through the frame of the building, and Darman felt it in his back. A'den and Sull were coming out. He checked that his sidearm was fully charged.

"*Master* Sull will be leaving Gaftikar in a few days," A'den announced, not looking at any of the squad. Sull trailed out after him, looking grim. "Keep him fully entertained until his transport arrives."

Niner just couldn't keep his mouth shut. Standing up for what you believed was terrific, but sometimes it was just missing the point. "But—"

"ARC trooper Lieutenant Alpha-Thirty died of his injuries following an unknown incident, okay?" A'den announced pointedly. "He was too decomposed to ascertain a cause of death. But I recovered his armor and I'm returning his tally to SO Brigade for records purposes. Got it? Because if you didn't, I can repeat it even more slowly."

Fi raised an eyebrow. "He looks pretty decomposed to me. We'll give him a decent burial. Can I have his boots and *kama*?"

But Niner wasn't giving in to A'den without a speech. That was Niner all over. Darman suspected he would have given Ordo an equally hard time. His ultrastraight decency anchored the squad.

Sometimes, though, he just needed to look the other way and shut up.

"At what point does *improvisation* turn into complete collapse of discipline, *ner vod*?"

A'den stared down at him as if he'd just noticed him. "You think I should stick him on a desertion charge and return him to Zey for due process."

"That's what the regs say . . ."

A'den looked away for a moment as if he'd taken sudden interest in the Marits, who'd now managed to demolish the training house even without ordnance. They emitted excited, triumphant little squeals, totally at odds with their ferocity. Then the Null took his comlink from his belt and held it out to Niner.

"Okay, *mir'sheb,* why don't *you* flash Zey and tell him we have a renegade ARC on our hands?" He got fed up waiting for Niner to take the link, reached down to grab his hand, and slapped the thing into his palm. "Go on."

Niner inhaled deeply, knuckles white as he gripped the device. Darman caught Fi's eye and wondered if either of them would stop their sergeant. Atin looked studiously blank.

"Go on, Mouth Almighty," said A'den. "*Turn him in,* if you've got the *gett'se* to do it."

"You didn't answer me." Niner stood his ground. "Where's the line between bending the rules out of common sense and failing in our duty?

"Duty my *shebs.*"

"I don't mean duty to the Republic. I mean to *our own.* So some ARC can choose to do a runner because he's so kriffing independent, but the poor grunts in the Galactic Marines have to stay and suck it up? When do *they* get to choose?"

A'den squatted down level with Niner. He grabbed his wrist and forced Niner's hand and comlink up to the commando's mouth. "So tell Zey, then. You want to know what happens next? This isn't like a proper army. Sull won't get a court-martial. He won't get jailed or busted down a rank. They'll put a blaster round through his head, because they can't trust him again and they can't have an ARC on the loose."

Niner and A'den were frozen, eyes locked on each other.

"Maybe that's what someone who leaves his buddies to do the fighting *deserves,*" said Niner.

"Go ahead, then. Finish it."

A'den let go of Niner's wrist as if he were throwing it away and stood up. Sull ambled around at a short distance, head down, arms folded, looking for all the world as if he were listening to comlink chatter in a nonexistent helmet. Darman suddenly found himself preoccupied with unknowns that Skirata had never covered in training: Who would fire the shot? Who executed renegades? He couldn't imagine a brother clone or a Jedi officer pulling the trigger. Maybe they called in Republic Intel.

They certainly couldn't call on CSF to do it. CSF was now very friendly with clones in general, thanks to Skirata.

"Shabii'gar," Niner snapped, and tossed the comlink back at A'den. Then he got up and stalked off. Niner wasn't sulking. Darman knew he was walking away from the temptation to hit the Null, because he'd never heard him use language like that before. "Just remember that if you ever expect us to haul your *shebs* out of the fire."

A'den watched him go and shook his head. He had weather-beaten skin that made him look older than Ordo and Mereel, and a distinctly paternal air. "Don't you get it?" He turned to the three remaining commandos. "What'll happen to any clone who can't be patched up and deployed again? Or when we get too old to fight?"

Darman found himself pinned down by A'den's intense stare. He had to answer. "Yeah, I think about it a *lot.*"

"And? You noticed any pension plans or retirement facilities?" A'den rolled his eyes. "Attended any career resettlement courses, did you?"

In quiet moments with Etain, the moments when he began to get a glimpse of what was tearing Fi apart, Darman tried not to dwell on it, because there was nothing he could think of doing that didn't mean leaving his buddies in the lurch, and—statistically—he wasn't likely to be around to worry about premature old age anyway.

But the idea of being too badly hurt to be worth saving did trouble him. He liked life, all right. He loved it. Anyone who thought clones didn't have a sense of fear or mortality was a fool—or maybe a civilian justifying that it was okay to use them, because they weren't like *real* humans.

The whole squad was silent. A'den seemed to be getting exasperated.

"You're *ex-pen-da-ble,*" he said, all slow deliberation, emphasizing each syllable. "All soldiers are, always have been, but you are *extra*-expendable. No rights, no vote, no families to kick up a stink about your treatment, and no connection to any community that'll fight for you. Bred, used, and disposed of when you're beyond economic repair or show too much dissent. Fine, be noble martyrs, but do it because you *choose* it, not because you're a cage-farmed nuna and you don't know how to think otherwise."

Fi was usually the one with all the chat and a knack for defusing situations, but he was disturbingly silent now. He seemed to have an increasingly uneasy relationship with the outside world. He craved it—Darman could almost taste the envy when Fi caught glimpses of other beings' lives—but he looked like he tried to put it out of his mind, too, maybe because he was sure he'd never have a life beyond the GAR. Niner had proved to be far better at shutting things out than Fi.

It must have been easier for the rank-and file-troopers. They saw almost nothing of the world beyond the battlefield. They hadn't been raised by father figures like Skirata or Vau, so they clung to one another. It was all they had. Yeah, cage-farmed nuna, and the cage could look like a safe haven when you left it. It was a good comparison. The outside world was unknown and scary. *Institutional neurosis,* Skirata called it.

"Problem with wars," Fi said at last, voice suddenly a stranger's, "is that they show people what they can really do when they put their minds to it, and that makes peace pretty uncomfortable for governments when it finally comes. You can't put them back in their box."

"You don't know anything about peace," said Atin. "None of us does."

Darman tried to lighten the mood. "Ordo's been telling him stories again." Sull was still waiting there. Darman wondered if he would have pulled the trigger on the ARC if he'd been ordered to. "Never teach clones to read."

"Ordo doesn't know anything about peace, either," Atin said.

Darman felt he was equally ignorant, but he reserved the right to keep thinking about it. If the point was winning the war, then someone *had* to have thought what would happen to the army afterward.

"Do you think Sev's got a girlfriend?" Fi asked.

"If he has, she probably escaped from the Galactic City violent offenders' unit." Darman nudged his brother. *Come on, Fi, don't obsess.* "Not your type."

"I'd never hold it against a girl for being a psychopath." Fi made a visible effort to be his other self. "Can't be too picky."

"Well, much as I love soaking up the wisdom of you great philosophers, I've got things to do." A'den gestured to Darman to get up. "Go retrieve Sull's kit. He'll tell you where he buried it. Meanwhile he's going to tell me all he knows about Eyat. Deal, Sull?"

The ARC shrugged. "So you can wipe 'em out better?"

"If you've got a little *friend* in Eyat that you want to rescue, now's the time to mention it."

Sull shook his head. "Nobody. Funny, even the lizards don't recognize me now. I must make a big impression."

"You going to debrief on Eyat or not?"

Sull seemed to consider it. "Okay, but there's nothing you don't already have from the guys who built the place."

Darman diverted to find Niner on his way to dig up Sull's armor. He was standing by a tree looking out over the escarpment, fingers hooked in the rear waistband of his undersuit, and he didn't turn around as Darman walked up behind him and put a hand on his shoulder.

"Armor up, Sarge. Let's find Sull's kit."

Niner turned, and Darman had expected to see some remnant of anger. But he looked more upset than bottling up fury. It was as if he'd had bad news.

"Okay . . . ," he said, still distracted.

"Are you all right, *vod'ika*?"

"Can I ask you a question?"

That wasn't Niner at all. He didn't edge around issues. Darman felt uneasy. "Well . . . yeah, go ahead."

"If you could go now—if you could get on a transport and go wherever you want, no consequences, even take Etain with you—would you go?"

"Leave the army?"

"Leave the *squad*. Leave us behind."

Darman chewed the idea over, and it made his gut churn.

These weren't the men he'd been raised with in his first pod of four clones: every member of Omega was the sole survivor from his last squad. But these were still his brothers in arms, men who knew exactly what he was thinking, how he felt about everything, what would make him annoyed, what he liked to eat, every last tiny detail of every breath taken each day. He would never have that degree of intimacy with anyone else—maybe not even Etain. He could hardly imagine a day without them. He wasn't sure how that would fit into the vague idea of being with Etain in some state of domestic bliss that he didn't understand and had only glimpsed around him, but he knew that being separated from his brothers would rip a hole in him that would never heal.

He'd never come to terms with losing Vin, Jay, and Taler, when they were all part of Theta Squad, and—just like Delta, even now—thought death happened to other squads, never theirs.

That was before they faced the real war. That was when an accidental death in training shocked them into silence for days.

Niner was still waiting for his answer. "It's not about serving the Republic, Dar. I don't even know what the Republic is now or why it's better than the Seps. All I know is that I go out each day trying not to get killed and making sure you guys don't die, either, nothing more than that. So . . . what fills that space when you leave your brothers behind?"

Niner was still thinking about Sull and why he could walk away while his comrades stayed. It was more than loyalty to the Republic and all that guff that Jango had hammered into them.

"Wouldn't you rather be somewhere nice, doing something other than fighting?" Darman asked.

"Dar, *would you leave*?"

"It's not going to happen," Darman said at last. *Is that yes or no?* He wasn't sure. He wasn't even certain what a Darman outside the army would be, let alone separated from his brothers. "So don't even think about it."

But Darman went on thinking about it as they checked

their position and hunted for Sull's armor. He was sure that Niner was thinking about it, too.

Tilsat, Qiilura, day three of the evacuation,
476 days after Geonosis

"This," said Levet, "is what happens when you give a lot of overpowered, easily portable hardware to locals who know the terrain better than we do."

Etain knew the farmers would use every trick General Zey had taught them during the resistance, but that didn't make capturing them much easier. So far, the troopers had seized five hundred or so alive and bundled them into transports; the rest had scattered into small groups, taking the abundance of Republic-supplied weapons with them.

If the farmers had been Separatists, the planet would have been cleared by now. But hands were tied. These were Republic citizens, and this was the Gurlanins' planet, which meant it couldn't be reduced to a wasteland.

It wasn't the way any of them wanted to fight, except maybe her.

But so far the fighting had followed a pattern. After the farmers had taken a few fatalities, they surrendered. They seemed to feel they'd made their point, and now that they were scared and exhausted, they wanted an end to it. With that in mind, Etain pursued the strategy of picking off a few in each group and inviting a surrender.

It didn't seem to be working this time.

The platoon was pinned down in the river valley north of Tilsat. The seven other platoons were scattered, chasing the largest rebel groups that had broken away. Five to one had looked like easy odds for clone troops, but the complication of trying to remove the colonists in one piece had handicapped them badly, and the time was fast approaching when Etain was going to give that up as a bad job.

"Incoming!"

An artillery round smashed through the trees behind

Etain's position, showering the line of troops with shards of ice and branches. She ducked instinctively, Force or no Force.

Levet, usually glued to her side, sprinted away behind the defensive wall that had been a merlie shed and dropped to his knees to operate an E-Web repeating blaster that was now standing idle on its tripod. The gunner lay sprawled with his leg at an awkward angle; another trooper was trying frantically to remove his helmet. Levet laid down fire as two clones worked on their fallen brother's injuries, and Etain realized that she could no longer prioritize as a commander had to.

All she could see was the wounded trooper.

Who is he?

She always tried hard to learn their names—they always had names among themselves, not just the numbers their Kaminoan masters gave them—and this one escaped her. She felt she was denying him. She couldn't let him be a stranger. But now she had to.

You have to fight. You can't fall back and play medic.

The farmers were spread across the hillside above the platoon, hiding in ice-glazed crags and hollows, and somewhere up there they had a small but devastating artillery piece, supplied by the Republic to help them drive out the Separatists. They also had a lot of blaster rifles—and what was effective against droids could also be lethal applied to regular trooper armor. Her lightsaber and Force powers were of limited use for attacking dispersed fire. All she could do was fend off rounds and debris, because her concentration had vanished. Once, she could have centered herself and visualized the threat, taking in the very fabric of the air and land and water, and deflected plasma bolts or sent snipers crashing against the rocks. Now she tried to locate each firing position to focus on that alone.

Pregnancy's changed me. Not that I was that strong in the Force to start with.

To her left, Levet directed fire into the hillside, placing E-Web rounds in a neat sequence that sent small avalanches down the hill, exposing grass and rock. Troopers were ranged around her, targeting sniper positions at either end of the valley. She waited for him to pause firing and adjusted her headset comlink.

"Casualties, Commander?" She should have had a lieutenant in command or a captain at most, not the services of a full commander, but every Jedi general got one, even insignificant Jedi Knights like her. "When this starts to cost too much, I think arrest isn't an option."

"Ten men injured, two serious."

"Get them casevacked."

"We'd have to recall the A-tee to do that at the moment, ma'am, and there's the small matter of where we evacuate them to anyway. If the bacta and med droids can't fix them, nobody can."

Some generals might have thought that ten men down out of a platoon of thirty-six was acceptable, but Etain didn't. "Let's take the hillside out, then."

"Let me confirm that . . . you no longer want to take prisoners?"

Etain could hardly believe what she was saying. "They're farmers. You're elite troops. With the gloves off, this would have taken you no time at all."

"You want one last try at talking them down, ma'am?"

Levet knew her better than she thought. He seemed to understand that she'd blame herself later if she didn't offer them one last chance to surrender. How many more times she had to offer she had no idea. They'd made their intentions clear.

"Okay. Bring up the A-tee."

Blaster exchanges continued, but the troopers seemed to be fighting in complete silence. They could hear their comlink circuit in their helmets; she couldn't. There was just the crack of blaster rounds and the rain of frozen soil as cannon rounds ripped into the farmland around them. When she remembered to click her teeth to activate the platoon comlink circuit, the voices switched on in her earpiece and she was plunged into the chaotic noise of battle, of men calling positions and range and elevation, and one voice repeating, "Is he okay? Is Ven okay? *Is Ven okay?*"

Ven. He *did* have a name. She knew it now.

Etain switched back to her closed circuit with Levet. "How long before the A-tee's in range, Commander?"

"Twelve standard minutes, ma'am."

"Okay." She concentrated on the hillside opposite, thinking into the minds of the men and women she'd known—trained—and tried to persuade them by thought influence that they were hesitant, uncertain if they wanted to continue this, anxious to leave for a better life. "Cease fire. Stand by."

The troopers lowered their blasters immediately and edged back from the wall, some dragging wounded comrades. One of them wasn't showing any signs of movement at all. Ven lay a little way from the E-Web, helmet beside him, bright scarlet blood leaking into the snow and melting it. His comrade was still pumping his chest two-handed.

The firing from the hillside tailed off into silence.

Etain could sense the emotions around her like patches of colored light; sharp yellows of fear, the blue-white pulsing intensity of ebbing life, and something she could only identify as *child-like,* faint and gray. It was an echo of what she'd first sensed of Darman. It wasn't innocence, though: it felt lost and in need.

The baby kicked again. For a moment she thought it was him. One day he would need to know that his mother had done everything she could to give the farmers a way out.

"Birhan?" she yelled. "Birhan, are you out there?"

The valley echoed. On rural Qiilura, sounds carried a long way. She thought she could hear the distant *ee-unk ee-unk* of the assault walker picking its way through the fields toward the road.

"It's not Birhan." The voice that called back to her was a woman's.

"You can stop this now. You can all walk out of here."

There was a long pause. "*You're* the ones who are cut off on both sides . . ."

"And *we're* the ones who've been trying to take you

alive . . . up till now." The yelling was making Etain's throat sore. She checked her chrono. "I'll give you five standard minutes to lay down your weapons and surrender."

Silence. Absolute silence, other than the backdrop of wild sounds that Darman had labeled NFQ—Normal For Qiilura.

"I suspect that's going to be a *no*," Etain said.

She waited, glancing at her chrono from time to time. It was so quiet that she could hear the snow flurries hitting the troopers' armor, rattling like beans. Levet worked his way back toward her and signaled to check ahead.

Narrowing her eyes against the snow, she could see movement. From the lower slopes of the hill, figures in drab working clothes, faces swathed in scarves, rose slowly and held their hands up in surrender. *Thank the Force. Some sense at last.* She watched carefully for weapons, but they really did seem to have thrown down their rifles. She risked standing up, lightsaber in hand.

"Ma'am, when will you learn to keep your head down?" Levet said sharply. "*Jedi* doesn't mean invulnerable."

"I've got armor," she said, "and I can deflect blaster bolts if they take a potshot at me." It seemed unnecessarily aggressive to activate her lightsaber, but she did it anyway. She wasn't taking any chances. As she edged forward, with the weapon held away from her body, more figures popped up from snow-covered crags, some with hands on heads, some simply holding blasters and rifles aloft. The farmers on the lower slopes had started to pick their way down toward the road.

Their resistance seemed to be a gesture now. They just wanted to show some fight, save face, and be able to tell their children that they hadn't gone quietly. Pride mattered to them. She understood that.

"Okay." She walked forward a few more meters and called out to them. "You've got nothing to fear. No reprisals, I swear. We're just going to take your weapons."

There was no response. They seemed to be taking a long time to get down the slope, but the snow was more like packed ice, and treacherously slippery. She turned to Levet, nodded, and then waved some of the platoon forward to relieve the farmers of their weapons. Fifteen troopers advanced through what had been a field of barq grain in the summer, ghosts against the white landscape picked out by the black of their bodysuits visible between the plates of plastoid alloy, and the single green rank flash of a sergeant.

Etain checked one more thing off her mental list. It was slow going, but they were getting there. "Levet, evacuate the—"

That was as far as she got. An explosion peppered her face with dirt and lifted two troopers meters into the air. One fell screaming, and the other couldn't because he was blown apart.

Mines.

The platoon froze, trapped in an uncharted minefield.

Trap. You don't do that, you just don't surrender and lure my men to their deaths—

Etain's sense of time evaporated. She saw some of the farmers grab their weapons again, and an instinct overtook her that wasn't Jedi at all, an instinct to kill for this act of betrayal. Levet was yelling over the comlink as the remaining men still behind cover opened up with rifle and E-Web fire.

Etain raised her lightsaber before she even realized she'd seen the muzzle flash of a blaster bolt, batting it away. Her comlink was filled with a cacophony of orders and responses, some from the assault walker. Another mine detonated. Another man screamed. Blasterfire and artillery rounds rained down from the hillside.

Etain took a moment to realize it was her own voice calling in fire from the assault walker. "A-tee, bearing five-five-six-zero, take it out, I repeat, *take it out*—"

Shouldn't get in Levet's way. He's the commander. He knows what he's doing. They're killing my men. They'll pay for that.

There was no moral argument left in her about who had first betrayed whose trust here. All that was left was her will to survive and to save her comrades. It was that visceral, that stark, that un-Jedi. She had no sense of anyone else around her except the dead and wounded troopers; she had no sense of *anything* beyond stopping the incoming fire and venting this red-hot rage that was choking her and tightening a band around her forehead.

She hadn't even realized she'd gone into the minefield. She felt she could see through the snow and soil to the devices beneath, devices they should have detected—no, they were custom anti-droid trip mines, plastoid and remotely armed. Somehow she was avoiding them all, but the troopers had no such Force-senses and simply knelt where they'd been forced to stop and returned fire.

Out of all the things she saw that day, that was the most extraordinary: men pinned down on an exposed field, still fighting, when the slightest movement might set off an unseen mine next to them. None of them was paralyzed by panic. No wonder fools thought that clones felt no fear.

"Ma'am, *stop*! Hold it, for fierfek's sake!" Levet's voice rang in her comlink. No, she *wasn't* going to stop. She couldn't. The hillside ahead of her erupted in a massive plume of snow and dirt that rose into the air and fell again like hail. Then there was a rumbling sound. A section of the hillside gave way, taking rocks and soil with it. The sheet of compacted snow slid off like frosting separating from a cake and came to rest like an avalanche.

The walker fired again, shuddering with the recoil, and the stony ridge near the crest shattered as if a fist had punched through a sheet of transparisteel. The explosion deafened her for a few moments and then she felt grit and ice pepper her face, and ducked. There was a second explosion, and a third, and when she raised her head again she couldn't see the hill through the storm of debris that was rolling toward her like a giant foaming wave. The soil beneath her shook as intensely as a groundquake. And then the airborne debris began to hit the ground, the huge billowing wave collapsing, leaving behind it a reshaped hill and a road blocked by rock, soil, and ice.

The rebel fire was now coming only from the position to

the south of them, not the hill. And men were still stranded in the minefield.

"Ma'am, I said *stay where you are,*" Levet shouted.

"No, *you* stay where *you* are, Commander." Etain's anger always got the better of her. She'd never learned to control it. If the dark side wanted her now, then it could take her as long as she got her people clear. "Take out the other artillery position. Just suppress it. Okay?"

And I'm pregnant. Am I crazy? I'm risking my child's life. It's not mine to risk.

But the AT-TE was already in action, pounding the southern position at the other end of the small valley with its cannon. It felt like a holovid was playing in the background, something utterly divorced from what was happening on the minefield. And it was: there was nothing it could do for them other than suppress fire. She was in a minefield surrounded by stranded men, some of them bleeding to death.

It was the sound that tipped her over the edge. They said wounded men cried for their mothers, but troopers had no mothers; they didn't even have a father figure like Skirata. They called for their brothers.

She knew now because one was doing just that. He was calling for Bek, or at least it sounded like that. Bek wasn't responding. Maybe Bek was one of the dead.

It broke her heart, and her last fragile ties to the Jedi.

She looked over her shoulder: Levet was edging his way through the minefield. She didn't just try to influence his mind. She put all her effort into making him stop dead. He hesitated for a moment, but kept coming.

"You can't detect these mines with your sensors, Levet. Don't try." She waved him back. "I can sense what you can't. I'm okay. Don't do this."

Something caught her peripheral vision, a flicker of movement, nothing more. She stared, and then the snow seemed to ripple like an oil-covered sea. Shapes emerged from it, white Gurlanin shapes, and a dozen or more crept into the minefield.

Gurlanins could sense variations in soil density. *Of*

course. Jinart had located gdan tunnels for her during Omega's first mission, so they could detect buried trip mines. One of the Gurlanins tiptoed over to her.

"Jinart," Etain whispered. "Go careful . . ."

"Valaqil," said the Gurlanin. It was Jinart's consort, once Zey's personal spy. "Can't you even tell us apart?"

"I can't even see you half the time."

"We'll mark a clear path so you can rescue your wounded. I'll lead your other men out of here."

"I owe you."

"Yes, you do, Jedi, and if anything happens to you then we may pay the price, so shut up and follow me."

"I can sense where the mines are. I'm okay."

"Pity you didn't sense they were there before you sent your men in."

It was brutally true. Etain's moment of qualified relief was destroyed by shame and guilt. This was *her fault.* She'd caused these troopers' deaths through her own incompetence, and not military incompetence at that: she hadn't used her own Force-senses well enough.

But she didn't have the luxury of self-pity now. She called to the stranded troops who could still walk, unsure if the anti-droid mines had emitted EM pulses, too. "Can you still hear me?"

"Yes ma'am."

"Follow the Gurlanins. Walk in their footprints. They can lead you out."

It was going to be harder moving the wounded men, but she'd do it. She wasn't going to leave a single man behind, dead or alive.

Levet clicked back into her comlink circuit. "Ma'am, a larty will be here in a few minutes. We'll winch them clear. Back out of there . . . *please.*"

"What about the downdraft? Might detonate some more devices."

"I have orders, ma'am. My general's safety comes first."

"No, it *doesn't.*" Etain thought again about her child, but his father was one of these men. None of their lives could count for less than hers, or there was no meaning to having this baby. "I'm a Jedi. I can *do* this."

There was one man she could reach easily. He was ten meters away, not moving, but she sensed he was alive. His right leg was shredded below the knee. Her Force-sense of danger was fully alert now, and when she looked at the snow, churned up with debris and blood, she could see where the mines were, like heat haze in her field of vision. She placed her boots carefully. If she could get a hold on him, lifting him with Force assistance would be relatively easy.

There was a meter-wide safe area she could see. Keeping her balance would be a problem, but if she could get him across her shoulders, she could lift him. She'd watched Darman lift Atin by rolling on him first, but she didn't have enough safe space to do that. All she could do was kneel— carefully, one foot a hand span from a haze that indicated a mine—and ease her head and shoulders under his body.

He made a sound as the air was pushed from his lungs, but he wasn't conscious; he'd lost too much blood. She was stuck now, the full weight of him across her back, and as she shuffled her legs into a kneeling position she nearly rolled him out of the safe zone. It took a little more maneuvering to get where she could straighten up and try the movement that needed a lot of help from the Force—to stand with an eighty-kilo man across her back.

After that, it was easy. *Relatively.*

Etain took a deep breath and was vaguely aware of the sound of the LAAT/i in the distance as she counted to three, tightened her grip on the margins of his armor plates, and then pushed upward, locking out her knees. For a moment the tendons felt as if they would never stretch out. She tottered a little. Then she found her balance and turned very carefully to walk, bent over at forty-five degrees, between the shimmering patches in the snow that only she could see.

The weight lifted off her shoulders and she gripped more tightly, thinking she was dropping him, but she found she was clear of the minefield and a couple of his comrades had simply hauled him off her back.

Levet caught her by the shoulder. "Enough, ma'am. Even if I have to slug you, you're not doing that again. Understand? Leave it to the winchman."

She didn't feel so clever now. She weighed forty-five kilos and she'd admit even to herself that she was skinny.

"Okay." She looked around at separate little scenes of despair, troopers receiving first aid from comrades while the med droid from the AT-TE hovered among them. She hadn't even noticed the huge six-legged walker move in. Now she could see the trooper hit earlier, Ven, and his buddy kneeling over him, face pinched and yellow with the cold. Once troopers took their helmets off to attempt mouth-to-mouth resuscitation, they were as vulnerable to the freezing conditions as anyone. She walked across to him, feeling unsteady, and squatted down.

"Can't get a pulse, ma'am," he said quietly.

"He's not dead." She put her hand on Ven's forehead and felt the life in him—weak, but holding on. She couldn't see where he'd been hit. The vulnerable points were the gaps between armor sections. "Extreme cold improves survival chances with some injuries. The med droid will be with him in a few minutes." Ven's skin felt like a corpse's. She knew *exactly* what a cadaver felt like. "Okay?"

"Okay, ma'am. Thanks."

She'd been at this stage before: numb, not fully aware of her surroundings, and unsure how much time had elapsed. The firing had stopped, so the surviving farmers—if there were any after the AT-TE's cannon bombardment—must have moved on. Most of the Gurlanins had vanished except for the few helping the gunship's winchman get a harness on the remaining dead and wounded.

It was odd to watch them. They could take any form they pleased, anything at all, yet instead of shapeshifting into something with hands, they remained in what she thought of as their animal form. It was as if they felt they didn't have to change any longer. They had their planet back, very nearly. It seemed like a kind of physical nationalism where they could be themselves again.

"You okay now, ma'am?" said Levet.

Etain watched the walker squat in the low position to open its hatches and take in the wounded on repulsor gurneys. Ven's skin was like pale wax; other men were suffering from blast trauma, shaken around inside their armor by mines or artillery rounds. Even a helmet didn't prevent brain injury, and their armor wasn't the expensive ultratoughened Katarn type that enabled Fi to throw himself on a grenade and come out of the encounter just badly shaken. The med droid was injecting medication to stop intracranial swelling; one man was having a temporary shunt inserted through his skull to drain off fluid.

"I'm not injured, if that's what you mean." She turned to look at Levet, unable to judge his degree of annoyance in the Force. He was a calm sea of self-control with undercurrents hidden so deep that she couldn't tell if they were violence, sorrow, or passion. "Sorry. I didn't mean to cause you anxiety."

See, all these horrible medical details I know about now? I didn't want to learn this the hard way. Maybe when I get out, I can use this, be a medic . . . not a Jedi, not after this war. Not if, but when.

It was more than worrying about Darman. It was all of them: the clone soldier she loved, the ones she knew as friends, the ones she didn't know and never would. It overtook her now. She worried that her anxiety would damage the baby, and slid her arms inside her cloak to put a surreptitious hand on her belly and send a sense of comfort to him. He was agitated. Her state of mind *was* affecting him. He seemed almost . . . *angry.*

It'll be all right . . .

But she had no name for him. She didn't dare. And if he was angry, it was something he'd inherited from her.

"We're done," Levet said. He stood listening, one finger held up for silence, and Etain heard a single shriek—a man, a woman, she couldn't tell—in the distance. The Gurlanins were picking off the rebel farmers who'd escaped the bombardment.

I ordered this. I started it. I did it. I made the mistake about the minefield.

Etain was simply dismayed to take stock of the person she'd become, and how far her Jedi training—contemplation, reason, nonviolence—had receded into the distance.

"Ma'am? Time to move on and track down the others. This is going to be a long, fiddly job."

"Okay." Etain needed a moment. She stared down at the compressed pink snow where Ven had lain while his buddies worked on keeping him alive. There was more blood than she'd expected, but it was hard to tell when it had stained the snow and spread. Blood in water or slush always looked worse than it was. "I'll be with you shortly."

She stood thinking of Darman, picturing him so that the baby might possibly see what she saw in the Force, and then made her way to the LAAT/i gunship. The speeder buses had already left empty, with no farmers to evacuate. Levet walked behind.

"Ma'am," he said. "Hang on."

"What?"

"You've been hit, ma'am. Look—"

Etain turned around to face the commander and saw what he'd spotted: she'd left a trail of blood droplets in her wake. Instinctively, she looked for injuries, knowing how easy it was to be numbed to them until the adrenaline wore off.

Then it dawned on her. The blood wasn't coming from an injury, but running down her leg. She could feel its brief warmth now as it cooled on her skin and froze where it soaked into her clothes. A searing cramp seized her and doubled her up.

She was hemorrhaging. She was losing the baby.

Nar Hej Shipping Company, Napdu, fourth moon of Da Soocha, Hutt space, 476 days after Geonosis

Sev stood to one side of the entrance, staring at Fixer on the other side as he had so many times before.

He couldn't remember the last time he'd walked through an unknown door without blowing it up, kicking it open, or melting its locks with a blaster bolt. One day he'd use the controls like everyone else. Scorch knelt between the two of them, edging the thin blades of the hydraulic spreader into the crack between the two halves of the door.

"I need an explosive fix," Scorch said. "I'm fed up with opening things *quietly*."

"We don't want an audience arriving to admire your work."

"Sev, I'm a *surgeon* among rapid entry artists." Scorch grunted with the effort as he braced the spreader against his chest and leaned on it. The blades finally slipped into the gap. "You're a nerf butcher."

"Want to be on the menu, too?"

"Patience. Or we'll lock you in a room with Fi and let him talk you to death."

Fixer let out a long sigh, one of his eloquently wide repertoire of nonverbal responses, and held up his hand to do a mute countdown: four, three, two . . .

One.

Scorch pumped the hydraulics and the blades separated, sliding apart along the length of the bar. The doors were now open far enough for him to wedge the hydraulic ram between them and part them wide. Sev stepped over him, focused on not letting Ko Sai's trail go cold.

So . . . they couldn't let Skirata know about this.

Or Omega, come to that.

It bothered Sev a lot. He understood the need to know and *not* know, but something that had to be kept from specific people he knew and trusted—and who *wouldn't* trust a brother commando?—troubled him.

We're not like ordinary men. We're professionals. We don't play games.

But what puzzled him most was the order not to tell Vau, either. Maybe Zey thought Skirata would wheedle it out of him. The Jedi certainly didn't trust Mandalorians, but maybe that was inevitable given the free-range nature of Vau's and

Skirata's black ops activities. They might have been old but they were still thoroughly bad boys.

The office was in darkness. Sev's helmet spot-lamp picked out desks, grubby mats on the floor, and doors that led to what his sensors told him was a long hollow space—a corridor. It probably led to living quarters. It wasn't unusual for traders to live in the same building as their offices on Napdu, because it was just a staging post for the sector's freight—no nice residential neighborhoods. Sev knew that because his HUD-linked database said so, under a red glowing header that read LOCAL CONDITIONS. He saw too little of the galaxy's day-to-day life to judge for himself, so he still relied on intel. He could see Scorch and Fixer's view of the dark office in their point-of-view HUD icons, and Fixer was already slicing into the computer records.

And Ko Sai's trail led here, after it was shaken and beaten out of reluctant informants. Vaynai, waterworld and smugglers' haven, stopping off at Aquaris, another waterworld rife with piracy and other scum, to . . . Napdu.

Fixer took a probe from his belt and slid it into the computer's port, then stood in a pose of frozen concentration as he watched the screen. "Business is booming," he said. "They really ought to shut the system down at night and password-protect the start-up."

Scorch prowled, taking flimsi out of files. Anyone who still used flimsi either had data they didn't want to commit to a sliceable medium or was neurotic about keeping backups for the tax office. "And that would slow you down how long, exactly? Thirty seconds?"

Fixer grunted meaningfully. Sev, half his attention on points of entry and exit, and the other half on Fixer's HUD view of the scrolling spreadsheets, could hear Boss clearing his throat. Their sergeant was a hundred meters away, waiting in a TIV—a special ops traffic interdiction vessel—that masqueraded as a packet courier, and the disembodied sound of someone coughing and swallowing irritated Sev a great deal.

"Boss . . ."

"Problem, Sev?"

"You, Boss . . ."

"When I can take my bucket off, I'll gargle with bacta. Got a cold. Okay?"

Fixer came to life again. "That's the contents of his data storage copied across. Scorch?"

Scorch was still sifting through a pile of flimsi, moving it from one stack to another and pausing to stare at each sheet. He was scanning the contents on his HUD holorecorder. "This is just old stuff. Might as well grab what I can, though."

Boss's voice rasped on the comlink. "This cesspit is orbiting another waterworld, Delta . . . Da Soocha. See a trend?"

Sev heard a faint creak and padded up to the interior doors. He listened carefully, then pressed a sound sensor to the panels. "Prepare to bang out. I detect signs of unintelligent life, and it's not Scorch . . ."

Fixer shut down the computer, grabbed a trashy ornament— a souvenir faux crystal vase from Galactic City with long-dead insects piled up in the bottom—and broke open a cash credit box to pocket the contents. Vau had taught them to make infiltrations look like robberies if they could, and Sev remained impressed by his old training sergeant's unerring eye for the choicest deposit boxes on Mygeeto. Whatever Vau did, he did it exceptionally well.

He's the best. Why should he expect any less from us? He made me what I am. He cares, whatever Skirata thinks.

"Okay, we're gone," said Fixer, and vanished through the doors with Scorch. Sev backed out after them, DC-17 aimed, in case the owner walked in and became another unfortunate statistic in a lawless sector. Burglars didn't usually wear Katarn armor; it would have been hard to leave a live witness.

The three commandos sprinted down the road—no street lighting, all properties shuttered, no prying eyes—and down a dark alley to catch up with Boss. The TIV sat like a crouching animal in a gap between two repulsor trucks. The hatch opened, and they piled inside.

"Okay, let's thin out and run through the data." Boss punched in the coordinates to take the TIV into a freight lane out to Nar Shaddaa and held his hand out for the datachip.

"C'mon, Fixer. Got to transmit it back to base for General Jusik to sift through."

Fixer dropped it into Boss's palm. "Bet I find it before he does."

"You can have a techies' race between you," Scorch said, taking off his helmet and rolling his head to ease his neck muscles. "He's okay, ol' Jusik."

Fixer pounced on the chip as soon as Boss had transmitted the contents and slotted it into his datapad. Sev, sliding across the bench seat in the crew bay to lean on his shoulder, noted that there were an awful lot of freight and passenger transactions.

Fixer shrugged him away. "Gerroff. Go pester Scorch." Sev heard his comlink click off and Fixer was in a world of his own, searching for all traffic that came from or connected with Vaynai in the last six months.

Sev eased off his helmet and gazed at the starscape. It was pretty. There were things out there he wanted to see and do, and probably never would, but he was determined not to think about it or else he'd end up a whiner like Fi, always regretting what he couldn't have. His life was too short to waste it like that. It took an effort to steer away from speculation and longing, but Sev prided himself on his singlemindedness even when it hurt—*especially* when it hurt.

"So what's Zey's problem with Skirata?" Scorch asked, kicking the back of Sev's seat. The benches were arranged one behind the other. "Doesn't he trust him?"

"Doesn't trust him not to make *tatsushi* out of Ko Sai," Boss murmured. "Papa Kal got off to a bad start with the Kaminoans . . ."

Scorch carried on swinging his boot against the metal frame. "Is it true he killed one?"

"Who knows? He's crazy enough."

"So what's Vau going to do with his stash?"

Sev turned around, grabbed Scorch's ankle, and twisted to

make the point. "Maybe he'll pay for a nice *beskar* saber for me so I can remove the source of this irritation."

"Come on, you'd miss me if I got killed . . ."

"*Nobody's* going to get killed. Except by me."

"Shut up, you two." Boss took a sudden intense interest in the TIV's rectenna display. "Busy lane. Don't distract the pilot."

Fixer, gaze glued to his datapad, suddenly stirred and pulled off his helmet. "Paydirt."

"What?" Sev asked.

"Fifteen flights booked in that originated on Aquaris or Vaynai. Five of those passed through both. Two of that five went on to Da Soocha. One paid for in cash credits."

Boss muttered to himself. "*Very* busy lane . . ."

"Vessels?" Scorch asked.

"One hydrographic survey vessel, one private charter. The droggy ship was the cash credit transaction."

"So she's doing the waterworld grand tour." Sev pictured the rough layout of the galaxy, mentally plotting a course from Kamino, then to Vaynai, then Aquaris, then Da Soocha. It looked as if Ko Sai had headed out along the margin of the Outer Rim toward the Tingel Arm and then looped back, maybe to cover her tracks, maybe to avoid something. Whatever she was doing, she was hopping from one ocean world to another. "Looking for a new house with a pool?"

"Better find the pilot and shake him down about the trip."

"What if it's not Ko Sai?" Sev was distracted by the fact that Boss wasn't joining in. "I suppose we start over from Aquaris, if the informant was telling us the truth."

"We'll pay him a visit if his memory needs help." Scorch rolled his eyes. "How many Kaminoans do you think go wandering around the Outer Rim, Sev?"

Boss interrupted. "I hate to ruin your travel plans, gentlemen, but this is a busier freight lane than anyone has a reason to expect. Check out the joker who's tailgating us."

All four commandos squeezed forward to stare at the rectenna screen. There was a small, fast vessel right up their tail, so close that if they'd vented their waste tank it would have spattered the viewscreen. It wasn't the kind of thing that bad pilots did. It was what someone in *pursuit* did.

"It's a big galaxy," said Sev, pulling on his helmet and sealing the collar for vacuum. He felt his stomach tighten and his pulse pounding in his throat. "He could overtake . . ."

Scorch helmeted up, too. "Maybe he wants your autograph."

Boss commed back to base. The sensors showed that the vessel's weapons were charging, and the transponder trace read UNKNOWN.

The cannon round that shaved past their port side was definitely known, though. It had trouble written all over it.

7

*Master Windu, I respect clone troopers as much as any
Jedi, and perhaps even more in some cases. But a certain
distance is required from our troops, clone or not. General
Secura is becoming a little too close to Commander Bly,
and while I applaud her dedication to the men under her
command, this can only end in tears.*
—Jedi General Arligan Zey, director of special forces,
stepping outside his area of responsibility in conversation
with Master Mace Windu

Aay'han, laid up on Bogg V, 476 days after Geonosis

Ordo watched a strange tableau unfolding in the crew
lounge of *Aay'han* as he worked on fitting the enhanced
weapons in the ship.

While he passed hydrospanners and connectors to Mereel
in the engineering section, he kept an eye on Skirata and Vau
through the open hatch. He was ready to step in and break up
an argument, because *Kal'buir*'s embarrassed and partial
thaw toward his old comrade couldn't. last. The Nulls had
grown up with the Skirata-and-Vau act—arguing, bickering,
even fighting; the only thing the two had in common most of
the time was their armor and their military skill. Skirata
thought Vau was a sadistic snob, and Vau saw Skirata as an
overemotional, uncultured thug.

But, for now at least, there was a truce. It felt uncomfortable, like borrowing someone else's clothing. Skirata was

trying be polite and grateful, and neither man seemed to know how to handle that. Their stilted conversation had suddenly given way to very focused and intense discussion in voices that Ordo couldn't quite hear.

He tapped Mereel on the knee. His brother's legs protruded from the open access duct as he tested power couplings. *Aay'han* was going to pack a lot more punch when Mereel was finished.

"Mind the actuator housing, *vod'ika*." Ordo laid the metal plate on the deck. "I need to check on *Kal'buir*. Something's going on."

"Call me if you need to break them up . . ."

Vau and Skirata were sitting facing each other on the square of sofas, and they were both talking on their comlinks. They also appeared to be listening to each other in a bizarre jigsaw of a four-way conversation.

"You're a good lad, *Bard'ika*, and I appreciate the risk you're taking."

"What do you mean, no med droid?"

"So where are they now?"

"Levet should have cleaned them out by now. They're only farmers."

"Shot at? Who knew they were even there?"

"Kal's going to have another meltdown."

Skirata paused and stared hard at Vau. "*Bard'ika*, can you hold on for a moment?" Vau held out his hand and they swapped comlinks. "So, Jinart, what exactly am I going to be angry about?"

Skirata listened, head down, and then shut his eyes. Ordo glanced at Vau, who shook his head. "Delta," he mouthed, and gestured with Skirata's comlink. "They followed Ko Sai as far as Napdu and then they ran into some competition. No further contact."

Napdu was one stage behind them in the hunt; events were getting out of hand. Ordo stood by Vau's seat and tried to follow both conversations, which was suddenly much harder now that he knew some of the facts and his brain was trying to fill in too many gaps. His mind wasn't on Delta's safety, and he felt guilty about that. Somehow getting hold of Ko Sai seemed much more important. There were millions of lives hanging on her, after all.

"We need to get a move on," he said. He glanced at his chrono; TK-0 and Gaib had a few more hours to come up with the pilot who transported Ko Sai to Dorumaa, but he needed that information *now*. If Delta were that close—they were physically closer to Dorumaa than *Aay'han* was, in fact—then they stood a chance of getting there first, provided they made the connection. "I'm not throwing away this lead."

The lead would be . . . a pilot. It was hard to move Kaminoans around and find them accommodation without somebody noticing, even if they didn't recognize the species.

Skirata seemed to be getting increasingly upset rather than angry. He had one hand shielding his eyes as if to ignore distractions; all that Ordo could hear was occasional grunts and sighs as if Jinart was telling him bad news in extreme detail. Eventually he spoke.

"Okay, I'm sending Ordo . . . no, don't let her move a muscle, Levet's perfectly capable of doing the job without her . . . he'll probably be happier with her out of the way, in fact. I'll call in later."

Skirata handed the comlink back to Vau, who resumed his conversation with Jusik. Mereel wandered up and stood beside Ordo.

"Where am I going?" Ordo knew perfectly well where he was going, but he didn't want to go, not with Ko Sai within reach. He wanted to be in at the end of the hunt. "*Buir?* I heard *Jinart,* so I assume it's Qiilura."

Skirata stood up and gave both Nulls a playful but half-hearted shove in the chest. "*Ad'ike,*" he said, "I need Etain out of there fast. She's bleeding where she shouldn't be, and the farmers have settled in for a fight. They're having to pick them off one at a time, asking them to surrender very politely each time."

"No wonder we're not winning, if that's how Jedi fight wars," Mereel said.

"Rules of engagement, son . . . last resort."

Ordo had never understood it, either. He could recite any statute or regulation, including all 150 Contingency Orders for the Grand Army—which all clone officers had to know by heart—with all the ease granted by his eidetic memory. But making sense of rules was another matter. Why start a killing war if you were going to slam on the brakes and declare one way of killing someone morally preferable to another?

"They'll end up killing them all anyway," Ordo said. He would never disobey his father, and he loved him too much to allow him to be even slightly disappointed, but he had to at least *ask.* "*Kal'buir,* are you certain you want me in Qiilura? I can be more use to you finding Ko Sai."

Father. Yes, he'd always felt like Skirata's son, but now . . . he actually *was.*

"Etain's used to you, *Ord'ika.*" Skirata had promised he would never lie to his men, but he'd admitted not telling Ordo everything. Perhaps he wasn't leveling with him now. "She might get *gedin'la* if Mereel or Vau show up. You know how cranky women are when they're pregnant."

"No, I don't."

"Well, they are. Hormones. And Etain's cranky enough to start with."

Vau looked up and put his comlink back in his belt pouch. "I got on very well with the young woman when we last worked together, actually."

Skirata gave Vau the long stare, the one that said he didn't think the comment added anything useful to the sum of the galaxy's knowledge. Vau shrugged and got up to wander around calling for Mird, who'd gone exploring, leaving only his pungent aroma to keep the sofa warm.

"Come on, *Mer'ika,*" Skirata said. "Let's contact your tinnie friend and find that pilot. Time is of the essence."

Ordo couldn't disobey. *Kal'buir* had his plans, and this was where Ordo fitted in. He didn't have to be happy about it, though. He was being handed a soft job, a nursemaid job, the kind he always did when his brothers were racing around the galaxy carrying out anything from assassinations to elaborate financial frauds.

Do they resent me? Maybe they pity me.

"Yes, *Kal'buir*," Ordo said. "I'll treat it as a medical emergency."

Mereel tossed him an identichip, the kind that opened security locks. "Take the shuttle I used to get here. I left it next to the cantina."

They lived that kind of life. Credits, transport, supplies, the cost was no object: if the Republic didn't bankroll it, they stole it, directly or indirectly. Ordo didn't have any more personal desire for wealth than his brothers. He was used to finding all his needs met, but his needs seemed nowhere near as rich and varied as those of the beings around him. All he wanted right then was a piece of the cheffa cake that Besany had sent him, so he took half from the galley, slicing it in two pieces with his vibroblade, and left the rest for the others—even Mird, if strills ate such things. Then he went in search of the shuttle, just another mercenary wandering around on a lawless planet, and sat in the cockpit chewing the cake for a few minutes.

It was dry and spicy against his tongue, like licking scented velvet. The comfort effect was immediate and from another time and place.

Sometimes Ordo felt just as he did when he was a small child and Skirata first towered above him: part of him was competent far beyond his years, and the rest was hollow terror because the *kaminiise* were going to kill him, but Skirata had snatched him and his brothers to safety and fed them all on *uj'alayi,* a sticky-sweet Mandalorian cake. It was a powerful act of salvation, one that had defined Ordo. He felt it as freshly now as he had then. It was the *cake.* That was it. The cake had brought it all back. He felt safe again.

And this was from Besany Wennen. She was saving him too, in her way.

Ordo folded the remains of the cake in a piece of cleaning rag, slipped it into the pocket on the thigh of his flight suit, and fired up the shuttle's drives to head for Qiilura. He had no idea—yet—what to do with a pregnant Jedi who was showing signs of miscarriage on a backworld planet a long way from competent gynecological help, but he'd find out.

He was Ordo. Nothing was beyond him.

Hutt space, 476 days after Geonosis

"He can't shoot straight," Boss said. "But he's spoiled my paint job."

The TIV jinked again to avoid cannon fire from the pursuing ship. Sev checked via the external holocams and there it was: a *Crusher*-class fighter. It harried the TIV, closing up and then falling back several times, loosing cannon rounds to one side then the other.

"You could have creamed it by now, Boss." Sev wasn't sure what his sergeant was playing at. "Or maybe just hyperjumped out of here. Forgotten what the Big Red Button's for?"

"Curiosity is the sign of intelligence, Sev."

Scorch had a tight grip on the restraining belt. "I'm not that curious."

"Think about it." Boss rolled the TIV as if he was enjoying it. "If this guy hasn't killed us, either he can't, or he wants us in one piece because we've got something he wants. I want to know who he is."

"Sometimes it's better to leave a little mystery in a relationship," said Scorch.

Sev felt the steady beat of his heart, nothing else. He'd passed the point of fear, and his body was on autopilot; he'd strapped himself in for a rough reentry somewhere almost without thinking about it. "So land and see if he follows."

"You get there eventually, don't you?"

Nar Shaddaa was the next planetfall, unless they landed on Da Soocha, and nobody ever landed there, not even the Hutts who named it. That was going to be cozy. The planet was all ocean except for a couple of small islands that broke the surface. But Delta had done their job and transmitted the data already, so if anything went wrong another squad could pick up where they left off.

Did I secure my locker back at the barracks? I've got the code key here. Fierfek, they'll have to force the door open if I get killed . . .

Sev had no idea why he was thinking about death or focused on such a trivial worry. Death hadn't crossed his mind that often before, not in a concrete way. Besides . . . it wasn't as if Boss couldn't handle a skirmish with a tourist, was it? Anyone who wasn't Grand Army was a tourist, by definition—an amateur.

The Crusher was chancing it, getting too close. If he tried that tailgating maneuver again, one of them would end up with a hull breach.

Scorch seemed intrigued by the idea. "What if he thinks we really are a courier shuttle and he's planning a robbery?"

Fixer came to life. "In a fighter?"

"He could have stolen the fighter, too."

"Oh yeah. I bet that happens all the time . . ."

"*We* do it."

"*We're* special forces."

"Okay. Time's up." Boss banked to starboard, and the array of lights on the navigations display tilted to show a course for the nearest planet—the third moon. "Let's find out."

Scorch went through the ritual of checking his suit's seal integrity again. "You got charts for that place, Boss?"

"Nobody has. Let's make some."

The third moon of Da Soocha had landmasses. Sev could see them as the TIV neared the atmosphere. If the pursuing Crusher really thought his quarry was a courier shuttle, heading for this deserted lump of rock would have tipped him off that it wasn't; but he was still on their tail. Sev closed his eyes and clenched his fists on reentry—it always bothered him to see the hull temperature climbing on the console display—and thought that it was good of Scorch not to rib him about his phobias. He never had.

"It's going to be fun when we land." Scorch was going through the motions of hitting the release catch on his restraints and swapping firing modes on his Deece, over and over, like it was all an Ooriffi meditation ritual. "He who disembarks first, wins."

"Nah," Fixer said. He was almost chatty today. "He who disembarks first is a nice target."

Boss brought the TIV down into a bumpy landing on grassland, skidding fifty meters through driving rain and slewing sideways before coming to a halt. Sev, concentrating on the charge level on his Deece, saw the Crusher's jets almost fill the front viewport as it dropped down in front of them and came about to land with its nose facing them. There was an awkward pause.

"He's charging cannons—" The TIV shook. Boss swore, and for a moment Sev didn't know if the vessel had been hit or if Boss had fired. Either way, the Crusher clearly hadn't been expecting the TIV to be anything other than a lightly armed vessel, because there was suddenly a cloud of steam building beneath it as it powered its drives again. Then its port wing shattered into fragments, sending a ball of fire into the damp air. *"Go go go!"*

Sev was first out as the starboard hatch swung open, dropping into grass that came up to his shoulders and smeared his visor plate with water. The ground squelched under his boots. He ran with his head lowered, shielded by the grasses, and Delta went into a sequence they'd drilled for a hundred times: storming an enemy vessel. Once they were close in to the fighter, there was little it could do, and with one wing missing it wasn't going anywhere in a hurry. Scorch fired a rappel line to hook onto the superstructure, then hauled himself up to slap a strip of flexible charge around the hatch.

"I'd knock," Scorch said, dropping down again and diving for cover, "but I think they'll be upset about the wing . . ."

Bang.

The hatch blew out, flinging twisted metal into the air, and Sev dodged a chunk that whistled past his helmet. His legs moved before his brain engaged and he leaned partway through the hatch, suddenly face-to-face with a human female pilot who had an impressive blaster. The shot knocked him backward, but blasterfire wasn't enough to penetrate Katarn armor, and he simply shook himself and raised his Deece again, finding his mind completely blank except for the single purpose of returning fire.

Sev fired. There was no such thing as winging someone or shooting them in the leg, whatever the holovids depicted, and he did what he was trained to do. The cockpit was full of smoke, the pilot draped at an awkward angle across the seat. It was only when the smoke began clearing that Sev realized there was a copilot, a man, and he was dead, too.

"Shab," Sev said. "Maybe I could have done that better."

Scorch peered into the cockpit. "Let's try that again without the *dead* bit, shall we?"

"I wanted a chat with them . . . ," Boss said. He hauled Sev back by his shoulder and rapped him in the chest plate. "Now how am I going to work out who they are?"

"Leave it to me." Fixer pushed past them and scrambled into the cockpit, hauling the bodies out of the way and pushing them out onto the grass with a wet *thud.* "At least I can interrogate the onboard computer and tell you where they came from."

Boss and Scorch contemplated the bodies in the grass, turning them over and rifling through their flight suits. Now that the adrenaline was ebbing, Sev felt a mix of vague dread flood him just as it had when he'd screwed up in training. There was no Sergeant Vau around to give him a good hiding for his incompetence, but it was as bad now as it ever was. Next time he saw Vau, he knew that his old sergeant would see the failure on his face and give him grief for it. There was no *good enough.* There was only *perfect.* Sev had no excuse for not being perfect, because he'd been designed from the genome up to be the galaxy's best. Anything he got wrong was down to laziness.

There were no excuses. Vau said so.

It was like waiting for the blow to hurt.

"Well," Fixer said. "Interesting." He jumped out of the Crusher and brandished his datapad. "They passed through

Kamino. And they transmitted data back. I'll unscramble that later."

Scorch sucked his teeth noisily. "Tipoca's not exactly the crossroads of the Outer Rim . . ."

So the Kaminoans had sent someone after them—after Ko Sai, in fact. Nobody popped into Tipoca City uninvited or stopped to refuel. You only went there if you had business with the Kaminoans.

"Bounty hunters?" Sev asked.

Boss examined a handful of chips and flimsi. "We can crack the identichips later. The important thing is that we know we're not the only ones who've tracked Ko Sai this far, and the aiwha-bait will know all about Da Soocha by now."

Sev was starting to feel anxious. They were definitely going up against the Kaminoans *and* the Seps now. It was going to be a race. Tipoca would send someone else as soon as they knew the Crusher was missing, if they didn't already.

"Better get a move on," said Scorch. "No telling who else we'll have to elbow out of the way."

Sev trailed the others back to the TIV, still uneasy and angry with himself for not taking the Crusher's crew alive.

"No," he said. "Could be anybody."

8

*Soldiers of the Grand Army, in honor of your courage and
service in the fight against oppression, you shall want for
nothing, and become instructors of the next generation of
young men to defend the Republic.*
—Chancellor Palpatine, in a message to all ARC troopers,
commanders, and GAR commando units on Republic Day

Gaftikar, 477 days after Geonosis

Darman was making sure the Marits knew how to lay
charges for rapid entry—they did, all too well—when the
woman walked into the camp.

He couldn't tell it was a woman at first because she was
wearing a freighter pilot's rig, multipocketed gray coveralls
that engulfed her, and a heavy pair of durasteel-capped
safety boots. But when she turned down the collar that was
shielding the lower half of her face from the wind, he could
see it was a female human about Skirata's age, with short,
light brown hair and a gaunt face that gave him the feeling
she checked out the latest in blasters rather than fashion.

She didn't walk like any of the women he knew, but maybe
that was the boots. He'd grabbed his Deece before it dawned
on him that A'den wouldn't be such a slacker on security as
to allow just anyone to approach.

Even so, Darman checked the charge on his Deece and
stood by just in case. If an Alpha ARC could be caught off
his guard, there was always the chance that the Nulls weren't

as omnipotent as everyone thought, either. A'den strode toward her, Sull ambling behind him in the same drab working clothes.

Fi and Atin wandered out from the main building to watch. Fi held Sull's gray leather *kama* in one hand with half the blue lieutenant's edging removed. He'd insisted on having it. With the blue bits unpicked, he said, it went with the red-and-gray armor he'd salvaged from Ghez Hokan. Fi liked order in his wardrobe.

"Who's she?" Atin asked.

"K'uur!" Darman strained to listen. "I can't hear with you yapping."

A'den obviously knew her. He shook her hand, indicated Sull with a jerk of his head, and handed something to her, which she waved away, but A'den shoved it into her top pocket. All Darman heard of her response was, ". . . rather have news of . . ."

The wind took the rest. There was a storm coming. At least Darman had the speeder to take him to Eyat to clear out Sull's apartment rather than trudging through the rain again. Sull seemed to be listening intently to the exchange between A'den and the woman, and then they both turned to him and A'den slapped him on the back. Sull's expression was set on what Darman now thought of as ARC default: deliberately blank, with one eyebrow slightly raised as if in disdain for the rest of the galaxy. That probably summed up ARCs pretty well.

"Come on, there's a good boy," the woman said, and beckoned to Sull to follow her. Astonishingly, he did. "Long way to go."

A'den called after her. "I'll do what I can, Ny, okay?"

So her name was Ny, and that could have been the entirety of it, or short for any number of names. She paused to glance at the squad as if she'd never seen clones together before—chances were she hadn't, he thought—and went on her way.

Darman could only imagine that she was Sull's transport out of the system, and that guaranteed his obedience at least for a while. But if an ARC wanted to leave Gaftikar under his own steam, he could have found any number of ways to do it.

Whatever A'den had said to him during that ARC-to-ARC chat must have been *very* persuasive.

Fi watched the incongruous pair vanish among the trees at the edge of the camp. The woman looked like a kid alongside Sull.

"Maybe it's his mother," Fi said, trying on the *kama* with a critical frown. "And he's grounded for a month for not doing his chores."

"Stop going on about *mothers*." Atin seemed to have lost interest. "You don't know what any of that means. It's all off the holovids. Like some new alien species learning about humans."

"Yeah, well, maybe that's what we *are*." Fi unclipped his helmet from the back of his belt and rammed it onto his head, shutting out the world again. His voice emerged from the audio projector. "Aliens in a society of human beings. Excuse me, will you, gentlemen? I have to go play with some lizards."

Cebz, the dominant Marit, scuttled around the camp but seemed to be keeping an eye on the squad. She could, after all, count, and maybe she was curious about the fluctuating number of clones in the area. If A'den hadn't leveled with her, then Darman wouldn't, either.

"I better go and clear any evidence out of Sull's place," Darman said to Atin. He prodded his brother in the chin, right at the end of the thin white scar that crossed his face from the opposite brow. It was still visible through his beard. " 'Cos I can look like him and you can't."

"You say that like it's a good thing . . ."

That was another advantage of being a clone. It was easy to take a brother's place; few folks would be any the wiser, except those who really knew you. Darman put on Sull's original clothes, noted that they were loose on him—had he lost that much weight?—and set off in the speeder for Eyat.

On the journey, he pondered the nature of mothers and what it might have felt like to have one, deciding it must have been a lot like having Sergeant Kal around all the time. *Kal'buir* said they'd all missed the necessary *nurturing* of a parent when they most needed it as babies. Darman often wondered if he would have been a different man had he been *nurtured*—whatever that meant in real terms—but he couldn't feel what was missing in his life, only that *something* was.

Lots of things were, in fact. He'd only known what some of them were when he touched Etain for the first time. And Fi seemed to see many more things that were missing than even he did.

Can't change the past. That was what Sergeant Kal said. *Only the future, which is whatever you choose to make it.*

Darman couldn't feel angry about Sull's decision to make a run for it, only a vague envy, and an uncertainty about whether he would have done the same.

Can't leave my brothers in the lurch. They put their lives on the line for me, and I do the same for them.

He put it out of his mind and concentrated on the road, knowing that if he ventured any further into those thoughts, then things would start to become confusing and painful. He distracted himself with finding the route to Sull's apartment again, reversing the route he'd taken out of Eyat.

Almost without thinking, Darman set the speeder down a little way from the apartment, walked around the block to check if he was being followed, and then ran up the external stairway to let himself in. A human male coming along the access walkway toward him nodded in acknowledgment to Darman, as if he knew him.

"Your boss was here, hammering on your door," he said, not stopping. He kept talking and walking as he looked back at Darman. "You been away?"

Darman was a lot more confident about his acting skills since the Coruscant deployment. "Yeah . . . I suppose I better explain myself to him . . ."

The man shrugged and went on his way. *So far, so good.* Inside the apartment, the place was as they'd left it after the scuffle with Sull: Darman hadn't cleared it out while he'd been waiting for Atin to return with transport, partly because he didn't know if they'd need to use the place for cover in the near future. The back of his hand still showed the neat purple depressions of Sull's no-holds-barred bite.

It wasn't the kind of place he would have picked to live, Darman decided. There was no rear exit, and the windows were poorly placed to keep watch. Sull must have felt unusually safe to risk living in such an indefensible location, and that in itself was unexpected in an ARC trooper.

Sull hadn't amassed a lot of effects in the couple of months he'd lived here. He had two changes of clothes in the closet, basic hygiene kit in the refresher, and a conservator full of food, as if he spent all his wages on it. *That's what we're all like, isn't it? No idea what to do with possessions, but always hungry.* Darman checked for anything else that might identify the ARC as being a GAR officer, and found a packet of crumbly, very sweet cookies that were irresistibly coated with seeds of some kind. He munched happily as he rummaged through the apartment. The place was military-tidy and anonymous, apart from a neat stack of holozines next to an equally neat stack of holovid chips that showed Sull stayed home at night.

Caged nuna. Yeah, even an ARC found it hard to step outside the cage when someone opened it. Maybe Sull had been sampling the outside world at a distance, through the entertainment that regular folks took for granted. Darman wondered where Sull was now: well clear of Gaftikar space, anyway.

The apartment's comm was flashing with unanswered messages. When Darman played them back they were—predictably—a broken stream of angry invective from a male voice demanding to know why *Cuvil*—not *Sull* to his new acquaintances, then—hadn't shown up for work again. There were also a couple of silent calls, brief clicks before someone shut the link again. Darman wondered where Sull had picked the name *Cuvil* and went on sorting through bins and other hiding places for any telltale links back to the Grand Army.

It wasn't the Gaftikari that he was trying to throw off Sull's trail. It was his *own side.* Suddenly that bothered him, because now they were all complicit in helping the man desert, and that was a lot more serious than going outside their rules of engagement on Triple Zero to take out a few terrorists. There was no way this could be spun as *getting the job done.*

Darman was still checking the holovids to make sure there
was no rental code on them that would lead back to Sull
when his fine-tuned instincts told him something wasn't
right.

It was the way the silence outside seemed . . . *heavy*.

Sometimes there was the kind of *quiet* that was just ambi-
ent sound with nothing to disturb it. Then there was what he
thought of as an effort to be silent. That was what he could
sense now. Somewhere in his subconscious, his brain had
processed something he hadn't even noticed hearing and
tripped his alarm.

There was someone outside.

The blinds were still drawn. Darman knelt on the floor and
placed a sensor on the exposed tiles, trying to detect the
faintest vibration. The red bars of the readout showed occasional spikes that usually meant footsteps, even though he
couldn't hear movement when he concentrated. He took out
his blaster, checked the charge, and squatted down behind a
chair to see what happened next, holding his breath.

When the doors opened—very quietly—he didn't dare
look around the chair and expose his position. Whoever had
let themselves in held the two sections of the door apart so
that it didn't close with a characteristic faint slap, but eased
slowly back again. Then he smelled something very familiar:
the faint scent of lubricating oil, the kind used on blasters
and vibroblades.

Darman wondered for a moment if Sull had given his key
code to a girlfriend and not mentioned it, but he knew what
females smelled like and this wasn't female. He wondered
what kind of company Sull kept at work, and if his boss had
run out of patience and sent someone around to teach him
what happened to no-shows.

But Eyat didn't seem like that kind of place. People here
seemed . . . almost *friendly*.

Darman watched a shadow fall across the carpet against
the hazy light filtering through the blinds. Then another one
joined it, and there was the faintest creak.

They knew he was here.

But maybe it was the local police, and the neighbor had realized he wasn't Sull after all, and alerted them to an intruder.

"So, Alpha-Thirty, you thought you'd try a new career, did you?"

He thought he knew that voice.

No, that wasn't something the Eyat cops would care about. The faint rustling of fabric and the occasional snatched breath came closer. Darman squatted with his sidearm steadied in both hands. Then the shadow fell on him.

He looked up into a masked face, eyes covered by a sun visor, and he was staring at a blaster muzzle as he fired. He pulled the trigger even before he consciously registered the blaster aimed at him because his training and common sense and raw instinct told the primitive, self-protecting parts of his brain that a masked man sneaking around was a bad, *bad* sign. He shot him in the face. It was a simple reflex.

The man fell backward with a grunt and a flash of blue light. Another shot sizzled past Darman's ear, but his brain didn't bother to get involved as his hand aimed of its own free will and sent blaster bolts—one, two, three—into another moving object that was in the wrong place at the wrong time.

The shots must have hit the second intruder: Darman smelled burned hair. He instinctively dropped and found himself lying on the floor next to the inert body of the first man he'd shot, a figure in black coveralls with a charred hood covering the face. He scrambled to grab the man's dropped weapon—a DC-15s sidearm—and took cover behind the angle of a wall, listening for movement.

The Deece handgun bothered him, because he had one, too; but Sull hadn't. It wasn't issued to ARCs, not that they didn't acquire whatever took their fancy. He folded the magazine flat and shoved it in his belt.

Now there was no way out of the apartment other than back through the doors—or out through one of the front windows. Getting cornered was a weird mistake for an assassin to make. Darman was trapped in an apartment with someone who was trying to kill him—or Sull to be precise.

Darman knew he should have simply rushed the second man, firing both blasters, but he'd lost his momentum. If this was Republic Intelligence, they were badly misnamed. They hadn't done a recce of the apartment.

Republic Stupidity, more like.

Or maybe they'd been very sure they could take Sull anyway.

Holovid directors would have been disappointed, he knew, but he didn't bother to call a challenge to the other man. He sprang to his feet and came out firing, because there was nowhere to hide in a place this small, and no real protection offered by the furniture. It was simply a matter of who hit who first.

Darman fired, and fired, and fired.

The man, all in black, stepped out from the alcove near the door and took the blaster barrage full in the chest. It knocked him back a few paces, but he didn't drop—and that was when Darman knew he was in real trouble and simply charged him. He knocked the man flat with sheer brute force and got a grip on his head, jerking it so hard to one side that there was a wet, muffled *snap* and the man went limp.

All Darman could hear now was his own breathing. He sank back on his heels and listened hard in case there were more men coming. But there was nothing.

Had the neighbors heard? Were the police on their way?

He had two dead men on his hands. That wasn't an unusual situation for a commando, but it was bad news in a city that wasn't supposed to know it had been infiltrated.

Before he decided whether to make a run for it, though, there was something he had to find out. Blaster aimed squarely at the head, he checked each body, grabbing the hood-like mask by the seam at the top and working it loose. Doing that one-handed was harder than it looked. The first man he'd shot was hard to identify with his face blackened and shattered, but he had familiar black hair. The second— he was recognizable, all right: and so was the gunmetal-and-purple armor disguised by his coveralls.

It was the face Darman saw every morning when he shaved.

He'd shot two clones, men just like him right down to the last pair of chromosomes. He'd killed two covert ops troopers.

The GAR was sending clone assassins after their own men.

Mong'tar City, Bogg V, Bogden system,
477 days after Geonosis

"I think you should leave this to me," Vau said as gently as he could. Laying down the law never worked with Skirata. "A little cold distance might be called for."

Skirata leaned on the rail of the bridge with one hand while he honed his three-sided knife on the metal. The thin rasping sound set Vau's teeth on edge; Mird rumbled with annoyance at each scrape, too. Beneath them, the most filthy and polluted river Vau had ever seen attempted to flow like curdled milk. There was more debris than liquid.

"I'm not sharpening it for the pilot," Skirata said.

"That's what I meant. Kaminoans don't answer questions when they're in slices."

Skirata didn't look up. His head was tilted down as if his focus was fixed on the blade, although it was always hard to tell where a helmeted man was looking. Eventually, after a dozen more intensely irritating scrapes of the knife, he sheathed it in the housing on his right forearm plate and paced along the bridge, then back again.

Mereel was late, and he hadn't commed Skirata.

"He'll be here," said Vau.

"I know."

"Even if he doesn't get the pilot, you've got the planet."

"He'll *get the pilot.*"

Maybe it didn't matter if Mereel didn't find him. Dorumaa was 85 percent ocean except for the artificial resort islands, so any landing was easy to track. There was nowhere that Ko

Sai could hide a laboratory on the surface, either; she'd have to go underwater.

It explained the equipment being freighted around. Ko Sai was looking to build a hermetically sealed lab, and maybe not just because she wanted it to be hyperclean.

Skirata flipped open his datapad and thrust it under Vau's nose. "There's the hydrographic charts, anyway."

Vau tried to make sense of the three-dimensional maze of colored contours. "Remember it only goes down to fifty meters. The developers were too scared to risk surveying any deeper."

"Then the same goes for her. And she'd have to pick a natural rock formation to hide in, or she'd need to import a lot of heavy engineering to excavate something."

"You better hope it's within the fifty-meter depth, then . . ."

"*Kaminiise* aren't a deep-sea species." Skirata held out his hand for the datapad. "If they were completely aquatic or could cope with depths, they wouldn't have been nearly wiped out when the planet flooded. They just like to be near water, preferably without too much sunshine. So . . . what better place to hide than a nice sunny pleasure resort? Who's going to look for her there?"

Vau snorted. "Delta Squad . . . the Seps . . . us . . ."

"I didn't say she had any common sense. Typical scientist. All theory. No idea how bounty hunters work."

"Well, she's evaded *you* for well over a year."

"Yeah? And now she's run out of road."

Vau hadn't actually disliked Tipoca in the eight years he'd been cooped up there. Inside the pristine stilt-city, it could have been any urban environment; he didn't miss shopping and entertainment, so it was largely indistinguishable from Coruscant, although the lack of hunting troubled Mird. The strill stalked Kaminoans instead. It even caught one once, but its prey was just the blue-eyed variety, the lowest genetic caste of Kamino, and the gray-eyed elite seemed only annoyed at the loss of a menial.

Yes, that was probably the day Vau's ambivalence toward

Kaminoans evaporated, and he joined Skirata in thinking of them as aiwha-bait.

"And what are you going to do when you get hold of her?"

"Take her research."

"And?"

"And what?"

"You think she'll have a file marked SECRET FORMULA FOR STOPPING THE AGING PROCESS IN CLONES—DO NOT COPY?"

Skirata clicked his teeth, impatient. "She'll need to be *persuaded*."

"No, you'll need to get her to work for you. That means no choppy-choppy slicey-slicey."

"Or get another geneticist on the case."

"Of course. They're ten a credit. They queue up at employment centers."

"Look, Walon, I'm not stupid. I know there'll be a gap to fill between getting hold of the research and making it into something my boys can use."

"Just reality-checking."

Skirata's voice had the tinge of a smirk in it. "And I can get my hands on a geneticist who knows her way around a Fett genome."

Vau kept his gaze on the riverside path, distracted slightly by a loud *glop* as something leapt from the river beneath and snatched a low-flying creature that might have been avian or insectoid. Either way, it was lunch now.

"Tell me you're not thinking what I *think* you're thinking," he said slowly.

Skirata ejected his knife from his forearm plate again and resumed sharpening. "Atin nearly got killed hauling her *shebs* back from Qiilura. Might as well make it worth the journey."

"Oh, you *are* thinking it. You're insane. Dr. Uthan's kept under tight Republic security. Chancellor's office level."

Skirata just laughed. Vau suspected he had no idea what his limits were, and that he'd get killed finding out the hard way. The fool should have grown out of it at his age.

"Last I heard," Skirata said, "was that she was bored out of her skull and reduced to trying to interbreed soka flies in her cell to stay sane. They don't care who they work for, these folks. No ideology. They just want to play with their toys. If she can develop a clone-specific pathogen for the Seps, she can apply Ko Sai's research—if you can take it apart, you can rebuild it, right?"

Vau had to hand it to Skirata. He always thought outside the box. "I'll consider that an incentive for getting Ko Sai to do the work."

Skirata sheathed his knife again, and the two of them leaned on the bridge rail to contemplate the twin evils of polluted waterways and having to wait so long at their time of life. Mird wandered around, rubbing its jowls on the bridge balusters to mark its territory.

"Here he comes," said Vau.

Mereel had acquired yet another form of transport. He had a great fondness for speeder bikes, and he seemed to be riding a different one every time Vau saw him. He had no idea whether Mereel came by them legally or not, but the Null trooper had a pillion passenger this time, and as the speeder drew closer it was clear that the being sitting behind him was a very scared green Twi'lek male. Vau could tell from the way his lekku looked rigid. It was the Twi'lek equivalent of white knuckles.

"He's very persuasive, is *Mer'ika*." Skirata ambled off the bridge and stood blocking the path, hands on hips. "So you stopped for caf and cake somewhere, son?"

"Had to take a call from A'den, *Kal'buir*." Mereel gestured to the Twi'lek to dismount. "But I thought you'd want a face-to-face chat with our esteemed colleague here." He slid off the speeder and nudged the Twi'lek. "Okay, Leb, tell *Kal'buir* about your job on Dorumaa."

"It was legal," the Twi'lek said. "I didn't do anything wrong."

" 'Course you didn't." Skirata always sounded at his most menacing when he was doing his paternal-reason act. "Just tell me about it."

"I delivered a consignment of six construction droids and

dry-lining materials to a barge half a klick off the coast of Tropix Island Resort."

Vau tilted his head at Mird, and the strill went into its softening-up routine, padding around the Twi'lek, brushing against his legs, and occasionally stopping to gaze up at him and display a yawning mouthful of teeth. It was a sobering spectacle. It sobered the Twi'lek right away.

"Can you show me on this chart?"

Leb the Twi'lek grabbed Skirata's proffered datapad and tapped frantically on the small screen, lekku quivering. "There," he said. "I checked the coordinates. The barge was *there*. Moored out to sea."

Skirata held the shaking datapad steady for him. "Did you collect anything later?"

"No. Nothing. One-way journey."

"What did the barge look like? Any propulsion unit on it?"

"Only a maneuvering repulsor. The kind the resort hotels use to round up the pleasure craft after a storm."

Vau started calculating in his head. "And you'd recall the weight of materials you delivered."

"I had to make several trips from the resort because the barge couldn't handle it all at once."

"So the barge was unloaded a few times?" Skirata asked.

"Oh yes."

"How long did that take?"

"I waited maybe twenty, thirty standard minutes after each drop."

"And who collected the stuff?"

"Human male, not very old, brown hair . . ."

The Twi'lek ground to a halt, eyes darting from Skirata to Vau to Mereel as if he was going make a run for it. It was easy to forget how intimidating a Mandalorian helmet looked to outsiders when they were deprived of all the visual cues of facial expression, and couldn't work out how well their information had been received.

Skirata moved his hand to his belt, and Leb flinched. He seemed surprised to get a credit chip rather than a blaster in the face.

"Thank you for your cooperation, son," Skirata said, and patted him on the cheek with exaggerated care.

Leb hesitated and then jumped on the speeder. So it was his after all: Mereel turned to watch it go.

"What a helpful fellow," Vau said. "Are you going to draw the search radius on the holochart or shall I?"

"Well, better find out the maximum speed of a Dorumaa resort barge first." Mereel took off his helmet and scratched his cheek. "I'm piloting, yes?"

Skirata nodded. "You okay with that?"

"If *Ord'ika* can drive the crate straight out of the manual, so can I. Let's get moving. And . . . A'den had some worrying news."

Skirata stopped in his tracks. "How worrying? Why didn't he call me?"

"He called *me*. It's tangential, let's say."

"Spit it out, *Mer'ika*."

"Someone sent two covert ops troopers after the ARC who went AWOL on Gaftikar. *Sent after,* as in assassination, but they ran into Darman instead and he slotted both of them. He's pretty upset."

Vau didn't need to see Skirata's face to guess what he was thinking. They made their way back to *Aay'han* in silence and sealed the hatches, preparing for takeoff. Skirata sat in the copilot's seat and flipped switches.

"Who ordered it, *Mer'ika*?" he asked quietly.

Mereel propped his datapad on the console, glancing at it as he carried out his instrument checks. "I don't know, but it's not necessarily Zey."

The news was a nasty little time bomb. Tangential—no, for once Mereel was wrong. It wasn't tangential at all. It was about trust and loyalty. It was the kind of revelation that would gnaw at all of them more deeply as time wore on, and combined with whatever Mereel had dug up on Kamino about the future plans for troop strengths, it proved none of them had quite as full a picture as they'd imagined, and also that there were things they weren't trusted with.

Like not being told that Delta is going after Ko Sai.

Vau strapped himself into the third cockpit position and tried not to think about the identity of the unfortunate covert ops troopers, because there was a good chance that Prudii— Null ARC N-5—had trained them. They were just ordinary troopers who'd shown a bit of promise for dirty work, selected from the ranks to backfill some of the roles that would have otherwise fallen to Republic commando squads.

"If it was Zey," Vau said carefully, "the *chakaar* should have told us they were operating on the same turf as Omega simply for everyone's safety."

"Covert ops gets tasked by the regular GAR as well as SO, Walon." Skirata was usually quick to pounce on any perceived Jedi failing: maybe he was developing a soft spot for Zey, who did seem remarkably understanding of Skirata's idiosyncratic style of command—a command Skirata didn't technically hold. He was a sergeant who pushed generals around. "Or maybe Zey knows exactly how I'll express my disapproval of putting down clones when they get too free-thinking, so he forgot to mention it."

"Then again, maybe it's Republic Intelligence."

"But that nice Chancellor Palpatine assured our lads that they'd have a secure future in recognition of their loyalty and sacrifice."

Mereel took exaggerated interest in the controls and lifted *Aay'han* from the landing strip. "Either way, we clone boys know just how much the Republic loves us when push comes to shove, don't we? And we won't forget that in a hurry."

Skirata put his hand on Mereel's shoulder. "We can only trust our own, son."

"Like the covert ops guys . . ."

"You think they had all the facts in front of them? You think they had any choice?"

These were almost certainly men they knew, and that made it hard to swallow. Vau wondered if they would still have carried out their orders if they'd been sent after Prudii—or Mereel, or Ordo, or any of the Special Operations men or Mandalorian instructors who'd taught troopers their commando skills. Vau marveled at Skirata's continuing ability to absolve clones of all blame, but he did have a point.

"Humans follow orders," Vau said. "Even human Republic Intel agents, of course. We're herd animals. We all default to training."

"Well, I'm defaulting to mine." Skirata gave his restraining belt a couple of tugs as if he didn't quite trust Mereel's ability to execute a smooth acceleration to the jump point. "Which is covering my *shebs,* and my boys'."

"How, exactly?" Vau asked.

"Safe haven, a few credits, set 'em up in a better line of work. New identity and a new life."

"Yes, I know all that, but *how* are you going to do it? You can't exactly place an ad." Vau traced the outline of an imaginary holoboard in the air with his fingers. "Troopers! Fed up with your life in the Grand Army? Feeling undervalued and unloved? Call Kal!"

Skirata scratched his forehead. "Word gets around."

"Word gets around to the wrong people, too . . ."

"Escape networks have always run that risk."

"That's not an answer."

"I'll just have to pick my network very carefully, then, won't I?"

Aay'han was clear of the atmosphere now, maneuvering carefully through the maze of gravitational fields in the Bogden system to reach a safe hyperjump point. Mird, who never liked takeoffs and landings, climbed onto Vau's lap and buried its head under his arm with a lot of whining and snorting to ensure that he knew it was displeased. He rubbed the strill's back to reassure it, and marveled at Mereel's ability to pilot a ship like a DeepWater with just the manual open on the console and a little intuition. They were clever boys indeed, these Nulls.

I think I like clones better than regular beings. They're superior in every way. Maybe we should keep them at home and send the Republic's random humanity to be the cannon fodder.

Vau had little time for anyone else, regardless of species,

but the men of the Grand Army were a different matter. It was, he realized, one of two things that stopped him and Skirata from killing each other: their mutual respect for the clone soldiers who had taken over their lives, and the fact that Mandalorians put aside their rifts when presented with a common threat from *aruetiise*.

"You do realize," he said to Skirata, "that if the troopers were given a choice, most would opt to stay in the army anyway?"

"I do. We all prefer the comfort of what we know best."

"They'd be as dead as volunteers as they'd be as slaves, Kal."

"But they'd have a choice, and that's what makes us free men."

"Actually, that's a load of *osik*. Plenty of free beings in the galaxy don't have a vote and don't get a choice about what they do each day. There's a very blurred line between slavery and economic dependence."

"Yeah, well, if you want to argue about the continuum of oppression, clones are still at the extreme end of the graph. So I'll concentrate on them rather than the downtrodden masses, thanks."

The landscape of loyalty was shifting with each passing day. First it had been a matter of worrying about what would happen to troopers when the war ended. Now they were discussing men who deserted while the fighting was still going on.

"Kal, would you rather fight for the Separatists?"

"Ideologically? You know I would. The Republic's a crumbling bureaucracy at best and a cesspit of corruption at worst. But I joined for the credits and I stayed for my boys. What's your excuse?"

Vau couldn't claim he'd joined for the credits, although he'd often led a fairly hand-to-mouth existence since forgoing his inheritance. But he stayed for the same reason Skirata did, even if he had no intention of admitting that to him.

Mird, satisfied that takeoff was over, pulled its head out

from under Vau's arm and deposited a skein of drool in his lap.

"On reflection," Vau said, groping for a cloth to wipe his pants, "I think it's the elegant lifestyle."

Teklet, Qiilura, 477 days after Geonosis

Ordo knew his limitations, and learning obstetrics from a manual was a lot riskier than piloting a new ship the same way. Requisitioning a top-of-the-line med droid from a supply base en route had cost him time but would greatly improve Etain's chances of carrying her child to term.

And if the droid couldn't hack it, then . . . no, he'd face that if he had to, and not before. He sprinted across the snow from the landing strip with the droid struggling behind him. It was big and heavy, and not adapted for rough terrain.

"Captain, I *still* need to know what procedure I have to perform," it said peevishly. It was a 2-1B model, and it—he—had a professional ego on a scale with his extensive surgical expertise. "I was awaiting deployment to a more *significant* theater of war. Where are my nursing assistants?"

Ordo reached the door of the HQ building as indicated on his datapad chart and bypassed the security locks almost without thinking. "Don't you take some sort of oath to help the sick and injured, Too-One?"

"No. And it's *Doctor.*"

"I'll make one up for you, then—*Doctor.*" As the doors opened, Ordo came face-to-face with a clone commander in yellow livery. "It starts with, *I pledge to keep my vocabulator offline as much as possible.*"

"Captain," said the commander. "I didn't know you'd be bringing a med droid."

"Specialist stuff, sir." So *this* was Levet: Ordo reminded himself that he was outranked here—technically. "We can't afford to lose any more Jedi. It takes longer to make them than to grow us. Where's General Tur-Mukan?"

Levet gestured upstairs. "Good luck. She seems not to realize that I know she's *yaihadla*."

Ordo was always surprised to find any clone outside the Special Operations ranks who knew more *Mando'a* than just the words to "Vode An." He was especially taken aback by one with enough fluency to know the word for "pregnant."

"Ah," Ordo said noncommittally. Levet had somehow earned the nickname of Commander Tactful, and now he knew why. *Mando'a* wasn't one of the languages generally programmed into med droids. "Really."

"I humored her, but she has her reasons for not discussing it, and I never argue with a general if I can help it." Levet slipped his helmet on. "The Jedi Council doesn't like fraternization within its ranks, so I imagine the poor woman is terrified."

Ordo waited for the next bombshell to fall, but Levet went no further in his analysis and seemed content to think that another Jedi was the father-to-be. Maybe he hadn't considered the possibility of a humble clone, although there was plenty of speculation about other generals and the nature of their social lives.

"I'll be diplomatic," Ordo said.

There was the small matter of making sure that the med droid kept his vocabulator shut, but that was a technical detail. Once he'd treated Etain, he'd need a full-spec memory wipe. Ordo hadn't mentioned that to him yet.

Etain was propped up on pillows, eyes closed and hands clasped in her lap, and there was no obvious sign of the shapeshifter. She looked past him at the droid, then sighed.

"Hello, Ordo," she said quietly. "Sorry you had to be dragged all this way. I know Kal's worried about me when he sends you."

She could always tell one clone from another even without looking, just from the impression he made in the Force. Ordo knew she found him disturbing. Maybe it was the waking nightmares and the frustration that swirled around in his unguarded thoughts: he could keep a lid on it, but she knew it was there just as surely as *Kal'buir* did.

"And how are you, General?" It was as good a place to start as any. "Are you still bleeding?"

"I think *I* should be asking those questions," the droid said. He pushed past Ordo and leaned over Etain, ejecting an array of sensors and probes from his chest. She stared at him in disbelief. "Any pain? I have to examine you—"

Too-One's arm came to a sudden halt, and Ordo thought he'd malfunctioned. He seemed to be struggling to move.

Etain gave him a narrow-eyed stare. She'd apparently declined help from the other med droids, but this was the equivalent of the chief of surgery. "You better warm those appendages of yours first, tinnie . . ."

"Ah. You're a Jedi. Of course." There was an ominous grinding whine from his servos and the faintest smell of overheating. "The sooner you release me, the faster I can complete the examination."

"I'm glad we understand each other." The droid's arms suddenly jerked, and he tottered slightly. Etain's use of the Force seemed to be a lot more precise these days. "I'm about ninety days' pregnant."

"I wasn't informed of *that.*"

"Well, now you know. I've been accelerating the pregnancy with a healing trance, so I'm probably in the fifth month in terms of development."

"My data banks make no mention of Jedi being able to do that. How?"

"It's not a precise science. I just meditate, really. He's been kicking, so I'm guessing how far things have progressed."

"*He.* So you've been under a physician's care, had routine scans—"

"No, I'm a Jedi, and we can detect that stuff." Etain glanced at Ordo as if appealing for support. "The baby's reacting strongly and I know he's been upset by the fighting, or at least to my reaction to it."

"Impossible," Too-One said. "Higher brain functions don't appear until twenty-six weeks, and even with acceleration—"

"Look, you'll just have to take my word for it. And I'm still losing a little blood, and having cramps."

Ordo stood back to watch the show. The droid and Etain seemed to be having a standoff, staring at each other as if she was daring him to lay manipulators on her. Then Too-One took out a scanner and passed it over her belly.

"Oh my," he said primly. "My database suggests this is the equivalent of a six-month fetus."

"Told you so . . ."

Too-One hesitated and then parted the heavy cloak that Etain was still clinging to. There was a visible bulge under her tunic, but nothing that would make anyone stop and stare.

Ordo found himself suddenly fascinated in a macabre kind of way. There was no mother's heartbeat in the artificial womb of the transparisteel tanks on Kamino, and no comforting darkness. Ordo knew that he should have begun his life like the child within Etain, and why the atmosphere of silence, isolation, and unbroken light—with only his own heartbeat to cling to—had helped make him the way he was.

He remembered too much. Maybe it was a bad idea to hang around while the details were being discussed. But *Kal'buir* had told him to ensure Etain was safe and well, and that meant waiting.

"Ordo . . ."

How did we ever learn to be human at all? If bloodlines and genomes don't matter to Mando'ade, *what makes me a human?*

"Ordo?" Etain gave him a meaningful look.

"What?"

"I know nothing fazes you, but . . . well, I'd prefer you to wait outside while the med droid completes the examination. Do I have to draw you a picture?"

Ordo took the hint and stepped outside the door, still in earshot in case something went wrong. There were times when he realized just how far adrift he was from normal humanity, and Etain's pregnancy, a universal human condition that showed how mundane and constrained by biology even

a Jedi could be, simply reminded him how much of an outsider he really was.

He didn't even have a mother.

He had a father, though, and *Kal'buir* made up for everything.

The buzz of conversation and the occasional raised
voice—Etain's—suddenly stopped. The droid opened the
door.

"You can come in now."

Ordo wasn't sure what he was going to see, but Etain was
just sitting on the edge of the bed rubbing the crook of her
arm. "Well?"

"I have problems with the placenta," she said. "And my
stress hormones are sky-high, which isn't helping."

"She shouldn't be fighting a war in her condition, and she
shouldn't accelerate this pregnancy any further," Too-One
said, addressing Ordo as if he was somehow both responsible
and her keeper. "I've given her medication to stabilize her,
but she should let nature take its course and find a less stress-
ful environment for the duration."

"Understood," Ordo said. That was clear enough. "Does
she require more medication?"

"For the next seventy-two hours, yes." Too-One produced
a pack of single-use sharps from his bag. "Normally I
wouldn't leave an untrained being to administer these, but
you've had emergency medical training, have you not?"

"Oh yes." Ordo took his collection of electrical disruptors
and data slicing keys from his belt pouch. They dangled from
a plastoid cord like an untidy necklace. "Battlefield first aid."

Too-One wasn't expecting it and he never saw it coming.
Ordo thrust the disruptor into the droid's dataport and Too-
One stopped dead, unable to process any signals or data.

"What are you *doing*?" Etain looked aghast. "You can't
just deactivate him like that."

"Uh-huh." Ordo checked the diagnostics on the slicing
key and found the time point in Too-One's memory where he
was first told he was being taken to Qiilura to treat a female
Jedi for unspecified gynecological problems. That was all

he'd needed to know to download the appropriate data resources. Now he didn't need to know that at all, and he certainly didn't need to know he'd been here and treated a pregnant Jedi. "This is *not* data you want hanging around in the system, General."

Ordo hit the DELETE & OVERWRITE command with his thumbnail. Too-One had never been here, as far as the droid was concerned.

"He's a doctor, droid or not. Patient confidentiality is part of his programming."

"Sadly, it's not part of anyone else's, ma'am. Data stored is data that might one day be found. Your child's existence has to remain a secret. If you need more treatment—we'll start over."

"Ordo, he's *self-aware,* even if he's inorganic." Etain had that expression of professional piety that really annoyed Ordo when it came to most of the Jedi he'd met. Politicians had that same look sometimes. It said that they knew better and that he didn't understand. "You can't just remove a chunk of his memory against his will. It's violating him."

"No, it's like not telling him about classified information, only retroactively. Happens to troopers every day." Ordo checked that the segments of memory were truly erased. "Are you going to mention the irony of clones mistreating droids, ma'am? Because I always find that amusing."

"It's tempting."

"Have you ever memory-rubbed an organic being? I know some Jedi can. *Bard'ika* told me."

"Only in training, for practice, and then only with consent, and—"

"Well, then."

"You've never forgiven me for messing around with that stop command, have you?"

"If you mean do I trust you not to misuse it again when it suits you and effectively switch me off like a droid for a fraction of a second, no. If you mean do I harbor a grudge—no, I don't."

Ordo now had to move Too-One to a plausible location to

reactivate him. That was going to be hard unless the tinnie walked, because he was too heavy to lift.

"I suggest you go and hide in another room while I fire him up again and fill in the gaps."

"And afterward?"

"I'm removing you from Qiilura for the time being. Get your kit."

"Can't I just take it easy here?"

"And what are you going to do when you hear the artillery, and Levet comes back to report to you on the day's casualties?"

Etain looked over Too-One as if seeking inspiration, then nodded. She got to her feet and disappeared along the landing to another bedroom.

"Okay, Doctor, wakey-wakey time . . ." Ordo rebooted Too-One and stood back to watch his reaction.

"Did I malfunction?" asked the droid, clearly disoriented. "I have an unreadable sector in my memory."

"Corrupted data," Ordo said casually. It was true, from one perspective anyway. He'd definitely corrupted it, so much that it was unrecoverable. "I rebooted you. You're on Qiilura. They're a little short of medical support, so I assigned you to Commander Levet. You might have to deal with the local militia's casualties, too."

"A patient is a patient, Captain." He pressed the diagnostic panels on his arm. "Most disturbing. I hope I haven't lost any significant data."

Too-One sounded a little humbler than he'd been pre-wipe. If Ordo hadn't known better, he would have said the droid was *worried* about his lapse of memory—scared, even. Everyone said droids couldn't feel fear.

What's fear anyway? A mechanism to save you from danger and destruction. All droids were programmed to avoid unnecessary risk to themselves, and only the level of necessity varied according to model. If that wasn't fear, Ordo didn't know what was.

He'd have to think about droids differently from now on.

But that didn't mean he wouldn't blow them to shrapnel if they got in his way.

He handed Too-One over to Levet, who was still waiting downstairs, and the commander dispatched the droid to the landing area to await incoming vessels.

"I'd like to keep the general's condition between the two of us, to spare her embarrassment," Ordo said. "The droid's been wiped. You can never be too careful. Funny people, Jedi."

"Indeed they are." Levet projected the holochart above the table in the cramped room he used as an office. It still smelled too strongly of Trandoshans for Ordo's liking. "Now, what was this about the general? Sorry. I have a terrible memory."

Levet *knew,* and there was only one way of permanently scrubbing a human memory that Ordo trusted. But his conscience, the rules of decency that *Kal'buir* had instilled in him, said to leave the man—this *brother*—alone.

"I'm going to have to remove her for a while. I assume you're happy to continue the removal of the colonists here on your own."

"Oh, I think we can blunder along . . ."

"How long until the planet's cleared?"

"Another week, maybe, depending on how they react. We're losing too many men to mines. The locals are very good at concealing them from sensors with metal chaff, so we're adjusting our tactics."

"Either they come out quietly and board the transports—"

"Or we'll call in air support." Levet traced his fingertip through the three-dimensional representation of the Tingel Arm and the northeast quadrants. "The Thirty-fifth is due to take part in the assault on Gaftikar, so we need to clean up here, even if that means getting a little heavy-handed."

There wasn't a better time to move Etain. Once she knew how tough things were getting for Darman, she'd be tempted to seek him out. Gaftikar was relatively close to Qiilura.

Ordo paused in the hallway to check the messages on his

datapad. Jusik had reported Delta's latest position on their way to Da Soocha; *Kal'buir* was on his way to Dorumaa.

Ordo thought of calling Besany, but it seemed a selfish indulgence while Etain and Darman were denied routine contact. And *Kal'buir* had left one more message:

Suggest that the name Venku is quite nice, son.

Naming the child seemed to be a harmless concession to Etain's anxiety. If Darman or the child himself didn't like the name in due course, then it could always be changed. Ordo tried to imagine how Darman would react when he found out that nobody had told him about the baby, and that he was the last to know. Ordo was sure he would have been upset if he'd been in the same situation, however necessary it might have been.

"General?" Ordo thudded up the stairs. "Are you ready to leave?"

Etain emerged with a rough bag over her shoulder that looked like it had one change of clothes in it. Jedi didn't have much by way of possessions, just like clones.

"I need to say good-bye to Levet," she said.

"He knows you're pregnant, by the way. He's not blind or stupid."

Etain paused on the stairs for a moment. "Oh."

"And . . ." *Come on, the name's important to her, and it's important to* Kal'buir, *or he wouldn't have passed it to you.* "Kal says *Venku* is a good name."

Etain looked totally distracted for a second and her lips moved. "Venku," she said at last. "*Venku.* Does it have a meaning?"

"It's derived from the word for 'future,' *vencuyot.*"

"In the sense of . . ."

"A *positive* future."

"Ah." She nodded and managed a smile. The future was obviously as tantalizingly fragile for her as it was for any clone. "Tell Kal it's an *excellent* name."

Ordo waited by Mereel's shuttle and took in the clean silence of the snow while he waited for Etain to say her good-byes. Every time he tried to be civil to her, he couldn't seem to make it work. It wasn't as if he even disliked her. He just couldn't find any common ground, despite the parallels in their lives.

She emerged from the building and trudged through the snow, seeking out the path already worn down by boots.

"Where are we going, then?"

Ordo opened the hatch. "A resort beach."

"You're winding me up, aren't you?"

"No. It's what I believe they call a tropical paradise. I'll acquire a change of clothes for you."

Etain settled into the copilot's seat and looked like she was having trouble taking it all in. Ordo suddenly had an insight into the mind of a Jedi who wasn't comfortable with authority like Zey, or happy being one of the ordinary people as Jusik was.

She's never done this. She's never been somewhere purely for relaxation. She's as institutionalized as any clone trooper. And there's no Kal'buir *to look out for her.*

Yes, he pitied her, as he'd told her once before. It surprised him that he could, if being grateful that he wasn't her was pity.

"I don't feel right about going to a resort when men are still fighting, Ordo."

"And indulging in self-flagellation when you're pregnant and in danger of losing the child serves no purpose at all."

"I suppose that's your unique way of telling me to be kinder to myself . . ."

It was so much easier to have a conversation with Besany. She was a precise woman, and endlessly patient when he didn't understand some finer point of civilian etiquette.

"Dorumaa," Ordo said, trying hard for Darman's sake. "Mereel says it's an excellent place to relax."

Kal'buir had only told him to make sure Etain was safe and well. He hadn't told him not to return to the hunt for Ko Sai.

Like Etain, Ordo didn't like sitting on his *shebs* while the people he cared about were facing danger.

9

*Millions of us were wiped out when the seas rose and
engulfed Kamino. We survived as a species because we
were willing to think the unthinkable. Some genetic
characteristics helped us survive the starvation and
overcrowding, and some did not, and there was no room
for sentiment or for weaklings. We culled; we refined;
we selected. The prospect of extinction forged us into
the species we designed ourselves to be, the purest
expression of the Kaminoan spirit, and at a level of social
maturity that weaker mongrel species will never attain,
because they lack the courage to cull. We are the masters of
genetics and sole arbiters of our fate, never to be at the
mercy of chance again.*
—Draft memoirs of former Chief Scientist Ko Sai, on
Kaminoan eugenics and the desirability of the caste system;
never published

Eyat City, Gaftikar, Outer Rim, 477 days after Geonosis

The bodies of the two covert ops troopers were much heavier than Darman expected.

The wait for Niner and Fi to show up—two hours—was
the longest of his life, and every creak and click made him
think the Eyat police were surrounding the apartment. When
his brothers finally arrived, he felt inexplicably guilty, as if
he had to explain himself.

Niner stood staring down at the two troopers.

"Have you tidied them up, Dar?"

Darman had done his best. Apart from the damage to the one he'd shot in the face, they both looked quite peaceful now. They looked like him, but dead—and he was having a hard time dealing with that. Their arms were neatly at their sides, legs straight.

"I felt bad leaving them lying around like meat. What are we going to do with them?"

Fi shrugged. "Can't leave them here as air fresheners . . ."

"Fi, they're our *own*." Darman couldn't bear looking at the faces any longer, and grabbed a blanket from the bedroom. "We have to dispose of them properly."

"We've got their armor," Fi said. "Sergeant Kal will want the tallies. He's funny about that."

"Okay, let me put it another way—what if that was *your* carcass lying there? What would you want done with it?"

"I'd want someone to shake their head and say, *What a waste of such a fine-looking and stylish young man!* and then give me a big state funeral," Fi said, taking the blanket out of Darman's hands and rolling one of the covert ops troopers in it. "With loads of women weeping that they never had the chance to sample my charms. But apart from that, I wouldn't give a mott's backside by then, would I? It's just a temporary shell. Only the armor lasts."

Niner sneaked a glance out of the window. "It'll be dark in an hour or so. We'll take them back to camp and bury them. Dispose of the armor somewhere remote."

"And tell the lizards not to dig them up and eat them."

"Dar, Marits don't eat other sentients. Just their own dead."

"Oh, that's all right, then."

"Dar, these guys tried to *kill* you—"

"No, they came for *Sull,* Sarge, and that's just what you were ready to do not so long ago—remember?" Darman had no problem killing. It was his job, he'd grown used to it, and he didn't even get the bad feelings and nightmares afterward that they said humans usually had. But he'd killed his own comrades, not an enemy. The circumstances didn't make him feel any better. "I don't think I could ever go after my own like that, no matter what. Not unless it was personal and they'd done something terrible to me."

He realized he was blathering. Even Fi gave him an odd look. Niner bundled the second trooper into a blanket, and Darman helped him. The dead troopers' muscles hadn't stiffened yet, and when Darman bent one of them over, the movement forced the air from the man's lungs; he emitted a distressing sighing noise that made him sound as if he'd come back to life. Darman had seen some unpleasant things in battle, but that moment was seared into his memory as one he knew he'd never forget.

By the time the bodies were trussed with fibercord, they could have passed for lumpy carpets in bad lighting.

"A'den's been told that the assault on Eyat is probably going to be in a week's time," Niner said, seeming unconcerned. "So it wouldn't matter if we left them here."

"No, we *bury them.*"

"Okay, okay."

"I mean it."

"Dar, am I arguing?"

It would have made more sense to run; the longer they waited here, the more at risk they were. It wasn't hot outside, and with the environment controls in the apartment turned right down and the windows sealed, it might have been a couple of weeks before the neighbors smelled that anything was amiss.

But that wasn't good enough, even if they *had* been sent to shoot Sull.

Fi wandered into the kitchen. The conservator door sighed open and then shut again; he came out with a plate of food in one hand and a single fritter cake in the other, which he held up to Darman.

"Eat," he said. "Go on, or I'll sulk."

Darman accepted the cake and chewed, but it stuck in his throat like sawdust. He had an urge to call Etain. It was the first time he'd ever felt the need to seek comfort from someone outside rather than from his immediate circle of brothers, and it made him feel disloyal, as if their reassurance and support were no longer enough for him.

"You should talk to *Kal'buir*," Niner said quietly. "He killed a commando by accident. Remember? He probably knows better than anyone what you're going through."

"I'm not *going through* anything." Darman suddenly felt transparent and exposed. "I'm just getting jumpy waiting for the cops to show up. How nobody heard the blaster noise I'll never know."

"The place is well insulated," Fi said gently. "Pretty well soundproof, except for the floors creaking."

Darman knew he wasn't fooling anyone, and retreated to the kitchen to wait for darkness on the pretext of clearing out the cupboards. Yes, he'd talk to Skirata. Whatever Kal had been through was worse: he'd shot a commando in training during a live-fire exercise, one of his own boys, and even though everyone knew accidents like that happened, Skirata was never the same afterward. It had to be much, much harder to live with causing the death of someone you cared about. The covert ops troopers were relative strangers.

But Darman had heard that ARC troopers were ready to kill clone kids rather than let Sep forces take them during the attack on Kamino, not for their own good or to save them from anything, but to deny them as assets to the enemy. Would Sull have hesitated to kill a brother clone who got in his way? Darman doubted it.

It was all getting too blurred and messy lately. He longed for the good old days, when the enemy was just tinnies and very easy to spot.

"Okay, let's make a move," said Niner.

Niner brought a speeder right up to the front of the apartments—so *that* was what had taken two hours, then, acquiring more transport—and they moved the bodies like rolls of carpet. A few people were about on the street but they took no notice, probably thinking someone was moving house. Then Fi went to collect Darman's speeder while Niner and Darman waited in the vehicle with the bodies in the back.

It was just a simple drive back to the camp. Darman felt he

could manage that, and began fretting about digging graves in the dark. He certainly didn't plan to leave the corpses overnight. He had an image of the Marits making a stew out of them, and it wasn't funny at all. It disturbed him in a way he hadn't thought possible, making his mouth fill with unwelcome saliva as if he was going to vomit, but he had to hold it together long enough to work with the lizards until the assault on Eyat began.

"Nice strong cup of caf when we get back," Niner said. His voice had every single intonation then that Skirata's did, all reassurance and concern. "You'll be okay, Dar."

What if they weren't actually going to kill me? I never waited to find out.

"Sarge, do you suppose they'd just come to *arrest* Sull?"

"No," Niner said firmly. "They came to *execute* him. And even if they'd arrested you, they'd only have been taking you back so someone else could kill you. So stop replaying the holovid in your head and accept it was them or you, *ner vod'ika.*"

Sometimes Darman thought that he alone knew what was going on in his mind, and then one of his brothers would tell him exactly what he was thinking. On balance, exposed or not, he was more comforted to know he wasn't alone or going crazy.

They drove out of town with Darman occasionally directing Niner, who was working from the holochart in his datapad. Fi followed behind in the other speeder. It was all going fine—fine under the circumstances, anyway—until the red and green strobing lights of the local law enforcement patrol vehicle shot past them.

"He's in a hurry," said Niner.

"Late for his caf break . . ." That was what Captain Obrim always said when he saw one of his CSF speeders misbehaving. Darman glanced in the rearview to check that Fi hadn't dropped too far behind. "Doesn't look like they get too much trouble in this place. Not exactly the lower levels of Triple Zero."

"Everywhere's got its lower levels, Dar."

He felt that if he kept chatting like a normal person, everything would be all right. He thought that right up to the moment when the police speeder braked and came to a halt, the illuminated matrix between its rear jets flashing a single word: STOP.

"*Osik,*" Niner muttered. "I think he means us."

"Tell me this isn't stolen, *ner vod.*"

"It's not. And we're not over the speed limit, either."

Niner slowed down. Darman could see Fi dropping farther behind to stop outside a tapcaf.

"Now, nice and calm," Niner said.

"Let's hope he thinks we're twins."

"How many folks know what clones look like, anyway? Especially here." Niner activated the comlink deep in his ear by clicking his back teeth; Darman felt his own embedded earpiece vibrate for a moment as it started receiving the signal. Then Niner lowered the side viewport and put on his sensible-but-blank expression as the red-uniformed officer walked up to the speeder with one hand on the blaster at his belt. "Good evening, Officer. What's the problem?"

"Keep your hands where I can see them, sir, and show me what you've got in the back." The officer leaned slightly to stare at Darman. "You—step out of the vehicle and put your hands on the roof."

For a moment Darman thought Niner was going throw the door open and knock the guy down, but he gritted his teeth and popped the rear hatch.

Fi's voice filled Darman's skull. "He's on his own, Dar. I can drop him from here."

"Wait . . ."

Darman got out of the speeder slowly and left the door open for a rapid retreat, but he edged far enough down the length of the speeder to keep an eye on Niner. The officer leaned into the small cargo space at the back of the speeder, still keeping his hand on the butt of his blaster as if it was some comfort to him. He didn't seem to realize that turning his back on a suspect—*two* suspects, in fact—was risky, and

Darman looked hard to see if he had some headset linking him to another officer nearby.

But there was nothing. He was simply not used to dealing with serious criminals—or commandos.

"Had a report of a speeder being used to remove items from a residence, sir," the officer said. His voice was muffled as he leaned in, one hand taking some of his weight on the tailgate. "This one, in fact. Now, what do you reckon you've got here—"

The moment the cop moved his hand to the tightly wrapped body in the cargo area, his fate was sealed. It was almost as if they'd drilled for it: Niner jumped him and pinned him flat, facedown, arm locked around his throat to silence him, while Darman stepped in and checked him for comlinks. Fi was now right behind them in the other speeder, shielding the tussle from view.

Unlike the holovids, there was no quick blow to the head to render someone conveniently unconscious while you made your getaway, with no harm done beyond a headache when they regained consciousness. This was just a poor cop, like any of Obrim's team. He'd stopped the wrong men at the wrong time. Darman's eyes met Niner's, and he knew he should have simply shot the cop as his instinct told him to, but he couldn't.

Fi stepped in and rifled through the array of weapons on the officer's belt. "Ah," he said—the only word spoken in the whole incident—and selected a stun baton. He shoved it into the cop's armpit; it crackled just as Niner let go of him. The man stopped struggling and convulsed a couple of times.

"There," said Fi. He hauled the officer onto the curb, where he slumped in a heap, hidden from the oncoming traffic by the other speeder. "Sorry about that, Sarge."

"It's okay, I broke contact before I got a shock . . ."

"Time to bang out, *fast*."

"Sorry." Darman jumped back into the passenger's seat. There was more traffic around than he expected, but Niner shot straight out into it and burned toward the city exit. "Sorry, I should have—"

"No harm done," Niner said.

Fi overtook them and disappeared into the distance. Darman took out his DC-15 and kept it cradled in his lap, checking in the rearview until they were clear of the city limits. He was starting to worry that he'd lost his nerve. He'd never hesitated over taking a shot before. His thought process wasn't supposed to kick in and start arguing with his risk assessment.

I could have compromised this mission. And that means I put my brothers at risk.

"If you'd shot him, it would have been another mess to clean up," Niner said, veering away from the road and weaving through the trees. "Can't leave civvy cops dead all over the place. It's not Galactic City, is it?"

"You're telepathic, Sarge."

"I was thinking what Skirata would have said, actually."

"We've still left a cop in Eyat who's seen us up close."

"Well, next time he sees us we'll have our helmets on, so a fat lot of good that'll do him."

A'den and Fi were already waiting in the makeshift ops room when they reached the rebel camp, which appeared to be in darkness like the rest of the base. All the windows were shielded by blackout material. Inside the fragile-looking house, the two of them were sitting at the table and gazing forlornly at a datapad, and A'den had his hand held against his ear as if he was concentrating on a signal he could barely hear.

Fi didn't look up. A'den did.

"Wow, you're good," the Null said wearily. "How many stiffs have you racked up tonight? Two troopers and a cop. You're going to beat your own dumb record at this rate."

"We never killed a cop," Niner said.

Fi simply looked over his shoulder at them. "I didn't *plan* to. Stun batons are tricky things if you don't know the medical history of your target."

"Oh, great. *Great.*"

Fi tapped his datapad, and a crackling stream of audio

filled the room: it was voice traffic from a police control room, judging by the jargon and codes.

"Say again, three-seven. Last call shown on the onboard log was a vehicle stop on Bidean Way."

"No clear surveillance holocam view available . . ."

"Confirm ID on the suspect speeder. Rental, fake identichip used to secure it . . ."

"Hey, did anyone know he had a heart problem?"

Fi silenced it again and got up. "Atin's digging a hole. I'll go and help him. I'm good at digging holes, really *deep* ones."

A'den shrugged and went back to listening to the circuit. "I think the cops got excited when they found the stun baton burn on their buddy. Joining up the dots to work out that it was actually a covert commando team cleaning up a spillage is a step too far for them, thankfully." He leaned backward as far as his chair would go and grabbed another datapad. "Now take a look at these aerial recce images."

Darman took the pad, but Niner was still focused on the previous issue. "So, Sergeant, what would *you* have done differently?"

"I'd have shot the cop," said A'den.

"And that would have solved the problem *how,* exactly?"

"It wouldn't have changed a thing. It just worries me that you put being nice before doing the job right. We do extreme stuff. That means some unlucky saps get caught as collateral damage. Deal with it."

Darman knew A'den was right, and he was troubled by the fact that he'd hesitated; he was reacting to an internal template of police as Jaller Obrim's kind—allies, comrades, friends—and it was wholly wrong and a recipe for disaster at some point in the future. He couldn't afford to judge anyone by their uniform. He couldn't even assume all Jedi were on his side now. If he found out that Zey was tasking Special Operations personnel to deal with deserters like that, he wasn't sure how he'd take it.

"I realize you're the explosive ordnance man," A'den said, "but can't you manage to interpret aerial images?"

Darman jerked out of his thoughts. "Okay."

"Well?"

Darman stared at the flat images of what looked like the two-dimensional map of a city with a chron that showed it was recorded a few hours earlier. It was part of Eyat, not as a schematic of the construction that the Marits had worked on, but a real image. He could see tiny dots moving along roads. A large compound in the heart of the city was packed full of repulsor trucks and armored vehicles of various types that hadn't been there a few days earlier when Omega was inserted. There was even mobile anti-air cannon. He handed the datapad to Niner for inspection.

"They're getting ready for our visit, then . . ."

A'den nodded. "No doubt their Sep allies have aerial reconnaissance of the accumulation of Republic souvenirs we've given the lizards. We can both spy on each other, when we know where to look."

So Eyat was bracing for a Marit assault. "Other cities?" Darman asked.

"All doing the same. I'm not sure if they understand how the lizards here cascade things. But it's unlikely they'll know about *Leveler* until she's looking for a parking space."

A warship had been identified to deploy to Gaftikar, then. It was imminent. *"Leveler."*

"With a few thousand of the Republic's finest embarked, Thirty-fifth Infantry and Tenth Armored. Just to soften up Eyat and a few other major cities to allow the Marits to move in, then pull out when the dust has settled."

Eyat wasn't well defended at all. From what Darman had seen, even one ship was overkill. "Shenio Mining has enough resources to roll over Eyat and the government on its own without any military support if it wants to strip-mine the place that badly."

"Yeah, but you know how companies like to look like they've been invited legally, or else people scream that it's corporate invasion."

"It *is* corporate invasion," Darman said.

"Maybe there's some strategy, some big picture we're not

privy to," A'den said. "But in the end, all wars are about someone wanting something the other guy's got. If I thought that throwing a hydrospanner in the works would change the nature of the galaxy, I'd do it, but this is the way life works, chum. Let's just do the job and hope we stay alive long enough to move on."

Niner didn't seem bothered. He looked much more interested in the recce data. Darman left the two sergeants to their own devices, retrieved his entrenching tool from his backpack, and went in search of Fi and Atin.

In the quiet night air, it was easy to follow the sound of a shovel biting into the soil with that familiar metallic chinking sound. Fi and Atin—totally silent—were hacking away in a clearing fringed by small bushes, somewhere that roots would be less of a problem. Darman paused to look at the two bodies and joined in the digging by the faint, shielded light of a glow rod laid on the ground.

Two meters was deeper than it sounded. The three of them eventually stopped to stare down into the pit.

"Should we have dug two graves?" Atin asked.

"Sergeant Kal said that *Mando'ade* use communal graves if they bury at all." Darman racked his brain, trying to remember what else Skirata had taught them about disposing of fallen comrades. He didn't care about what the book said about concealing signs they'd ever been there. This was about respect for men who were one simple designation prefix away from being *him*. "And no soldier wants to be separated from his brothers."

"Unless they're particularly *di'kutla*," Fi said.

Atin squatted down over the bodies. "Okay, let's roll them in."

"Can't we *lower reverently* instead?" Darman went over to the pile of purple armor and pried the ID tallies from the breastplates. When he ran his pocket sensor over them, they gave him the readouts CT-6200/8901 and CT-0368/7766. There was no indication of what they actually called each other, of course; the Grand Army didn't give a *motla'shebs* about how clones liked to be addressed, on the record at least. He did what he'd been avoiding for the last few hours, and interrogated the copy of the Nulls' database that Ordo had given them all back on Triple Zero. Once he knew their real names, he would feel even worse. But he needed to if he was going to give them any sort of farewell rite. "They're . . . Moz and Olun." And this was the worst bit. "Jaing trained them at one time."

If Moz and Olun had harbored any ambitions beyond surviving the war, Jaing might have been the only one who knew what they were. Those dreams probably didn't include getting killed by another clone. Fi and Atin lowered them into the pit, still wrapped.

"Ni su'cuyi, gar kyr'adyc, ni partayli, gar darasuum," Darman said. It was the ritual remembrance of those who'd passed on, recited daily with the names of all the people the mourner committed himself to immortalizing: I'm still alive, you're dead, I'll remember you, so you're eternal. Sergeant Kal said that *Mando'ade* got straight to the point, even in spiritual matters. "Moz and Olun."

Fi threw a few handfuls of dirt into the pit, then picked up his shovel. "You know you've got to recite that every day for the rest of your life now, don't you?"

"I know," said Darman, pitching loose soil back into the grave.

And how many more names by the time this war is over?

It wasn't going to be hard to remember them. It was going to be much, much harder to forget.

Ore terminal, Kerif City, Bogg V, 478 days after Geonosis

Twi'leks were much heavier than they looked. Maybe it was the lekku, because that tissue had to be pretty dense; or maybe they were all muscle. Either way, it took a little more effort than Sev expected to restrain one.

"My, my," he said, grabbing Leb Chura in a headlock and slamming him into the warehouse wall. "You get around, don't you, delivery boy?"

The Twi'lek hit the permacrete slabs with a loud wet grunt, and Sev was sure he had a good grip on him until the pilot struggled free and made a run for it across the pitch-black landing strip.

It was always a challenge when you couldn't immobilize targets the quick way. But Delta needed this one alive and talking. Sev tracked him in his night-vision visor, a speed-blurred green figure with head-tails flapping as he ran.

"Coming your way, Fixer . . ."

Leb ran full-tilt toward his ship on the freight pad, and Sev raced after him. One downside of Katarn armor was that it was heavy—okay for short panicky sprints, but over any distance it slowed a man down—and Leb was opening the gap between them.

No problem. Fixer and Scorch were waiting.

The Twi'lek cannoned into a solid wall of commando, plastoid, and Deece as the two men intercepted him the hard way. Sev heard the *ooof* of air expelled from his lungs. Leb was knocked flat on his back before being hauled upright and pinned between Fixer and Scorch.

"I know Sev's weird, pal, but it's rude to run away when he tries to be sociable." Scorch could put a charmingly menacing leer into his voice that Sev couldn't emulate. His gloved fingers tightened slowly on the Twi'lek's neck. "He doesn't mean to bite. He's just being playful."

"What do you want?" Leb gasped, getting his breath back. "I've done nothing. I'm all legit. Who are you, anyway? Mandalorians? 'Cos I've—"

Boss ambled across the landing strip. "Don't break anything. General on deck." He tilted his head to indicate that Sev should look behind him. "*Bard'ika* on your six . . . *very* anxious to do some interrogating."

"Leb, now's the time to enjoy the hospitality of the Republic," Scorch said, hauling the Twi'lek bodily toward Delta's traffic interdiction vessel. "We just want to ask you a few harmless questions about your itinerary."

"Yeah, the *questions* might be harmless, but *you're* not . . ." Leb now looked past Scorch and spotted Jusik jogging across the permacrete, Jedi robes flapping. "Oh yeah, now the Jedi's going to zap me with his Force powers, isn't he? Shove a lightsaber in—"

Jusik caught up with them. He always looked as if a strong breeze would knock him over. "No lightsaber necessary, my friend. You haven't got any reason to withhold information, have you?"

When Jusik used that especially quiet, reasonable tone—and he never raised his voice anyway—Sev wasn't sure if he was using Jedi mind influence or not. There was always something disturbing about Jedi, even the approachable ones like Jusik. Sergeant Vau said it was a good idea never to turn your back on one. They weren't like regular folks.

Would I know if he was using that mind stuff on me?

Sev thought about that more and more lately. He still liked Jusik, though.

It was a tight fit in the TIV crew compartment now—four armored commandos, a scared Twi'lek, and General Jusik—and Leb seemed not to realize it was hard to give a prisoner a good hiding in such a confined space. His eyes went from visor to visor. He really didn't have a clue who they were. But then very few beings ever got to see a Republic commando close up, and the helmet always seemed to bother them when they did. Eye contact was everything for most humanoid species. Without it, they couldn't gauge how much trouble they were in.

"So you've been delivering *specialist equipment* shipped in from Arkania," Boss said. "And you don't have a permit for it."

"I don't need one. Do I?"

"You're from Ryloth, so you're a Republic citizen, and that makes trading in cloning equipment illegal."

"I'm not trading in anything, and I don't look in the crates—"

"Arkania. They don't export fruit, do they?"

"I'm a delivery boy, like you said."

"Your name showed up in a list we happen to have."

"Okay, arrest me, then."

Boss turned his head slowly to Sev, his silent cue to play the heavy. Jusik just watched, impassive.

"We don't do arrests," Sev said. "We get answers. Give us one and we'll go away."

"Or . . . ?"

"Or I'll be very upset." Sev could make his knuckles crack alarmingly just by closing his fist. "Tell me where you took the consignment."

Leb's gaze wandered to the hatch as if he was calculating what he'd have to do to escape. Maybe it was just a reflex. His lekku were moving slightly in some wordless reaction. "Why's everyone so interested in this stuff? Is it really glitterstim or something? The Mandalorians asked me the same thing—where I took it. I thought it was just vats and permacrete and stuff."

"What Mandalorians?"

"Three of them. One young, two older, judging by the voices—'cos they have helmets like you, don't they?—and they were wearing—"

Jusik cut in, suddenly very intent on the question. "Green armor. They wore dark green armor, didn't they?"

Leb blinked. "Yeah." He defocused for a moment as if he was trying to visualize something. "Yeah, they wore dark green. How did you know?"

"A hunch," Jusik said. Sev was almost pushed aside now. Whatever Jusik had on his mind, whatever intel he had, he hadn't shared it with them. He'd busted a gut to get here, though. "I can work out who they are. Now tell me where you took the equipment."

"Dorumaa."

Jusik leaned back as if he had his answer, as if the identity of whoever else had shaken down Leb mattered more to him than the delivery destination—Ko Sai's likely location. Sev was distracted by that, trying to construct a scenario in which that information mattered more.

"You want to pin that down?" Boss asked, and indicated Sev. "Or do I let my colleague ask you?"

"Tropix island resort." Leb sounded fluent, as if he'd rehearsed it, or at least given the same answers before. "You want the coordinates? Here they are." He put his hand inside his tunic and froze. "Hey, it's just a datapad . . . take it easy . . ."

Sev realized he must have looked as if he was going to hit him. He wondered how he managed to give the impression of being more violent than his brothers, because any armored commando with a Deece looked like bad news. He wasn't trying to act like a psycho, whatever buildup Boss gave him, but folks didn't feel comfortable sharing a space with him, and whatever he intended didn't seem to affect that.

"I'll take the data," Jusik said quietly. He held his hand out for Leb's datapad, tapped the controls, and keyed something into his own device. Then he handed it back.

"Hey!" Leb stared at his datapad in horror. "You erased it!"

"I'm so clumsy," Jusik said. "Come on. Let's see you safely on your way, shall we?"

"But my data—"

Jusik crooked his finger at Sev to accompany him, and they bundled Leb out of the TIV so fast that he almost fell out of the hatch. The two of them held on to an arm each and steered him toward his freighter.

"Don't I get some creds for my trouble?" Leb said.

Jusik slapped something into his palm. "Not just that, citizen, I'll make the problem disappear, too." He stared into the Twi'lek's face and put his hand flat on his chest for a moment. "In a few minutes, things will be back to normal for you. Now off you go."

Leb stood at the foot of the ladder up to his cockpit and seemed to be contemplating the contents of his palm as Jusik and Sev jogged back to the TIV. There was a small anonymous-looking shuttle a little distance from it, one that Sev had seen Jusik use before.

"What did you give him, sir?" Sev asked.

"A few hundred creds and a spot of amnesia."

"What?"

"I mind-rubbed him."

"Oh, you can do that, too, can you?"

"No point deleting the records on his datapad if he remembers them and remembers *us*."

There was a low rumble behind them. Sev turned to see Leb's ship powering up, driving clouds of dust and grit into the air with the downdraft of its thrusters.

"But whoever's after Ko Sai can still find him, except he won't be able to give them an answer this time, so how does that solve his problem?"

"I didn't say it would solve *his*," Jusik said. "But it certainly solves some of ours."

It wasn't very Jedi of him, but then maybe Sev didn't fully understand their beliefs. "What about those Mandalorians? You sounded like you knew something."

Jusik shrugged and opened the hatch on his shuttle with a gesture of his hand. It might have been some Force trick or simply a remote control. "Let's just say Ko Sai's in demand."

"But who *are* they?"

"Competition. I'll catch up with you later."

Sev accepted need-to-know even if it annoyed him. He watched Jusik disappear into the shuttle and rejoined Delta in the TIV, trying to work out what he felt about Mandalorians, and whether they were all like him.

"The general's scrambled the Twi'lek's brains," he said, slumping into a seat and fastening his restraining belt for takeoff. "So he isn't going to be discussing his travel arrangements with anyone else, at least."

Boss tutted in annoyance. "We should have asked him for a bit more detail about where he did the drop. But Jusik seemed really keen to get rid of him."

"Well, he knows something we don't."

Nobody said it, but Sev knew they were thinking it. *Mandalorians*. It was always sobering to run into them—or the mention of them—and find they were on the Separatists' side, or on no side at all, but not the Republic's allies. Like most of the commandos, Delta Squad had been raised and trained by Mandalorian sergeants; men like Walon Vau had done what generations of *Mando* fathers had done, raising their sons to be self-sufficient warriors, passing on a Mandalorian culture that made strong, tight-knit armies.

Yeah, but there's Mando, and there's Mando. Is that me? Is that who I really am? And how do real Mandos see us?

Omega were *very Mando* now. All Skirata's squads were; he was a real hard-liner, old Kal, all tradition, emotional sentimentality, and—if anyone got in his way—complete no-holds-barred violence. Sometimes Sev preferred Vau's cold distance, because it was for their own good. But there were times he envied Omega; Vau said Skirata was too soft and made weak soldiers, but all Sev saw was someone he didn't have to be afraid of and who would let him make mistakes.

Too late to think about that now.

"Okay, Dorumaa it is," said Boss. "Hope you packed the swimwear, Fixer . . ."

Tropix island resort, Dorumaa, Cularin system,
478 days after Geonosis

Tropix was a manufactured paradise with every facility a sun-seeking visitor might want, and as far from Skirata's idea of bliss as he could imagine.

It was all bright colors, noise, and heat. Lulari trees imported from Hikil tinkled like wind chimes in the breeze, and their heady scent was pungent enough to give him the start of a headache. Mird bolted along the shell-paved beachfront path ahead of Vau, whipping its tail and whimpering with excitement as it picked up strange new scents.

It was a Separatist planet, at least as far as the Cularin system was Sep-loyal. Skirata felt everywhere was enemy territory regardless of whether it was red, blue, or yellow on the charts, and didn't let the stereotyped idyll weaken his guard.

"Well, this is classy," he said. Beings of various species lounged on a white sand beach lapped by a turquoise sea so vividly blue that it could have been dyed. Twi'lek waitresses whose skin almost matched it wandered among the vacationers with trays of drinks. Droids trundled between, raking sand and somehow managing to leave no tracks behind them. "Imagine being stuck here for two weeks. What do you reckon, *Mer'ika*?"

Mereel shrugged. Out of armor, in a plain white shirt and beige pants, he suddenly looked so ordinary—so *civilian*—that Skirata could only think of all the routine things he was denied.

"I could probably find something to occupy me," Mereel said. "Do you two realize how much you look like glitterstim dealers?"

Vau looked back over his shoulder, a rather splendid pearl-inlaid blaster shimmering in his holster. "I'm going for the casual but menacing look. Glad I pulled it off . . ."

"It's the Arakyd special, Walon. Says more about you than credits ever can." The gangster look was less conspicuous here than full Mandalorian armor. The idea was to look like they'd come for sportfishing so that submerging *Aay'han* offshore didn't attract the wrong sort of interest. "Looks rather *expensive.*"

"Another bauble from the Vau deposit box. My great-grandfather is said to have shot a servant with it for serving his caf too hot."

Skirata almost went for the bait. "You're just saying that to make me mad, aren't you?"

Vau's expression was unreadable. "You know I'd never do such a thing."

Mereel put a restraining hand on Skirata's shoulder as he overtook him. The terrible thing about Vau and his family was that it was perfectly possible. Instead, Skirata tried to concentrate on the inexplicably generous Vau, the man who'd just given him millions for the frankly sentimental and unselfish purpose of rescuing clones, rather than the sadistic martinet who'd nearly killed Atin to toughen him up.

"*Udesii,*" Mereel muttered. "Take it easy, *Kal'buir.*"

Skirata did his best. He took a deep breath as he walked into the lobby of the resort's huge hotel complex and focused on being a glitterstim baron on a short break. He was a non-descript, short, gray-haired, middle-aged man who could pass unnoticed as a vagrant in the right clothes, or bring a room to a halt simply by walking with the right degree of swagger.

Today he could play a prince. He had a fortune in the safe on board *Aay'han,* so thinking like the idle and disreputable rich was easy. He was both.

A tall female Rek looked down at him. Skirata had seen them working as bounty hunters—their ultrathin whip-like bodies came in handy for accessing awkward locations—but it was a surprise to come across one in the hospitality business.

This one didn't appear to have a sense of humor. He decided to skip the diet jokes.

"Do we need a permit for angling here, ma'am?" Skirata asked innocently. "We've come for the rifi fishing."

"Yes," she said, not exactly personifying *hospitable.* She fixed him with a disturbing purple eye. "Are you guests?"

"No, we have a marine vessel moored here."

"Well, there'll be a fee for berthing. Do you wish to hire tackle, too?"

"Oh, we've come *very* well prepared, thanks . . ."

"And you'll have to sign a waiver, because Tropix Resorts cannot be held responsible for any death, injury, damage, or other untoward incident caused by, or relating to, hunting, fishing, or exploration in any area more than ten meters offshore, or beyond a depth of fifty meters—"

Skirata smiled indulgently, waste of time though it was, and took out a stylus. "We're used to taking risks, ma'am. Where do I sign?"

"How long will this permit need to cover?"

How long to find the hiding hole that Ko Sai had created for herself? Maybe hours. Maybe days. If they were unlucky, weeks, and when they found it there was always a chance that the aiwha-bait would have moved on again.

"Give me a week's pass," Skirata said, slapping his credit chip on the desk. "If we find we have . . . more time to kill, I'll extend it."

The Rek checked the chip in her scanner. "Thank you,

Master Nessin." Skirata flinched at the bogus ID. "I must advise caution if you fish beyond the five-hundred-meter limits. We do have people go missing from time to time when they ignore the warnings. But that's part of the appeal for many anglers and divers who come here."

Vau did his icy I-know-something–you-don't smile. "Sport-fishing isn't sport unless you run the risk of being caught yourself, is it?"

"There's always relaxing on the beach," said the Rek. "Or a pleasant walk around the harbor."

She seemed to have classed them as two old guys trying to rediscover their youth through destructive machismo, maybe with Mereel as the fit young minder who could haul them out of trouble. It was perfect: whoever Ko Sai had as a contact here—and she'd need one, if only to get hold of supplies—wouldn't be tipped off to the fact that Mandalorian bounty hunters were in town.

Aay'han didn't look too conspicuous on one of the pontoons that stretched out into the azure water. Most of the vessels alongside showed no signs of ever having slipped their moorings, but there were a few more rugged craft that were clearly from offworld. Skirata took out his datapad and aimed the scanner discreetly in their direction to check the passive transponders, just in case. He found no registrations that worried him.

"You have to hand it to the investment group here," he said as they tried to look casual. "They take a disaster and turn it into a USP."

"You're so crass," Vau muttered.

"What's a USP?" Mereel asked.

"Unique selling point, son. As in, they made a complete *shu'shuk* when they terraformed the place, not knowing just what kind of wildlife was in the ice when they thawed the planet. There are some real nasties lurking underwater, but instead of saying, *Ooh, that's too dangerous, let's scrub the resort idea,* the tourist board touts it as an opportunity for wild adventure. I have to respect that kind of resilience in business."

Mereel smiled to himself. "Until the lawsuits come rolling in."

"Just operating costs," Skirata said. "Overheads."

The three men climbed onto *Aay'han* and sat on a flat section of her casing, backs resting against the curve of the port cargo bay, looking out to sea. Mird sat with its nose pointing into the wind, sniffing happily. Skirata didn't know a lot about sport angling, although he could manage to catch fish if he ever had to, and he hoped there wasn't some giveaway sign of a real angler that was conspicuously missing. If push came to shove, he could always play the stim baron on his first fishing trip.

"The aiwha-bait has to have a resupply route," he said. "She can't just go to ground here and have no contact with anyone. How does she get her food? She's not the kind that lives off the land. She's used to having *minions*."

"Sea," said Mereel.

"What?"

"Live off the sea, not the land."

"Well, Kaminoan discipline or not, she has to eat something."

"Let's do a little exploring," said Vau. "We have the chart. *Oya,* Mird!"

Mird stood up, paws slipping on the smooth hull, and looked around frantically at the command to hunt. The strill couldn't sense any prey. Vau leaned over and ruffled its loose folds of gold fur, pointing at the water. Strills could fly and glide, but swimming wasn't their forte. Mird rumbled with disappointed frustration.

" 'S'okay, Mird, I'll let you hunt *kaminiise* soon," Skirata said. He wondered if he was getting soft: he'd always disliked the animal, even if he couldn't blame it for its savagery given a master like Vau. Now he saw its talents, if not its charm. "*Soon.* Okay?"

Mird's eyes had that focus and intensity that suggested it understood Skirata perfectly, and it settled down again with its huge head in Vau's lap. Mereel slid his sun visor into place and leaned back against the curve of the hull, fingers meshed behind his head.

"Let's narrow down the search range first," he said, pointing. "Look. Check out the speed."

Moving across the harbor, well within the safe turquoise shallows, was a powered barge with aquata divers getting ready to explore the underwater world, wearing a bizarre array of brightly colored swimwear that said they didn't dive for a living. The hull looked like the barges tied up on nearby pontoons in Tropix resort livery: this was what the staff here used to get around the perfectly planned, ideally spaced island chain, and this was what the Twi'lek must have used to move Ko Sai's equipment and droids out to sea.

If they worked out the speed the barges could cruise, and factored in the weight of the cargo the Twi'lek had delivered, they'd get a radius within which to search.

Skirata aimed his datapad, laying it flat on his knee and letting it track the barge. "I was never very good at this . . ." It was just a matter of timing it across a set distance, using the datapad like one of those gizmos that CSF sometimes used to track speeders. "Well, I make that fifteen klicks an hour."

Mereel slid along the hull and checked over his shoulder. "So that means if the barge went out to some RV point and returned in half an hour, we're looking at a maximum range of maybe ten klicks, if it was moving faster, and that's being optimistic."

"Let's take the search out to the fifteen-klick radius, then, just to be sure."

Vau keyed in the data and projected the holochart onto the hull. "This is three-dimensional, remember." A concave relief chart formed like a mesh basket in blue light that was hard to see in the sunlight. "That's the underwater topography in a fifteen-klick radius from the coordinates the Twi'lek gave us."

Even in these lighting conditions, Skirata could see the indentations of cave mouths under the waterline. The charts only went down as far as fifty meters.

It was as good a place as any to start looking.

"Who did the hydrography for the developers?" Mereel asked. "They put that fifty-meter limit in for a reason, because they must have known what was below it. They didn't just stop looking because it was time for a caf break."

"I don't think there's the equivalent of city hall here," Skirata said. "We can't just stroll in and ask the local planning chief if we can look through his database. That's the problem with commercially owned planets."

Vau opened the top hatch and motioned Mird inside. "Where's your spirit of adventure, Kal? Have overpriced DeepWater hybrid, will explore . . ."

"I got this tub for a good price." Insulting Skirata's ability to drive a deal was marginally worse than questioning his courage, and he realized Vau had baited him yet again. "And I wonder what you'd do with yourself if you didn't have me to torment."

Vau raised one eyebrow—now, *that* was annoying dumb insolence, it really was—but Skirata ignored the impulse, thought of the fortune Vau had handed over to him as if it were a cred chip he'd found on the street, and stood up. Mereel slipped the mooring line and prepared to get under way.

The islands were constructed on the tops of natural peaks jutting from the sea, like porceplast crowns on the stumps of teeth. Once submerged, it was simply a matter of doing what he'd do on land if he was hunting an animal in a lair: looking for signs of activity, checking out cave mouths, and venturing inside.

It was just a recce, just a discreet dive to scope out the topography that wasn't shown on any of the charts, so they could come back later to stage a planned assault. But if an opportunity presented itself, they'd take it.

Outside the transparisteel bubble that formed a clear dome over the cockpit, a tourist brochure of an underwater world drifted past them in vividly colored serenity. Mird seemed fascinated, pressing a snotty nose to the transparisteel and making excited grumbling noises, and Skirata risked reach-

ing out to haul the strill back by its collar and wipe the viewport clean. *Filthy thing, but it has its uses, just like us.* Vau
took the hint and beckoned to Mird to sit on his lap.

Relations had definitely relaxed between Skirata and Vau.
There was a time when they'd have brawled over less.

Aay'han dropped below sixty meters, past the charted
depth. The water was surprisingly clear; lacy weeds swayed
gracefully in the currents. Brilliant pink and yellow fish like
ribbons wove themselves between the fronds, flashing displays of lights like a Corsucant casino.

"That's more like it," Mereel said, sounding pleased. The
navigation displays stripped away the layer of marine life
and showed a three-dimensional landscape of slopes marked
with fissures and channels that penetrated deep into the face
of the submerged mountain forming the one island within
the fifteen-kilometer zone. *Aay'han* came alongside a deep
shadow that appeared as a hole on the sensors.

"Worth a ping," said Mereel. "Let's just line up the sensors
and see how far into that feature we can map."

"You okay with this, son?"

"Yes, *Kal'buir.*" He turned the vessel ninety degrees and
pointed *Aayhan*'s nose at the opening for a deep scan. "Now,
that's a likely one. Goes back a hundred meters at least. Mark
that on the chart, please, Sergeant Vau." He turned to Skirata.
"I'm several pages ahead of Ordo in the manual now . . ."

There'd be a contest later, Skirata could tell. Ordo and
Mereel, a double act right from the time he'd met them as
two-year-old clone kids—no names, no numbers, and already handling blasters—sometimes indulged in a little ri-
valry and one-upmanship. It explained Mereel's love of risk
taking. He had to edge out of Ordo's shadow somehow.

They worked along the thirty kilometers of submerged
coastline, checking and scanning cave after cave. Some were
immediately obvious as dead ends when the sonar scan was
mapped onto the three-dimensional view, just depressions in
the rock that went nowhere. Some were so deep and twisted
that the sonar didn't find an end, and those were marked. As
Mereel eased *Aay'han* through the extraordinary forest of

weed and marine creatures—some of which slapped sucker-
like mouthparts onto the cockpit bubble as if testing the ship
for flavor—Skirata kept an eye out for signs of disturbance
to the environment that might indicate recent construction
work. If Ko Sai was here, she'd only been in residence for a few
months. Signs of activity might still be around—fresh-cut
rock face, debris from cave mouths, any number of telltale
signs that she'd had a hideaway built down here.

Vau stared out of the dome, too, with Mird mirroring his
posture as exactly as a six-legged animal ever could, blinking
from time to time and pausing once or twice to turn and gaze
at its master before giving him an enthusiastic and slobbery
lick across the face with a dripping gray tongue.

Skirata shuddered. But at least there was one being in the
galaxy that loved Vau unconditionally. Fierfek, if he'd started
feeling sorry for the *chakaar* after so many years, it was a
bad sign. The fortune was just creds Vau had no use for, Skirata told himself, something he wanted to deny his own priv-
ileged class and that simply happened to be useful in the plan
to rescue clones—an afterthought.

It's not true, though, is it? He's a Mando *too. The same
thing that drew him to Mandalore is the same thing that kept
me there. We chose it. Maybe I hate him because of the parts
of him that are too much like me.*

"All stop," Vau said suddenly.

Mird stiffened, always sensitive to Vau's reactions. The
strill was hunting, even if it couldn't get out there and taste
the scents and currents. Mereel brought the ship to a halt and
she drifted, silent except for the hum of the shields and environment controls.

Vau pointed ahead, slightly to port.

"In that weed forest. Look."

Aay'han's exterior holocams trained in the direction of
Vau's finger and Mird's snout. The weed was thick and populated by shoals of glowing orange discs that could have
been fish, worms, or swimming crustaceans. The impression
was one of a tapcaf courtyard strung with decorative lights.

Not all the weed was pale green. Some looked white in the

aquamarine light. Skirata strained to focus, and then a current moved the weed a little more and he realized he wasn't looking at weed at all, but bones.

It was a skeleton.

"Shab," Mereel muttered. "I think we're too late for resuscitation, *Kal'buir.*"

"I hope he bought travel insurance." Skirata couldn't see any marks on the bones at this distance. "Or *she.*"

Who'd died down here? And why?

The skeleton was swaying in the current as if dancing with the weed. It was definitely a humanoid of some kind, picked clean and as white as an anatomical specimen, although a closer inspection—as close as they could get without leaving the vessel—showed a few colonies of pale yellow growths that looked like closed shadow barnacles. It was hard to see what was holding it down. If the flesh was gone, the connective tissue that held the bones together should have been gone, too. Skirata couldn't think of a species that fitted the bill, but it didn't matter. He—or she—wasn't going anywhere.

"Diver who ignored the hazard warnings?" Vau asked.

Skirata's instinct for bad signs was more reliable than any sonar. "What kind of marine life eats a diving suit and apparatus as well as the meat?"

Mereel, engrossed in the controls for the external security holocam, let out a long breath.

"And when did you last see a fish with fingers?" he said quietly, switching the holocam image to one of the large monitors. "Look."

The close-up view of the weed bed that swayed around the skeleton's ankles like a deep-pile carpet showed a splash of bright orange. As Mereel magnified the image and went in for a close-up, Skirata realized what it was.

Mereel was right. There weren't too many marine species that could take a length of fibercord and secure a body to a rock.

The close view on the monitor showed a knot: a competent, nonslipping, textbook Keldabe anchoring bend. In a galaxy of loop rings, gription panels, and a hundred high-tech ways of attaching things, few people bothered to learn to tie knots properly, let alone one as distinctive and complex as that.

Very few people indeed: only clone soldiers—and Mandalorians.

10

Naasad'guur mhi,
Naasad'guur mhi,
Naasad'guur mhi,
Mhi n'ulu.
Mhi Mando'ade,
Kandosii'ade,
Teh Manda'yaim,
Mando'ade.

No one likes us,
No one likes us,
No one likes us,
We don't care.
We are Mandos,
The elite boys,
Mando boys,
From Mandalore.
—Mandalorian drinking song, loosely translated; said to
date from a ban on Mandalorian mercenaries drinking
in local tapcafs, when employed by the government of
Geris VI

Republic Treasury building, Coruscant,
478 days after Geonosis

Besany closed the doors to her office and obscured the
transparisteel walls with a touch of the button on her desk.
She didn't want to be disturbed.

Centax II. Do I concentrate on that?

She fondled the blaster that Mereel had given her and wondered what it would take to make her use it; she'd never fired one in anger. She hadn't even been trained to shoot, but now seemed a pretty good time to learn. Then she began trying to work out how she might take a closer look at Centax II—in person, or at a distance—and work out what was going on. It was a military area, and no member of the public could stroll in there unannounced. There weren't that many excuses to pay a visit even for a Treasury agent.

The public accounts showed a number of contractors providing services to the Grand Army that could be cross-referenced to Centax, and one of them—Dhannut Logistics—also showed up on the health budget. It was worth a look as long as she was thinking *medcenter.*

I could be totally off beam, of course.

And I got Mereel his answer anyway. I should walk away from this.

But she couldn't, because Ordo couldn't walk away, and neither could Corr, or any of the others. She realized how empty her life must have been to have filled up so fast and so easily with people who—possibly—didn't give her a second thought except as a useful contact.

I'm not stupid, Kal.

But they had something she wanted, too, and it wasn't just Ordo. She wanted a share of their closeness, that belonging and camaraderie, and an end to feeling she was on the outside of life.

She thought suddenly of Fi, and how—so Ordo said—he knew there was a complete element missing from his existence, and he resented it. She at least knew what hers was, and where she might get it.

But there was also the lure of a wrong to be righted, and she knew she wasn't alone in that. Senator Skeenah from Chandrila was getting very vocal about the Grand Army's conditions and clone rights. He might prove to be a handy excuse for investigating further.

Her private comlink stared back at her from the palm of

her hand, daring her to choose between calling Ordo and contacting the Senator. Still scared that she might call while Ordo was gambling whether to cut a red wire or a blue one as a detonator counted down, she sent him a delayed message instead. He could choose when and if he wanted to read it.

I hope you enjoyed the cake. What else could she say? She had no idea who else might see it, secure link or not. *You have to try my home cooking when you get back.* She could imagine Ordo reading it with a frown, taking it at face value, while Mereel—who seemed to be leading a totally different life, and relishing it—would have given her a knowing grin.

Besany sent the message with a click of her thumbnail on the keys, then tapped in the code for the Senate switchboard.

No point leaving an audit trail on the office link, just in case. He's a known antiwar activist. They'll be watching him—whoever they *might be.*

Senator Skeenah's administrative droid made an appointment for her to meet him later that day, which indicated just how few lobbyists were courting a man who opposed the war, and asked if she preferred "off site."

"I'm at the Treasury building," she said. Visiting the Senate was routine for a government employee; it would draw less attention than a meeting in a tapcaf or restaurant. She'd be picked up on any of a dozen security holocams as she moved around Galactic City, and even by the surveillance satellites that kept watch over Coruscant. "I'll come to his office."

On the way to the meeting, sitting in the back of an air taxi, she felt that the small blaster in her pocket was visible to the whole planet. She didn't even know what type it was. It was a smart dark blue with a stubby green-gray barrel and a little red light that showed it was charged, quite a pretty object. When she peered at the engraved plate on the butt—she was sure the end of the grip was called that—she could see the words MERR-SONN.

"Lady, you're making me nervous," said the taxi driver. "You going to assassinate someone?"

Besany hadn't realized he could see that far over the back

of the seat, but there was a lot she didn't know about the visual field of a Rodian's faceted eyes. She slid the blaster off her lap and back into her pocket.

"I mix with unsavory characters," she said.

Taxi drivers had an opinion on everything. "Senate's full of them . . . they're called politicians."

She thought that way, too, but then realized she'd never actually met one socially. Where did she get that idea? From the holonews? From the courts? The power of stereotypes was astonishing. She wondered how she could ever gain any headway in making Coruscanti see the anonymous troopers fighting the war for them as living, breathing men.

She couldn't even say they were all someone's son or husband or father or brother. They were utterly outside of society. The size of the task almost crushed her.

One step at a time, girl. Do what you can.

Senator Skeenah met her in one of the cell-like private interview rooms kept for Senators to meet members of the public. He was much more ordinary than she'd imagined, not terribly well dressed, but he had an earnest passion that hit her like a tidal wave. Another stereotype crashed and burned.

"Of course I'm concerned about what happens to these men," he said. "Whatever other member planets might do, Coruscant hasn't tolerated slavery in millennia. It's intolerable that we adopt it now simply because it's expedient. But I'm a lone voice."

Besany took it carefully. "I'm having some difficulty identifying medical provision for the Grand Army, Senator. I can identify expenditure on what I think are medcenter facilities, but it's not . . . let's say the audit trail isn't transparent."

That careful comment meant a great deal in political code if the listener wanted to interpret it. Skeenah seemed to. "Yes, I've asked repeatedly about casualties—the medical field units are woefully inadequate, and I can't find out what happens to those killed in action. To the best of my knowledge, the bodies aren't recovered. There's no heroes' return for these poor men. So if you see large sums allocated to clone welfare, I can assure you there's no sign of it being used to that end."

Besany had a sensation of dread like cold water spilling in her lap. It was something she could have found out easily enough from Ordo; he'd know what they did with bodies, but it was one of a long list of things she'd never thought to ask. The inference was that troopers were simply discarded like waste, and that stoked her anger. She hovered on the edge of asking Skeenah if he knew anything about facilities on Centax II, and decided that it was too dangerous to have that kind of discussion with a man she didn't know.

"I audit some of the Grand Army accounts," she said. That much was true, and hardly a secret if news of her meeting got back to her bosses. She slipped a plastoid contact card from her pocket and pressed it into his hand. "If there's ever anything you think I should look at—discreetly, of course, because I'd be investigating other public servants—do let me know."

"Ah, you're the internal police . . ."

"I look after the taxpayers' credits."

"And here was I thinking you might be concerned about the welfare of our army."

Besany bit her tongue out of habit but it was too painful a comment to let pass. "Oh, but I am," she said. "They're not just theoretical charity cases to me. I'm dating a trooper."

Skeenah looked taken aback for a moment, and she wasn't sure if he was reacting to her cutting comment or the unsolicited personal detail.

"Well," he said, "there's no point my haranguing you about the fact that they're all human men like any other, is there?"

It was time for a little humility. "I know a lot of clones, by most people's standards, and yes, I care what happens to them."

"You might *know*, then, what happens to them."

"In what sense?"

"When they're wounded but can't return to active duty. You see, I can find out what happens on the Rimsoo medical stations—or at least I get some limited answers from the Defense staff—but I'm getting no answers about the men who can't be patched up and sent back."

Besany thought of Corr, temporarily assigned desk duties after a device he was defusing blew up and took his hands with it. He was awaiting the arrival of specialist prosthetics, and if Skirata hadn't grabbed him for commando training, he'd have gone back to ordnance disposal.

"I would imagine they die," Besany said. "The army seems to go to a lot of trouble to send them back."

"Ah, but life isn't that tidy," Skeenah said. He lowered his voice, even though the doors were shut. "There'll be injuries that a man can survive, but that means he'll never be fit for service again. I can't seriously believe something like that hasn't happened in more than a year of this war. And yet there are no homes for these men, who must surely exist, and we *know* they don't end up being cared for by family— because they have none. So where do they go?"

Besany didn't even want to think about it, but she had to. The only answer she could think of right then was that the most badly injured who might otherwise have been saved were left to die.

But some mobile surgical units had Jedi advisers. No Jedi would let such a thing happen . . . would they?

She had to talk to Jusik. He'd tell her.

"I'm going to see if I can find out," Besany said.

"And I'm going to carry on pressing for proper long-term care facilities." Skeenah looked troubled. "Meanwhile, I'm also going to help raise funds for charitable care. There are some citizens out there who want to help, you know."

"I'll keep you posted," Besany promised.

She took the long walk back to the Treasury building, pausing for a caf on the way, and found that the Senator's question was now eating away at her. Yes, it could only mean that clone troopers lived, or died, and there was no middle way or disability provision. The war hadn't reached the eighteen-month mark yet. Governments were always poor at thinking things through, especially when wars caught them on the hop.

Maybe this was what Dhannut Logistics was doing, then: care facilities out of the public eye to hide the signs that the war might not be going as well or as cleanly as the civilian citizens imagined, just as she'd first thought. She decided to check out their other projects when she got back to her desk, but while she sipped her caf, she checked them out via her datapad simply to get a street address from the directory.

And that was where things started to get interesting.

There was no entry in the public database for Dhannut. It could have been a subsidiary of another company, of course, or even one that wasn't based on Coruscant; but either way, it would have to be registered to tender for government contracts, and it would have had to register for corporate taxation even if it was offworld, and so it would require a tax exemption number.

Jilka could come in useful now. She was the tax officer; she was an expert in finding companies that earned revenue and didn't pay their taxes in full.

Besany Wennen, who'd played things by the book all her life until she fell in with a crowd of misfits and men who didn't exist, put on her best liar's face and prepared to spin a plausible story to Jilka, crossing the line from merely accessing records for unauthorized reasons to entering a world of deception—with consequences she knew she could never imagine.

Rebel camp, near Eyat, Gaftikar, 478 days after Geonosis

The Marits were scuttling everywhere in a state of excitement, and there were a lot more of them today than Darman had seen before.

He leaned against the doorway of the hut, brushing his teeth, collapsible plastoid bowl in one hand as he contemplated what was going to be a busy few days.

"Shift it, Dar." Niner was in full armor. He'd had word, then: they were going in. "Thirty-fifth's moving. They're finishing up on Qiilura. Let's make sure they've got an open door."

Qiilura. Darman spat foam into the bowl. "Have I got time to call Etain?"

"Do you have to?"

"Well, I might get killed, and . . ."

Niner's expression was hidden behind his visor, but Darman knew every nuance of his breathing by now, every faint sound that indicated swallowing or licked lips, every click of the jaw when words didn't emerge.

"You'll be fine," Niner said at last, and slapped him on the shoulder. He was playing the reassuring *ruus'alor,* the sergeant; the word was derived from *ruus,* a rock, and it summed up his solidly pivotal role pretty well. "But call her anyway. Say hi from me."

Niner walked away toward the Marits. He never talked much about what he wanted from life. He never confided in his brothers about fears and loneliness, or talked about girls, or showed any sign that he didn't think the war was a good idea. It was the last bit that worried Darman most. Niner probably kept his yearnings to himself for the sake of maintaining morale—did he think they didn't *know* that?—but everyone griped about the war and every aspect of it out of habit and custom. It was the only leeway clone troopers had—to express opinions that the command was clueless, that the food was garbage, that the kit was *osik,* and that it was all a waste of time, but it was better than being a civilian. And it was a veneer, a kind of bonding ritual to show how much you didn't care, when in reality you were scared witless, always hungry, and usually disoriented. Being the best army in the galaxy didn't stop any of those feelings. At first, Darman—like all of them—had thought their role in life was noble and inevitable; now the indoctrination had been worn thin by seeing the galaxy beyond Kamino, and even some ARCs were deserting. The rank and file were grumbling—in private. If they'd had somewhere to go and the bonds had been weaker, Darman suspected a lot more would have vanished from the ranks.

But they stayed for their brothers. They stayed because their only source of self-esteem was being the best at what they did.

And they had nowhere else to go.

Once more of them worked out what happened to those who couldn't—or wouldn't—fight any longer, what would happen?

Yes, the GAR might have been better off with tinnies. They never worked things out.

"How many teeth have you got, Dar?" Niner yelled. He'd stopped to look back. Darman paused with the brush still in his mouth. "Because you're taking an awful long time cleaning them."

Darman mumbled through a mouthful of foam. "Sorry, Sarge."

He went back to the refreshers to rinse his mouth and clean up, then changed from his fatigues into his bodysuit before washing the clothing in the refresher's basin with a rock-hard lump of the local soap and shaking it out so that it dried in minutes. Habit—ritual—was a soothing thing. By the time he'd attached his armor plates to the bodysuit, the fatigues were dry and he could fold them tightly into a small roll that he slipped into his backpack.

He couldn't even recall putting on his plates. His mind was on Etain. He shut the door and commed her.

She took some time to answer. He was on the point of just recording a message when he heard her voice, and he felt instantly foolish, tearful and excited. It was audio only, no holoprojection, but he never questioned that because she was on deployment and she had her reasons for not showing him where she was.

He worried anyway. He wanted to see her again, quite literally. He was worried he'd forget her face.

"Can you talk?" he asked.

There was a brief pause. "Are you okay, Dar?"

"I'm fine. I got bitten by an ARC trooper."

"That's gross. Are they poisonous?"

She seemed to think he was joking. Darman wondered

whether to blurt out that Sull had been under a death sentence, but decided that kind of thing needed saying in person. "It's okay, I just sucked out the venom and shot him. Anyway, Fi wanted his armor. Hey, I miss you. What's happening on Qiilura?"

Another pause. "It's not good. Most of them went quietly but some dug in, and . . . well, you know."

"Casualties?"

"Yeah."

"Ah."

"Not me, obviously."

"I'm glad." He caught a note in her voice that said she was holding back; maybe there was someone with her. The holovids showed clandestine love affairs as exciting, but Darman just found the secrecy miserable. "What's Levet like?"

"Solid guy."

"We'll be working with his battalion pretty soon. Does that mean you'll be coming back to Triple Zero? Sorry—I shouldn't ask. Just thought you'd be finished there, and . . ."

"It'll be a few more months. Three, maybe."

"Oh." *Where? Why?* "Okay."

"I miss you too, Dar. Think of something you'd like to do when we meet up. I'm not good at planning things like that."

Darman wasn't, either. He suspected she didn't mean a drink from a grimy glass at Qibbu's sleazy cantina for old times' sake. "Mereel might have some ideas. He seems to know every tapcaf between Galactic City and the Outer Rim."

"Okay. I don't mind as long as you're there."

"Me, too." Darman worried that he didn't have any smart talk or witty lines. He sounded like a total *di'kut,* he knew it.

There was a loud rapping on the door. "Dar?" It was Fi. "Dar, are you in there?"

Darman rolled his eyes and addressed the ether. "*What,* Fi?"

"Are you going to be in there all day? I'm not going to dig a latrine because you're still doing your hair . . ."

"Okay, okay. Give me a moment." He lowered his voice. "I'm sorry, *cyar'ika,* I have to go."

"I'll call you in a while. Stay safe. I love you."

"Look after yourself." Darman was working up to saying that he loved her, too, when the link closed from her end of the channel, and the moment was gone. He took a deep breath before yanking the door open, brokenhearted that he might never get the chance to tell her. He had a bad feeling about the coming assault on Eyat. It was vague and nagging, probably just his growing awareness and resentment of the way things were, but possibly—just possibly—an omen. Mixing with Jedi made you almost believe in that kind of stuff. "Fi, I'm going to break your *shabla* neck . . ."

Fi stepped back with his hands held up in mock submission. "Steady on, *ner vod.*"

"You really pick your moments."

"I want to use the 'freshers."

"Yeah, and I was—" Darman stopped himself. There was no point ranting at Fi for interrupting a call to Etain. It would be particularly tactless. "Okay." He patted his brother's cheek with exaggerated care, and realized he was doing a very Skirata-like thing. "I'm going to check the ordnance again."

"Atin's been through it twice."

"Then I'll do it a third time."

"Dar . . ."

"What?"

"You can talk about Etain, you know. I'm not going to burst into tears or anything."

Fi closed the door behind him, and Darman heard the sound of running water. Fi wasn't stupid and he'd probably heard every word anyway, but Darman still felt guilty at having a part of his limited life that put any kind of barrier between them.

Outside the hut, Niner and Atin were laying out equipment, checking it, and taking no notice of A'den's spirited argument with one of the Marits. It was another dominant one with a red frill at its throat, but it wasn't Cebz. The lizards were gathering: where there had been fewer than a hundred in the camp, there were now a few thousand in the area, coming to the rendezvous point from villages scattered throughout the countryside.

Darman stared at the pile of ordnance. There were enough thermal detonators to remove a large chunk of planet.

"Overkill," he said.

Atin looked up. "Whatever happened to *P* for plenty?"

"You've seen Eyat. They've got triple-A and traffic cops, not Acclamators. So we hammer them with the Thirty-fifth and then the lizards overrun them. Don't you think that's a waste of resources?"

"Dar, it's still a capital city," Niner said. "And we're not just fighting the Gaftikari. We're denying the place to the Seps."

"And we're not footing the bill for it, either," Atin said.

Darman pondered what possible use this planet would be to anyone except the mining companies. Did they even use kelerium and norax to build droids? Maybe it was the Republic doing a favor for Shenio Mining in exchange for services rendered elsewhere. The galaxy seemed to work that way. *Help us out in the war, buddy, and we'll see you right when it comes to building your profits.*

And it didn't matter to him at all. He had no stake in it, no interest, and no consequence to him except his life and his brothers' lives on the line, which was simply the job he did.

He bent down to pick up a small thermal det and rolled it in his hands, seeing the little restaurant opposite the Eyat government building. The minced roba pastry rolls washed down with sweet caf had been delicious; a charge of this size, detonated within twenty meters, would shatter the restaurant's transparisteel frontage into a thousand blades and send them flying at three thousand meters a second into anything and anybody within a thousand-meter range. Sometimes it paid not to think about it too much.

"Can I do the power station?" he asked.

Niner didn't turn his head. "You recce'd the government buildings area."

"Doesn't mean I can't take out the station."

"I don't like changing plans this close to time."

"What plans? We didn't even complete the first recce. We've scrubbed the assassinations. We're going to run the same risks."

Niner didn't answer. They'd become so used to doing things on the fly with little or no planning that Darman began to wonder if they were getting sloppy. Special Operations was as much—no, *more*—about detailed surveillance, observation, and rehearsal than going in with Deeces blazing and blowing stuff up.

"A'den's going to brief us in around an hour," Niner said at last.

"Great." Darman tossed and caught the unprimed det like a toy a few times and then laid it back on the fabric sheet with the rest of the ordnance. "I'm going for a walk."

Niner could always recall him. He slipped his helmet over his head, sealed it, and strode off into the camp, seeing the world through the filter of his visor's HUD again, targets in an environment rather than beings in a landscape. Skirata said they were at the stage of life where they were making emotional connections that regular folk made much earlier in childhood, able to imagine themselves in the situations they created. But, he said, it was hard to picture yourself as the guy strolling past the restaurant at the moment the charge detonated when you'd never done ordinary things like that and had been given only a detached academic grasp of blast radii, overpressures, and fragment velocities.

Omega Squad, like all the clone army, had been little more than highly trained, superefficient, ultrafit children when the war started. It struck Darman that they were living life the wrong way around—given the maximum ability to fight long before they had the experience to identify with beings on the sharp end of the fighting.

Too late to worry about that. What am I going to do, warn Eyat? Join the Seps? Cry over dead strangers?

There was nothing else he could do but fight to win, and survive to . . . what, exactly? The question never went away.

When we win, what happens? What do soldiers like us do in peacetime? Maybe he'd end up doing refugee relief. Etain said Jedi did that sometimes. Maybe they'd still end up working together.

He walked among chattering, excited Marits with jewel-like scales who didn't seem to be anxious about the coming assault. They were swarming around artillery pieces, drilling with E-Webs. This was clearly something they'd been looking forward to for a long time.

Darman paused to watch them, realizing his main fear was that he'd get killed before he told Etain that he loved her, and wondered where the remaining humans would fit into a society run by efficient, orderly Marits whose lives seem to run like flow charts.

He gestured to the red-frilled boss lizard to come to him. They didn't seem to be offended by being summoned.

"What's going to happen when you take over?" Darman asked. "What's going to happen to the people in Eyat?"

Boss Lizard did a bit of baffled head-cocking and looked as if he was calculating. "There'll be roles for them in proportion to their population, of course."

Darman realized he should have expected a sensible, numerical answer like that. "So no bloodletting. No purges. No species cleansing."

"Not for its own sake, no. What's the purpose of wanton destruction? We just want what we deserve. We are the *majority.*"

"What if they refuse to fit in with that?"

"That," said Boss Lizard, "would be pointless."

"What are you going to change when you seize power?"

"Nothing. Except we shall live in the cities and we shall have the majority of the elected posts according to our population."

Darman could now see the mismatch between Gaftikari humans and their Marit workforce. They weren't even competing for the same thing, a nice tidy two-sided I-want-what-you've-got. The lizards thought differently. The two viewpoints didn't quite overlap, and the lizards were far more concerned with being proportionally represented than having power.

He didn't always understand politics and he was glad of it. This was the point at which he preferred the order to go *there* and blow up *that*.

"We should have made a joint government a condition of building their cities," Boss Lizard added, almost as an afterthought. "Next time, we'll remember to do that."

They were born engineers, all procedure and ratios. Darman nodded and walked on, out into the heathland to the south of the settlement. Now he could see across the flat terrain for kilometers: smoke from scattered clusters of huts in the distance threaded its way into the clear sky, and the occasional ancient speeder tracked across his field of vision, throwing up range and speed data onto his HUD.

He thought of the aerial recce images of Eyat, with its modest defense resources preparing for an attack, and wondered how long it would take.

Where do I belong? Where's home?

It sure as *shab* wasn't Tipoca City. Most days he didn't even think it was Coruscant.

Darman stood watching the late-afternoon sun slanting across the heath, wondering what it was like to have a job where you could stop work at the end of the afternoon and do anything you liked, when the audio link came to life in his helmet.

"Niner to Dar, RTB. Seps incoming."

He activated his HUD displays, expecting to have data patched through to him. The image that filled his field of view was a chart of the Gaftikar system, way out near the Tingel Arm—so close to Qiilura, close enough that it would have taken only a few hours to reach Etain—and the peppering of red points of light showed Separatist vessels on a course for Gaftikar.

There were a few blue lights, too. They were generated by the transponders of Republic vessels: the Third and Fourth battalions of the 35th Infantry embarked in *Leveler*, another two companies from the same regiment not far out of Qiiluran space, and a fleet auxiliary converging on the same point at 180 degrees at sublight speeds.

"ETA?" Darman said. Life slipped immediately into acronyms and jargon, the language of the military comlink.

"At those speeds . . . a day."

"What's keeping them?"

"Officer commanding—some nonclone captain called Pellaeon—says it's brinkmanship."

"Back in ten . . ."

"We're digging in. Surveillance sat shows Eyat's bringing in fighters from outside."

"How many?"

"Six. And that might not be a problem for an assault ship but it's bad news for us, so get back here."

That, at least, answered Darman's question about what use Gaftikar was to anyone. Apart from the mining corporation's interests, it was just another handy place for a fight.

And they were sending in the mongrels now, nonclones, some of the service personnel from the fleet. *Pellaeon*. Who the *shab* was he? Darman wondered who the 35th's Jedi general might be, because it wasn't Etain.

She said they'd finished on Qiilura.

Whatever it was, wherever they were sending her, she could tell him, couldn't she? Maybe she didn't want to worry him. *Of course I'm worried. I'm always worried.* Ordo . . . yeah, he'd ask Ordo. Ordo always obliged, always got the messages and letters through somehow.

The rebel camp had taken on a different air by the time Darman got back, and he'd only been gone thirty minutes. The Marits had thinned out, and E-Webs and cannon stood concealed under camo netting. He sprinted for the main building, realizing even as he made for the doors that it was so flimsy he was better off outside.

"Sarge?" Darman clicked through the frequencies on his helmet link. "Sarge?"

"Ops room," Niner barked.

Darman entered, pulled off his helmet, and stood over the ops table, trying to get a better look at the holochart that

A'den had projected onto it. It showed the whole central region, with the scattered Marit villages and the occasional Gaftikari town, like small planets around suns. When he magnified Eyat and superimposed the latest aerial reconnaissance images on it, the sudden preparations became clear.

"That's as of fifteen minutes ago," A'den said.

Eyat's boundaries were ringed with vehicles and vessels, and there was no steady procession of civilians out of the city as was usual when attacks were expected. There was nowhere else for the Gaftikari to go. They were marooned on islands in an ocean of enemies. All they could do was dig in.

"You reckon they really know what's coming?" Atin asked. "I mean, *really* know?"

A'den, fully armored, tilted his head as if listening to a separate helmet comlink. "No. Not a clue."

"This is them reacting to the Seps reacting to our inbound ships, yes?"

"That's their only source of surveillance," said A'den. "I'm not sure who they're more worried about, us or the Marits. But they know we're coming, so I'm not prepared to risk a squad in there to prep the battlefield if we've got two battalions, a squadron of Torrents, and Captain Pellaeon's nice big cannons arriving within a day. Unless Eyat's got some hidden superweapon we failed to spot, the place is just one big target."

Darman still couldn't work out why the two task forces couldn't simply engage in space and leave the planet alone. But taking Eyat without a bit of muscle and cannons behind them meant very messy fighting if there was no air cover to make the point. He wasn't sure which was the worse outcome for the civilians.

"We're not really the main game in town now, are we?" Niner said. "Are we going forward with the Thirty-fifth?"

A'den must have switched his audio feed from *Leveler* to the general circuit, because Darman's helmet was suddenly full of the voice traffic between vessels. They seemed more concerned with keeping an eye on the Separatist flotilla, waiting for it to power up to hyperjump. A'den cut the link again and sat in silence, as if he was staring at the holochart lost in thought. He was waiting for instructions.

"Who's the Jedi in command?" Darman asked.

A'den looked up. "General Mas Missur. Did you want to stay on the circuit?"

"No . . ."

"It's that woman of yours, isn't it?"

"She wouldn't tell me where she was but she's been with Levet for some months, so yes—I want to know if she's with that flotilla and not telling me."

Personal business didn't matter on the brink of a battle, but nobody argued with him. A'den switched to another channel, head barely moving. Darman heard the slight pop as he switched, and he guessed the Null was on a secure link to someone, either finding out or asking why he'd been saddled with a commando who couldn't save his private life for off-duty hours.

"Levet says she's not with the Thirty-fifth and she's not in a combat zone," A'den said, unusually kindly. "So stop fussing."

Darman could have called her. He had a secure link: it wasn't as if he was going to give away a position to the enemy. He dithered, trying to decide whether to slip into the refreshers and comm her discreetly, just to be sure she wasn't somewhere even worse. He just wanted to tell her . . .

Niner, as ever, seemed to read his mind. He shoved Darman with his shoulder plate. "Go on," he said quietly. "Be quick about it, though."

Darman stepped out into the corridor, opened his helmet link with a couple of blinks, and voice-activated Etain's code. The display in his helmet told him what he could hear: NO RESPONSE. He carried on paging the system for a couple of minutes, telling himself she might have been taking a shower or even asleep, and then he left a message. It was hard to say the words to cold dead air instead of to her standing in front of him.

"It's me, *Et'ika,*" he said. "I never told you I love you."

When he closed the link he felt embarrassed, but he'd

done it, however inelegantly. If anything happened to him, at least she *knew.*

A'den and Niner walked out of the ops room, heads moving in a conversation that couldn't be heard outside their helmets. Fi and Atin followed. Darman's audio circuit popped again.

"Change of plan, Dar," Niner's voice said in his ear. "The general wants us to play forward air control. As soon as it gets dark, we'll move up to the outskirts and recce the positions of their mobile triple-A. Levet says *Leveler* will be on station a couple of hours before dawn."

"Lovely," said Fi. "It'll all be over in time for breakfast."

The squad spent the next hour or so stripping out the rental speeder to make room for a couple of E-Webs. Atin removed its ID transponder and poked an assortment of probes into it to scramble the registration details.

"Just in case we need to go right inside the city." He held up a small rectangle of plastoid. "We're going to have a hard job walking in dressed like this."

"I still think I should go in and blow the main power station," Darman said. "If only to give us the cover of complete darkness."

A'den wandered over to them, obviously eavesdropping on their circuit. "I'll be going in to place a few EMP charges in sensitive spots around their communications centers, because we don't want them chatting to the Seps once this kicks off. All you have to do is call in the air strikes. Okay? Once we've neutralized the big targets like their triple-A, and *Leveler*'s made a few holes in the infrastructure, then the Torrent squadron can provide air support for the Marits to go in. I don't want *any* of you deviating from that plan."

"Yeah, where are the lizards?" Fi asked, straightening up. "I thought this was their big night."

"Oh, they're all here . . ."

It was almost dark now, and when Darman looked toward Eyat, he couldn't see the city. In the last few nights, he'd got used to the glow from its street lighting, all the more noticeable for being set in the middle of an unlit rural location. But it was in darkness tonight. He flicked his visor through its magnification and night-vision settings and still couldn't see much. Even in infrared, it was just a faint green flattened dome of heat.

"They've switched off the lighting," he said. "They're expecting air raids."

"Shame that they're going to get creamed," Fi said. "It looked like such a nice place."

Nobody said it, but Darman thought it: there was no reason to fight here, beyond the fact that the Republic had staked a claim by way of supporting the Marits, and so the Separatists felt they had to front up, too. Darman wondered if it was treason to think that way, or just a difference of opinion on strategy.

"I wonder where Sull is now," he said, but nobody answered. He glanced over his shoulder at the scrubby woodland to one side of the camp, night-vision visor still in place, and thought it was malfunctioning until he realized the points of light—thousands of them, as if the display had massive interference—were actually *eyes*.

It was the Marits. Suddenly, they were an army, silent and motionless, waiting for the signal to kill.

Seven kilometers south of Tropix island, 478 days after Geonosis

Mereel stepped out of the drained-down air lock in his briefs and pulled the aquata breather from his mouth. Then he shook himself like Mird, showering water across the cargo bay, and slapped a cold wet skull into Vau's hands.

"If we're going to run DNA tests," he said, "this seems to have teeth in it." Skirata handed him a towel, and he rubbed himself down. "Not a shred of meat or clothing on the thing. Whoever it was, I'm guessing that they were stripped of any identification and tied to an anchor so that the body wouldn't float to the surface and so the local wildlife could remove soft tissue and everything else that identified him. It's a *him,* by the way. Had a look at the pelvis."

"Killed first?" Vau turned the skull over in his hands while Mird watched. It might have mattered; a disposal was a different crime and motivation than weighting someone down to drown. Not all humanoids drowned fast, either. "Or punishment?"

Skirata shrugged. "I don't think he died of old age, so it's probably irrelevant."

Mereel looked anxious for a moment, as if he'd let Skirata down simply by being unable to give him an answer. "I can't tell, *Kal'buir.* No obvious fractures or marks on the bones."

"It's okay, son. Get dressed, 'cos we need to carry on looking."

Mereel padded off, hitting the heel of his hand against his ear to shake out the last of the water. They needed proper diving suits if they were going to work outside the hull for any lengthy period. Vau put it on his list of things to acquire.

"I'm going to guess," he said, "and you know I don't do that very often, but I bet we'll find this is the last person to see Ko Sai."

"What makes you say that?"

"The Twi'lek. He delivered the equipment to whoever was piloting the barge, and if that had been a Kaminoan, he'd have noticed. Someone had to hand the stuff over, which meant seeing her or the location. Not someone a crafty piece of work like Ko Sai would have wanted around to blow her cover."

Skirata swabbed down the water on the deck. "When we go ashore again, I'll see if any staff went missing. I can't see Ko Sai having a human sidekick."

"Well, maybe she didn't—not for long, anyway." Vau listened carefully and caught a faint beeping. "Is that the cockpit alarm?"

Skirata paused and straightened up, frowning. His hearing had taken a pounding from standing too close to artillery over the years, even though he managed to hide the fact.

"Unless you know it *isn't,* why are you standing around asking the question?"

They made for the cockpit, but Mereel was already leaning across the pilot's seat, talking to a familiar voice on the other end of the open comm. Vau caught the word *Delta* just as he squeezed into the compartment.

"It's General Jusik," Mereel said. "Delta are on their way here. Want to talk to him, *Kal'buir?*"

"Osik." Skirata raked his fingers through his hair. "What happened, *Bard'ika?*"

"They caught up with the Twi'lek pilot. Not much I could do, but at least I stopped him from giving them too much detail."

"What did you do, shoot him before he could talk?"

"Bit of the old Jedi magic. He got as far as saying he'd told some Mandalorians about Dorumaa, so I suggested they'd been wearing green armor. If he'd said gold, and black, and . . . well, Delta know your armor, Kal."

Skirata closed his eyes. "Thanks."

"And I made sure he didn't get as far as giving them coordinates for the drop. But they know it's Dorumaa, and they've had to divert to pick up some scuba armor. I estimate you've got ten to twelve hours, but I'm going to be there in six."

Vau cut in. "To do what, exactly? Not that we don't appreciate your assistance, but—"

"You haven't found Ko Sai yet, have you?"

"We're close," Skirata said.

"Well, if you haven't found her in six hours, I'll *help* you."

Vau nudged Skirata in the ribs. "And if we haven't found her by the time Delta get here, you keep them busy. How are they planning to insert, anyway?"

"Land during the night and just pose as sport divers if they have to."

"Thanks, *Bard'ika.*"

They couldn't have expected Delta to be far behind. The problem with hunting for someone was that the hunt itself tended to bring debris to the surface, and even if Delta didn't quite have the Nulls' remarkable access to information, they'd been trained in the same techniques. Vau felt a little flush of pride that his squad hadn't done so badly compared with Skirata's precious boys and all their genetic enhancements, but he decided not to rub it in.

"Come on," Skirata said wearily. "More caves to ping." He settled down in the copilot's seat.

Whatever differences Vau had with him, the man had an extraordinary tenacity; the size of the task ahead was so huge, the chances so flimsy, that any sane individual would never have bothered to start. It wasn't just a matter of finding one Kaminoan who didn't want to be found. Vau wondered if she was even capable of doing what Skirata wanted.

If this is all a wasted effort . . . how's the little chakaar *going to take it?*

The quest—oh yes, it *was* a quest, a sacred calling for Skirata now—seemed to sustain him. It was as powerful as religion. He was so fixed on his boys' welfare that he seemed to have no plans for himself, and his definition of who qualified as *his boys* was now so all-encompassing that it seemed in danger of sucking him dry. It was more than the Nulls, who had been his sons in fact if not in name from the day he met them. His obsession had then spread to the commandos, and now to any stray trooper who came into his orbit, like Corr. It was as if Skirata was desperate to avoid any thought of himself, to erase himself in every waking moment.

Maybe his memories were unhappier than Vau knew; he seemed to be reinventing himself a day at a time, and he rarely talked about his past now, not even his father.

He never talks about his mother. And apart from the knife—does he recall anything of his birth parents?

Toxic things though they were, Vau still found families interesting. The best thing he'd ever done was to run away from his own. As if on cue, Mird appeared at his side and clambered onto his lap, the only family he had, and maybe the best kind.

"Did you ever think of asking Arkanian Micro to take a look at some clone tissue?" Vau asked. "Just in case."

"I did." Skirata was staring straight ahead at the shifting three-dimensional display of the sonar mapping scanner, reflected onto the transparisteel viewport. "But it'll be my very last resort. Once they have a genome to play with . . . well, I don't want to see any more lads bred to die."

"What if they hadn't been Jango's clones?"

"What?"

"*Mando'ade* don't care about bloodlines. What if they'd been from a Corellian donor, or a Kuati? Would it still tear you up to see them used?"

Mereel seemed to be making a point of staying out of the conversation. Skirata sucked his teeth thoughtfully.

"If I'd met them as little kids about to be exterminated, I think I'd have done the same." He looked distracted by the idea, as if he hadn't ever considered it. "Being Jango's blood just made it more relevant. But Jango or not, they'd still have needed a sense of belonging, wouldn't they? And it would still have been my duty to give it to them. And that would have made them *Mando'ade*."

"Interesting formations ahead," Mereel said. Vau thought he might be trying to change the subject, but maybe not. "Going in for a closer look."

Vau looked at Mereel in profile and tried to see Jango in him, but it was surprisingly hard. Odd as that might have sounded to an outsider, it was true: the clones usually didn't remind him of Jango Fett at all. Part of that was living among them for years, and becoming blind to the superficiality of appearance, but there were many ways in which they didn't even look like their progenitor. Jango—born of parents who lived hand-to-mouth, undernourished as a youngster—hadn't been much taller than Skirata, but the Kaminoans had managed the clones' nutrition carefully from the day the egg was fertilized, and they'd turned out tall and muscular. In a hundred and more ways, they *weren't* exact replicas of Fett.

Nor was his son, Boba. Poor kid: it was a terrible age to lose a father, and the boy had nobody else in his life. He was worse off than any trooper. If he managed to survive, Vau predicted he'd turn into the hardest, most bitter, most messed-up *shabuir* this side of Keldabe.

Even I had a second father to adopt me . . . too late, maybe, but better than never . . .

"What's that?" Skirata said suddenly. He pointed forward. "Lots of debris."

They were on the northwest quadrant of the island's shelf, and the slope on their starboard side was pocked with dark depressions that could have been caves. Strewn across the smooth seabed was a sharply delineated area of small fragments. They were visible even in the filtered sunlight, but when Mereel directed the external lamp ahead of the vessel they stood out in sharp relief.

"That's not a rockfall," he said. "If it was scree, it'd cover the whole area from the foot of the slope, because it *slides*. But there's a gap, about ten meters. Rock doesn't jump, does it?"

Mereel brought *Aay'han* up twenty meters and maneuvered to a dead stop right above the debris. From the exterior holocams, the aerial view projected onto the cockpit monitor reminded Vau of a bag of flour dropped on a clean floor.

"Relatively recent, too," Skirata said. "Or the silt would have covered it."

"Looks like someone dropped a load of spoil from an excavation a long time after the island was terraformed."

Vau actually felt excited. It was an odd hunt, but every bit as exhilarating as a chase. Mird picked up on his excitement and slid off his lap, rumbling in anticipation. "It's very tempting," Vau said, "to work out a direction of travel from the shape of that spoil . . ."

The three men looked at one another.

"Let's go for it," Mereel said, with a big grin.

They were above the fifty-meter limit now, and as *Aay'han* circled slowly above the island shelf, the sensors picked up the throb of drives and the churning sounds of propulsion units from submersibles and surface vessels exploring the turquoise shallows. The scan showed them as points of light, most of them well within the ten-kilometer safety zone. They wouldn't be disturbed down here.

"I never completed the diving course," Skirata said suddenly. "I just thought you ought to know that."

"Might not even need to get our feet wet, *Kal'buir.*" Mereel took *Aay'han* deeper, facing the submerged cliff. "Look at the three-D scan."

Head-on, the sonar showed a complex pattern of holes, although none of them seemed to extend far into the rock. But there was an overhang that was more or less in line with the patch of debris. Mereel skimmed the seabed, stirring silt into the clear water, and came in close to the jutting shelf of weed-coated rock.

And there it was. From this angle, the scan picked up a deep tunnel, mostly hidden from casual inspection by the overhang, but now visible as a rectangular shaft with rounded corners and an aperture about eight meters by five. *Aay'han* had a twenty-meter beam.

"Well." Skirata shrugged. "We can't just drive in, can we?"

"You're so *nautical,*" Vau said.

Mereel still had that grin on his face. "There's always the chance we'll find that it's only a waste outlet, and that there's a hungry thing twice the size of a dianoga living in there."

"Let's find out."

"If Ko Sai's in there, then she'll be using transport to get in and out. Let's head back to the resort and see what they've got for rental."

"This means diving, doesn't it?"

"Not necessarily, *Kal'buir.*"

Whatever Mereel had in mind, it amused him. Dangerous things usually did. Vau raised an eyebrow. "I'll put Mird ashore, if that's okay with you."

"Trust me," said Mereel.

Aay'han surfaced well clear of the harbor and skimmed through the gap in the breakwaters toward her berth. As they drew nearer to the pontoons and slowed almost to a stop to come alongside, Mereel pointed across the water.

"*That's* what we need," he said. "I *knew* they'd have them here. *Perfect.*"

Vau and Skirata followed his finger, but Vau could see nothing except choppy waves. Then something broke from the surface, like a Whaladon breaching, and arced three meters into the air before crashing back into the sea again. At first, Vau thought it was an enormous silver fish, but by the time it had progressed across the harbor in extravagant, corkscrewing leaps, he'd managed to focus on the thing long enough to see that it was an extraordinary ship shaped like a firaxa shark, minus the head fin. It was five sleek meters long with a brilliant scarlet flash on one flank and the words WAVE-CHASER picked out in gold.

Fierfek, it looked like fun. Vau could barely recall *fun.* The craft would also fit neatly through the entrance to what he hoped was Ko Sai's laboratory, as well as *Aay'han*'s cargo hatch.

"Let's go rent one," Mereel said. "They're two-seaters and they've got a top speed of twenty-five kilometers an hour. Not that I researched them earlier, of course."

Skirata just looked blank. It was the expression he wore when he wanted to say *nu draar*—the most vividly emphatic of *Mando'a* refusals—but felt he had to keep up appearances. "*One.*"

"Someone has to pilot *Aay'han,* because those things won't have much range," Vau said. "And I'm volunteering. I had my midlife crisis about ten years ago, so you can go play boy racer this time, Kal . . ."

"*Shabuir,*" Skirata muttered, but he looked nervous.

The Wavechasers turned out to be for sale or rent. Price had long since ceased to be an issue for any of them now that time was the rarest and most precious thing imaginable, so Skirata bought one.

"Handy runabout for *Aay'han,*" he said, staring at his boots. "And if we dent the thing, we won't have any explaining to do to the rental office." Then he looked up at Mereel, a head taller than him, and slapped the passcard in the

Null's palm. "All yours, son. High time you owned something *nice.*"

Vau was usually immune to Skirata's polar extremes of emotion, but for a few seconds the old *chakaar* and his surrogate son simply looked at each other as if there was nothing else that mattered in the galaxy, and Vau felt genuine envy.

It wasn't Skirata he envied. It was Mereel, for having a father who doted on him so much that he could do no wrong. Like time, it was something his wealth had never bought him.

11

*There's one thing that bothers me, sir. They say Master Yoda
referred to the war as the* Clone War *right after the Battle
of Geonosis. It was the very first battle of the war. Why did
he identify the war that way, by the clones who are fighting
it? Have we ever said* the Fifth Fleet War *or the* Corellian
Baji Brigade War? *What does he know that we don't?*
—General Bardan Jusik, confiding in General Arligan Zey

**Shuttle, en route for Dorumaa from Qiilura,
478 days after Geonosis**

"**W**hat does *cyar'ika* mean?" Etain asked, gazing at something in the palm of her hand.

Ordo could guess where this was heading, and as they were stuck in the cockpit of a small shuttle he had no option but to have a conversation. He was afraid things would stray into areas where he felt woefully ignorant, and not having the answers always troubled him. He expected to be perfect.

"It means 'darling,' " he said. "Sweetheart. Beloved. Dearest."

Etain swallowed audibly and didn't look up. "And it's okay for a woman to use that word to a man?"

"You can use it to anyone," Ordo said. Ah, she was groping her way through the minefield of a relationship in a foreign language. "Anyone or anything you love. Child, spouse, pet, parent."

"Oh." There was a slight drop in her tone as if she hadn't expected to hear that. "Okay."

"If Darman uses it, it's not because he regards you as his strill, General . . ."

She made a little sound as if she was trying to laugh but had forgotten how. "So does everyone else know about the baby except Dar?"

"Just *Kal'buir,* Sergeant Vau, and my brothers. And *Bard'ika,* obviously." Ordo respected Jusik's ability to sit on the news for as long as he had, but it made him wonder what else the Jedi didn't tell him. He longed for a day when none of this subterfuge was necessary. "Because we have a duty to look after you."

"I—I appreciate your concern."

"No pain?"

"No."

"Any more bleeding?"

"No . . . Bardan knew before I told Kal, actually. He sensed it." She let out a long sigh and clasped her hands on her belly as if it were much larger than it actually was. "Is he still angry with me?"

"You'd know if he was. *Kal'buir* just tries too hard to put the galaxy right for us, but it can't be done, and it isn't his job to do it now that we're grown men."

"Have you ever told him that?"

"Not in those words, exactly."

"So you're scared of him, too."

"No. I'm scared of not being worthy of him."

"No pressure, then . . ."

It was hard when someone devoted their entire life to your welfare, a mounting debt that never got paid. Ordo wanted to see *Kal'buir* get a decent night's sleep in a proper bed, and have his ankle fixed. He wanted him to find a nice woman to take care of him; in fact, he wanted all the things for his *buir* that the man wanted for his sons, more or less. "I'd better warn him we're coming when we drop out of hyperspace."

"Why didn't you call him earlier?"

"Because he would have told me to take you back to Coruscant, and I would never disobey him."

"Even if he's wrong?"

Ordo didn't always agree with Skirata, but that was a long way from his *being wrong*. "He needs me there."

"And am I going to be any use like this?"

"You don't have to be useful."

"What's the big deal with Dorumaa anyway? Because I know Kal would never take a leave, let alone in the middle of a war."

There was no point keeping it from her. She'd find out as soon as they touched down. "Ko Sai."

"What about her?"

"I think they've found her, and that means her research, too."

Etain was suddenly very quiet. He could hear her breathing but kept his eyes on the streaked starscape in front of him.

"Kal wasn't just ranting, then."

"No." She didn't understand him at all. "Mereel has been tracking her for months. Unfortunately . . ." Ordo wondered whether it was wise to tell her that Jusik had tipped off Skirata. It wasn't. If they wanted to confide in each other as Jedi, that was up to *Bard'ika*. "Unfortunately, Delta caught up with one of his informants and so they're heading for Dorumaa, too, on the Chancellor's personal orders to capture her."

This time he did glance at Etain, and she looked like a scared child. Her mouth was slightly open and she was an awful color, almost gray; he should never have mentioned it. The last thing she needed in her state was another thing to fret about, but if she didn't worry about it now, she'd have to worry about it when they landed, and he couldn't possibly have left her on Qiilura any longer to do more worrying with only the shapeshifters for company.

"You really are crazy, aren't you?" Etain said.

"Me personally?"

"Kal and the Nulls going up against Delta . . . and defying Palpatine?"

He struggled to reassure her. "We're not *fighting* Delta. We're just getting there first. No harm done."

"Ordo, this private-army thing has to stop. You can't do this. You'll end up being shot for treason."

That rang all the wrong bells with Ordo. She might have said it as a general warning, but it was a little too close to the hidden reality of Sull and the other ARC troopers who wanted out of the GAR.

"So you know they put us down like animals, do you?"

"I was just—"

He wanted to put it to her straight: did the Jedi know about executions? Did they ever discuss what went on once the battles were over? But he knew *Kal'buir* would be angry if he raised Etain's blood pressure and harmed the child, so he bit his lip—literally—and let his anger and mistrust pass.

She's just a kid. She's just like Bard'ika, *only not as confident and as good at the job. You* have *to back off.*

It was a physical effort to shut up. Ordo could taste salt and metal, blood wet on his lip. "I'm sorry." He focused on what Skirata would want and fought down the impulse to take out his resentment and frustration on Etain, not because it was unfair but because it might lead to events that would upset *Kal'buir* and Darman. He wanted to ask her why only a handful of Jedi objected to a slave army, and why they could claim to believe in the sanctity of all life and yet treat some life as being exempt from that respect. It was a question he should have put to Zey, too. Instead he parted his lips and heard himself say, "Let's change the subject. If Besany's offered to cook dinner for me, does she mean dinner, or . . ."

He trailed off. Etain was staring at him with the look of someone who'd seen a terrible accident, and he had no idea how to phrase the question anyway, but he did want to know the answer. The width of the cockpit was just over two meters. Etain reached across and grabbed his arm so hard that he flinched.

"Can we roll this back a bit, Ordo? Please? Who's putting down clones? Does Zey know about this?"

He didn't have to be Force-sensitive to know she was disturbed by what he'd said. "Seeing as it's ARC troopers being hunted down by covert ops troopers, maybe Zey *authorizes* it, even if they're not all in his chain of command. He wasn't slow to give the nod to *Kal'buir* to carry out illegal assassinations that can't be traced back to him, was he?" Ordo wiped his lip on the back of his hand. "I just don't know. And I shouldn't have told you."

"But you *did,* and now I'm mad about it."

"Nobody leaves the Grand Army except in a body bag, Etain." He decided to soften the impact by dropping her rank, which would have sounded like an accusation right then. "Once that story gets around, what do you think that'll do to loyalty, let alone morale?"

Etain seemed to be framing difficult words. "Ordo, I can't help being a Jedi. I never had any more choice than you did, and I can't turn off my Force abilities any more than you can switch off your brain. So you scare me, because I can sense the dark side in you, all the violence and anger, but it's all pushed down, and I just wonder when you're finally going to erupt and lose control."

It was nothing he didn't know already. *Kal'buir* said you couldn't breed men the way the Kaminoans did and expect anything else—and the aiwha-bait had no interest in producing happy, well-adjusted clones, just lethal and disciplined ones. It wasn't as if they were going to be around long enough to ponder the meaning of their existence and work out that they'd had a raw deal.

Is that what Besany sees? A psycho? She never seems afraid of me. Would she say if she was?

"Etain, you're not responsible for the whole Jedi Order," he said. "But I don't feel much when I kill, because it's just something that needs doing, and I don't kill for fun. I don't even think all life deserves respect. All I care about is me and mine. If that means killing some more, I won't lose any sleep."

"If it helps," Etain said, "I reached the point where I didn't care how many farmers got killed on Qiilura as long as no more of my troops did. I don't think the Jedi Council would

approve of that, but I'll learn to live with it. I think they justify turning a blind eye to the reality of the army by the in-
verse process."

As small talk went, it was one of the worst experiences
Ordo had ever had. He had nothing more to say, and swiveled
a few degrees in his seat to check the course and revise the
deceleration point to drop out of hyperspace. No wonder
Mandalorians had generally taken the Separatist side in this
war: the Republic was rotting from the core outward, soft
and corrupt, detached from everything outside the orbit of
Coruscant unless it could milk it dry. But taking out his disgust on a frightened, pregnant girl who was as disenfranchised as he was—*disenfranchised,* that was it—wasn't the
Mando way. Ordo felt deeply ashamed, as if his anger had
been an entirely separate person for those few moments, not
even part of him. He always did when it got the better of him.
Etain had a point.

"What are you going to do if Venku turns out to be Force-
sensitive?" he asked, striving for a truce.

"He will be." Etain patted her belly. "I can tell. And I
won't let him be taken like I was. I'll teach him how to handle the powers he develops, if Kal will let me, but he won't
be a Jedi. I don't need Kal to forbid me."

"Did you realize he'll probably have a normal life span?"

"Sorry?"

"Mereel's been slicing the data from Tipoca for a while, to
see which genes they were targeting in the accelerated aging
process."

"I had no idea you were doing this."

"Not something we'd want to advertise, is it?"

"Tell me. Please. I need to know."

"Some of the genes they use to accelerate aging are recessive, and others have to be switched on and off chemically.
The *kaminiise* tailored us at every stage, you see. If we were
hybrid plants, they'd say we didn't breed true. That's the interesting thing about epigenetics—"

Ordo stopped dead because Etain had put her hand to her
mouth and her eyes were screwed tight shut. His immediate

thought was that she was miscarrying, and while he would never use the word *panic,* he was stuck between systems in a small shuttle with just a first-aid kit and his eidetic recall of the medbay manual.

Then he realized she was crying, and trying not to sob out loud. She'd never struck him as the crying type. *Kal'buir* would have rushed to comfort her, but Ordo wasn't quite up to that. Eventually she opened her eyes and wiped her face with the sleeve of her frayed brown Jedi robe.

"I'm sorry," she said. "I've worried about that so much. Kal's right—outliving your children is the worst thing imaginable. I can handle whatever comes down the line as long as Venku gets a normal life span."

"Trust me, the aiwha-bait wouldn't want their rivals to be able to just *breed* clone characteristics like that—they'd want *total* control over their product. But Mereel's getting very adept at this, so he knows what to test for."

The relief was transformational. Etain's pinched little face softened into something approaching prettiness, and she settled back in the copilot's seat with a beatific smile on her lips. Ordo thought of all the times that *Kal'buir* had told him how being a father to the Nulls had been his salvation; maybe it would be the same for him, although he had a range of mountains to climb before that could even be mentioned to Besany Wennen, who he had never even kissed, despite the strong bond between them.

"Do you think Kal ever wonders where his first family is?" Etain asked. "It seems so unfair on him. He'd been divorced for years."

It was a delicate point, the one secret that Kal had kept from his Null boys: that his biological sons had declared him *dar'buir*—no longer a father, parental divorce *Mando*-style—when he vanished from the galaxy with the rest of the Mandalorian training sergeants. The army-in-waiting on Kamino was so secret that they could tell nobody where they'd gone.

Yes, Skirata's sons still denounced him for vanishing, even

though they would have been grown men themselves by that time. Two sons and a daughter: Tor, Ijaat, and Ruusaan.

"He gave them every spare credit he had after the divorce," Ordo said. "For years. It's why he had to accept the Kamino contract."

"Mandalorians take family duties to extremes, don't they?"

"It beats the alternative."

"Ordo, whatever arguments I've had with Kal, I respect his commitment to you all. I'm not sure I'd have had the guts to let my kids denounce me rather than tell them about the clone program."

"It's hard to live with being the cause of that."

"Maybe, but to have someone care about your welfare that much is a wonderful thing."

Etain and Jusik were the only Jedi Ordo had met who seemed to yearn for the imagined family they'd been taken from, because Zey, Camas, and Mas Missur seemed perfectly content with their lot in life, and so did all the little Padawans who danced attendance on them. For all Etain knew, her mother could have been a religious fanatic and her father a domineering brute, like Walon Vau's parents. Maybe the Jedi had done her a favor. She'd never know.

"Not much farther," he said, struggling to learn unfamiliar social skills. "Then I can comm *Kal'buir* and we'll find you somewhere relaxing while we get on with the business."

"You know what would make me feel better, Ordo?"

Ah, a lifeline. He grabbed it. "Just say."

"I'd like to know exactly where Darman is and what's happening to him. I used to be able to call or at least get information from Brigade HQ, but it's hard to talk to him without feeling that urge to tell him about Venku."

"I'll check as soon as we drop below light speed."

"Thank you."

"No trouble at all."

"And she doesn't just mean dinner."

"Who doesn't?"

"Besany. You asked."

"Ah. So I did."

Ordo debated whether to call in advice from Mereel, who was the expert on that sort of thing, and suddenly found that the neon indicators on the shuttle's console were absolutely riveting at times like this. Eventually he brought the vessel down to sublight velocity to drop out of the Corellian Run, and the galaxy came to a crash stop as the stars snapped back into points of light. However many times he did it, he still felt as if he were falling forward for a few moments afterward. He corrected the course for Dorumaa and took out his comlink.

"Before you ask, *Kal'buir*," he said, "Etain's better. No more bleeding or pain."

Skirata sounded breathless. "Where are you?"

"Not on Qiilura . . ."

"Did something go wrong?"

"No, but Etain can rest more comfortably on Dorumaa than she can on Qiilura. Levet's finished up there and you need all the help you can get."

"You're a naughty boy, *Ord'ika*."

"I'm sorry, *Buir*."

"Ahh, c'mon." There was a loud grunt as if someone had winded Skirata in a fight, then a series of hollow thuds. "You know I'm always happier when you're around."

"Mind my asking what you're doing?"

"Mereel's got a brand-new toy for hunting *kaminiise*. It made me throw up. We're just practicing with it."

Ordo tried to imagine a weapon that would turn Skirata's durasteel stomach. "Any news?"

"Oh yes. It's just a matter of infiltration."

"She's there?" The elation made his stomach lurch. "Is that confirmed?"

"High probability. Not certainty."

"When are we going in?"

"Right now."

But the shuttle was still a couple of hours away from Dorumaa. Ordo took a moment to register that and felt oddly betrayed, then instantly ashamed at harboring even the slightest resentment. *My father's putting himself on the line again to save us, just like he did when we were kids. I don't have the right to be annoyed.* He summoned up all the acting skills he'd learned while passing himself off as Trooper Corr so as not to ruin Skirata's moment of triumph.

"Be careful, *Kal'buir*. She won't be alone."

"*She's* the one who needs to be careful. *I'm* the one with the tatsushi recipes."

"We'll get there as soon as we can."

"I'm sorry we can't wait for you, son. Delta's going be here in less than a day."

"I understand. Where's *Bard'ika* now?"

"On his way to divert Delta when they get here, just in case."

"Have you identified a place to hold Ko Sai while we persuade her to our way of thinking?"

"Plan is to get her offworld as soon as we can. I was thinking of Mandalore. Rav Bralor owes me one. So does Vhonte Tervho. There are still some *Cuy'val Dar* around."

"Better transmit the location and an RV point in case you've banged out by the time we land."

"Will do. I'm sorry I haven't been keeping up with the squads. When we get this *shabuir*, I'm going to take a little time to check in with them all."

"Tell Mereel to enjoy his toy, whatever it is."

Ordo hoped his disappointment didn't show on his face. But Etain was a Jedi, and she didn't need body language to work out that kind of thing.

"I've never hated anyone like that," she said. "We're not supposed to have extreme passions, we Jedi."

"It's probably better that I'm not there when they find her." Ko Sai decided which clones met quality control standards and which didn't. She'd passed a death sentence on him and his brothers, two years into their lives; Mereel would discuss the many ways he wanted to kill her. "Extermination is rather personal."

"He's not joking about the recipes, is he?"

"What makes you say that?"

"Mandos." The borrowed slang sounded odd in that formal little Jedi voice she had. "They—you like your trophies. You keep armor from dead loved ones. I hear some wear scalps and . . . other things on their belts."

That was how *aruetiise* saw Mandalorians, then: savages, but handy when you needed them to fight for you. No wonder clones latched on to that identity so easily. "There was a time when we couldn't bury our dead—or anyone else's. But I'm not sure we ever descended into cannibalism. Loud drinking songs, perhaps." It was always sobering to hear a stereotype of yourself. "I'm told *kaminii* tastes like jaal flesh, though, a blend of meat and fish."

Judging by her expression, it took Etain a few seconds to work out that he was joking. But the body was a shell, a thing for doing deeds and passing on knowledge, and once its purpose was completed it didn't seem to matter if it was buried, eaten, or left for the scavengers.

Ordo wanted to savor life for as long as the next being, but part of him was relieved by the thought that if he didn't outlive his father, he would be spared the pain of losing him one day. It was a selfish thought. Life without *Kal'buir* was unimaginable.

"Funny, I lost my taste for meat when I became pregnant," Etain said.

They were in enemy space now. Ordo browsed through a stack of false identichips and inserted one into his datapad to reprogram it with new details. He'd posed as Etain's partner before on surveillance; they could even act like a jaded couple who'd run out of things to discover about each other.

Etain studied the information on the new woman she'd be on Dorumaa. "If you and Besany marry, she'll have to do the whole *Mando* thing, won't she?"

Ordo avoided thinking that far ahead. "Eating prisoners and wearing their teeth for necklaces, you mean?"

"Seriously. It just occurred to me that . . . well, I have to do it, too. For Dar. Guaranteed to upset the Jedi Masters, that."

"You'll have some catching up to do with *Bard'ika*."

"What's expected of a Mandalorian wife?"

"Fight for eight hours, stop to give birth, then have your old man's dinner on the table. Except on your day off, of course."

"Seriously . . ."

"It can be a very hard life. Nothing that would faze a Jedi like you, though. Just get used to braiding your hair. Fits under a helmet better, I'm told."

Jedi had more in common with *Mando'ade* than they wanted to admit. Ordo watched the chrono with growing frustration, hoped that *Kal'buir* might run an hour or so late so they could be there for the abduction, and decided that if the Dorumaa visit was scrubbed, the best place for Etain to hide until the birth was Mandalore.

Skirata could always persuade Zey that she needed a few months to check out whether the Seps were getting *beskar*, super-resistant Mandalorian iron, from Keldabe. Zey knew when not to ask too many questions.

He certainly hadn't asked them about ARC trooper A-30, Sull.

Island shelf, approximately nine kilometers from
Tropix island, Dorumaa, 478 days after Geonosis

Skirata checked his weapons with a ritual that had been unconscious habit since he was six years old, when Munin Skirata had found him cowering in the ruins of a bombed building on Surcaris, clutching his dead father's three-sided knife.

The weapons had changed over the years: technology, credits, and experience meant that he now favored small and silent kit, especially if working in *aruetyc* clothing. But now he was armored for combat. He wanted Ko Sai to understand that she was dealing with *Mando'ade*.

There was also the possibility that she had protection. Those droids that the Twi'lek had transported had to go somewhere, and there was no telling what countermeasures were waiting down in her lair.

Assume the worst.

If it did turn out to be just a dianoga lurking in a sewage vent, he was determined that the disappointment wouldn't slow him down for one single heartbeat. He'd get back on the hunt, because that loathsome *gihaal* had definitely passed through this planet. He could feel it.

But it would be nice not to have to keep dodging Zey. I'm tired of kissing his shebs. *I'm tired of the Republic.*

"Tight fit?" Mereel said. He seemed to be having the time of his life, and Skirata was glad to know the boy could find joy in the most unlikely situations. "Not really built for two men in armor, is it?"

Skirata went through the litany—knife in his forearm plate ejector, short-track Verpine shatter gun, custom WES-TAR blaster, knuckle-dusters, durasteel chain. He didn't count the stun grenades and ordnance in his belt pouches, just the small self-defense items.

"Throwing up in a helmet isn't something I'd recommend, no . . ."

"You haven't—"

"I came close."

"I'll try not to roll her too much."

"Ko Sai?"

"This ship."

"Ah." It was definitely the roll, that corkscrew movement, that made his stomach run for the exit. "Where did you get the harpoon gun?"

"It was in *Aay'han*'s tool locker."

Yes, Mereel was on top form. And he really hated Ko Sai. Skirata loved his sons without reservation, but sometimes they made him nervous, and their phenomenal intellects were no guarantee that—just occasionally—they wouldn't get out of control.

It's a miracle they're this normal. But I'll be ready to step in if he loses it with her.

The Wavechaser's two seats were set one behind the other, as in a gunship cockpit, and there was a small cargo compartment abaft—around four cubic meters—for small items like food and diving equipment. It was just a sport vessel. Transferring Ko Sai to a suitable location for a nice friendly chat was going to be a logistics challenge, but the whole craft was under two meters wide, and that meant it could pass through the air lock with its hydroplanes folded. *Shab,* if it came to it, he'd stun the aiwha-bait with the butt of his blaster, shove an aquata breather in her mouth, and haul her underwater if he had to.

One way or another, Ko Sai wasn't walking out of here.

Vau followed at a discreet distance in *Aay'han.* Skirata only knew where he was because the blip showed on his HUD display, and Vau was on the comlink circuit. There was no turning around in this cramped cockpit to take a look.

The *chakaar* seemed to be making a pretty good job of piloting her, too.

"Don't damage that boat, Walon," Skirata said.

"Ah, you're *learning.*" Vau seemed horribly cheerful today. Maybe he disliked Ko Sai more than Skirata knew. "It is indeed a *boat* in this mode. Not a ship."

"When did you get to be such a stickler for naval terminology?"

"My father was an admiral in the Imperial Irmenu Navy." Vau had a special contemptuous drawl that he reserved for references to his original family, a way of dragging the air over his larynx and swirling the sound around his sinuses so that it emerged like metal scraping across brickwork. It always put Skirata's teeth on edge. Hatred had its own sound. "Did I ever mention that? Ceremonial uniform like the drapes in a Hutt bordello and a vibroblade five centuries old. I wanted to join up, you know. He said I wasn't good enough."

"But the *Mando* navy will take any old *osik,* right?"

"Have we ever had a seagoing navy?"

"Our own, or one we borrowed? Why, do you want to buy one?"

"Just curious. Making small talk before I tell you that I managed to slice into the Dorumaa utilities mainframe, and the supply grid shows a rather extravagant amount of power being piped to a location that would, were I to map it onto a chart, line up pretty well with the area around the cave entrance."

Mereel chuckled. "Maybe the dianoga watches a lot of HoloNet."

Skirata smiled. "Lady needs a lot of lighting, refrigeration, autoclave, and computing power for cloning research, I'd say . . . is there any other large facility on the surface at that point?"

"Just the bolo-ball field, and that isn't eating a lot of power. Not like pumps . . . lighting . . . refrigeration . . . you get the picture."

"Oya!" Seasick or not, Skirata's hunt had now acquired a celebratory atmosphere, and he hoped this wasn't overconfidence.

Oya. Let's hunt.

It was such a small word, but it was embedded in the Mandalorian psyche as everything positive in life: from *let's go* to *good luck* to *well done* to . . . *it's the best news I've had in ages.*

The Wavechaser had no built-in sonar or external holocams, so once they were in position they navigated by chart and Mark One Eyeball, as he liked to call it. The vessel— now nicknamed *Gi'ka,* Little Fish—slipped into the shadow of the rock overhang and lined up with the slot-like tunnel.

"Did you check how deep this thing can go?" Skirata asked, noting the occasional creak from the hull.

"Crush depth?"

"That's such a depressing term, son."

"Two hundred meters. No problem. *Udesii.*"

"Okay."

"Hand me the sensor."

It was easier said than done. Skirata squeezed it past the gap between Mereel's shoulder and the bulkhead so he could grab it. Skirata was still mentally rehearsing the drill for getting his helmet off and inserting the aquata breather if the hull was breached, accepting that water bothered him a lot.

Mereel aimed the sensor, a small sonar gun, and an icon of

the readout appeared in Skirata's HUD. *Worth every cred. I should have had this upgrade years ago.* When he magnified the image, it looked like a dead end deep inside the shaft, unnaturally smooth, and if the calibration was right, then it was nearly a hundred meters long.

"My bet," Mereel said, "is that this is a sump, as in cave exploration, but *designed* as a barrier." He took a deep breath: so *Mer'ika* wasn't as confident as he looked. *"Oya."*

Gi'ka crept forward into the mouth of the shaft, silent except for the slight burbling sounds of her drive, and now they were in total darkness with only the sonar gun to tell them where the next hard surface was.

Slowly, slowly . . .

Vau's voice was a whisper in the helmet comlinks. "All clear this end. Ordo's ETA is fifty minutes, Jusik's two hours."

"What's Delta's?"

"Five, maybe six."

On a mission like this, with so many unknowns, that lead might evaporate.

"Might lose our signal, Walon. The abort point is—"

"I don't *do* aborts, Kal. I'll wait here until the oxygen runs out. That's two months . . . at least."

"I hope you brought a holozine to read, then. . . ."

"Oh, I won't be bored. I'll be counting your proceeds from the robbery."

Vau always knew how to wind him up, but making it obvious was as close as the man could ever come to being friendly. Skirata could feel the sweat beading on his upper lip, the sort that cooling inside the *shabla* bucket could never prevent. He thought the water was getting lighter. But it was his imagination.

If there were any alarms they'd tripped without knowing it . . .

No, the water *was* getting lighter. He could see a definite green glow to it now. *"Mer'ika,* what's that?"

"If it's a sump," Mereel said, "there'll be a vertical shaft leading up into a dry zone."

"You're a smart lad."

"I know how *kaminiise* think. Remember the older section of Tipoca? How they first built the stilt-cities when the planet flooded?"

"I didn't explore as widely as you kids did. In fact, I *still* don't know all the places you managed to access."

The Kaminoans loathed the Nulls. *Uncommandable,* Orun Wa said. *Deviant. Disturbed.* Ko Sai even sent Jango Fett an apology for how inadequate her product had turned out, promising to put it right in the Alpha batch after they'd "re-conditioned" the failures.

It would be good to see her again, and show her just how her "product" had grown up.

Now the vessel was in hazy water, meters from what looked like a break in the ceiling of the tunnel, and finally they edged forward into a pool of light. Mereel craned his neck.

"There you go, *Kal'buir.*"

Above the transparisteel cockpit canopy was a water-filled shaft, and it was clear enough to make out the surface. It didn't look like fifty meters, though. Thirty, maybe. A dark shape sat motionless at the top: a hull.

"So that's going to eat some pumping power," Skirata said.

"Yeah, I think that's below sea level. Might be limited by the geology, which I doubt, given the terraforming. Might be designed to flood the inner chamber in an emergency."

"Let's just crack it," Skirata said.

"This is where it gets interesting, then."

Skirata checked his blaster and blade again and felt his stomach churn then settle, the way it always did when he was ready to fight. "Take us up, *Mer'ika.*"

It was hard to tell if anyone was up there waiting for them, or if there were any traps. But there was no dianoga, just brilliant pink-orange growths on the stone, and when *Gi'ka* broke the surface and the water ran off the canopy in rivulets, Skirata could see that they were in an empty chamber like a swimming pool with tiled edges and a bank of lighting in the ceiling. A dull gray ship a little bigger than the Wavechaser sat in the water, secured by a line and bobbing slightly as *Gi'ka* made waves.

Mereel took out his blaster, Kal prepared to jump out behind him, and the canopy popped open.

Gi'ka wasn't stable on the surface. She threatened to roll like a canoe until Mereel hit something on the console and she stabilized. He brought her alongside the jetty and looped his fibercord line around a large cleat set on the permacrete rim. If they'd needed to make a fast exit from the craft, they'd have been out of luck. Skirata extracted himself from the hull and fell onto the jetty. There were times when the age difference weighed heavily.

"I think we go in here . . ." Mereel indicated a single large bulkhead hatch set in one wall, and looked around for controls, which turned out to be set behind a watertight plate. He pried it open while Skirata stood ready to take on whatever might lie on the other side.

"Ready?"

"Ready, son."

"Knock, knock . . ."

Mereel pushed a circuit disruptor into the control panel. The hatch opened, lifting from the lower edge and receding into a recess at the top. Skirata, one weapon in each hand, cycled through the range of visor options from infrared to EM and found he was staring straight ahead into another tunnel, but one whose walls were lined with pipes; at the end, it looked like a T-junction, with a passage off to either side. He moved along it with Mereel, each covering the other as they reached the end and checked either side.

The left-hand fork looked much more promising. The smooth floor looked a little less shiny, as if it got a lot more foot traffic, and there were conventional doors at one end. They'd just passed through what seemed to be a flood barrier, and now they were entering the complex proper.

"I bet the Dorumaa Fire Department doesn't have schematics of this," Skirata said.

Mereel grunted. "At times like this, you realize just how

handy *Bard'ika* is. He'd have worked out the layout and Force-opened the hatches."

"I never said Jedi didn't come in handy." Skirata edged up toward the doors, shoving his Verpine in his belt. "Got an EMP grenade ready?"

"If this place is all electronic fail-safes, I'd rather try brute force on any tinnies first. Might fry the doors locked . . ."

"Okay."

"Must be tough to have half the worst enemies in the galaxy after you."

Skirata couldn't hear the faint crackle on the comlink any longer: Vau was out of range. He flicked through the frequencies with a series of blinks, listening for anything down here that he might pick up.

"Open the doors, son."

Mereel flourished his disruptor. "If we've got the wrong house, we just say sorry and run for it, right?"

"Got the roads mixed up, yeah . . ."

"Ankle okay?"

"Been worse."

"In three, then . . . two . . . *one.*"

The brilliant light and glossy white walls that dazzled them as the doors snapped apart were familiar; they didn't have the wrong address. This was Tipoca chic, plain white only to beings without the Kaminoans' heptachromatic vision. Bulkheads slammed down to the floor somewhere behind them, and the corridor ahead echoed with a distant chiming that didn't sound urgent enough for an alarm.

Then there was a silence that didn't sound . . . *silent.* Skirata could sense someone nearby, an animal sense that made his nape prickle. He almost didn't need his HUD sensor's grainy image to tell him there were figures on the other side of the archway, just six meters away, two pressed against the left-hand wall and one to the right, rifle-shapes raised, their arcs of fire overlapping.

Shab.

If both of them died here where they stood, Vau was waiting and Ordo was on the way, so there was *still* no way out for Ko Sai. Skirata's mouth was dry. He steadied his Verp one-handed and felt for a laser dissipating aerosol grenade. In this tight space, an instant fog of LDA would reduce blaster fire to a painful slap—even on durasteel armor.

And we've got Verps, projectiles. Nothing LDA can do to stop that . . .

In this confined space it was going to be a close-quarters melee—personal, dirty, and desperate. Mereel nodded in the direction of the bottleneck and took out a detonite grenade. "Might need to cook off, too . . ." he said on the helmet com-link. He meant detonating the grenade before it hit the ground. "Hold on to your *buy'ce, Kal'buir . . .*"

Skirata resigned himself to more than a few bruises when the thing detonated. "It's only pain." Cooking off was risky, but he and Mereel had *beskar* plates, so they'd take their chances with percussive injury. The Null darted to the opposite wall. This was damage limitation, and the least damaged guys survived. "In three. One, two . . ."

Skirata lobbed the LDA canister. It snapped to life with a loud crack, fogging the air right at the moment that blue beams sliced through the mist at crisscrossed angles. Dissipated blaster bolts hit Skirata in the chest but only knocked him back a pace, like a drunk in a cantina who couldn't land a punch; he returned fire to cover Mereel for a few extra seconds, hearing the Verpine's slugs shatter the wall tiles.

They'll have to close the gap. They'll have to come forward now—

"Cover!" Mereel lunged forward and tossed the det into the cloud. "Down!"

Skirata fell more than ducked, feeling a cold searing sensation in his knee and tasting blood in his mouth, but he was on his feet again somehow, crashing against Mereel's armor as they stormed into the LDA fog. He tripped over something solid on the floor—a body, a man down—but kept his Verp level. Then the image filled his visor at the same time his HUD-slaved targeting showed him the outline of a—

T-slit visor. Shab, they're Mandos like us.

His body did the thinking and he fired at close range.

Mereel cannoned into a figure that was just an outline in Skirata's HUD; Skirata heard the *pa-dack-pa-dack* of two slugs smacking into metal but the Mandalorian blocking his way—fierfek, *they're* vode; *they're our own*—just reeled as if punched and came back at Skirata with a spiked gauntlet. Their plates clashed chest to chest. *Beskar* had a sound like no other metal, all heavy dull solidity, no high tinny frequencies like durasteel when hit. Skirata took a punch under the jaw that filled his sinuses with what felt like molten metal. His knife dropped from its housing into his hand and he brought it up hard under the only really vulnerable place in a suit of *beskar'gam,* the toughened fabric seal between the gorget and the chin.

The struggle moved in quiet slow motion, and there was no scream—just the start of a yelp and then choking—and blood everywhere, but he knew it wasn't his and for that moment it was all he cared about. The man clutched at Skirata's grip on the hilt as he aimed the Verp one-handed into the gap and fired point-blank.

Skirata didn't think he'd ever forget the sound, not a ballistic crack but a wet sheet slapping in a gale. The man dropped. Skirata struggled to free his knife, wondering why he could still hear gurgling and panting in his audio feed, then silence punctuated by a dull thud.

"*Kal'buir!* You okay?" Mereel sounded breathless. "Three down. All clear."

The blaster sounds had stopped but Skirata could still hear them like a muffled echo. Mereel came out of the dispersing fog condensing on the floor and walls, and caught him by one shoulder.

"*Shab,*" Skirata said. The few seconds of relief at not being the one who was dead gave way to a vague anger. He adjusted his HUD sensors. Nothing moved. "That's the lot, then."

There were three bodies in Mandalorian armor on the floor. One kill was his, one was Mereel's, and the third must have been killed by the blast. Where was Ko Sai?

We shouldn't be killing each other. This is insane.

Mereel backed along the wall, rifle raised, checking visually. "I'm not picking up any more activity."

"Okay, door by door now, Mer'ika." Skirata put his self-disgust aside. "She's here."

"I bet the place locks down when the alarm kicks in," Mereel said, trying the first door. He took out a sensor and scanned for security circuits while Skirata listened for signs of life.

Maybe he should have yelled for Ko Sai to come out and face them. She must have known they were there. A firefight among *Mando'ade* wasn't the kind of thing you missed because you were making a pot of caf.

And it was definitely a laboratory.

It reminded Skirata of Tipoca City, all clinical white surfaces and sterile areas, doors with hermetic seals, a temple to order and perfection and disregard for life. He couldn't smell it with his helmet on, but he knew that if he took it off, he'd feel that slight tingling in his nostrils and smell the sterilizing fluid.

"The doors are on two circuits, *Kal'buir*," Mereel said. "I'll fry one set at a time. That means all the doors open at once."

"Then she can make a run for it," Skirata said. "Or wait for us to drag her out."

There was nowhere for her to go. Skirata thought that this might have been a decoy, and that the right-hand fork near the entrance was where they should have been, but Mereel beckoned to him and indicated a security panel. It was the kind that had an outline of the floor plan with small lights indicating the status of each compartment or room.

"Emergency generator," Mereel said, tapping his fingertip against the panel. "That's the plant room on the right-hand side. This is the only accommodation."

"She hasn't got an army down here, then."

"Probably just enough bodyguards to cover three shifts. The more folks down here, the more supplies she has to bring in. But we can check the rooms."

"You reckon the next shift will be along soon?"

"Make sure you reload."

"Let's just find the *shabuir* and drag her out."

"I need to strip the data out of her systems, too."

Snatching someone off the street was basic work for any jobbing bounty hunter, fast if risky. Kidnapping a scientist and stealing all her research—all of it, nothing left to fall into the wrong hands—was a much bigger task if you were in a hurry.

Bard'ika, *let's see you persuade Delta to stop for dinner, and maybe take in a holovid, too.*

"Ten doors each side, *Kal'buir*."

The whole place was one giant waterproofed tank with interior partitions, so unless he'd got this badly wrong, there was only one way out, and that was past him.

Skirata took his helmet off one-handed for a moment and inhaled deeply. He always claimed he could smell Kaminoans, but what hit the back of his palate galvanized him almost as much: the place *did* smell like the labs in Tipoca City. The reminder brought back more resentment and loathing than even he could recall. The adrenaline flooded him again, and he found his second wind.

"Lucky dip, *Mer'ika*. Fry 'em."

Mereel stabbed the disruptor into the panel. The lights flickered, and ten pairs of doors sighed open. Skirata had never seen a Kaminoan with a blaster, but he didn't dismiss Ko Sai's capacity to use one. He edged up to the side of each door and darted inside, blaster ready. There were banks of conservators, sealed transparisteel boxes with remote handling apparatus, empty tanks—he didn't know how he would have reacted had there been something *alive* in them—and one room full of what looked like computer storage, rack upon rack of it. Genetics took a lot of data crunching.

"I know you're in here, you sadistic *shabuir*," Skirata yelled. He'd risked leaving his helmet off. He wanted her to see his face, his loathing, his promised vengeance come to pass. "You going to come out? Or can I have the pleasure of *dragging* you out? Because I'm not a nice man, and age isn't mellowing me."

Mereel opened a pouch on his belt with one hand, taking

out data blanks, ready to strip the information out of Ko Sai's lab right down to the last spreadsheet and shopping list. "Say the word, *Kal'buir*."

"Open the hatches."

The last ten doors made a chunking noise as the locks withdrew. Skirata slipped the set of knuckle-dusters over his left gauntlet and flexed his fingers. Then he walked slowly down the run of rooms, blaster held out level with his shoulder, confident he could fire before she could. He killed for a living.

So did she, in her way.

He drew level with the fifth door and stared in.

Ko Sai didn't have a weapon. She sat at her desk, her clean white desk, just as she used to in Tipoca City, staring back at him with those disturbing gray eyes. She still wore the thick black cuffs that showed her rank as chief scientist of the entire cloning program, even though she'd abandoned Kamino and left her government in the lurch.

There was something repellent about someone who wore a rank to which she was no longer entitled, especially when she worked alone. Her status was her life.

"And who sent *you*?" she demanded. "Lamu Su? Dooku? That deluded creature Palpatine?"

"I bet it's nice to be the most popular gal in school," Skirata said. He'd always shot first and insulted the corpse later. But he couldn't kill her, not yet. She had work to do. "Can I pick *none of the above*?"

"It'll be credits," she said. There was *nothing* Skirata could find to like about Kaminoans. Where others heard gentle fluting voices, he heard condescension and arrogance. "How much do you want to go away?"

Skirata couldn't believe she didn't remember him. But then he was just another lump of human meat, and maybe she really didn't know him from Vau or Gilamar, or the Mandalorians dead on her shiny white floor.

"I'd like all your research, please."

"Oh, Arkanian Micro. Of course."

"Cut the *osik*. You know exactly who I am."

"For a moment I thought you were one of Palpatine's thugs. Everyone hires Mandalorians. You're such a cheap people, easily purchased."

Skirata had wanted to see shock on her face, or at least hatred. He was disappointed. No, he was *furious*. He beckoned to Mereel.

"Bucket off, son. Say hello to the nice scientist."

Mereel paused for a moment, but when he lifted his helmet off he was smiling, a wonderful artless smile that made him look like a harmless lad who didn't know the first thing about the weapons he had slung about his armor. He walked forward and leaned against the door frame.

Skirata could see her pupils dilate. Her head jerked back.

Oh yes, it's all flooding back now. Let's all get nostalgic, shall we?

And Mereel remembered, because he had perfect recall, way, way back to when he was a baby, before Skirata had even met him.

Mereel's perfect white smile never faltered. He took a short rod from his belt, an electroprod of the type farmers used to herd nerfs.

"Hi, Mama," he said. "Your little boy's back."

Treasury offices, Coruscant, 478 days after Geonosis

Audit trails were the fabric of Besany Wennen's life. They were like the laws of physics: there was no transaction without an equal and opposite transaction. Where credits were spent, someone received. And when someone poured a great deal of money into a project, then it wasn't something they did alone.

There was no monopoly on information. If a thing existed, somebody designed it, manufactured it, delivered it, or in some way *touched* it. And with enough time and effort, then that somebody could be found.

Besany wandered into Jilka Zan Zentis's office with as casual a manner as she could and perched her backside on the low filing cabinet. "I have to ask you a big favor," she said. "And you can say no."

Jilka looked up slowly. "If it involves doubling up on a date, I remember the last time . . ."

Besany thought of Fi for a moment. "Actually, it doesn't, but if that would seal the deal, I can introduce you to a very pleasant young man."

"Let me think about it. What's the favor?"

"I need to know about a company called Dhannut Logistics. They caught my eye but I can't find out where they're based even though they're an approved Republic contractor."

"Oh, you just don't know where to look, sweetheart." Jilka loved a challenge. Nobody in their right mind would have done a job like hers unless they *enjoyed* hunting corporate tax defaulters and all the risks that went with it. "If they're taking our credits, we'll be squeezing corporation tax out of them. And if we aren't, I'll be delighted to introduce them to the experience of filling out form two-slash-nine-seven-alpha-eight-alpha."

"Dhannut Logistics," Besany said. "Dee, aitch, ay, double enn, yoo, tee. They probably build medical facilities."

"And how much has poured into their coffers from the unfortunate taxpayer's pocket?"

"I can identify about fifty billion."

Jilka's eyes lit up. She had her funny moments: maybe Fi *would* like her. "That's just the teensiest bit over the taxable revenue threshold, isn't it? Let's see what I can find."

Besany only wanted a lead. She didn't want Jilka to start digging too far, because the fewer people who knew, the better. But Jilka was off and running, scrolling through records and even consulting another computer screen.

"You're right," she said, sounding a little disappointed. "No street address. But they paid their tax in full, and I have their accountant's details here. Odd."

"Why?"

"You shouldn't be able to file a tax return without the address of your head office, but this has gone through the system."

"I'm going to tell you that it doesn't surprise me."

"Medical equipment, you say?"

"Facilities. I'm guessing construction or specialist fitting out. Maybe they're not even based on Triple Zero."

"Triple What?"

"Sorry, fleet slang. Here. Coruscant."

"Oh, they're based here, all right. They wouldn't file the returns in Galactic City otherwise. This has a GCCC code."

"Any chance of slipping me the accountant's address?"

Jilka scribbled it on a scrap of flimsi. "Never came from me. Didn't go through the message system. And I've never seen you before in my life."

"If anything else crops up . . . Dhannut, anyone dealing with Dhannut . . . let me know?"

"Certainly. You've got me intrigued now. What's rung your bell? Fraud?"

"I think it's a front for other activity. Because I'm missing their details on the database of approved Republic contractors, too. Which also shouldn't be possible."

"Sounds mucky. I notice you're packing a blaster now. Sensible idea."

"Just think about it. Dhannut appears in *two* databases that it shouldn't be able to get an entry in. If it's not legit, and they haven't sliced into the system, then someone with government access has *let* them in."

"You just can't get the staff these days."

"And folks think we just shuffle files all day . . ."

"So do I get the very pleasant young man? Is he tasty?"

"He's very fit and you certainly wouldn't lose your appetite looking at him."

"Deal."

"I'll ask him next time I see him."

"If he's that wonderful, why weren't *you* interested?"

"I've got one just like him."

"Ah. *Ah.*"

"Don't knock it till you try it."

Jilka's expression dropped a fraction, suddenly serious.

"You've changed, Bez. And I don't mean that you look like you're in love, either."

Besany did her noncommittal smile, the slightly chilly one that she reserved for suspects when she hadn't amassed quite enough damning evidence but was certain she would, given time. "Thanks, Jilka. I owe you."

She decided to detour to Dhannut's accountant's office on the way home rather than spend any more time in the Treasury building; she wasn't on an investigation at the moment, just tied up in annual reports for the Senate committee, and attention from her bosses was the last thing she needed now.

And she'd gone a lot further than Mereel had ever asked her to go.

Quadrant T-15 was well outside her area. She stared at the flimsi, worked out a meandering route—a couple of taxi changes, interspersed with walking to blur the trail—and tried to forget about it until it was time to leave, but when things started eating at her, she found them hard to drop. It was her single-minded persistence that made her good at her job. It also kept her awake at night.

Her problem was that she was conspicuous. People remembered her: she was tall, very blond, and striking. Sometimes that was an advantage in investigations, because people tended to underestimate her, but it also made it hard to do undercover work. She needed to dull her shine a little.

Skirata called it *going gray.* He had a gift for behaving and dressing in such a way that he could pass completely unnoticed, drawing no attention. He could also stop traffic, if he wanted to. Funny little man; Ordo worshipped him. He certainly had a ferocious charisma.

As she crossed the walkways that connected the catering district from one of the retail zones that all looked the same now wherever they were on the planet, she took care to keep an eye out for trouble.

The Chancellor's office. Well, if the taint goes that high . . .

No, this was stupid. She'd never been intimidated before, and she refused to be now. One more taxi hop and a ten-minute walk brought her to Quadrant T-15. She thought she'd found the road, but then realized it couldn't be the right one; it was a long run of textile manufacturing units, not offices. She walked on, but the sector numbers were getting higher, so she was heading the wrong way. She retraced her steps.

It still didn't look right.

Besany fed the address into her datapad to check the coordinates, but it was adamant—this was definitely the right place. She walked the entire length of it, both sides, and found herself staring at Unit 7860, which should have been an office tower, but was very obviously a textile mill. Some of the walkway-level doors were open; she could see the machinery and occasionally some workers passing the doors.

Nonexistent accountant. Nonexistent company. Real credits. What was going on here?

Whatever it was, it was now clearly illegal, although she still had no idea of how trivial or how serious it might be. Regulations said that she should have logged it right away, but she couldn't, not now. She wasn't even sure whether to tell Jilka, because knowledge like that could put her at risk, too.

Besany kept her hand on her blaster, deep in her pocket, all the way back to her apartment. When she slipped her identichip into the lock and her doors closed behind her, she felt able to breathe again.

She looked at the chrono: late, *very* late, too late to eat, or else she'd never get to sleep. Grumbling to herself, she poured a glass of juice and watched the holonews headlines, not really taking it in but noting that the coverage of the war was now a long way down the menu behind the love lives of waning celebrities and cantina brawls involving grav-ball players. One of the more sober news channels had a defense analyst from the Republic Institute of Peace Studies putting forward theories about the nature of the Separatist droid threat, but it seemed folks wanted to skim over the depressing news as fast as they could. It was also getting harder to find any front-line reporting—organic or droid—lately. For Coruscant, it was business as usual, so who cared about fighting on the Rim? Trooper Corr didn't agree with her, and had told her he was happier without a holocam peering over his shoulder, but *she* cared. She wanted to know *everything* about the war. It was as if watching it would give her some protective power over the threats facing Ordo and his brothers. Not watching every scrap of news felt like sneaking off sentry duty, which she could only imagine.

"Moron," she mumbled at the screen. The analyst was throwing out numbers, huge ones, and because her business *was* numbers she found herself reaching for a stylus and doodling a few figures on the nearest datapad. "I bet you don't even know how many zeros there are in a quintillion."

She did, though, and numbers comforted her, so she considered his argument. Then she started wondering how much metal went into a battle droid—forty kilos, at the very least—and multiplied it by a quintillion just out of curiosity, and then started wondering where all that metal came from if 90 percent of the average rocky planet was silica, and not all the remaining 10 percent was the right kind of metal, or could be mined anyway, and mining and ore processing ate up a lot of resources . . .

No, quintillions of droids didn't sound feasible. But it was a lovely big unprovable number to throw out to frighten people. She was settling in to scrutinize all the analyst's numbers when she heard a scratching sound that made her start.

Her apartment was on the five-hundredth floor, and armored rats didn't make it into her neighborhood, let alone know how to use the turbolift. She looked around, realizing she'd left the blaster on the table, and as her gaze swept past the sliding transparisteel doors to the balcony, she saw it: a salky, a domesticated version of the Kath hound, a popular pet among the trendy set in Galactic City because it didn't shed fur and didn't need much walking. The animal stared at her, head cocked appealingly on one side, and put one paw against the glass in a mute plea to be let in.

It must have jumped across from an adjacent balcony. Some people had no idea how to look after their pets. Besany tutted loudly and opened the doors just wide enough to talk to it without letting it in. It thrust its muzzle through the gap, whimpering and trying to lick her hand.

"Aww, sweetie, where did *you* come from?" Salkies had a thick mane that covered their whole head from shoulders to eyes, and looked a much cuter creature than the savage predator they were bred from. "Did some silly person leave the doors open? Where's your collar?" She risked fumbling through its mane to look for some identity tag; these creatures were *expensive,* so it was certain to have one. "We'll get someone to collect you, sweetheart. You just hold still—"

"What *is* this?" said the salky in a liquidly rich male voice. "Has your building got a no-pets rule or something? Let me in before somebody spots me."

Besany yelped and jumped back, stunned. Before she could even begin to panic about hallucinations, the salky deformed into a smooth shapeless mass and squeezed through the gap like molten metal before changing color. Now Besany was looking at a pool of black glossy material that resolved into a four-legged, fanged creature like a sand panther.

"Fierfek," she said, and that wasn't a word she used often. "It's *you.*"

The Gurlanin narrowed brilliant orange eyes and padded over to the sofa. "I'm not Jinart, but I suppose we all look the same to you. Am I allowed on the furniture?"

"Look, I—"

"Don't worry about the name." He sniffed around the room as if checking for something. "Your people kept your side of the bargain. The last human has left Qiilura. So as a parting gesture of goodwill to those charming soldier boys, I have some information for you."

The Gurlanins had said they could be anywhere and nobody would know. She almost asked this one if he'd thought about a career in Treasury Audit, then had a chilling thought that a Gurlanin could have been working right next to her or following her in the street at any time. What *did* you say to a shapeshifting spy? "That's very kind."

"One, make sure you keep that blaster with you at all

times, because your meeting with Senator Skeenah did *not* go unnoticed, and you're under surveillance by Republic Intelligence, and I don't mean Sergeant Skirata's men. I mean the highest level of government." He shoved his snout into the kitchen and snuffled again. "Two, you won't find Dhannut Logistics, because they don't exist. They're a front for moving credits around inside Republic finances. You did well to find the connection with Centax Two, but if you keep crashing around you're going to get caught, so I'll save you some time. Yes, there are clones now being produced in facilities outside Kamino—some here, most on Centax, and a *lot* of them. No, the Grand Army command hasn't been told, because those Jedi generals will want the extra men to deploy right away, but they won't get them. So you can pass that on to your contact."

Besany didn't think she'd been *crashing around* anywhere. She was mortified. "Why should I believe you?"

"Because Qiilura has a fragile ecology and we know Skirata is a vengeful little piece of vermin who really *could* persuade the fleet to melt it to slag. We want to be left alone now. *Really* alone."

"I see."

"We'll maintain a presence here, by way of insurance," said the Gurlanin. "Not that you'd notice."

"Okay, but can I ask—"

"No."

"Just the—"

"I said *no.* And don't be tempted to dig further, because you have no idea what you're really dealing with." The Gurlanin sat back on his haunches and looked as if he was shrugging his shoulders, rippling long muscles, and then she realized he was changing form again. "Things can always get a lot worse."

"Did I really crash around?"

"Actually, you did exceptionally well—for a human. But that's not going to be good enough. And things might be getting too dangerous even for *us.*"

He lapsed into silence without explaining what that

meant, and then became a shapeless lump of marble before extruding—there was no other word for it—into a man, upright and all too familiar.

Gurlanins were perfect mimics. She'd seen one posing as a civilian employee she *worked with,* and never spotted it. They could pass as anyone and anything.

It seemed they could also pass as clone troopers. Besany stared back at a man in white armor who could have been Ordo, except he wasn't behaving like him, and he didn't have a helmet. The replica smiled coldly at her; her stomach churned, and it took every scrap of strength to stop herself from thinking through the implications of that chilling little trick.

"I'll let myself out the front door," he said. "It's not as if people don't know about Ordo now, is it?"

For a long time after the Gurlanin left, Besany couldn't bear to sit down on the sofa or even use the refresher, because she no longer had any idea what was real and what was illusion. She paced around, horribly awake with no prospect of getting to sleep tonight, and wondered what she could safely do and say even within her own home. But she had her secure comlink, and she needed to trust something right then.

She keyed in Ordo's code and tried not to think of the Gurlanin who could metamorphose into him so fast, so easily, and so convincingly.

Outskirts of Eyat, Gaftikar, 478 days after Geonosis

A cluster of blue-lit T-shapes wobbled toward him in the darkness, and Darman checked the chron in his HUD.

"Lights out, *vode,*" Niner said, and the blue lights vanished. Omega Squad were now invisible to infrared and EM scans, and very nearly invisible to the naked eye as well, although it was still easier to see them than detect them with sensors. "Torrents approaching from the south, time on target eight standard minutes."

"I'm shifting the remote," said Atin. "There's activity on the eastern side of city, vehicles moving. Has *Leveler* got any high-altitude scans online yet?"

Darman's HUD display was a mass of image icons: the views from the remote they'd sent up earlier to observe the positioning of mobile anti-air cannon, the point-of-view screens from each of his brothers—Fi's was shaking slightly in a definite rhythm, showing he was back in his private world of deafeningly loud glimmik music—and a composite feed from *Leveler,* currently displaying a Torrent pilot's view of a low-level approach over the unspoiled countryside.

Darman never liked having time to think too much, especially now. He kept seeing the restaurant and the mini mall in the unirail station. A'den told him he was *overidentifying* as part of adjusting to the presence of the civilian world, seeing what he could have been in that world, and that it'd settle back down to worrying about his own *shebs* very, very fast. He hoped so.

Niner opened the link to Leveler. "*Leveler,* this is Omega, do you have any real-time imaging you can show us yet?"

"Omega, we do, and we're trying to identify the civil defense headquarters and the comm station."

"*Leveler,* we have anti-air units moving around here. Please advise Torrents."

"Omega, can you confirm *this* marked coordinate as the comm station?"

"*Leveler,* affirmative, but is that now a target?"

"Omega—only for ground forces. We're targeting the relay satellite from orbit."

Niner made his impatient-Skirata noise, clicking his teeth. "*Leveler,* we'd like voice links to the Torrents. Please advise on frequency."

It wasn't supposed to be done that way because it made for confusing voice traffic, but Niner always wanted the option of aborting a strike himself rather than relying on a relay via the ship. *Leveler*'s end of the link went silent.

"I hope he's asking Pillion or whatever his name is for permission, and making it snappy," said Fi. "Six minutes to target."

Atin huffed. "Two triple-A units on the move, Sarge. I'm transmitting the coordinates anyway."

"Leveler," Niner said, "triple-A units moving. You should have new coordinates. Can you confirm you've identified those?"

"Omega, confirmed."

"Leveler, I'll run through the frequency range and identify the Torrent channel . . ."

"Omega, please avoid direct comm because of risk of conflicting orders. Stand by for sitrep."

Niner snapped over to the closed squad link for a brief, angry moment. "In your dreams, *di'kut.* If I lock on, you can't block me." Then he flicked back to the ship's link. *"Leveler,* understood. Omega out."

"Mir'osik," Fi muttered. "We're the ones on the ground."

Niner checked his Deece. "We're going to have to teach them respect for special forces someday."

"Etain thinks Commander Levet is a good *vod,*" Darman said. "But I'd still feel happier if I could interrupt and point out if they were hitting the wrong target. It gets a bit frantic in the comm center sometimes."

"Heads up, larties incoming . . ." A'den's voice cut into the circuit.

The Null was a thousand meters or so east of them with one group of Marits, who'd brought up an impressive range of cannons and artillery as well as thousands of troops. When Darman focused with his visor on maximum sensitivity, the area looked like an undulating sea, and then he realized it was actually the mass of lizards getting ready to overrun the city. It bothered him. He didn't know or even care who was right in this planet's oddly restrained dispute— restrained up to now, anyway—but helping it happen didn't sit well with him, and it was the first time he'd felt that so clearly.

He could hear the LAAT/i gunships now, the larties, a

wonderfully reassuring *chonker-chonker* sound that said extraction, air support, and friendly faces.

"This is like using thermal dets on insects," Fi said, more to himself than anything. "They might knock out a few Torrents if they're lucky."

"We don't often have this much of an advantage, *ner vod,*" said Niner. "Enjoy it while you can."

The chonking note of the larties was overlaid now with much higher-pitched drives, the equally familiar sound of V-19 Torrent fighters that rose to a deafening crescendo as they streaked low overhead. Darman's helmet audio shut down briefly to protect his hearing. Seconds later the first fireball rose into the night sky above the eastern approach road, and the battle started.

Darman found it unsettling to stand waiting while other troops went forward. Omega were used to being the first in, softening up position, sabotaging, preparing the battlefield. Forward air control—if they were fulfilling that role at all with *Leveler* in orbit—was something a droid could do: observing, confirming, relaying accurate coordinates and data. They didn't need scarce resources like a commando squad to do it.

Adrenaline without an outlet was a bad thing. Darman fretted. Fifty meters west of them, one of the larties landed and a squad of 35th Infantry jumped out.

"You want a ride in?" the sergeant said. "We're securing the HoloNet center. Don't want to break it before we can send out all those uplifting Republic messages, do we?"

"We had an op order once," Niner said, mock-wistful, "but obviously some officer lost the thing. *Shab,* why not? We're just watching the show otherwise." He opened the link to Leveler. "*Leveler,* Omega requesting confirmation that you want us to take the HoloNet center . . ."

The comm officer on the line didn't sound like a clone. He did sound under a lot of pressure, though.

"Omega, confirmed."

Niner jogged after the 35th's sergeant; Darman's tally scanner showed him as Tel. "He's a man of few words."

"That's because he doesn't know many," Tel said. "We've got mongrel officers now, for fierfek's sake, and that one only got through the Academy because his dad's some ranking captain. If he could read a chart, he'd be dangerous. You should hear Pellaeon having a go at him." Tel paused. "Pellaeon's all right, though. They're not all useless."

Omega piled into the gunship through its open side, and Darman grabbed a safety strap. *Mongrels:* more nonclone officers, then. He hadn't had contact with many. Fi and Atin peered out of the crew bay with the confidence born of armor that could take a lot more punishment than the average trooper's. Darman watched the slight tilt of white-helmeted heads as the infantry checked out the commandos' kit, like they always did. When it was the only focus in your life, you tended to notice what kit others had and you didn't.

"That matte-black rig," said one of the grunts. "Is it so we can write interesting things on it in lumi-markers?"

"They teach you to write?" Fi feigned comic shock. "No point being that overqualified, *ner vod*. Is that why you go around in threes?"

"What?"

"One who can read, one who can write, and one who likes the company of intellectuals . . ."

"Tell me that one again when I'm on the winch end of your rappel line, will you?"

It was all banter. Nobody called them *Mando*-loving weirdos, anyway. The larty zigzagged between streams of triple-A and the smoke trails from flares.

"Just for your notebook," Niner said quietly, "we usually go in and secure the strategic targets *before* the shooting starts. It's idiosyncratic, I know, but it seems to work."

"Tell the mongrel in the fancy uniform," Tel said wearily. "I just go when sent."

It was a surreal experience. The larty touched down briefly to drop the squads in an empty market square lit by the yellow glow of fires blazing nearby. There wasn't a human being in sight: no defending army, no fleeing civilians, nothing. But they'd known the attack was imminent, and the Mar-

its said there was an extensive network of underground service passages that would double as shelters. Darman felt a
little better about that. They ran for the HoloNet building
that was helpfully identified by a large sign reading HOLO-
GAFTIKAR CHANNEL TEN.

Tel checked the datapad on his forearm plate. "Well,
they're still broadcasting. The satellite's supposed to be neutralized, though."

Atin fired a grapple over the edge of the roof and tugged
on the line, testing for weight. "I'll see what I can disable at
the uplink anyway." He winched himself up, and Niner and
Fi stacked either side of the entrance with the 35th while
Darman unrolled a strip of det tape with a flourish and stuck
it on the doors to form a frame charge.

"Cover!" He counted down while everyone turned away
from the direction of the blast. "Fire!"

The doors ripped apart in a burst of smoke and debris.
Niner went in a breath before Tel, saving a scrap of squad
pride, and the process of clearing the building began the hard
way via the emergency stairs because the turbolift was stuck
between floors. Darman covered Niner as he smashed open
doors to offices, finding nobody inside.

"They can transmit days of programming from a datachip
array, Sarge," Darman said. "They might have done that."

Fi's voice came on the HUD link. "I think I've found the
studio."

"Why?"

"It says STUDIO TWO on the door."

"Well, we know there's a Studio One as well, then."

Darman consulted the meticulously mapped construction
database the Marits had given Omega when they arrived, but
it wasn't clear from the floor plans which were recording
areas and which were transmission. Maybe it didn't matter if
the satellite relay was compromised and Atin could disable
the uplink.

"If this place is still staffed at all," he said, "there'll be the
obligatory lone hero keeping the patriotic resistance messages going while we kick down the door."

"Try not to damage the kit, that's all," Tel said. "Otherwise we'll have to ship in replacements before the propaganda and psy ops spooks can move in."

Darman had another moment of wondering how this all fitted in with his overall mission, then ran up the stairs to find Fi. He was crouched outside the studio doors, holding a sensor against the metal.

"There's a transmission signal coming out of here," he said. "Might as well knock."

Darman looked up. "Red light. Means live to air, don't go in, and so on, doesn't it?"

"Yeah," Fi agreed, and put a few Deece bolts through the control panel at the side. "It does."

Darman never found out if there was the last brave broadcaster in Eyat still sitting at the console, spreading defiant messages to repel the invaders. The next thing he knew was that he was being thrown upward on his back, hurtling toward the ceiling, and that his audio circuits cut out with a snap as a ball of light lifted him. Somehow he was expecting an explosion to be much louder. The ceiling rushed to meet him and he smashed into it, feeling motionless in midair for a moment before crashing back down and feeling his chest plate hit something very hard as he fell. He was aware of bumping helplessly down a flight of stairs on his back, flailing to grab anything to stop his fall. When he finally stopped moving, he couldn't hear a thing except the rain of falling debris hitting his helmet.

The HUD was still working. He just didn't have audio. He tried the comlink channels and got nothing, but he had Niner's POV icon, and Atin's, and they were moving: they were shaking like the view of someone working frantically to move something. It looked like smashed masonry and durasteel beams. There was a filter of dust around him as thick as smoke.

But Fi's icon wasn't moving at all. The horizontal was canted at a steep angle, as if Fi was lying on the floor on one side. Debris was visible, blurred as if it was too far inside the focus range, pressed to the input cam of the visor.

"Fi?" No good: he wouldn't hear him. Darman pulled off his helmet, knowing he was battered but not feeling anything. "Fi? *Fi!*" he yelled. His mouth filled with dust and he spat it out, dribbling some down his chest plate. "Fi, *vod'ika,* are you okay?"

But there was no answer. Darman hooked his helmet onto his belt and began tearing through the rubble, looking for Fi.

12

They grow up loyal to the Republic, or they don't grow up at all.
—ARC Trooper A-17, preparing to destroy Tipoca City's clone children during the Battle of Kamino, three months after the Battle of Geonosis

Ko Sai's research facility near Tropix island, Dorumaa, 478 days after Geonosis

Skirata had taken an instant dislike to Kaminoans the day he'd found himself stranded on an indefinite contract to train a secret clone army in Tipoca City. After that, the relationship with them got worse by the day.

But compared with Mereel . . . no, he hadn't fully understood the depth of the Nulls' loathing until now. And it was the first time he'd heard a Kaminoan scream. It was a long high shriek that went off the audible scale and made his sinuses ache.

"Easy, son." Skirata kept his voice low and caught Mereel's arm, applying just enough pressure to show he meant it. "Not yet."

Mereel looked like a stranger; face drained of blood, knuckles white, pupils wide. He'd always seemed the most carefree lad of the six Nulls, the one who could be most charming, sociable, and entertaining. Skirata's grip seemed to pull him back from across the border of an uncharted dark wasteland. He flicked off the electroprod with his thumb.

"I'm not going to kill her," he said, voice hoarse. "I know too much about Kaminoan physiology to make a mistake like that."

He wasn't bluffing. Ko Sai, slumped in her chair, seemed more skeletal and fragile now than elegant. Her long gray neck was curved down like the stem of a wilted flower. It was amazing what a few volts could do.

"I said you were savages, and I was right." She raised her head and fixed Mereel with those awful eyes. It was the black sclera that did it: if the areas of pigment had been inverted— dark iris on a pale sclera—she might have had a serenely benign expression. As it was, to a human she looked permanently enraged. "Torturing me won't make you any more worthy of survival. You're genetically inferior. You weaken your species."

Her gray pupils marked her as the ruling caste, bred to rule. Mereel flicked the electroprod back on and rammed it into her armpit. The convulsions weren't a pretty sight.

"You created the recipe for my genome, sweetheart." He sounded a lot more controlled now. "And just look what you made me do."

Mereel pulled back and stood flicking the switch back and forth with his thumb. Skirata still hadn't heard every detail of what had happened to the Nulls before he first met them two years into their development—the equivalent of four- or five-year-olds—but he knew far too much already of the way they'd been mistreated. And the botched attempt to improve on Jango Fett's genome had given them a whole raft of problems beyond being traumatized and disturbed. Ko Sai was finally getting practical evaluation of her experiment.

"We had a dirtbag geneticist like you once," Skirata said. "Yes, a mad *Mando* scientist. Liked experimenting with kids. He's been dust for millennia, but we still know what the name *Demagol* means. The irony is that it can mean either 'sculptor of flesh' or 'butcher,' so I reckon you two would have had a lot of cozy chats about how to screw up living beings."

"I find the idea of an academic Mandalorian quite amusing," Ko Sai said, all venom and syrup. He hated that voice. "You're not a culture of thinkers."

"Shame on you, Chief Scientist. Have you forgotten the erudite Walon Vau? If you think Mereel's a bad boy with a nerf prod, you need to meet Walon . . ."

"Your threats are predictable."

Skirata gestured to Mereel. "Start stripping the data, son. Clear the mainframe."

"Arkanian Micro won't know what to do with it," Ko Sai said. "They don't have the expertise."

"So who does? Who's bankrolling you, aiwha-bait?"

"Nobody."

"All this came from charitable donations, then?"

"I was given credits to carry on my research, yes, but I work for nobody now. Science can't breathe with a paymaster pressing down on it."

"And that's why you've got the Seps and your own government after you. You stiffed them, hence the *Mando* bodyguards. You did a runner with the creds."

"Charming phrase." Her case-hardened arrogance began to crack a little. The faintest note of worry tinged her voice, and she swayed that long skinny neck—just like the ones Skirata had been tempted to grab so many times—to watch what Mereel was doing to her precious data. "If you're not in the pay of Arkanian Micro, then you must be working for Chancellor Palpatine."

Mereel actually laughed, but carried on plugging chip holders and bypass keys into the slots on Ko Sai's system. The wall of the office was rack upon rack of data storage.

"Yeah," Skirata said. "I bet *he* thinks we work for him, too. What made you leave Kamino? How much did they pay you?"

"I didn't leave for some paltry *fee*."

"You didn't leave for a sunnier climate, either."

"I left to prevent my research from being exploited by *inferior species*."

"Oh, you mean the ones that keep your economy afloat by buying slave armies from you?"

Mereel tutted, now fully engrossed in transferring the files. Indicator lights danced and shivered, adding a welcome rainbow of colors to the sterile white décor. "*Kal'buir*, just hit her, will you? You can't have a meaningful ethical debate with the thing."

Ko Sai seemed genuinely outraged. Even sitting down, she could draw herself up to an impressive height. Skirata wondered where to land a punch on something that skinny.

"Your Chancellor wanted me to use my research into aging to prolong his own life indefinitely. I told him it was a massive waste of my skills to do that for such a corrupted and diseased species."

That was interesting. No, it was *more* than interesting: it was bizarre. "I bet that went down really well. You need to work on the bedside manner, Prof."

"He's a most *disturbing* man."

"Yeah, he's a politician." And she was weapons-grade professional vanity through and through. It was worth a shot. "Could you even do it?"

Ko Sai's head swayed like a snake as she glanced at Mereel's back. Maybe she thought he couldn't bypass her encryption. She seemed to have no idea that he'd done it on Tipoca, too.

"Do you think I'd tell *you*?" Her attention was fixed on Mereel, and she was looking as worried as a Kaminoan ever could. "You're going to corrupt that data, clone."

"I'm not your *clone*," he said, an edge in his voice. "I have a name."

"I spent my *life* collating that. It's unique. You might destroy the most advanced body of genetic research in the galaxy. There are no copies of it."

Mereel burst out laughing. "Now, that's funny. No copies of cloning data?" He looked over his shoulder at her and gave her that harmless smile again. "But that's why we came to see you, Mama. Actually, I meant to ask you something. We're somatic cell clones, right? So where did the original enucleated eggs come from? Did you manufacture those somehow? Or was there a prime donor? No, don't tell me. I'd hate to think you found a way to use *kaminii* eggs."

Skirata watched with fascinated horror as Mereel managed to press every button on Ko Sai's eugenicist board.

Kaminoan emotion was so subtle as to be invisible to most humans, but living among them for those years had taught Skirata plenty. She was *offended*.

"That is *repellent*," she said. The words didn't match that gentle voice. "We would never pollute Kaminoan tissue that way."

"Good," Mereel said. "Just checking."

"You don't understand."

"I understand fine."

"The only reason we survived the environmental catastrophe on our planet was that we found the courage to weed out every characteristic that didn't make us stronger. Are you Mandalorians so different? How much do you know about your own genomes? You breed selectively for qualities, too, whether you know it or not. You even *adopt* to add those genes to your pool."

"But we didn't put down the *defectives*," Skirata said. "We didn't *kill innocent kids*."

Skirata stared into her face. He'd felt sorry for only one Kaminoan in his entire life: a female who'd produced a child with green eyes. He'd found her hiding in the clone training area, sneaking out to find food during the downtime hours. Green eyes weren't allowed. Gray, yellow, blue—that was the hierarchy that told Kaminoans where they stood and stayed in the scheme of things, whether they were genetically perfect for administration, skilled work, or menial labor. There was no room for any other color. It betrayed intolerable genetic difference.

The aiwha-bait found her, of course, but they only killed the kid. The mother's blue eyes meant that she could live.

"I fail to understand how you can judge us for being selective," Ko Sai said, "when you allowed the clones you claimed to love as sons to be killed."

It wasn't just Mereel who knew how to hit the raw nerves, then. For once Skirata managed to ignore the bait.

"Let me offer you a deal, Ko Sai." He shouldn't have done this on the fly, but he had no choice: it was next to impossible to make use of her data unless someone with her expertise could put it into action. It wasn't like following a recipe for *uj'alayi.* "We've got your data anyway. Nothing you can do about it. But I'd like your expertise, too."

"Not until you tell me who you're working for."

She wasn't a closed door, then. "I'm not working for anybody. This is for my boys. I want to stop the accelerated aging so they can live out normal life spans."

Mereel didn't turn around. He just pulled out full datachips and inserted new ones. "Yes, let's talk about gene switching. Boy, you've got a lot of data in here. More than the Tipoca mainframe. You took a *lot* with you when you bolted."

Ko Sai didn't answer. Skirata checked the chrono and tested the signal to *Aay'han.* It was working again.

"Walon?"

"I wondered when you'd remember me."

"Tatsushi to go, soon."

"Ahhhh. Give the good lady my regards. Private suite waiting for her."

"Any news from Ordo?" Skirata asked.

"Not yet. But you need to get moving."

"Understood."

Ko Sai was getting rattled now. Kal could see it. "How we doing, *Mer'ika*?"

"Another ten minutes, even with this fast transfer. Then I've got to erase all the layers just in case. When this is gone, it's *gone.*"

Skirata turned back to Ko Sai and took a set of restraints out of his belt pouch. "Either I'm more deaf than usual, or you didn't answer me."

"You can't make me work for you."

"I don't think you can do it." ·

"And you can't manipulate my self-esteem, either."

"Okay, I'll leave that to the Chancellor, because one of his personally tasked commando squads is coming for you in a few hours, but my boys' need is greater than his, whatever it is." Skirata could see from the head movement that Palpatine had really disturbed her. "Maybe he wants you to front up his secret clone production on Coruscant." No response: did she even know about it? "Whatever made Tipoca agree to exporting the technology?"

"A grave mistake."

"Must need Republic creds pretty badly."

"Using second-generation cloning, the Republic might as well hire Arkanian Micro—"

Mereel cut in. "Yes, they'd have to, with Jango dead. Hasn't been quite as successful. Has it?"

"No doubt you divined that from the Tipoca database, too," Ko Sai said. "But I can't think of anything you could you offer me that would persuade me to cooperate with you."

"What's it to you if clones live or die?" Skirata decided to let the Nulls exorcise their demons on her if she proved useless in the end. "You might even learn something from stopping the process."

Her head stopped that slow swaying. He had her attention for a moment, which suggested it was a challenge that might lure her.

"I don't have to beat it out of you, of course," Skirata said slowly. "Plenty of folks around who can extract information by pharmaceutical methods."

"And if they were expert enough to understand Kaminoan biochemistry, you wouldn't need me to unlock the aging sequence."

"Let's see." Skirata gestured with the restraints. "Now be a good girl and let me slap these on you, and don't tempt me to *make* you wear them."

She paused for a few moments, then offered her wrists with the grace of a dancer. It wasn't the time to negotiate with her; there was a mountain of data to assess before he could be certain he needed her at all, and if she was driven to do this research without wanting to make a profit on it, then the prospect of being able to carry on with it might prove to be enough.

But he could test that.

"You done now, *Mer'ika*?"

Mereel had a small pile of datachips in one hand, jingling

them like creds while he waited. "Just waiting for this erase program to run through the whole system. I don't think anyone's going to recover the data after we've trashed the place, but no point being careless."

It had always been part of the vague plan—asset denial—but Skirata wasn't sure if Mereel was playing the psychological game. It was as good a time as any, though. Skirata took a couple of thermal dets out of his belt and examined them, adjusting the controls with his thumbnail.

"Twenty minutes should be enough time to get clear."

Mereel shook his head. "Make it half an hour. We don't want to still be on the planet when this blows. It's going to attract attention."

"Good point."

Ko Sai watched them like lab specimens. "You're bluffing."

Skirata set the dets for remote detonation, then placed one in the center of the floor and the other by the exit. Ko Sai wouldn't know the difference between a timing device and a remote trigger. Mereel watched him with faint amusement, then put his helmet back on. "Fierfek, no. I can't afford to leave anything that Delta could recover. Come on."

Skirata hauled Ko Sai to her feet—she was more than two meters tall, so it wasn't an elegant maneuver—and shoved her out ahead of him, blaster in her back. If she reacted now, fine. If she didn't—they were out of here.

And now he had to pass the bodies of three Mandalorians. Somehow he'd put that out of his mind while shaking down Ko Sai. Now he had to look at them, wonder who they might be, and work out how he would inform their next of kin.

"Hang on to her, *Mer'ika,*" he said. "I have to do something."

He squatted down and eased off the helmets, possibly one of the most unpleasant and distressing tasks he'd ever had. No, he didn't know any of them; and one was a very young woman. That finished something in him. Females were expected to fight, and it was often hard to tell from the armor alone if the wearer was male or female, but it left him feeling hollow. He couldn't even recall if he'd been the one who killed her. A search of their pockets turned up little, so he took the helmets to trace them via their clan sigils later, and to give their families something for remembrance.

Mandalorians ended up killing one another for all kinds of reasons, personal and incidental. It still didn't make it right. The covert ops troopers sent after Sull, now these strangers—the thought of nek dogs came back to him, dog set on dog for sport, or just a killing machine to do the master's bidding. Skirata felt it was time *Mando'ade* stopped being everyone's nek.

Mereel patted him on the back. "Us or them, *Buir.*"

"They're still our own."

Skirata stacked the helmets and carried them with his own. It was going to be a tight fit even with two vessels to make the short journey back down the tunnel.

Ko Sai stopped dead. "Wait."

"Dets are counting down. That's not a good idea."

"This is a foolish game." Ko Sai turned around. "I have to go back."

"Why?"

"I have materials I need to remove."

"Terrific," said Skirata. "You could have mentioned that earlier."

But Mereel pushed her along. "If it doesn't help me reach a ripe old age, then it can stay here."

"But—"

"Move it."

"No! I *insist* we retrieve it."

Skirata walked ahead to the jetty area. "Too late."

"It's biological material."

He paused. "Alive?"

"Cells in cryostasis."

"You've got ten seconds to do better than that."

"It's a template for a new army, better than—"

Skirata waved Mereel on. He didn't even want to know whose cells they were.

"No, you can't destroy it, you must—"

"This is where it stops, Ko Sai." He thought of telling her that he'd named all twelve Null ARCs, even the six who'd died before they were recognizable as embryos, but this creature wouldn't understand why, and she wasn't worth the explanation. He kicked the mooring line of her runabout submersible with his toecap. "*Mer'ika,* open this crate for me, will you? Shove her in and I'll drive. I can manage to follow *Gi'ka.*"

She was still berating him as the two submersibles emerged from the tunnel into sunlit water, and Skirata wondered how he'd ever stood an ocean planet for years. Ko Sai's vessel was too big to dock in *Aay'han,* so they surfaced and did a hurried transfer through the top hatches.

Vau smiled silently at Ko Sai, pointed to one of the cabins, and ushered her in.

"Mird," he said, "keep her there. Understood?" He indicated the imaginary line that separated the cabin from the rest of the deck. "If she crosses it—" He snapped his fingers, and it seemed to be a code between them, because Mird got very excited and bounced up and down, whining like a pup. "Got it? Clever Mird!"

Mird remembered her, that was clear. Vau locked the hatch shut anyway.

"If you're going to make a habit of abduction, Kal, we really need to invest in a jail."

"I'd probably throw away the keys."

"What are you going to do with her?"

"She can't ever forget what she knows," Skirata said. "And I can't keep her around forever. What do you think?"

Vau shrugged. "Just checking."

Skirata followed Mereel into the cockpit and settled into the seat with a sense of partial closure. He refused to believe Ko Sai was the only geneticist who could ever manipulate aging, and he could never be sure that any solution she offered wasn't a biological booby trap. Once someone who knew what they were doing had sifted through all the data, he'd decide whether he needed her at all.

Aay'han passed the tethered headless skeleton as she surfaced, and Skirata felt purged of all guilt where Ko Sai was concerned.

In the end it was simply a matter of when, and where.

"I'm glad we don't have to file a cargo manifest, *Mer'ika.*" The breakwater was in sight now, and beyond it a white beach dappled with the shade of gaudy parasols and scented, chiming trees. He hoped there'd be at least one day's respite here for his motley clan—if they had any idea what to do with it. "Millions of credits in stolen goods, and a kidnapped scientist."

"And stolen industrial data."

"Oh yeah . . ."

"Better not get pulled over by the cops."

Aay'han came alongside the pontoon between two pleasure boats. Skirata felt bad about Ordo racing across the galaxy to be here and then having to turn around again, but at least he'd have the satisfaction of the look on Ko Sai's face, and a brightly colored drink in a tacky theme cantina like any normal lad. Maybe it didn't matter where they took Ko Sai in the end, because everyone wanted a piece of her.

"Here." Skirata handed Mereel the remote for the thermal dets. If the signal didn't work from here he'd have to go back and blow the tunnel entrance, because he wasn't about to walk back on a live det. "You ought to do it. Very cathartic."

"My pleasure. I declare this facility . . . closed." Mereel closed his fingers around the small cylinder and rested his thumb on the button. "But it's not over yet." He squeezed slowly. *"Oya manda."*

The button clicked, and then there was a moment of silence before a sound like an instant, distant storm disturbed the tranquility of the beach. A couple of tourists stopped to look around as if expecting to see some spectacle. And then it was over: Ko Sai's legacy had vanished in flame and tumbling rock, unseen, and the only archive of her life's work was a pile of data chips in Mereel's belt pouches.

"That felt better than I expected," he said. "Thanks, *Kal'buir.*"

Sometimes, just sometimes, even the most pragmatic and

rational of men needed to lay their ghosts with a little symbolic gesture.

Mereel's smile—harmless, charming, and no guide to his state of mind—still didn't waver.

Eyat City, Gaftikar, 478 days after Geonosis

"Medic!" Darman yelled, but there was no response, and he knew he was stupid to expect one.

He popped the seal on Fi's helmet and pulled it off. The built-in armor diagnostics said his brother had a pulse and was breathing, but he wasn't responding. There wasn't a mark on him—no sign of penetrating injury, and no bleeding from mouth, nose, or ears—but Darman couldn't tell about the rest of his body. Katarn armor was sealed against vacuum, and that meant it was also good protection against lethal pressure waves. Darman could recall the whole grisly lecture during training.

"Vod'ika, talk to me." Darman pushed back Fi's eyelids: one of his pupils reacted a lot more than the other. That wasn't good, he knew. Then Fi lifted his arms and batted Darman's hand away.

"Oww," he said. "I'm okay . . . I'm okay."

"Can you feel your legs?" Darman asked. Fi could obviously move his arms, so at least that part of his spine was intact. "Come on." He pulled off Fi's greaves and tapped his shinbone. "Feel that?"

"Oww. I'm *fine.*" Fi drew up his knees and tried to roll over to get up. "Just—did I fall? What happened?"

"I don't know if it was a booby trap or what. The whole wall's gone. Come on, let's get you out before anything else collapses."

"Might be worse outside."

Astonishingly, Fi stood up with minimal help from Darman and managed to put his helmet on. He stumbled a few times trying to pick his way over the rubble, but he was moving under his own steam. Darman knew that didn't mean much when it came to blast injury, but Fi had once tested the Mark III armor the hard way by throwing himself on a grenade, so it was going to take a lot to kill him.

He's okay. He's okay.

"Where's Niner?" Fires raged outside but it was eerily quiet, the noise of blasterfire and explosions muffled by distance. Darman found the front of the building gone, and remembered Atin had been on the roof. "*At'ika?* Atin, it's Dar. You there?"

Atin's voice crackled over the comlink. "I think I've broken my *shabla* ankle. I can see Niner. He's giving first aid."

They were all accounted for, then. Darman could spare a thought for the 35th Infantry now that he knew his brothers were alive. The larty had come back to extract them; it touched down in the middle of the road, the port-side hatch of the troop bay closed and blocking the line of sight between the ruined holostation and the buildings opposite. Troopers struggled forward carrying comrades between them, but one trooper was still flat on his back while Niner struggled to place a hemostatic dressing on his chest wound.

"I should be doing that," Fi mumbled. "I'll do that. I'm the squad medic . . ."

Atin appeared, limping badly. "Well, we stopped enemy broadcasts just fine. I think that was incoming."

"Ours or theirs?" Darman asked. Atin took hold of Fi's arm, but he stumbled and Darman had to catch him. "Hey, you okay?"

Fi swayed a little. "Just dizzy."

"You should get that checked out. Sounds like concussion. You're the squad medic, Fi, you should know that."

"That's what I said, didn't I?"

"Fi?"

"Okay."

"What's wrong, Fi?"

"I'm going to throw up."

Darman started to get scared at that point. This wasn't Fi. He'd seen Fi under stress, in pain, and at every other extreme, but nothing like this. Fi managed to get to within five meters of the larty and then stopped to tear off his helmet, throw it aside, and brace his hands on his knees to vomit. That was as far as he got on his own. Darman and Atin managed to haul him into the crew bay, and Niner was briefly forgotten as they propped Fi on the narrow bench seat along the aft bulkhead and tried to keep him talking.

Sergeant Tel was yelling at Niner to get the chest injury case inboard. Whatever else was happening in Eyat and the surrounding area, Omega Squad's stay on Gaftikar was over. Darman tried to comm A'den to update him, but didn't get a response.

He's probably busy, not dead. Worry about Fi. Fi's the one in trouble.

Both blast hatches dropped down to seal the crew bay and it was a full casevac to *Leveler* now, only minutes from liftoff to docking, always minutes too long. Darman relived the extraction from Qiilura, Omega's first mission as a reformed squad, which had nearly ended in Atin getting killed. *Atin made it. Fi will, too. That's what happens, isn't it? We all lost our squads the first time around, and it can't happen again.*

"Come on, Fi." Atin tapped his cheek to keep him conscious. "Keep talking. I've never had to ask you to do that before." Fi was barely coherent now, mumbling about something he'd left behind in the camp and complaining that everything was blurred. Against the opposite bulkhead, the onboard IM-6 droid was busy with the chest injury. Niner couldn't move across the deck because of the number of wounded, and stood hanging on to a safety strap.

They'd all done the basic training; they knew what was wrong. Almost nothing penetrated Katarn armor, but it was a sealed box, nothing more, and being shaken around in a box hard enough was still going to cause brain injury. That fitted the uneven pupils and the puking. Darman looked on the positive side. At least he now knew that he had to make the triage team treat Fi as a priority.

The helmet comlink clicked. "Dar, I don't care who I have

to kick out of the way," Niner said, "but he gets seen first, soon as we dock."

"You got it."

But it wasn't like that at all. When the larty disgorged its wounded, the hangar deck was almost empty, because they weren't taking heavy casualties on Gaftikar. *Leveler* had already crippled a Sep assault ship and taken minimal damage. The battle on the ground seemed completely artificial, divorced from the size of the engagement or the importance of the planet below. It was a pathetic, pointless skirmish for Fi to get injured in. It felt more like senseless bad luck.

Niner and Dar pounced on the med droid at once. "Head trauma," they chorused. "Loss of balance, headache, vomiting, gradual loss of speech and coherence." Fi, unmarked and looking like he was simply settling down again after thrashing around in a nightmare, lay on the repulsor as the droid mapped his skull with a small scanner. Atin tried to limp across to join them, then gave up and hopped the rest of distance.

"Correct," the droid said. "Intracranial pressure is increasing. We'll chill him down and insert a shunt to drain the fluid before we put him in the bacta tank. That'll reduce swelling in the brain."

Darman felt instantly deflated, faced with cooperation when he was pumped with adrenaline and fear, primed to fight. The repulsor moved off to medbay and Darman kept up with it, telling Fi it was going to be fine, even if he couldn't hear him now, until the twin doors closed in his face and left him helpless. Niner put a hand on his shoulder plate and steered him back to the hangar.

"Don't worry," he said. "Accurate diagnosis and quick treatment. He'll make it. Now let's look after *At'ika*. And get yourself checked out, too."

"Yes, Sarge."

"Nothing more we can do right now."

There *was* one more thing, but Darman didn't want to call Skirata and get him worried when he only had half a story to tell him. Ordo, though, would kill him if he wasn't kept informed; he'd taken a shine to Fi in that blindly devoted Null sort of way, and he'd want to know. He was also the right man to judge when Sergeant Kal should be told.

Darman went reluctantly to the med droid when the last man from the 35th had been assessed, and wondered who would take Fi's place in the squad until he recovered. It would have be Trooper Corr, an accidental recruit to the commando ranks who'd settled into the special forces way of life with remarkable ease.

And it would be temporary.

It had to be.

Tropix island, Dorumaa, 478 days after Geonosis

Etain felt something scared and abandoned rippling through the Force, like someone running after her and calling her name, but who was never there when she turned around.

It's not Dar. It can't be, not now. I have to see him again.

She tried to identify its meaning as she walked along the bleached planks of the marina toward the berth where Skirata's ship was moored. Whatever it was, it was unhappy and it would be coming her way, so she slowed down, concentrating to make absolutely sure nothing had happened to Darman.

"Ordo," she said, "something's really wrong."

He seemed to have learned a lot of restraint very fast. The vague warning didn't spark a diatribe on why she needed to *narrow the range* and work on making the Force a little more specific. "Here, or elsewhere?"

"I'm not sensing immediate danger."

"I'll put in a status check to everyone, just to be certain." He checked his comlink. "I've had one troubling message today, and I doubt it'll be the last."

Moored at the farthest end of the pontoon was a streamlined dark green vessel with a curving transparisteel dome, about forty-five meters long, rising and falling on the swell.

From the position—closest to the mouth of the harbor—Etain got the idea that Skirata was always ready for a fast getaway. Ordo approached it as if he was walking into a fight, leaving a wake of anger, unhappiness, and more fear than she'd ever detected in him before.

"I'm not looking forward to seeing her, either, Ordo."

"I didn't mean Ko Sai. But I can think of better ways to occupy my time than begging her for help. She had the power of life and death over us once, and I'm not handing it back to her now."

"This is the first time I've met a Kaminoan," Etain said. Darman mentioned them very rarely, and usually in terms of keeping out of their way, like a grumpy Master at the Jedi academy. "But I can probably tell you if she's lying. Her only use to you is if she knows how to stop the accelerated aging, isn't it? Because you already have all her research. You could hire someone else to crunch the gene sequences."

"Oh, she knows *that,* too."

It really was a beautiful late afternoon. The sun was low on the horizon, with just enough gilded clouds to add a little punctuation to the sky. There was something about seeing beauty while struggling with dark thoughts that was uniquely upsetting, like being shut out from the world. Etain couldn't stop worrying about the disturbance in the Force that was close to Darman. She'd have to contact him or go crazy worrying, but in the meantime she made do with reaching out to him, hoping he wasn't too preoccupied to feel it.

As she followed Ordo down onto the pontoon that stretched out into the harbor, she could see faint cockpit lights on the ship.

"What does *Aay'han* mean, Ordo?"

"It's a state of mind. An emotion." He walked a little way ahead of her now, not a clone captain at all, just a young man in plain blue pants, sport shirt, and sun visor who could have been one of the professional slingball coaches at the resort. With most of his features obscured, even Zey might not have recognized him except by that very upright walk. "Enjoying time with loved ones but suddenly recalling those who've passed to the *manda,* and still feeling the pain, but embracing it."

The concept hit Etain hard enough to elicit a kick from the baby. She wasn't sure whether *aay'han* upset her or if she craved that emotional intensity, but it seemed the polar opposite of the Jedi avoidance of attachment, and gave her an insight into why the ancient mistrust between Jedi and Mandalorian never healed. The two communities seemed only to have areas where they were identical, and areas where they were diametrically opposed, with no regions of neutrality or apathy. It made for uncomfortable relations.

Ordo jumped onto the flat section of *Aay'han*'s casing and reached into an open hatch. Someone she couldn't see passed him a long strip of durasteel sheet, and he hooked the curved end over the hatch coaming to form a brow onto the pontoon.

"Up you come," he said, gesturing to take her hand. "Can't have you leaping onto decks at the moment."

Etain could easily have Force-jumped across the whole pontoon and landed safely, pregnant or not, but it was such a touching gesture that she accepted it graciously and walked onto the hull. Ordo had his moments. On the other side of the cockpit dome, Mereel and Skirata sat with legs outstretched, leaning back against the transparisteel and passing a carton of some drink back and forth between them. Both men were staring out to sea, lost in thought.

It wasn't quite how Etain expected to find them, given what Ordo had told her was waiting below.

And this was the first time she'd seen Skirata since their blazing row when she told him she'd let herself conceive without Darman knowing, and he'd exiled her to Qiilura. She felt stupid and selfish now, looking back on how she expected him to be the instantly doting grandfather, but one thing remained certain: the Force showed her she was right to have this child.

She braced for either a frosty reception or a renewed rant on her shortcomings, one of which was being a Jedi. Skirata looked up.

"Ad'ika!" he said, not a hint that they'd ever argued. "How are you, girl?"

Oh. "I'm . . . okay, Kal, all things considered."

"Look, I'm sorry Qiilura went to *osik.* I'd never have suggested it if I'd thought the *vhette* were going to put up a fight." He stood up and faced her with the awkward air of someone trying not to notice or comment on her bump, but it seemed to trigger some anxiety in him. Mereel still looked as if he was meditating. "Jusik's intercepted Delta. He can't steer them away from Tropix, not since our chatty Twi'lek buddy mentioned it to them, but he's giving them a very rambling and unspecific briefing on the geology of the islands."

Ordo's comlink chirped, and he walked a few meters aft to sit on the cowling of the port drive to answer it. Mereel got to his feet and went to join him.

Etain had expected Skirata to get as far away from Dorumaa as he could. "Aren't Delta going to be a little conspicuous in their full Katarn rig on a tropical island—in Sep space?"

"If you've seen some of the fashions we've seen parading by in the last hour, *ad'ika,* I'd say they might get away with it."

"I don't understand why you're still here."

"You think we'll be any more secure on Coruscant?"

"Maybe—"

"Guess who Ko Sai was running from."

It took Etain a few moments before the light went on. "Oh. Our respected leader?"

"Head of the queue. Plus the Kaminoan government, the Seps, and us. Coruscant's the last place I can stash her."

Etain didn't think that would be a problem for Skirata given his business contacts. "Can't your Wookiee associate find her a soundproofed apartment where Vau can beat the living daylights out of her without upsetting the neighbors? Like last time?"

"She's scoping out other locations, *ad'ika.* Besides, Vau won't get a look in. My boys don't have happy memories of Ko Sai."

"I'm missing a few details in this, aren't I?"

"That's why I think we should go down below and have a quiet discussion, all of us."

The hatch set abaft the cockpit turned out to have a ramp rather than the ladder Etain was dreading. A pungent scent of strill wafted up from below. She thought Skirata was right behind her, but when she looked, he was still up top, and Walon Vau was waiting for her with Mird, who seemed to remember her if the excited grumbling and snuffling were any guide. The crew cabin was oddly un-ship-like, with a square of scruffy sofas facing one another around a low table bolted to the deck. She sat down and Mird laid its head in her lap, slobbering happily.

But there was something else on board. Etain's Force-senses detected what she could only articulate as a cold *void:* the three-dimensional shape it conjured up somewhere behind her eyes was a smooth concave, not the rippling, multi-layered, and colorful impressions she got from most beings. She didn't need to be told who or what was in one of the crew cabins that opened onto the main crew lounge. Ko Sai was in one of the compartments, disdainful and unrepentant as she awaited her captors.

"My father would have called this the *mess deck,*" Vau said. When it suited him, he had an effortless patrician charm that was hard to square with how he disciplined his men. "I admit I still flinch when I hear Kal using terms like *backward* and *on a ship.* I also admit that it's confusing to have a vessel that's both a maritime and air asset, though."

"So what do you plan to do with her?"

"Ko Sai or *Aay'han*?"

"Ko Sai."

"It's rather like watching a kragget rat chase a delivery speeder in the lower levels. If they catch one, they realize they have no idea what to do with it, and just sink their fangs into the fender."

"Oh, I think Kal knows what to do."

"Etain, I'm quite used to judging who'll want to divulge

their innermost thoughts to me after a little persuasion, and I don't think her cooperation is likely."

"What's she holding out for?" Etain was now distracted slightly by the delay up top, and the foreboding she'd felt earlier was now solid and spreading like an oil slick. "What does the life span of a clone matter to her anyway?"

"Professional ego, my dear. She can create life, or shape it to her design, or snuff it out. That god-like power warps anyone. She's not bargaining with us."

"You've got everything she ever worked for."

"Yes, it must be sobering for her to realize that we only need a fraction of it and we don't care about the rest."

Etain noted the *we*. "Kal's not going to sell it . . . is he?"

"Absolutely not. He's pretty cavalier about the property of others, but this has become his life's cause. It's literally do or die for him." Vau frowned slightly and went to the foot of the ramp to peer up into the fading light. "What are they doing up there? Delta's going to pass this way and see them, and that'll blow everything." He took a few steps up the ramp and called to them. "Special sea duty men to stations, secure all hatches . . ."

Vau was almost smiling, clearly in a good mood and playing the sailor, but that smile faded as Ordo came down the ramp with his comlink clutched tight in his fist. Mereel and Skirata followed him, all of them with that same dazed look.

Etain could see her bad news coming. *I'd know if it was Dar. I really would. It's not Dar. It can't be.* She waited, one hand resting on her belly, refusing to even consider it in case thinking it made it happen.

"Who is it?" she asked quietly,

"Fi," said Ordo. "He's been wounded. He's in a coma."

Etain found she had suddenly veered from accepting the reality of warfare to believing it would never happen to the men she knew, and that it wasn't fair when it eventually did.

"That was Darman calling. He said they were caught in an explosion during the assault on Gaftikar, and Fi took a pounding. He's in *Leveler*'s medbay, in low-temperature bacta. Ruptured spleen, too, but it's mainly the head trauma.

He's stable. That's a good sign. Really, it is. It's just a matter of waiting until he regains consciousness."

Ordo was reassuring himself. It didn't seem to have occurred to him to let Darman speak to Etain, but the fact that he'd swept past that told her everything was okay. She felt angry with herself for thinking of Dar first and not concentrating on Fi. Now she was painfully aware of Ordo's distress. He and Fi were close.

"Better let *Bard'ika* know," Skirata said. "*Leveler* will be on station out on the Rim for a few more days yet, so if you give me an order, General Tur-Mukan, I'll recall Corr and he can make up the numbers for Omega until Fi's fit again."

"Of course, whatever you need to do." Skirata usually did as he pleased, but he was in a conciliatory mood today. "Where is he, anyway?"

"Doing some asset denial with Jaing."

"I had to look up the data on Gaftikar when I knew where Dar was deployed," Etain said. "What a marginal thing for us to get involved in. Somehow I always thought the casualties would be in the big battles."

The gathering had taken on a somber tone, and they all sat around trying not to meet one another's eyes. Eventually Ordo broke the silence.

"I'll go visit as soon as he's transferred from *Leveler*."

"Which facility do troops get taken to?" she asked. "Does Fi end up in a neurological unit?"

"I don't know." The look on Ordo's face said it was more than just being uncertain which of Coruscant's many hospitals would receive him. "Men normally get treated by mobile units or in theater. They either recover, or die."

"Atin was treated at Ord Mantell base last time," Skirata said. "He's got a chipped bone in his ankle, by the way. Dar's fine. Niner's fine. A'den's fine, too."

"I hadn't forgotten them, Kal." He sounded a little pointed. Etain was still processing the previous sentence, feeling uneasy. "But I don't understand the medical system. Do they have that level of care within the Grand Army? Jedi gossip as much as troops do, and I hear that the mobile units are seriously under-resourced. I'd hate to think of Fi waiting in a long queue to be healed by one exhausted Jedi."

Etain didn't know why she hadn't asked the question before. She'd asked what happened to the bodies of those who died in action, and had no answer; but from that point she'd been working with special forces, and—after the initial disastrous casualty rate when they were deployed badly by novice Jedi generals—they didn't lose many men. The question went away. But now it was back.

Ordo glanced at Skirata as if asking permission to mention something, and got a barely perceptible nod.

"There's a Senator Skeenah who's made a nuisance of himself by demanding answers on what happens to badly injured men, and about long-term provision for troops in general." Ordo's impression in the Force was still tinted with fear, but it was more like anxiety for the welfare of others. Etain knew him well enough to work out who was at the top of that list. "But somehow I don't think his well-meaning campaign to set up charity homes for us when we're basket cases is actually addressing the problem."

"Of course," said Skirata, "we don't know if he's aware that the Republic sends out hit men to execute clones who want to try their luck in Civvy Street, either."

Vau was watching the conversation with an air of boredom, which usually meant quite the opposite. He kept looking across to the one closed cabin, which had to be Ko Sai's holding cell, and exuding impatience. "If you broadcast that on the hour, all day on HNE, nobody would care, Kal. I guarantee it."

"They'll care if the Seps start attacking Coruscant and interrupt their holovid viewing, all right."

"But there's not going to be this massive wave of protest on behalf of Our Brave Boys. You'll be knocked flat by the wave of apathy. Goodness, our slave army, bred to fight, disposed of when it's too much trouble? What a sensible system! Good for the Chancellor! That's what we pay our taxes for!" Vau dropped the bored act and came very close to exposing emotion for once. "It saves all those civilians from having to look after their own democracy. The most you'll get is a few creds dropped in a charity box on the anniversary of Geonosis. No Senator is going to change a thing."

Skirata jerked his thumb in the direction of the cabin door. "Time we had another chat with Ko Sai now that we've got our Force-powered lie detector on board."

Etain bristled. "It's good to feel valued, Kal."

"You can do something none of us can, *ad'ika*. Yes, it's valued."

Mereel stood up to open the cabin, and Mird padded across the deck to intercept. Etain noticed the electroprod hanging from the Null's belt. *I'm not even appalled. I know I ought to be, but if he handed me that thing and said a little encouragement would make Ko Sai hand over information that would give Dar and all the others a normal life span—I know I'd use it.* That was where attachment led, then. She couldn't muster up much guilt.

But she'd also done unthinkable things to total strangers, like the Nikto terrorist, and the slippery path to that had begun when she was trained as a Jedi to use tricks like mind influence and memory-rubbing.

As he slid the magnetic bolt, Mereel was forming a little black vortex in the Force, not unlike the impression Etain first had of Kal. Ordo appeared to forget Fi for a moment as the door opened and the tall, thin, gray-skinned figure in a monochrome uniform with black cuffs stepped into the center of the crew compartment.

"The longer you hold me here," Ko Sai said, "the greater the risk you take that someone else will find me."

This was the first Kaminoan that Etain had seen in the flesh. It was hard to believe that this graceful, soft-spoken species could be so monstrous. But she only had to look at Mereel and Ordo, radiating hatred, and the matched contempt of Skirata and Vau to see the scars Ko Sai had left in others' lives.

"Sit down, Ko Sai," said Skirata. "Let's pick up where we left off. Can you, or can you not, switch off the genes that cause accelerated aging?"

Ko Sai folded her long, two-fingered hands in her lap as if she was meditating. "It's possible."

"But can *you* do it?"

"Sergeant, you know perfectly well that I identified the relevant genes for each characteristic we wanted to introduce into the basic Fett genome, so you *know* I can switch genes *on* where there are genes that need activation. You also know that I have unique expertise that no other Kaminoan has—or you wouldn't be one of a number pursuing me."

It wasn't an answer. She was going to make Skirata—or Mereel, more likely—plow through petabytes of data to find the relevant gene clusters. Etain focused on Ko Sai and let the Force impression wash over her. The Kaminoan's sense of being right was immense, but it didn't overwhelm a detachment so total that if Etain hadn't seen people around Ko Sai, she might have thought the scientist was talking to herself. Skirata, Vau, and definitely Ordo and Mereel—they didn't register as living beings with the Kaminoan. They were *objects,* no different from Mird or the table. There were always connections in the Force between beings, the element that Etain's brain interpreted as threads and cables, and it was the complete absence of them around Ko Sai that made Etain take notice. It was like seeing jagged holes cut in a fine painting. What was *not* there was more striking than what was.

That scared Etain more than any signs of violence lurking in Skirata. It was the void she'd sensed, and it explained everything. No wonder the Kaminoans showed no hint of brutality or anger: they just didn't see other species as anything more than a fascinating living puzzle whose pieces could be taken apart and reassembled closer to their idea of perfection.

Skirata wasn't going to get anywhere, Etain knew it. It *was* possible to beat basic information out of people if they had it, but any complex answer—or trying to force them to do complex work—needed a bit of cooperation.

"Ko Sai, what other cloning projects have your people worked on?" Etain asked.

"A number of armies, as well as civilian workforces—

miners for Subterrel, agricultural laborers for Folende, even hazmat workers. Our specialty is high-specification, large-volume production for labor-intensive industries where droids are inappropriate, and a product that's tailored exactly to the client's needs."

"Is all that sales-babble in your brochure?" Mereel asked. "Because I think I'm going to puke. Perhaps you'd like me to leverage your synergy with my vibroblade."

Ordo put a restraining hand on his brother's arm and said nothing. Etain caught Skirata's eye; he shrugged and let her continue. Ko Sai would never see living beings in her hatcheries, only product, and so she could never feel pressured by guilt or shame.

She was, however, indecently proud of her reputation as the finest geneticist in the galaxy. That was a great height from which to climb down.

"So what would your personal reputation gain, or lose, if you just told us how the aging process could be normalized?" said Etain. "Or is this about protecting a secret industrial process?"

"Every cloning facility knows how to mature clones rapidly," Ko Sai said. "But there's no advantage in adding a feature that the client doesn't ask to have incorporated."

Etain's temper had never been brought fully under control by Jedi discipline, and hormonal upheaval in the last few months didn't help. "Isn't it your role to advise them on the options?"

"Life expectancy in a war is compromised for everyone."

"If you want to create an ideal army, though, I can understand rapid maturation—but it seems odd to allow that deterioration to continue once the product is at its peak." Etain threw Ko Sai's detached business-speak back at her. "Wouldn't you want the product to maintain optimum efficiency for as long as possible? Preserve them at their best? I think you didn't halt the process because you *have no idea how.* And in that case, we have no use for you."

It was out of Etain's mouth before she could stop it. Skirata didn't twitch a muscle, but Ko Sai wasn't looking at him anyway. She was blinking and swaying her head slightly, all ethereal grace, and Etain would never have picked her out in a crowd as a supremacist and a sadistic tormentor of children.

"Our client wasn't concerned about their longevity," she said. "Just that they should be ready when he needed them."

Etain sensed the Kaminoan's defensiveness and resentment. She pushed carefully, trying to steer that arrogant intellect into thinking and believing what she suggested. Jedi mind influence *was* a legitimate weapon. "And your product isn't as reliable as you tell your customer, is it? You don't manage to identify all the defective clones for culling. They're not blindly obedient anyway. Some even desert. You oversold the genetic factor and failed to mention that human beings aren't that predictable."

Ko Sai didn't respond. Maybe she was considering the idea that she was less than perfect, which must have stung a bit. But this wasn't about winning a playground argument. Etain had to help Skirata establish whether Ko Sai *could* undo what she'd done, and then if she could be *made* to do it.

What did Ko Sai really dread? Where could that lever be placed to shift her?

"I think I've had enough," said Ordo. He got up from the sofa and walked around behind it, then leaned over Mereel with his hand held out. "Give me the datachips, *ner vod.*"

Mereel opened the pouch on his belt and handed over a tight-wrapped block of storage media, bundled together in a small colorful brick. Etain watched Ordo cautiously: he walked a fine line between self-control and chaos far more often than anyone seemed to realize, and news of Fi's condition hadn't helped.

"Are you going to collate the files?" Mereel asked.

"No." Ordo unwrapped the brick of plastoid cupped in his hand. "Just having a moment of clarity." He looked across to Ko Sai. "Your entire life's work contained in a thousand cubic centimeters of plastoid, Chief Scientist. Not unlike mine, in fact."

Ordo folded the wrapping tight again and walked into the

passage that separated the cockpit from the crew compartment. Etain thought he was heading for the computer terminal in the storage compartment, but she heard the hatch mechanism hiss open and the thud of his boots as he walked up the ramp.

"Ordo?" No answer. *"Ordo?"*

The realization must have hit Skirata at the same moment it hit her. Everyone bolted for the hatch, cramming into the short passageway, even Ko Sai. Looking up through the canopy, Etain watched in horror as Ordo drew his hold-out blaster, threw the package of datachips high into the air, and fired at it like a claydisk shoot.

Fragments of plastoid flared and rained like a pyrotechnic display.

She couldn't see Skirata or Mereel from this angle. But Ko Sai let out a long gasp and slumped against the bulkhead, weaving her elegant head from side to side in shock. Every precious line of research was gone.

"Oh, *shab* . . . ," said Vau, hands on hips, and hung his head. Etain was too stunned to speak. *"Shab."*

It wasn't just Ko Sai's entire life and purpose that had just turned into embers hitting the water. It was Darman's, too.

13

Of course Ordo's messed up. They're all messed up. They used live rounds on exercise at five years old, they fought their first war at ten, and the lucky few got their first kiss as grown men aged eleven. Almost all of them—millions—will die without ever having heard someone say, "Welcome home, sweetheart, I missed you." You think you'd be totally sane after all that?
—Kal Skirata to Captain Jaller Obrim, CSF Anti-Terrorist Unit, discussing life in uniform

The Marina, Tropix island, Dorumaa, 478 days after Geonosis

"*Ord'ika?*"

Skirata tried not to show his shock, but it wasn't working. His voice jammed in his throat and struggled to shake loose.

Ordo stood forward of the hatch, looking out to sea in the growing dusk, and folded his arms. "I'm sorry, *Kal'buir.*"

What am I going to do? How the shab can I start over now? We had it, we had it all, we were so close . . .

"Just—just tell me why, son." *How could he do this to me? What did I do to tip him over the edge?* "I know you're upset. I know you're worried about Fi."

Mereel caught Skirata's arm. "Nothing you can do, *Buir.* Let's start again and shake everything out of Ko Sai."

Skirata resisted Mereel's pull at his sleeve. "Give me a minute, son. You go warm her up for me. I need to talk to Ordo."

Skirata knew there was no point in being angry with the

lad: this was all *his* fault. It was so easy to see only the clever, courageous, loyal side of Ordo and his brothers, all their wonderful qualities, and forget how badly damaged they all were at their core. No amount of love could erase what had been done to them at a critical time in their development. All he could do was patch them up, and he was willing to do that until the day he died.

He stood beside Ordo and put his arm around him, not sure now if that would result in a flood of tears or a punch.

"Son, you know how much I love you, don't you? Nothing will ever change that."

"Yes, *Buir.*"

"I just need to know why you did that after all the trouble we went to in getting that data."

Ordo's jaw muscles twitched. He didn't look Skirata in the eye like he usually did. "This is all about having a choice. That's what matters, isn't it? But even now, we're still under a Kaminoan's control because she's got information she won't give us. Well, I'd rather live fifty years on my own terms than a hundred on hers. And now she'll know it. The information she's withholding is worthless. I've taken her power away for good."

"But I just wanted to give you a full life. You deserve that."

"But we're men, *Kal'buir,* and I know you've given up everything for us, but you can't keep making decisions for us like we're kids."

That *hurt.* The physical pain in Skirata's chest, like a heavy stone pressing down inside, got a little worse. "But what about your brothers, *Ord'ika*? What about *all* of the *ad'ike* who didn't get to choose?"

"There'll be other ways around this."

No point arguing. He'll feel bad enough about it when he comes to his senses. "Sure. We'll forget it for the while and concentrate on Fi, and Etain's baby, and then we'll have a rethink. Ko Sai isn't the only geneticist in the galaxy. Is she?"

But even the Kaminoan ones need to get her back, and they're the best. It's over. I'll keep trying, but unless there's a miracle . . .

The galaxy didn't do miracles. It only gave you what you took from it. Skirata was persistent to the point of wasted obsession, and maybe even beyond, but even he reached a point where he sank beneath the weight of a task. There'd been just too much bad news today. Perhaps tomorrow would be better.

They still had a fortune to fall back on.

Ordo turned around, looking like a scared little boy again for the first time in ages. There was nothing Skirata couldn't forgive him.

"I've hurt you, *Kal'buir,* and I can't undo that. But I'll make it up to you, I swear."

"You don't have to, son." *I forgot they hadn't seen Ko Sai up close since she finished testing them and told them they were going to be put down. I stuck abused kids in front of their abuser and expected them to cope. What was I thinking?* "You don't owe me a thing."

Down below, Ko Sai was in bad shape. Skirata wasn't shocked to find himself satisfied to see it. She was behaving like a bereaved human, head bowed, making a little cooing sound—whimpering, in fact. If anyone thought aiwha-bait were emotionless, they were wrong. It was just that different things mattered to them. She looked up into his face and he knew that, for once, they understood that they shared the same emotion, if for very different reasons—irreplaceable loss.

Etain and Vau had retreated to the seating on the opposite side of the crew compartment, leaving Mereel to deal with the Kaminoan. He stood in front of her, arms folded.

"Sooner you stop wallowing in self-pity, the sooner you can start rebuilding that work," he said. "If you're nice to me, I'll give you a hand."

She raised her head slowly. "That was *decades* of my work, you imbecile. *Decades.*"

"*Ori'dush,*" Mereel said. "Too bad. But that's what you get for building us crazy. Sure you don't want to make a start on recording it all again? Might as well do it while your memory is still fresh."

"I can't even access the material on Kamino."

"Maybe I should make sure they can't, either, next time I drop in. Tipoca City security's no better than when I was a kid . . ."

"You're savages. Why should I cooperate with you now if I didn't before?"

"Because you're stuck in a ship with four creatively sadistic people who hate your gray guts, and maybe the strill and the Jedi aren't too fond of you, either, and all you've got is the clothes you stand up in. Not even a scrap of flimsi to make notes. See how long you last . . ."

Skirata met Ko Sai's eyes. She looked back and forth from him to Mereel and Ordo a few times as if calculating something—*don't even think about it, aiwha-bait*—and then settled on Mereel again.

"And you'll starve me into submission, you think."

"Oh, you'll get well fed," Mereel said. "I want you healthy for a long time, so I can watch you suffer. I might not get a long life, but seeing you go crazy is cleaning some *osik* out of my heart that's been there for far too long."

"Cathartic," said Ordo. "It really is." He turned to the cockpit. "I need to check up on Fi's condition, and then we have to make a move, *Kal'buir*. Any preferences?"

The one place Skirata could guarantee to find some Sep-proof, Republic-proof, Jedi-proof accommodation was Mandalore. He had business to take care of there as well. He turned to Etain.

"Want to see the home turf, *ad'ika*? Visit *Manda'yaim*?"

She still looked in shock. There were no fancy Galactic City doctors on Mandalore, but plenty of women who knew how to handle a pregnancy.

"What do I tell Zey?" she asked. "He was sold on your story that I was staying on after Qiilura was cleared to help the Gurlanins for a few months."

"I'll think of something. I always do."

She shrugged. "Okay. I've never seen Mandalore. What's it like?"

"I'd like to say it's paradise," Skirata said. "But it's as rough as a bantha's backside, and half as pretty."

"I never liked beach vacations anyway."

Vau held his hand out to Ordo. "Better give me the code key for your shuttle. I'll take it back to Coruscant and meet you all there, as and when."

Maybe Vau had business to sort out. He had his inheritance, after all, and there were probably items he wanted to fence, because he had his expenses like everyone else. The shuttle needed to go home, too; they couldn't keep abandoning small vessels and charging new ones to the GAR budget. Enacca the Wookiee couldn't retrieve everything they were forced to dump.

"Thanks, Walon," Skirata said.

"I might take a detour to Aargau, actually . . ."

His bank was on Aargau. Business, then. That was fine.

Skirata strapped himself into the third cockpit seat so Ordo could take the copilot's position with Mereel at the helm. Ordo was now talking directly to *Leveler,* whose comm officer seemed to think he was calling from Arca Barracks on Coruscant. A code scrambler was a wonderful thing.

Vau released the mooring lines and gave Skirata a mock salute from the pontoon, and Mereel took *Aay'han* out past the breakwater, accelerating her gradually toward the speed at which she'd rise on floats and then lift clear of the water. Skirata opened his comlink and keyed in Jusik's code.

"We're out of here, *Bard'ika.* Thanks."

"Thank you for keeping me informed," Jusik said stiffly. So he had an audience: Delta must have been with him. "Is everything all right?"

"No. But it will be."

"Niner informed me about Fi."

"Ordo's on the case. Don't worry. And you don't have to worry about Ko Sai any longer, either."

"Okay . . ."

"Call me when you can talk freely. We're off to Mandalore."

Jusik was a good lad, Skirata reflected. He'd been good

right from the start. They were lucky to find a few *aruetiise* with that kind of loyalty.

Aay'han took off in a storm of spray, lifting into the night sky. As she passed above the island that had once housed Ko Sai's base in its bowels, Skirata checked the sensors and couldn't help but notice that there was now an area of subsidence on the sports field, a shallow bowl about a hundred meters across. He could even see it; the shadow created by the illumigrids made it look like a big black lake.

"*P* for plenty," Skirata said. "I think we brought the ceiling down."

Mereel checked for himself. "Oops."

"You're taking this pretty well." Skirata now worried what was happening behind Mereel's cocky veneer, because he'd badly underestimated what was going on inside Ordo.

"There's always a bright side," said Mereel. "One day, we'll look back on all this and laugh."

Skirata doubted it. But one thing, at least, was settled: he didn't have to hunt for Ko Sai any longer.

He just had to work out what he was going to do with her.

Tropix island, Dorumaa, 479 days after Geonosis

"So this is how the other half live," Sev said.

Delta Squad, clad in the dull but all-encompassing coveralls of a utilities maintenance crew, tried to look routine as they made their way along the shoreline collecting garbage. There wasn't a lot, but the management liked the white sand to look pristine before the hotel guests emerged after breakfast. Some poor *di'kut* was even combing it with a big rake.

"I'm glad I'm in this half, then," Boss said. "The novelty of cleaning up after civvies would wear off fast."

"I meant the lounging-around-in-the-sun bit."

"Overrated." Fixer speared a scrap of flimsi wrapping with a special sharpened pole designed for doing just that, although Sev could think of much better uses for it. It was the first enemy contact Fixer had had for a while. Sev considered requesting a transfer to the infantry, where they seemed to be getting more droid action. "Ruins your skin. Gives you blisters. You have to coat yourself in slimy sun filter to stop it from killing you in the end."

Scorch stood back and let him kill another scrap of litter. "So how long *have* you been promoting the benefits of a vacation on Tropix?"

"Look, any job would be better than mine, because right now I feel I'm wasting my time." Fixer shoved his finger hard in his ear, adjusting the hidden comlink bead. "This is boring. Even the police comlink channel is tedious. Drunks, lost valuables, and collisions between rental speeders."

Jusik had finally let them loose on the island itself. Fixer and Boss weren't happy about the delay, but the Jedi had a point: it was hard to blend in here in a suit of Katarn armor, and they didn't have what he called Omega Squad's *social skills*. Scorch had helped him liberate a few maintenance crew uniforms overnight, a task so easy it was almost an insult to their skills at getting into places they shouldn't have been. As for the locks—he could have busted them open just by scowling at them. It was pathetic.

It was a bummer about Fi, though.

Sev didn't like the thought of being in a coma, just in case it was one of those conscious ones where you knew what was going on around you but you couldn't respond. Whatever happened to him, he decided, would be fast and final; no hanging around. At one point he thought of talking it through with the rest of the squad, but they'd noted Fi's state and then shut it out of conversation, so Sev knew they were as scared as he was.

"I know that Jedi *sense* stuff," Boss said carefully, "and that generals are privy to intel we don't get, but I get the feeling *Bard'ika* isn't leveling with us."

"Maybe he's too embarrassed to tell us he brought us all this way to buy us a Neuvian ice sundae," said Scorch. "Part of this new management drive to make us feel valued."

"Does Zey know he's having an identity crisis?" Boss asked.

"Who says he is?"

"Aw, c'mon . . . the durasteel-underwear syndrome?"

"So he likes Mandalorian stuff," Scorch said. "Maybe it's comforting for guys who aren't allowed to have violent feelings. He can act out a bit."

"He's got a lightsaber. He acts out violence just fine with that."

Sev didn't have a Jedi's Force radar but he certainly had a trooper's sixth sense for an officer approaching. Just as he looked up from the blinding white sand, feeling uneasy, he saw Jusik striding down the boardwalk in what Sev thought of as his "half Jedi," the anonymous white tunic and pants that they all wore under the layers of robes.

"Why don't you put your theory to him, then, Dr. Scorch?" said Sev. "Go on, ask him."

"Yeah, I always wondered where he keeps his lightsaber when he dresses like that."

"Result," Fixer muttered.

Sev prodded him with the litter pole. "What?"

"Police channel chat." This was as near as Fixer ever got to excited. "Folk were calling in saying they'd heard a mystery explosion, but no location. Now they've had a report of a sports field subsiding on the next island."

"As in *underground* explosion?"

"Maybe. Rescue Service is going over to check it out."

Jusik caught up with them. "I've rented a fishing vessel so we can move our ops away from prying eyes. How's the maintenance business?"

"Explosive," said Scorch. "Fixer says the locals reported a big bang followed by a hole in the ground not far from here. And as this isn't a big-bang kind of planet, we might as well check out the lead."

"Good idea," said Jusik.

"Sir, are you okay?"

"My apologies, Scorch. My mind's not wholly on the job. If anyone would like an update on Fi's condition, let me know." He looked around him, almost as if he'd heard something and was trying to work out where it was coming from, but it was just one of his mannerisms. "No? Okay, let's take a look at this hole in the ground."

Fixer was still eavesdropping on the police comlink frequencies. "What cover are we going to use?"

"No need. Overfly it in the TIV, get a few coordinates out of it, then work out a way of assessing the point of the explosion."

"Might not be anything to do with Ko Sai, of course."

"Want to skip it?"

"No sir. But maybe the Twi'lek was decoying us."

Jusik picked up a scrap of litter, examined it, and dropped it in the collecting sack that Fixer was carrying. "What makes you say that? He ran for his life pretty convincingly."

Boss cut in. "Because we've turned up nothing, sir, except the traffic manager here who remembers someone hiring a utility barge for a delivery offshore, and then it was found drifting minus the employee."

"And nobody went looking for him."

"When they say don't go beyond the safety limits, they mean it. They have no idea what's lurking under the surface, and they're not too keen to find out."

Jusik shrugged. "Just as well we're made of sterner stuff. What a shabby attitude toward employee welfare."

Sev had seen Jusik hunting targets before, and he behaved like a man with a mission: single-minded, resourceful, and tenacious. On Coruscant, he'd even worried Sev with his wildly risky tactics. Now he was behaving differently. The fire had gone out of him. It was as if he didn't care if he found Ko Sai or not.

It could have been that he didn't *want* to find her, and that worried Sev for all kinds of different reasons. But maybe it was, as he said, because he was preoccupied by Fi. That was worrying in its own way, because an officer who was distracted when one man out of his commando group of five hundred was wounded really didn't have what it took.

"Yes sir," Sev said.

The aerial view of the island sports resort to the south of Tropix—ActionWorld, a name Sev found hilarious given its extensive array of visitor safety measures—was educational. Yes, it was an instant lake all right, minus the water. From the TIV, he could see how the ground had collapsed beneath the grass without breaking up much of the surface. Something underneath had caved in.

"Not too low, Boss," Jusik said. "What's our transponder telling their flight control?"

"Delivering ice desserts, sir," Scorch said, checking the charge on his Deece. "Yeah, put some syrup and crushed nuts on *this*."

Folks didn't use their eyes any longer. They believed everything their gadgets told them. Sev studied the chart on his database, mapped in the position of the subsidence, and compared it with the divers' hydrographic chart.

"The hole might not be directly above whatever blew up," he said, "but it's a fair assumption. That gives us a search area underwater."

"You're gagging to wear that scuba trooper's rig, aren't you?" said Scorch.

Sev didn't answer. He was starting to wonder what he'd say to Ko Sai when he found her. She was still a figure of dread, a name that even the Kaminoans used to mention in hushed tones, and not just because of her expertise; she had the power of life and death, the authority to say who came up to scratch and who didn't. Now that Tipoca City was far behind him, he was starting to realize why that wasn't such a great idea.

It was turning into a long, slow day. Transferring the kit from the TIV to the diving vessel without being spotted ate a couple of hours, and then they had to work out a search pattern without even knowing what they were looking for—except maybe a lot of rock.

And those scuba suits just processed oxygen from the surrounding water. There was no excuse for coming back to the surface because they were running out of air.

Fixer and Boss took the first shift, transmitting optical and sensor images back to the vessel. Sev, Scorch, and Jusik sat on the bridge, watching the output screens.

"Come on, Sev, cheer up." Scorch nudged him. He was suited up, slapping his flippers on the deck in a rhythm that annoyed Sev more with each *thwack*. "This is better than most of the stuff they show on HNE. It's really *interesting* rock. Great weeds, too."

If they didn't find Ko Sai, Vau would have something to say about it. Okay, he didn't know they were on the case, but he'd find out sooner or later if they *failed*.

Somehow that mattered to him more than coming up empty for Chancellor Palpatine.

Boss and Fixer surfaced after an hour and Sev and Scorch flopped over the gunwale into the crystal-clear water. Sev had done the compulsory diving course as part of his basic training—and why call it *compulsory,* he wondered, when *everything* was compulsory for a clone?—but just because he could do it didn't mean he *liked* it.

He didn't. Scorch did.

"Wow, this is amazing. Look at *that*!"

"It's a fish, Scorch. You'll get over it. So will the fish."

"Come on, how many folks get to do this? Savor the privilege, man."

"I will, next time I'm getting my *shebs* shot off."

Sev wanted to say a lot more right then: a terrible unguarded moment ambushed him, and he wanted to blurt out that he was fed up with hearing that voice within telling him he wasn't good enough when he was almost bleeding from the effort, and that he wanted . . . fierfek, he didn't *know* what he wanted, but he knew he didn't have it.

That was when he realized why Fi wound him up so much, because Fi asked the questions that he couldn't face. And Fi had a sergeant who was a *father,* who thought he was terrific whatever he did or however much he screwed up.

So the jewel-like fish and luminous coral around him had a long way to go to make up for that gnawing void in his chest. He ignored them, and swam without jet assistance to avoid churning up silt, scrutinizing the seabed of the island shelf and the rock formations around him for signs of recent activity.

Up ahead, there was a sloping pile of rocks extending from the cliff that wasn't on the chart. As Sev swam over it, he couldn't see anything growing there; no plants, encrustations, or any of the life that was quick to colonize every surface. *How do I know that? I've never dived anywhere like this. It's all from databases in my helmet systems. Flash-learned stuff. Things I've been trained to trust, unseen.* The rock face opposite was equally scoured, as if this pile had been the large chunk that had shattered and fallen away from it.

"General Jusik, sir," Scorch said, "is any of this showing up on your disturbance-in-the-Force meter?"

"I see it."

Sev picked up some of the smaller fragments and moved them, checking for any debris that wasn't part of what nature intended. This would take forever: he let the rock drop and swam away from the cliff to get an overall perspective, maybe even see some channel open to the sea. It was just as he was backing away that he brushed against something and turned, thinking he'd snagged weed fronds, and found himself looking at something white and vaguely familiar.

It didn't have a head, but the rest of it was a humanoid skeleton.

"Fierfek—"

"Sev?"

"It's okay, Scorch." But they could all detect that his pulse rate had shot up, because armor always had a sneaky little system for monitoring life signs. "Looks like the speeder buses run really late here, judging by how long this guy's been waiting . . ."

Scorch swam across to him, rocks and big bangs forgotten for the moment.

"What is it?" Jusik asked. "I can't see."

Scorch adjusted the unfamiliar helmet cam controls that linked his POV to the comm system. "See it?"

"Ah." Jusik sighed. "Any sign of what killed him, Scorch?"

"Let's ask Sev. He's a dead-body-ologist."

Sev, feeling embarrassed by his reaction, examined the bones. The left arm came off in his hand.

"Yep, he's dead all right."

Scorch sucked his teeth noisily. It was extra-amplified in the scuba trooper helmets. "Sure you don't want a second opinion, Doc?"

"Nah, I'm prepared to go out on a limb." Sev dipped down and retrieved the arm from the weed around it. He followed the length of orange fibercord to its origin, which turned out to be a nonslipping Keldabe anchoring bend tied on a mooring ring of some kind. "But I can tell you who made sure he didn't float, more or less. Can you see this, sir?"

"It's a knot," Jusik said.

"A special one. Mandalorian. Used only by Mandos and folks trained by Mandos."

Sev's first thought was the Twi'lek pilot, Leb, saying that he'd told some Mandalorians about his delivery route. There was a connection here, and it would have been a lot easier to make it if Jusik hadn't scrubbed the pilot's memory a little too soon for Sev's liking.

"Retrieve the arm," Jusik said. "We can at least try to ID the owner. Get what penetrating scans you can of the rock face and we'll examine it later."

Sev and Scorch looked back at the cliff face in silence. From here, the volume of rock brought down was apparent, and it was more than two or even five men could shift in the hope of finding anything behind it.

If Ko Sai had built a hidden research lab back there, and she'd been home when the explosion happened, then she wasn't going anywhere, ever. If someone else had found her before they trashed the facility—like the mystery *Mando'ade*—they probably hadn't offered to relocate her to a nice unit in the Keldabe business park.

It wouldn't be good news for Palpatine. But then Sev wasn't the one who had to break the news to him.

14

*Let me see ... by your logic, it's acceptable to use these
clones and spend their lives, because they were only
created for war, and wouldn't have existed otherwise. The
problem I have with that, Lieutenant, is that they do exist,
so they know how sweet life is—even from their limited
experience—and therefore their lives are worth as much to
them as ours are to us. So I'm sure you won't object to
accompanying the men on the next ground assault—and I
mean on the ground. Will you?*
—Captain Gilad Pellaeon, commanding officer of *Leveler,*
discussing clone troopers with a junior lieutenant

Republic assault ship *Leveler,* Outer Rim,
480 days after Geonosis

Darman was used to going where he pleased on board a
ship, so the med droid's attempt to stop him from entering
the medbay came as a surprise.

"Unauthorized personnel," it said. "You're an infection risk."

"I want to see my brother," Darman said. "RC-eight-oh-
one-five, Fi. Head injury."

The droid docked one of its probes into the console at the
nursing station, checking the central database. "Admission
record shows he's still in bacta and hasn't regained consciousness yet. Bay Eight."

"I know he isn't going to be sitting up in bed and wisecracking, but I want to see him. And if he's in a tank, how can I infect him?"

"It's not him I'm concerned for," the droid said. "It's the other casualties."

"Okay." Darman took his own probe out of his belt and docked it in the console. "Priority override five-five-alpha." The droid stood back to let him pass. "And I promise I won't go near any other patient, okay?"

Special forces weren't supposed to use the override access command except in emergencies, but this counted as one in Darman's eyes. There was no point being special forces personnel if you had to fill out forms asking permission to visit the refreshers. He went in search of Bay 8, past what were now packed wards. He paused to stare for a moment, surprised by the numbers.

The droid had followed him. "He's not in there. Move along."

"Where did they all come from? Not Gaftikar. That was a stroll in the park." But not for Fi: that was galling, and Darman still didn't know if it had been a booby trap or a cannon round, hostile or friendly fire. For some reason, it mattered a lot, even though he knew no good would come of knowing the answer. "Shouldn't they be shipped out to Rimsoos?"

"No, very few casualties were sustained on Gaftikar," said the droid. "These men are from a number of engagements in this quadrant. The Mobile Surgical Units can't handle any more at the moment, so they're sending them to vessels with spare medbay capacity."

So the Republic could order a top-notch army and all its kit, but they didn't get around to providing the medical support. Darman wanted to go and slap some sense into the Republic, but didn't know who to start with even if he could.

"Show me Bay Eight," he said.

Darman tried not to look to either side of him, but he did, and in one of the emergency bays med droids were working on a trooper. He couldn't see the type of wound because the man was lying flat and the droids were obscuring his view, but he *could* see the deck of the bay, and it was covered in blood. A small cleaning droid was mopping it clean, working its way around the equipment unnoticed.

For some reason, the scene stopped Darman in his tracks. *A mop.* They were using a domestic mop to wipe up the blood. Somehow it summed up how routine this was, how much a part of the daily round, how mundane, that men bled out their lives and the cleaning droids carried on keeping the ship spick-and-span. Where was HNE and its holocams now? This scene never intruded on the holonews bulletins. All Darman's vague resentment and fears suddenly found a sharp focus, and he was angry in a way that he hadn't been before.

"Bay Eight, tank one-one-three," the med droid beside him said sharply. "I have patients waiting."

At least Fi had been first in line for a bacta tank. The droid left Darman in a forest of blue-lit transparent tubes full of men, and for the first time since he'd known Fi, Darman had the panicky sensation of not being able to recognize him; the fluid distorted like a lens, and the men inside were sedated, so there was no way to recognize him by facial expression or scars. But he had the tank number.

Fi's injuries were all internal. Darman wished he could have said the same for some of the troopers he passed: bacta could heal a lot, but regenerating limbs wasn't one of its properties.

In tank 113, Fi hung suspended in a surgical harness, breather mask held in place by filaments looped behind his ears, a very regular trail of bubbles rising slowly to the surface of the bacta; he was on assisted breathing, then. He looked peaceful. But Darman didn't like that because he'd seen more than enough dead men with that same look of absent serenity.

"Hey, Fi," he said quietly. He put his hand flat on the transparisteel. They said coma patients often heard what was going on around them, so Darman treated Fi as conscious. "You're going to be okay, *ner vod.* Better hurry back, because Corr's taking your place, and you don't want him to get all the girls, do you?"

Darman watched Fi for a while, drumming gently on the glass with his fingers. They'd all started life in a tank a lot like this. Darman was determined Fi wouldn't end it in one. Now that he could stand outside all this, he could see it for the loveless, isolated, sterile excuse for life that it was.

Someone walked up behind him, very carefully. He knew Niner's gait anywhere.

"The med droid's getting annoyed with us trooping in here," Niner whispered, draping his arm over Darman's shoulder. "Fi's stable. They say they've stopped the swelling in the brain, so they'll drain him down and take him off the sedation in a couple of days and do scans. Then they'll know what shape he's in. We're going back to Triple Zero anyway even if *Leveler* isn't—we have to meet up with Corr and get a new squad in shape."

"Why do they need to sedate him when he's in a coma?"

"In case he wakes up in that thing and starts thrashing around."

"Ah."

"He'll be okay."

"What happens if he isn't? What if he's still in a coma? What happens then?"

This was where it got difficult. Men were wounded all the time, and some died, and some survived and were sent back to their units. It was the first time Darman had wondered why it was all so tidy.

"I don't know," said Niner. "I'll ask Sergeant Kal."

Darman knew why he hadn't asked the question before, though. The answer was brutally pragmatic. If it took too much effort to save a man, he wasn't a priority. He died.

Darman thought of the surgical expertise available to the Republic and just how much was medically possible these days—as long as you weren't a meat-can like them.

I thought we were expensive assets. You'd think we'd be worth a little more spent on repairs.

"Come on, Dar." Niner pulled him away, hooking his fingers into the back of his belt. "We'll come back later." Darman, reluctant to leave Fi in this cold and lonely place, put his hand on the tank again. "I'm not abandoning you, *vod'ika*. You didn't abandon me on Qiilura, and I won't leave you. Okay? I'm coming back. I promise."

Fi didn't react, but then Darman knew he wouldn't. The point was that he'd said it, and that meant he'd do it. Reluctantly, he followed Niner back to the mess deck, and found a quiet corner to pour his heart out in a message to Etain.

He could have unburdened himself on his brothers, but they all knew what he was thinking anyway.

Kyrimorut, northern Mandalore, 480 days after Geonosis

Etain stepped out of *Aay'han*'s cargo hatch and looked upon a wilderness of ancient trees huddling together for warmth against a biting wind that swept off the plain. The palette of sunset colors was remarkably like the tropical island she'd just left, all intense violets and ambers, but the temperature difference was thirty degrees.

Despite what Skirata had said, it wasn't unattractive. It was just dauntingly isolated.

"Okay, it's not Coruscant," Mereel said, offering her a hand down. "You can't comm the local tapcaf for a banquet-to-your-door delivery. But in the warmer months, it's beautiful. It really is."

Etain tried to believe him. It didn't matter, anyway: she'd be out of here in three months, maximum. For some reason, freezing her *shebs* off here—that was the right word, *shebs,* she knew that now—was a lot better than being exposed to the same temperatures on Qiilura. She had a connection with this place, however tenuous it was. There was something right about having the baby here. She understood all about bloodline and geography counting for little with Mandalorians, but it mattered to *her* because this was, technically, her son's home.

But she couldn't see any houses. There wasn't a light or a road out there, just the wild landscape.

"They have tree houses here, don't they?" she said, realization slowly dawning. Accessibility was an issue for a woman with a rapidly expanding waistline. "Like Wookiees."

Mereel laughed. For a man whose crazy brother had just junked his chance at a normal life span, he didn't seem too crushed. "Only in some places. Here, you need something a little more substantial in the winter. Think of it as your private retreat by the lake. Fishing, bracing country walks for a few hundred klicks . . ."

Skirata stuck his head out of the hatch. He had his comlink in one hand and seemed to be talking to someone who had dumped more bad news on him. He paused, oblivious that he was blocking the exit, and rubbed his forehead, eyes closed. He was back in his gold armor now, a regular *Mando* on home turf.

Enemy territory. Remember that. These people fight for the Seps.

Etain heard the word *Fi* a few times. *He's not dead. I'd know if he was.* Then Skirata closed the link and keyed in another code, stepping out and wandering around the landing area with his free hand deep in his pocket, left leg dragging a little.

"Ah," said Mereel, holding up a forefinger and cocking his head toward the sound of an approaching speeder. "Our gracious enabler."

"Has Kal got a home here?" she asked.

"Not until now," Mereel answered.

"I don't understand."

"He's looking at retirement properties, let's say. In the meantime, Rav Bralor's looking after his interests."

That meant absolutely nothing to her. "Who's he?"

"She. Another *Cuy'val Dar.*"

Skirata only trusted his own. Etain couldn't blame him: it was a dangerous galaxy, and Skirata was playing a very risky game indeed, even here. She wondered how he bankrolled all this, and suspected General Zey was going to get a heart-stopping shock one day when the auditors went through the SO Brigade accounts.

But Skirata had Besany Wennen on the team now, which was . . . convenient. A Treasury agent always came in handy.

And I think Kal's taking risks? I'm a pregnant Jedi general, and here I am in enemy territory, paying a social visit, looking to them for safe haven. Force preserve us . . .

A mud-spattered speeder drew up alongside them, and a figure in *beskar'gam,* the traditional Mandalorian armor, jumped out of the hatch.

. "*Rav'ika,*" said Skirata. They hugged with a metallic *clack.* "I owe you."

"Too right you do, you old *shabuir.*" Bralor pulled off her helmet, revealing thick, gray-streaked chestnut braids and a surprisingly unlined skin, and looked Etain over with a practiced eye. "So this is the little mother, hah? *Shab,* kid, you need to put some meat on your bones *fast.* Your baby needs it." She walked up to Mereel and patted his cheek. "You're looking fit, *ad'ika.* Good to see you again."

"Mereel," he prompted.

"Been awhile. I could always tell you apart back then."

Bralor was everything Skirata had said *Mando* women should be. If she'd had kids, Etain had no doubt that she'd endured a five-day labor in stoic silence, handed the newborn a blaster, and then zapped Trandoshans with the infant clutched under one arm. She looked frighteningly fit.

Venku, is this where you want to be?

"Thank you for your hospitality," Etain said, having no idea if Bralor knew who the father was. "I realize this can't be easy for you."

"It's okay, kid." Bralor had vibroblade housings on her gauntlets, *both* of them. "I know what you are. Kal and I go back *way* before Kamino. No problem. When you join this team, nobody cares where you came from. Only what you do from now on in."

That didn't answer the question, but Etain made a mental note to check with Kal about who knew what. It was impossible to keep track now.

"Okay," Bralor said, "follow me. Five minutes, tops."

"There's something else," Skirata said.

"There always is, *Kal'ika* . . ."

"*This.*"

Ordo emerged from the hatch with a handcuffed Ko Sai. Bralor's expression was a picture. She didn't quite gape, but she parted her lips as if to speak and then just laughed her head off.

"*Wayii!* Bringing meat for the barbecue?" She held her helmet hugged against her chest, an oddly girlish pose for a veteran commando. "This is something of a comedown for you, Chief Scientist, isn't it? Slumming it with the cannon fodder. Well, well."

Skirata looked suddenly exhausted, as if he'd been worried about Bralor's reaction and could now relax. "Ko Sai was a little reluctant to accompany us."

Bralor grinned. "You *kidnapped* her?"

"Yeah. I suppose you could call it that."

"*Oya!* Nobody can say you haven't got *gett'se,* Kal. You know what the bounty is on this aiwha-bait?"

"Oh yes," Skirata said. "But I liked her so much I decided to keep her."

"So how long do I have to hide her?"

"Until she tells me what I want to know."

"No problem, *Kal'ika.* I'll take good care of her while you're gone. I'm sure we can find lots of girly stuff to talk about from the Tipoca days." Bralor put her helmet back on. "You do still talk, don't you, Ko Sai? I used to enjoy our chats."

The Kaminoan still seemed stunned. Etain almost pitied her: at the top of her profession, second in terms of power only to her Prime Minister, and then on the run, hunted and humiliated and finally reduced to a hostage without even a change of clothes. But Skirata and Bralor obviously didn't see it that way. Bralor was relishing it.

"The only thing I can say," said Ko Sai at last, "is that you're ignorant savages, and I wasn't as adept a geneticist as I thought, because I failed to breed that out of your kind."

"I take that as a compliment," said Bralor. She pointed to the speeder. "Follow me."

Bralor's homestead was fringed by trees, seemingly in total darkness until they set *Aay'han* down in a field of stubble at the back of the house. The building itself was circular, partly submerged in the ground with a strange grassed roof that camouflaged it from the air, but flickering lights were visible through slit-like windows as she approached the main doors.

It was a bastion. Etain reminded herself this was a warrior culture, and knew that sooner or later she'd find out why it was embedded in the ground and not on a high vantage point.

The house was deserted, smelled of wood smoke just like Qiilura, and looked partly derelict. It seemed to be in the process of restoration. Bralor took them to the main room in the center of the building and gave them a rapid orientation. Rooms were set around the main room like a rim around the hub of a wheel.

"I don't expect you'll have trouble," she said, "but if you do, the exit's here." She pointed down at a point on the floor covered by rope-like matting. *Ah, tunnels.* It made sense now. "And the best lockable place to put *her* is the armory. Plenty of headroom."

Ordo was wandering around the place, making notes on his datapad for reasons best known to himself. Ko Sai's head drooped. Either she was utterly demoralized or she was taking a sneaky look at the tunnel exit. Etain decided to keep an eye on her.

Bralor seemed to be keeping one eye on her, too, but then she'd been stuck on Kamino for eight years just like Skirata and Vau, and she probably had her reasons. "So what information are you going to beat out of her, Kal?"

"How to switch off the accelerated aging in clones."

Bralor snorted. "If she could do *that,* she'd have tried it out by now. You know how this *demagolka* loved her experiments." She patted Skirata's shoulder. "I know you talked about it, but I never thought you'd actually do it. *Kandosii, ner vod.*"

"You'd be amazed," Skirata said quietly. "Come on, *ad'ike*. It's been a long day. Let's eat and then get some rest."

Ko Sai looked back at Etain as Bralor led her away. "The genome of your child will be *fascinating*."

So she'd worked it out. Skirata was right. Kaminoans had few facial expressions that Etain could recognize, but she knew *avarice* when she felt it. Ko Sai could think of nothing but a new puzzle to solve and rebuild. Then the fire of that new enthusiasm waned in the Force, and Etain suspected she'd remembered that her personal research was now melted plastoid fragments in the silt of an idyllic crystal harbor on the other side of the Core.

Etain drew her lightsaber out of her pocket and simply let Ko Sai see the hilt.

"Come anywhere near me or my child," she said, "and you'll find out just how little I've embraced the peace and serenity they tried to teach me at the academy."

Skirata winked at her. *"Mandokarla . . ."*

Mereel sat Etain down on a wide, deeply upholstered bench against the wall and shoved a few cushions behind her back. "He says you've got the right stuff."

So she was back on Skirata's good side, for the time being anyway. The meal turned out to be an assortment of dumplings, grains, and noodles smothered in various spicy sauces, preserved meats, and a pot of small red fruits swimming in what looked like syrup—the only thing she didn't try. Bralor seemed to have raided the contents of her store cupboard to feed her guests. Etain devoured it in the full knowledge that her stomach would rebel later.

The meal was taken in grim silence, which could have been exhaustion, but Etain sensed that Skirata was more crushed than tired. He drained a little syrup out of the pot into a small glass and gulped it down.

"Rav still makes good *tihaar*," he said hoarsely, and then started coughing. It was the throat-searing, colorless fruit alcohol that he had a taste for. "Best painkiller there is."

"You haven't been taking your daily dose, *Kal'buir*." Ordo

sounded a little strained, as if the realization of what he'd done to Ko Sai's research was now catching up with him.

"I found I could sleep without it." Skirata wiped his plate clean with a chunk of dumpling speared on a fork and chewed as if it hurt him. "Anyway, time for a sitrep. Work out what we do next. We've got Fi in bacta, we've got to go back through the Tipoca research stuff and see where we can pick up, and we've got confirmation that the Republic's got its own clone program without Kamino's involvement. And I've got to persuade Jinart to keep up the pretense that Etain's helping the Gurlanins get back on their feet now that the farmers have gone."

"She'll do that," Etain said. "She really thinks you'd maneuver Zey into trashing the planet if she doesn't cooperate."

Skirata finished his last dumpling. "Oh, I really would."

"Leave the research to me," Mereel said. "I think I know where to start shaking down Ko Sai. I'll go through the Tipoca data with her and see what sets her off. She's devastated about losing her own material. It's really broken her."

"Can't you just compare the trooper genome with Jango's and see what's different?" Etain asked.

"That only tells us which genes have been added, mutated, or removed," said Mereel. "It doesn't tell us what's been turned on or off. You can even turn them down, and make them work just a little. It's about expression—how the machine gets built from a blueprint—and that's messy, because if you tinker with one gene, it can have an effect on another set that's got nothing to do with the area you're working on. And then there's identifying what aging really is, because it's not just one factor. Am I boring you yet?"

"No," Etain said, but wasn't sure that she wanted to be depressed any further by the size of the task. It would have been daunting enough even before Ordo destroyed the datachips. "But I suppose if it was easy, Arkanian Micro would be doing this, too, and Kamino wouldn't be able to charge top price."

"She *can't* be the only one in the galaxy who can do this kind of work," Skirata said. "There *have* to be others."

"Best bet is to look for a gerontologist and an embryologist with an interest in genetics. But it'll cost."

Skirata shrugged. "If I invest the fund right, we'll be able to buy as many scientists as we need."

The word *fund* worried Etain. "Zey's going to spot the black hole in the budget sooner or later, Kal."

"It's not from the GAR budget, *ad'ika*." He gave her a knowing smile. "Okay, it's sabacc-on-the-table time. I have a slush fund. Creds from my *Cuy'val Dar* payoff, invested sensibly. Creds the Jabiimi terror cell paid me in that explosives sting. And now upward of forty million from a little expedition of Vau's, which I need to convert to cash creds and launder fast so it can earn interest and get invested again."

Etain wasn't an accountant, but it didn't sound like a lot of credits compared with the many trillions needed to run an army. The word *launder* registered on her but failed to shock any longer. "Is that going to be enough?"

"To establish a safehouse here and an escape route? Yes. To develop a gene therapy to counter the aging? I don't know. Possibly not. So I'll build up as much in the coffers as I can."

Etain had to admire his determination. She'd had no idea that he'd moved from anger and I-wish to calculation and action. The Force hadn't shown her the entirety of the man, just his headlines.

Venku kicked again, and she put her hand on her belly.

"You okay?" Skirata asked, all instant concern.

"He's kicking," she said.

"Ah, he'll be a limmie player. *Meshgeroya*. The beautiful game."

"I think he's permanently angry that I'm putting him through so much, actually."

She thought of the way Ko Sai looked at her, that clinical curiosity, and understood Skirata's initial anger. It scared her, too.

Ordo and Mereel took turns to pat Skirata on the shoulder before returning to *Aay'han* for the night—maybe because it was more comfortable, or they might have been guarding his valuables—and Skirata settled down in one of the chairs with his weapons laid out on a small table right beside him. He didn't use a bed, Etain had found, not since his first days on Kamino. It couldn't have been good for him. No wonder his ankle played up so much.

"I'm going to wander around the place," Etain said, regretting wolfing down so much food on an increasingly cramped stomach. "Give my meal time to settle."

"You should be doing plenty more of that now. Eating and resting." He opened one eye. "Give the baby the best chance."

She decided to risk it. "I just wanted to say that I'm learning a lot from you about being a parent. You're so patient with Ordo."

"He's my boy. I love him, even those times when he turns into a stranger. You'll understand when you hold yours for the first time."

"Your favorite."

"You can't have favorites. But he's probably the one I overprotect most, yes."

"What are you going to do if you succeed with this scheme and they . . . well, leave home?"

"I have no idea, *ad'ika*." Skirata rubbed his face wearily with both hands. "I forgot how to be Kal Skirata a long time ago. It's probably better that he never comes back."

Redemption came from the strangest sources; perhaps it was easier to find in the dark, extreme places that forced a man to sink or swim. Etain walked around the homestead, which was even bigger than she'd first thought—more a chain of connected redoubts than a farmhouse—and when she pressed her face to the transparisteel insets in one of the walls, she could make out the faint boundaries of fields backing onto the complex.

It was the perfect spot for vanishing without a trace. It was exactly what the *Cuy'val Dar,* soldiers so disconnected from normal life that they could step out of it indefinitely at a moment's notice, would think of as a safe haven. It was a remote, well-defended spot on a remote planet with a popu-

lation smaller than most Core world neighborhoods, let alone
cities.

It struck her then that this wasn't Rav Bralor's home.

It was Skirata's. This was the retirement property Mereel
had alluded to. Bralor was looking after it for him. If she'd
lived there, it would have had all the trappings of a real
home—*yaim'la,* that was the word. Lived-in, warm, familiar.
This was a construction site.

Etain found she'd walked in a circle and now was back at
the main entrance. Pulling her cloak up over her head and
mouth to keep out the cold, she stepped outside to check if
Aay'han was still there—with Nulls, she could never predict
anything—and saw Ordo and Mereel. They were sitting on
the coaming of the open port-side hatch, chatting in the faint
yellow light of the cargo bay, their breath emerging as mist.
They really are crazy—it's freezing out here. She caught a
word or two of the conversation before they noticed her.

Whatever they were talking about, Ordo was saying he almost wished he hadn't started it, because it broke his heart to
see *Buir'ika* like this. Mereel assured him *Kal'buir* would
understand.

Buir'ika. She could work out even from her smattering of
Mandalorian language that it was an affectionate word for
"father." Everyone seemed to be wallowing in guilt tonight.

"I don't care how genetically superior you are," she said
loudly. "Go to bed like good boys."

Mereel laughed. Ordo just looked uncomfortable. "Yes,
Buir," Mereel said. It was the same word for "mother" or "father." *Mando'a* didn't bother with gender. "We'll brush our
teeth, too."

Etain waited for them to close the hatch before she shut
the doors and made her way back to the heart of the complex.
Skirata was asleep, or at least in that doze from which he
seemed to wake so quickly. She found a blanket, shook off
the dust, and laid it over him, as she'd once seen Niner do.

Maybe it wasn't such a terrible thing to hand Venku over
to him after all.

Medbay, Republic assault ship *Leveler,*
482 days after Geonosis

"I'm not accustomed to working with an audience," said
the droid. "Please let me get on with my task."

Atin had taken on the role of enforcer today. The med
droid didn't seem to care which clone it was arguing with.
Darman and Niner stood on either side of Atin, making it
clear that it would be easier to give in than have to argue with
them four times a day.

"I spent serious time in bacta," Atin said. "*Twice.* I don't
have happy memories of it, so when Fi wakes up I want him
to see his brothers as soon as he opens his eyes. *Reassurance.*
It's a scary experience for us. Reminds us of the gestation
tanks."

The droid was only partially moved. "How very *primal.*
Move behind the observation screen, then."

"Okay."

"And after brain damage like this, he might be very disoriented. Do you understand? He might have problems even
recognizing you at first."

Darman didn't care if Fi swung a punch and thought they
were Neimoidian accountants as long as he was conscious.
They could sort out the rest later.

"We get it," Atin said.

The three commandos stepped out into the passage, helmets held one-handed, and peered through the transparisteel
like med students watching a master surgeon.

"Pity that *Bard'ika* isn't here," Niner said. "He'd have
sorted this lot out."

Darman felt a little wounded by the omission. "Or Etain.
But Jedi can't influence droids."

"I meant a spot of creative slicing. Sometimes I think he's
better than me."

The technician droids moved the bacta tank out of position on repulsors and onto a recessed platform in the treatment area. Fi, breather mask still in place, hung more heavily
on the suspension straps as the pale blue liquid was pumped

away and the cylindrical tank descended below deck level. The droids moved a repulsor gurney into place and maneuvered Fi onto it, placed a temperature sensor somewhere that would have raised a loud objection had he been conscious, then covered him in a padded blue wrapping. The mask was still breathing for him.

"He looks awful," Darman said. He placed his forearm on the transparisteel and rested his forehead against it. Bacta didn't leave you wrinkled and white like plain water did, but Fi looked dead; the contrast between his pallor and his black hair was stark. "Is he still chilled?"

Niner shrugged. "Well, that blue thing could be a heating pad."

They waited. A droid kept hovering back to check the sensor readout, and eventually Fi didn't look such a waxy yellow color.

"Here we go." Darman wasn't keen on seeing a needle go into flesh—his own or anyone else's—but he made himself watch as the senior med droid moved in with a cannula and slipped it into the vein on the back of Fi's hand. What Darman might have been able to do if he'd seen anything go wrong, he had no idea, but he had to keep watch for Fi's sake. The droid took a syringe and began injecting a pale yellow liquid into the cannula. "So this stuff reverses the sedation?"

Atin nodded. "I was all bright and breezy pretty fast. He might not be, remember."

Darman's gaze darted between the chrono on his forearm plate and Fi, and the urge to protect him—from what, from a med droid?—was hard to suppress. The minutes flicked by on the display, and the droid was joined by another. The two began attaching sensors to Fi's scalp, shaving off more small patches of hair—oh, he'd be really mad when he saw what they'd done to his hairstyle—and sticking the discs in place. They seemed to be checking brain activity.

"How long is this going to take?" Niner said. "Shouldn't he at least be conscious by now?"

But he wasn't. The senior med droid repositioned the sensors, checked the readout, and then stood back in processing mode for a few moments, the panel on its chest flickering through a sequence.

Then it unhooked the filaments from the breather mask and removed the tube from Fi's throat. Darman couldn't work out what was going on at first. But Fi's chest wasn't moving, no rise and fall of steady breaths, and that was the point at which Darman started to think in terms of going in there and resuscitating like he'd been taught. The droid seemed to be watching Fi intently. Then it turned away to the trolley full of instruments, slipping items into the steribag for autoclaving.

"That's it, I'm going to—"

And then Fi took a long gasping breath and coughed. The droid spun around as if it hadn't been expecting that at all. Fi was breathing on his own again, but he certainly wasn't conscious.

Darman was a stride from the doors when Niner stepped in his way and pushed through ahead of him.

"Droid," he said, "you want to tell me what's going on? What happened there? Is he okay?"

The med droid placed more sensors on Fi, this time on his chest and throat. "He's breathing unaided, and I wasn't anticipating that outcome."

"So why did you take the *shabla* tube out of him, then?" Darman snapped. He got the picture now, all right. They thought Fi was *dead*. "What's that about?"

The droid just followed its protocols. It dealt with a steady stream of wounded and dying men every day, and Fi was no more special to it than the next trooper. It was nothing personal at all. "His brain scan showed insufficient activity."

"You mean you pulled the plug on him?"

"I assessed him as brain-dead. That's still my professional opinion. The medical protocol is that we don't continue life support if a patient is still showing isoelectric scans after forty-eight hours." The droid paused. "Flatlining, I believe you call it."

The words hit Darman like a punch in the gut. It wasn't supposed to be like that. Republic medical care was the best there was: prosthetic limbs, bacta, microsurgery, nanopharmaceuticals, you name it, the stuff of which miraculous recoveries were made. Fi couldn't end up like this. Darman refused to accept it.

Niner had his fist clenched, held against his leg. For a moment Darman thought his sergeant was going to vibroblade the med droid like he'd done to so many combat tinnies. But Niner could always keep control.

"What happens in a regular medcenter?" he said, voice cracking.

"They have separate medical protocols. The Grand Army operates under different terms."

And Darman didn't need to be told what those were. He wanted to take it out on the med droid, but it was just a machine and had no more rights than he did. "You can't just leave him there. What are you going to do?"

"This has never happened before during my service. I have no instruction to keep a patient on extended life support in these circumstances. This medbay is for emergency and acute care only."

"I'll take that as a don't-know, shall I?" Niner said. "Put him back on life support."

"He's breathing unaided."

"Then keep him hydrated, because if you don't, that's basic combat first aid for us. If you don't put a line in the IV cannula, we will. Got it?"

The droid was genuinely perplexed. It had a very specific specialty, and what it was faced with now wasn't how to do something clever, but whether to do it at all. Darman didn't wait and moved in between Fi and the droid. If the tinnie came anywhere near him with anything but a helpful suggestion, he'd use an EMP on the thing. Atin pushed past it and took a big carton of saline sacs, and between them they hooked Fi up to a drip.

"Now either he stays there, or you let us move him to a nice quiet bay where we can keep an eye on him until we get back to Triple Zero," Niner said patiently, fist relaxing. "I think a bay would be best. We'll liberate that repulsor gurney and move him, if that's okay with you."

If Darman hadn't been so focused on Fi's plight, he might have felt sorry for the droid.

"Clones can be *very* disruptive to the orderly running of this unit," it said. "I tire of explaining our protocols to you, which is why I usually bar your kind from the treatment areas." So this wasn't the first argument the droid had had with a man's comrades, then. "But I have no authorization to transfer a patient in this state to any facility, so what happens to RC-eight-zero-one-five when we transfer the wounded is outside my authority."

Niner stood back to let Darman and Atin steer the gurney across to the treatment bays. They now had an audience of droids and walking wounded. "You mean you don't know what to do with him."

"That's what I said, isn't it?"

The droid let them take Fi. It was a busy droid that didn't have time to argue with RCs who weren't going to take no for an answer, and Darman felt brief guilt for tying up resources when there were wounded *vode* with less clout in dire need. But Fi was his brother, and if Darman didn't look out for him then the whole fabric of his tight-knit world, the small circle of people who were his life, meant nothing.

Niner pulled the bay shutters across to give Fi some privacy, and the three men crowded in as best they could, shoulder plates scraping one another. They had no idea what to do with Fi, either, except lay him in a coma position, make sure his saline line was clear—Sergeant Gilamar's combat medic course back in Tipoca was ingrained in them—and get on the comlink to someone who'd be able to sweep aside the bureaucracy and *osik* back on Coruscant: Kal Skirata.

15

The difficulty is knowing not who to trust—nobody, absolutely nobody—but who can be allowed to know how much about a given situation. It's no secret that we hold Dr. Uthan in a Republic jail, and the assumption is that we need her expertise to prevent the Separatists from creating another anti-clone virus like hers, or even force her to create a countermeasure. But I prefer to think of her as my insurance policy. Should I ever need to remove the Grand Army—if the clones are not as loyal as the Kaminoans claim, and we all know the claims merchants make—then I have my means.

—Chancellor Palpatine, private memoirs, on the uses of enemy scientists

**Special Operations Brigade HQ, Coruscant,
482 days after Geonosis**

"So it was a *big* pile of rock," said General Zey.

"Yes sir." Jusik could do calm like nobody else, and it seemed to be getting to his boss. "I estimate a few tons."

Jusik sat completely composed, fingers meshed as his hands rested on Zey's lovely blue desk. Sev, in I'll-wait-to-be-spoken-to mode like the rest of Delta Squad, sat to his right, helmet on lap, staring straight ahead, managing to feel that the conversation didn't involve him or his brothers at all. It was, Vau said, probably like a Jedi being in a state of meditation: aware, but not distracted. It was handy to be able to do that when your CO was getting a subtle roasting from his boss right in front of you.

"But we don't have any confirmation that there was a facility under that island," Zey said, staring out the window with his back to them. "Or that Ko Sai used it. And even if she did, we don't know if she was at home when Master Disaster came to call, do we?"

"We don't, sir."

If Zey leaned on Sev, he wouldn't be able to tell him anything different from Jusik even if he wanted to. That was exactly how it had happened, a very unsatisfactory outcome, and they were now back to square one and casting around for new leads—if Ko Sai had ever left Dorumaa, that was.

No—they were back to *minus* one. Before Dorumaa, they'd at least known for sure that the aiwha-bait was still alive.

It was funny how that phrase stuck. *Aiwha-bait.* All the Mandalorian *Cuy'val Dar* used it in the end. Even some of the non-*Mando* training sergeants did. Kaminoans weren't lovable when you got to know them.

"So if the facility was *blown up,* to use the technical phrase, did someone else get to her before we did, or did she do it to throw us off her trail?" Zey asked. "Because I'm getting a very hard time from the Chancellor, in that charmingly polite way of his, and if it's not him on my back then it's Master Windu, and I don't know which is giving me more pain."

"We just don't know, sir. All we know is that she had one pair of bounty hunters after her, who were almost certainly tasked by the Kaminoan government, and that a lot of equipment that could be used for cloning was shipped to Dorumaa—"

"—or that could have been used to pickle vegetables."

"—and that we found a body with signs of Mandalorian activity right next to a very recent explosion."

"Anyone can learn to tie a Mandalorian knot if they want to leave a message for the trusting saying, *It's okay, she's dead, the Mandalorians got her . . .* can't they?"

Jusik looked unmoved except for a slight twitch in his jaw muscles. Sev was at the right angle to see it.

"They could, sir," Jusik said at last. "But we do derive some certainty from the Force, do we not?"

"We do, but Chancellor Palpatine doesn't deal in Force certainty, or in the Force at all. He *wants* her, preferably alive, but he'll settle—reluctantly, although I shall no doubt *feel* his reluctance—for definitive proof of death. And I don't mean some half-wit Twi'lek saying he was pretty sure he dumped her body but he can't remember where." Sev felt the Force that time, all right, and it was probably a largely spent shock wave compared with the one that Zey had to be getting from above. Jusik's calm almost deserted him, and he blinked a few times. "Find me something solid."

"It means excavating."

"Then excavate."

"But if she surfaces again, she'll show her hand when she starts re-equipping a laboratory. She can't work with a data-pad and a stylus alone."

"Unless she goes to work illegally for Arkanian Micro or any of the other clonemasters. Does she have any research that Tipoca City isn't privy to, do you think?"

"I have no idea."

Zey turned to Boss. "Three-Eight, do *you* regard the corpse you found as significant?"

"Just the nature of the knot, sir. Especially as it was a long shot that we would find the location based on what the Twi'lek told us. If anyone signposted it, they were subtle."

"They might have known you weren't stupid." Wow, the old man was in a real mood today. "No option but to go back to the last good contact and start over. Although I don't like the idea of digging holes under sports fields deep in enemy territory on the off chance there might be a squashed Kaminoan under the rubble, that's all we've got. Perhaps I should have brought Skirata into the loop on this after all."

It didn't matter why he said it: he might have meant it be-nignly, or sincerely, or spitefully. But the end result was the same. It was a slap across the face for all of them. Jusik might have taken that as part of the learning curve of being a baby general, but Delta didn't *fail*. Dread crept through Sev like the onset of a strained muscle. At least they weren't yet at the stage where Vau had to find out that they couldn't cut it.

No. That I *couldn't cut it.*

"Leave it with us, sir." Jusik gave every impression of being okay about the dressing-down—Jedi never shouted or swore, although they did have a savage line in humiliating understatement—but he had to be bruised now. He'd already told them more than once that he was never going to make the Jedi Council. He didn't strike Sev as the type of man who wanted that kind of position anyway. "Is there a deadline on this?"

"Yesterday, at the latest," said Zey. "I can repeat the explanation from the top if you like."

"No need, sir. Resources?"

"You learned your trade from Skirata, young man. Whatever it takes." He paused. "If you really feel you're not getting anywhere, I might countenance investigating the Mandalorian angle via him or Vau."

Jusik managed to return some verbal fire. "They won't like finding out that they weren't trusted to know about this to start with, sir."

Zey just raised an eyebrow.

"Do it now," he said. "I want to be able to tell Palpatine that you're still out there on the case, and not lie. I haven't even told him where you were. Just in case he gets other ideas."

"Yes sir."

Jusik dismissed himself and beckoned to the squad to follow. They trooped after him in silence.

"We let you down, sir," Boss said. "Sorry about that."

"Don't worry, Boss, it's not your fault." Jusik's comlink bleeped for attention and he looked down at the display, pausing for a moment as if it was either baffling or important. "General Zey was just expressing his frustration. It's a job best suited to Intel, and he knows it. They should do the tracking and call you in when they need some serious soldiering done. Look, can you give me half an hour? I have to take care of something before we go."

It sounded like Jusik was saying they were only good for the brute-force end of the job. But maybe he'd just picked up on the fact that the squad wanted to be out on the front line.

"We'll have the TIV ready on the landing pad in thirty standard minutes, sir." Boss knew how to give Jusik a deadline in the kindest way. "And an appropriate wardrobe."

Jusik seemed agitated, turning his comlink over and over in his hands. "Excellent." He paused. "By mentioning that he might bring in Skirata and Vau, has General Zey given me a nod and a wink to do that in a deniable manner?"

"Not a question we're qualified to answer, General," Boss said. "Although if anyone can find out what a bunch of Mandalorians are doing, it'd be them. Or the Nulls."

"You talk as if Mandalorians are foreign to you, Boss."

"Well, they are. Some of them, anyway."

"Sorry, I didn't put that very well. I meant—do you think of yourself as Mandalorian in any way?"

"Probably as much as you think of yourself as a Jedi, sir. Raised that way, more or less, but the enthusiasm depends on whether your own kind are putting you in the line of fire or not."

Ouch. Sev winced, waiting for the reaction. None came. Jusik nodded as if that meant something, and shot off at a run toward the administration area.

Jusik was taking this whole *Mando* thing too far; the kid had no sense of danger. He'd dress up in that *beskar'gam* and end up with his throat cut, Jedi or not, because even if Skirata liked him and treated him like one of the family, the average *Mando* would take him for the Jedi spy he would certainly be.

"What's got into him?" Fixer asked as they made the final checks on the TIV.

"Hard to tell with a Jedi," Scorch said. "I get the feeling there's something going on, and Zey knows Jusik isn't leveling with him, but it's all happening on some higher plane while grunts like us just watch the outward show of business-as-usual. You can never tell what they're picking up in the Force while they're smiling politely."

That was *it*. Never knowing what Jedi could see and you couldn't really got to Sev, and it went beyond the *different skill set,* as Jusik insisted on calling it. The word *powers* annoyed the general, but powers they were. The squad carried on the conversation in hushed tones, as if Jusik might have some Force method for eavesdropping on them.

Scorch just confirmed Sev's bad feeling. "He's going to get himself killed. Skirata and Vau can play these games, but they've been around a long, long time."

"We're *all* going to get ourselves killed." Sev knew what he meant, though. "It's in the job description. The line that says don't take out any long-term loans."

"You think he'd rather be *Bard'ika* or General Jusik?" Scorch asked.

"Are you asking if I think he's loyal?"

"I suppose so."

Sev didn't enjoy the thought. "He's loyal to *us.*"

"They're great to have on your side, Jedi."

Fixer heaved a crate of supplies into the TIV's cramped cargo area. "I liked it better when we just blew stuff up and splattered Geonosians. All this thinking is bound to end in tears."

"Yeah, but not yours," Scorch said, taking out his datapad. "I'm going to work out how much thermal plastoid it'd take to launch ActionWorld into orbit."

"Or excavate a hole."

"You enjoy your hobby, Fixer, and let me enjoy mine."

Sev sat down on one of the crates and calibrated his Deece again, something that he'd begun to see as a nervous habit. Zey, he thought, was being way too hard on Jusik. He couldn't give a brand-new officer that kind of latitude without support and still expect him not to screw up. Okay, *everyone* was thinly stretched lately, and every time Sev looked at the deployment chart and worked out where all the Jedi were in theater, they really were getting more and more scattered, more physically separated from one another. But that was no excuse for not picking up a comlink and giving Jusik a how-are-you chat. Skirata called all his squads, all ninety men or however many it was right now, at least once a month just to see what they *needed.* He knew what they were doing operationally anyway. He said it wasn't enough to have an open door: if he checked on them regularly, they didn't have to worry if he'd think they were weak or whiny for raising a concern. And sometimes they just needed to know that someone still cared if they lived or died.

That was probably why Jusik gravitated to Skirata. Zey only had himself to blame if the kid liked playing *Mando* now. That subtle difference in handling soldiers was why Mandalorians made better armies.

Jusik's going to get in over his head one day, and if Zey hasn't got the time to keep an eye on him when Skirata's not around, then we'll have to do it. And if he does something dumb—well, Zey let him go off and do it.

Yes, it would be down to Zey. Before you handed someone power, you had to ask yourself if you'd be happy with the worst possible thing they could ever do with it.

Galactic City, Coruscant, 482 days after Geonosis

It might have been someone at the door, or the chrono alarm, or even a warning from the environment controls, but the beeping woke Besany. Then she realized it was the comlink on her bedside table making a sound she seldom heard.

She'd set it to make a different sound when calls came in from any of her secure codes—meaning Ordo, mainly. She didn't want to miss him if he tried to contact her. Fi's situation made her realize more than ever that she had to make more of what time she had with Ordo. But when she fumbled for the device and answered, it was Skirata.

"I forgot the time on Coruscant," he said. "Sorry. I woke you, didn't I?"

"It's okay. Just getting an early night." She sat up and shook herself to try to clear her head. "What is it?"

"Fi. Don't worry, he's still in one piece. But I need you to do me a favor."

It didn't even occur to her to hesitate. "Let me get my datapad." She felt around on the table for it and sent a glass of water tumbling over the carpet. "Ready."

"We're having a little trouble over his care, and if you could keep an eye on him, it'd be appreciated."

"Of course. Anything." The alarm bell that went off now was real but silent, deep in her head: she probably knew more about the absence of medical support than Skirata did. "Where is he?"

"Jusik managed to get him admitted to the main neuro unit at Republic Central Medcenter by making a few calls, but now there's some argument about keeping him there, and you're the nearest one to the medcenter to smooth it out. I wouldn't dump this on you if I could get one of my boys there faster, *Bes'ika.*"

You're very good at making me feel like one of the family. How well you know me. "I'd do it anyway, Kal, even without the psy ops. Consider me co-opted by reason of vulnerability, the general desire to do what's right, and the fact that I fell for your son."

There was a pause. Maybe she'd been too frank.

"I didn't mean it like that." Skirata sounded frayed; things were probably worse than he was letting on. "Sorry. I don't even know I'm doing it half the time. But if I didn't trust you to do what I'd do myself if I was there right now, I wouldn't ask. It's just a bureaucratic thing."

"I'll make sure Fi is getting the best medical care, whatever it takes. I'm good at bureaucracy . . ."

"Ordo updated you, then."

"I know he's in a coma, that's all. What level?"

"Niner said zero response to stimuli last time." It had all slipped into the unemotional world of medical jargon. "No brain activity, but still breathing unaided. I'm sending you the patient ID details now so you can get past the receptionist droid."

"I'll get over there right away."

"Thank you, *Bes'ika*. Everything hit us at once this time, or else—"

"Anytime. No need to apologize."

"You go careful with the other stuff, okay?" He meant her investigation of the cloning activity. "You got us some solid-gold intel, but it's not worth getting killed for."

"Isn't that the risk you all take?"

Another pause. "Even a manipulative old *chakaar* like me feels guilty sometimes. Whatever it costs, you know I can pay."

Or General Zey can. "I'll call you as soon as I've resolved it," she said. It was Treasury-speak, but she'd flipped into that persona now. "Whatever it takes. It's nothing a budget code can't resolve."

It could have been worse, she told herself, automatically putting on her work suit. It could have been three in the morning, when she'd be too sleep-befuddled to be any use. She tied her hair back in a severe tail because loose blond hair got her instant attention, grabbed her bag—and blaster, because Skirata wasn't joking—and called an air taxi.

RCM was a small city of a medcenter with its own traffic system, and it took several passes around the internal sky-lanes for the pilot to find the entrance to the neurology unit. Besany didn't like medcenters, and the moment she walked into all that bright-lit, antiseptic state-of-the-artness, she felt agitated. It was where her father had died. That was all it would ever be to her, and no amount of exquisite fresh flowers in the lobbies could change that. Skirata probably knew he'd plugged some gap in her life, but he couldn't know how well.

"New admissions," she said to the orientation droid, holding her anonymized datapad up to its port. There was a lot to be said for knowing how to cover your tracks. "Here's the patient ID."

The droid digested the code and when she withdrew the datapad, the text SKIRATA, FI: LEVEL 96, WARD 5, BAY A/4 appeared on the screen. So Fi wasn't a number any longer, but a man with an inevitable surname. The sensor system took over from the droid, and Besany followed a flow of instructions, from a reminder from the turbolift to ALIGHT HERE to the sensors in the corridors directing her left and right via the datapad. A city-planet of a trillion beings needed medcenters on an industrial scale, but there was something soul crushing about a complex so vast, it needed its own global positioning system. It was no place to be when you were sick, scared, or dying.

But the GPS worked. Besany found herself facing a small room in a side ward with SKIRATA, FI—TEMP ADMIT DNR visible on the viewscreen next to the doors.

They opened as soon as she stepped forward, and there was Fi with a line plugged into the back of his hand, lying on uncreased white pillows with his arms neatly on top of the blankets like a man newly dead awaiting a final visit from the family. The only difference from what she recalled all those years ago was that Fi was wired up to sensors, with his vital signs displayed on a small panel on the wall.

He did look very young indeed. Besany hadn't been imagining that, and somehow she'd expected to see visible injury even though Ordo had said there was none. It seemed perverse that Fi could look so perfectly whole and yet be so close to death.

"Fi," she said. "It's Besany. Kal sent me to keep an eye on you. Just checking you're okay."

She stood there for a while, working out what she was going to say to the administrators, and then the doors opened behind her.

"This is an unauthorized entry," said the med droid. "Who are you?"

Besany did it more out of habit than intent. She pulled out her Republic ID and shoved it in front of the droid's photoreceptors, but didn't put it in the data slot so it could identify her or her department. Something told her she was going to have to bend the rules again, and she didn't want to be traced. "Government business. What's happening with this patient?"

"There seems to have been an administrative error, Agent . . ."

Besany let the pause hang. "What kind? Billing?" It almost always was, and she could fix that. "Notification?"

"Are you from the Department of Defense?"

It was all pure reflex now. "Would I discuss it with you if I was? Just update me on this patient. I understand some difficulty arose over treating him here."

"He can't stay here."

"If this is about budget codes, my department will be *most* displeased."

"No, we have to terminate the treatment."

"You've got a line of saline in his arm and there's nothing on the drug chart. You're not short of beds. *What* treatment? I don't see the chief of neurosurgery in here."

"He's not a citizen. He's a clone soldier."

"I know. And?"

"We have no agreement for long-term care with the Grand Army. In fact, as far as the Republic is concerned this patient doesn't exist, and as he's been declared brain-dead by the duty neurosurgical team, we would normally terminate life support, except he's still breathing, which is highly abnormal." The droid paused as if to check if Besany was following its train of logic with her inadequate organic brain. "Withdrawal of life support in his case means withdrawal of hydration or feeding, or both."

"Starving him to death, for us lay-beings."

"Indeed. This is clearly ethically undesirable, so euthanasia will be administered."

Besany thought she'd misheard, but she hadn't. "No," she said, hearing her voice as if she were standing outside herself. "No, it will *not* be administered. I'll get his care authorized. In fact, I'll get him moved to private care."

Did I hear that right? Do they really put patients down like that? Like sick pets?

"He's Grand Army property, so unless you have a Defense requisition, you can't take possession of him."

"He's a *human being*."

"I don't make the rules."

"His name's Fi. If he hadn't been engineered and hatched, he'd be about twenty-four years old. He's a sniper, He's a trained combat medic. He likes glimmik music. He's an elite soldier."

"He's brain-dead."

"He's *breathing*."

"I *said* this was a perplexing case."

"Well, if you or any of your colleagues want to try euthanizing him, or whatever tidy euphemism you have for killing people in their beds, you'll have to get past *me.*"

"You're not from the Defense Department, are you?"

"I'm from the Treasury. If he's government property, he's *mine.* So I'm taking him."

"I cannot allow this."

"Try stopping me."

Besany rarely said things she regretted, but she realized she was now terrified. *What of? Injury? Getting into trouble with my boss? What, exactly, when Fi's lying there?* But her primal defensive instincts—for herself, for Fi—had taken over, and her mouth was pursuing its own panicky agenda.

"You have to leave now," the droid said.

If she walked out of here now and abandoned him, Fi was definitely dead, *really* dead. He was breathing fine. She didn't care about definitions of brain death or depth of consciousness. This was about what she believed in and thought was right, from the time she'd first met Trooper Corr and realized what her government sanctioned in her name.

If I don't make a stand now, what's the use of expecting Senator Skeenah to make a difference?

"Then you'll need to have me thrown out—bodily." Besany reached inside her jacket and drew the blaster Mereel had given her. "I'm not going quietly, and I'm not leaving without Fi."

She aimed the weapon squarely at the med droid's central section, where the power packs were located, and flicked the charge indicator so that it could see she was serious about using it.

She had no idea how she was going to get Fi out of here. She had no friends or family to call upon, and her small band of special forces contacts were scattered across the galaxy; she was on her own. *Order* and *precise planning* had always been her watchwords, but there was no time for that now, and the best she could hope for was to stall for time—time for what, and how long?—or make such a scene that they backed down.

"I'm calling security," the droid said, and backed toward the door.

Besany could see that it already had, or had at least alerted someone to the argument: there was a small crowd of white-coated figures and droids outside in the corridor. She followed it to the threshold with the blaster aimed, and when the staff outside saw it, pandemonium broke loose. They ran for it. Some screamed. The security alarm boomed and flashed along the corridor.

Besany shut the doors and seared the panel lock with the blaster, something she didn't believe would actually work, but that Ordo had mentioned in passing. It worked, all right. She was now stuck in the room with Fi.

Okay, I've done it now. I'll get arrested. I'll lose my job. What happens to Fi then? But what happens to Fi if I just cave in to them?

It was sobering to think how fine a knife-edge stood between an early night after a boring holovid, and plunging into an abyss of anarchy where she pulled a blaster on a med droid and made a stand against a system that stank.

Besany pulled up a chair and sat at Fi's bedside, blaster still on the door, and put her free hand on his. It felt warm and surprisingly smooth, but then the commandos always seemed to wear gloves.

"Sorry, Fi," she said. "But I asked Jilka if she wanted a date. She's nice when you get to know her."

Chances were that he'd never see her, but he wasn't going to leave here with the rest of the medical waste. She needed help, and there was only one person she could think of who could give it. She let go of Fi's hand and opened her comlink to call Skirata.

"I don't want to worry you, Kal," she said quietly, "but I've started an armed siege at the medcenter. I've got my blaster, and Fi's okay for the time being, but if you've got any advice . . . I'd welcome it right *now*."

Kyrimorut, Mandalore, 482 days after Geonosis

"We've got to go, Etain." Skirata grabbed a chunk of meat from the table and wrapped it hastily before cramming it into one of his belt pouches. Ordo was in the doorway, wearing his ARC captain's armor for a change. "We need to get back to Coruscant fast. Besany's run into a spot of trouble."

Etain was plowing through the list of members of the Republic Academy of Genetics, identifying likely scientists for future discussions—voluntary or otherwise—while Mereel was holed up in a room with Ko Sai. The Kaminoan wasn't adjusting well to captivity, and she wasn't feeling chatty.

"What kind of trouble?"

"She was trying to get Fi released from the medcenter and ran into a few problems."

Problems didn't usually mean "admin" in Skirata's vocabulary. "Tell me they're both okay."

"They will be. I just asked Jaller to give her a hand." If Skirata had called in a favor from Jaller Obrim, the head of CSF's Anti-Terrorist Unit, then it wasn't just admin problems. He hesitated, looking guilty, which Etain found painful under the circumstances. "Okay, Besany started an armed siege. They were going to terminate Fi."

The declining value of life in Etain's personal galaxy depressed her more each day. The war seemed to be eroding everyone's decency, or maybe it had always been that way but she was noticing it close to home now. Darman had joked that droids were more valued than clones because they had a scrap value, but it wasn't funny anymore. She hardly knew how to react.

And as Jedi, we're supposed to defend this Republic?

Etain settled for pragmatism rather than outrage. "Kal, she's a very competent woman, but she has no experience with firearms. She'll get hurt."

"Jaller will sort things out. He always does."

"Then why didn't you call him first? And isn't Vau around?"

"Vau was on Aargau but he's on his way back now—and I thought this was just some argument over budget codes. We're not abandoning her, *ad'ika*. Got to go. I'll keep you updated."

Ordo was completely silent. She watched his retreating back and guessed that he was going to have a rough few hours in transit, fretting about both Besany and Fi, and struggling with his own feelings about the datachips. She could taste his guilt. Every time she caught him looking at Skirata, it was with a regret that was eating him alive.

But Skirata was, as she'd thought on first meeting him, a gdan—one of Qiilura's assortment of carnivorous wildlife, very small aggressive creatures armed with dreadful little teeth, and who'd take on any prey regardless of its size. *Feisty* didn't begin to cover it. And Skirata, like gdans, bounced back from a drubbing fast.

Mereel came out of what Etain had started to think of as the interrogation room and laid a couple of datapads on the table. "Did I hear right? The lovely Agent Wennen started a shoot-out?"

"You gave her the blaster . . ."

"Just aiming at levity, although I don't feel like it." He scrolled through the datapad screens while he sliced a chunk from the leg of nerf one-handed and chewed it thoughtfully. The roasts seemed to sit on the table most of the day, losing a chunk or a slice every so often, and only the bone was left by the evening. "It's funny how scaring someone in an interrogation can be more effective than giving them a good hiding."

"You're talking as one professional interrogator to another, of course."

"You did a nice job with the Nikto, as I recall, when Vau hadn't made much headway."

"So what scares Ko Sai? Found it yet?"

"Anonymity."

"She's a Kaminoan. They don't take prime-time ads on HNE."

"I mean that she won't go down in her own history as one of the greats. With her work gone, she's nothing. Even when she betrayed her government and did a runner with their most lucrative industrial secrets, she could still think of herself as one of the greatest geneticists of all time—maybe *the* greatest. Now she's got *nothing* to show for her work. We trashed her lab and the last of her cell cultures, too. She's effectively erased from science history, which is probably worse than being dead for her."

"So what do you offer someone to get them to cooperate when they already think they've lost everything?"

"To rebuild her lab here and put her back on the map."

"But she knows she can't ever apply what she discovers. You won't let her. She knows you well enough for that."

"She's quite interested in Jedi genetics . . ."

"Oh no. No. Absolutely *not.*" Etain was instantly furious. "How *could* you?"

Mereel looked genuinely wounded. "I was only *lying* to her."

"You're using my child as some bargaining chip!"

"I'm using the *idea* of your child as a way of getting its father a normal life span, *General.*"

"You want me to go in there, don't you? You want me to work on her."

Mereel shrugged. "Here's my problem. I find it hard to separate what I want to do to her from what I want to get out of her. She hurt me and my brothers badly from the day we were . . . hatched, to the day two years later when *Kal'buir* showed up and stopped her. They don't really understand human pain and stress, except written on flimsi as some theory, and they don't care anyway as long as the flesh machine that they build works. Think about your child, and then think how you'd feel if she did to him what she did to us. And that's *without* being put down at the end of the experiment for fighting back."

Mereel always knew how to target her worst nightmares. That was probably why Skirata had let him loose on Ko Sai: he knew how to hurt, and he was much more subtle than Vau.

Etain didn't answer.

"So, *Et'ika,* you can see why keeping my mind on cooperation is hard."

What harm could it do? Ko Sai couldn't touch her, and Darman had everything to lose.

"Okay," she said. "But you're going to do a lot of babysitting to make up for this."

"I'd love that," he said. He smiled, and he had such an artless, genuinely joyful smile that it was hard to square what he did with what he was. "It's going to be *wonderful.*"

Etain spent a few minutes composing herself before she went into that room. She walked the circular path through the corridors that had quickly become her routine in the last couple of days, concentrating on a Force-bond with the baby. She could feel *him* growing now: before, she'd been in control of accelerating the pregnancy in healing trances, but now it was as if he had taken the reins and was deciding on his own pace. She had the strongest sense of him being impatient, of wanting to be out in the world and doing things, and it alarmed her. It was as if he felt she was a dangerous place that he needed to escape before she took him into any more battles or traded him for a deal with a scientist whose ethics were repellent.

Venku, we live in an age of chaos. You're going to change many lives. Maybe this is where you start, saving your father and your uncles before you're even born.

She could have sworn he calmed a little within her. Venku was the future, and Skirata acted as if he *knew* it, or at least was an instrument of the Force.

"Okay, aiwha-bait."

Etain took a breath and walked into the room. Ko Sai didn't look half as impressive or elegant in a borrowed shapeless gown, which was all that Bralor had managed to find to cover a being more than two meters tall. It had probably been furnishing fabric hurriedly sewn together: Mandalorian women didn't wear dresses. Without the well-cut, close-fitting suit with its spectacular high collar, Ko Sai looked faintly ludicrous, like a tau serpent trying to escape from a sack.

"I hear Mereel has been talking about my baby," Etain said, sitting down opposite her with a slightly exaggerated effort that announced how pregnant she was. It also let Ko Sai see that she had not one but two lightsabers on her belt. "Being a Jedi, I'm very pragmatic. We're trained to find peaceful compromises."

"Are you really a Jedi? You're not exactly General Kenobi . . ."

Etain concentrated on the most powerful Force grab she could muster and sent a chair crashing from one side of the room to the other, shattering it into splinters against the wall.

"Jedi enough for you?" she asked. She patted her bump. "I could run through my list, but I've got heartburn, so can we take it as read?"

"Impressive." Ko Sai could never sound impressed, so Etain took it at face value. "It's hard to tell from appearance."

"You're not interested in my conjuring tricks, though, are you? You want to crack a Jedi genome and take a look at those midi-chlorians."

"It would be fascinating."

"And instead of being the chief scientist who ended her career in disgrace and obscurity, you could be the preeminent authority on Force-user genetics."

"What do you care about scientific knowledge?"

"I don't, unless it can help the people I love."

"I find it staggering that anyone could destroy so much precious knowledge on a whim."

Ko Sai meant Ordo. If he'd tried to design a way to really get back at her, he couldn't have come up with a better one than vaping those datachips.

"Yes, that did come as a shock," Etain said.

"I thought it was one of Skirata's little games until I saw

the effect it had on him. He's lost a great deal, too, or you wouldn't be in here—would you?"

"No." Etain stood up and walked around the room slowly, just to give Ko Sai something to ponder. The more interested the Kaminoan seemed—and she did exude a powerful curiosity—the bolder Etain felt. "If it means giving you a few cells to play with in exchange for the clones having a normal life span, it's worth it to me. Not an extra-prolonged life. Not whatever the Chancellor wanted you to do for him. Just undo what you did, for these few men, and nobody cares what you do in the future."

"Skirata cares."

"Skirata is a practical man who loves his sons, not a moral philosopher."

Ko Sai looked her in the eyes. Etain understood what Skirata meant when he said they were creepy. It was a good description: no warmth, no understanding, just intense, pitiless scrutiny.

"We all sell out in the end," she said.

"Even me," said Etain.

"The father of your child is one of the clone units, isn't he?"

Etain had never heard them called *units* before. But Darman—all of them—were just organic machines built to order as far as the Kaminoans were concerned: product, merchandise, *units*. "Yes. Imagine it. One genome you know intimately, combined with one you've never been able to get your hands on."

Ko Sai's face didn't exactly light up, but Etain sensed a slight lifting of her dark mood.

"How can I trust you?"

"I'll give you a cryosuspended sample of my blood now." Etain wasn't sure where she might get a cryocontainer out here, but Rav Bralor would know. It was the kind of kit that even veterinarians kept for sending livestock samples for testing, so the next farm might have some. "You give me a list of some of the genes you regulated to achieve rapid aging, and how they're switched to reverse the process. I'm not even asking for them all at this stage. Just a demonstration that we understand we both have something to lose and gain in this."

"And what after that?"

"When the baby's born? Multipotent stem cells, maybe, from the umbilical cord."

Ko Sai did seem taken aback by that. "You've done your homework, Jedi."

Well, Mereel had, but Etain was reassured that she could still act convincingly. "Do we have a deal? Is it really worth holding out just to remind a few clones that you had that power over their life span, when you could move into a whole new area of research?"

Ko Sai went very quiet and made that odd weaving movement of her head, back and forth, very snake-like. It struck Etain as the equivalent of a human drumming her fingers on the table while thinking hard.

"Very well," she said. "There are many things I can cite from memory, even without the research from Tipoca."

Etain sat down and tried not to look triumphant. The heartburn helped a lot. Ko Sai marked screen after screen on her datapad, and then handed it to Etain.

"Those are the first sequences that can be switched back with zinc and methylation," she said. "Mereel should be able to check that those are valid."

"Thank you." Etain still wondered if the scientist actually knew the whole solution yet, but even if she didn't, they now had an extra something they didn't have before. "I'll get the blood container, and you can keep the sample with you. It need never leave your sight. Can I get you anything else?"

Ko Sai swayed her head. "Without my datapad connection to the HoloNet, I have little to read. Could you obtain the latest edition of the *Republic Institute Journal of Endocrinology* for me?"

"I'm sure I can."

Etain closed the doors behind her and breathed again. *Sorry, Venku, but she's never going to be able to put it to use, is she?* When she walked into the main room, which she'd come to think of as a cross between a kitchen and a salon, Mereel was finishing off the nerf. She wondered if slowing down the aging process would reduce the clones' prodigious appetites.

"Here," she said, laying the datapad in front of him. "All you have to do is offer her your firstborn and she's as good as gold."

Mereel stopped chewing and swallowed hard. He stared at the data.

"Et'ika," he said, "you're not just good for opening doors, are you?"

"We're taking it a step at a time."

"What did you offer her? Seriously?"

"First payment? A cryosample of my blood, and a holozine—the *Journal of Endocrinology.*"

"Maybe she misses the jokes page."

"Let's keep her as sweet as we can keep a Kaminoan, shall we?"

"Seriously—well done, Etain."

"Jedi stuff." She was starting to feel good again, useful and competent. "And I've found that most beings can't look away from a pregnant female. Psyched her out a little, especially given her life's work."

It was a job well done, for the time being. Mereel made her a pot of *shig*—a tisane made from a plant called *behot*—before getting on with examining the data.

"I'll have to get this checked," he said, "and that means farming it out in sections so they don't know what it is I'm working on, but it's a hopeful start."

Etain sipped. The *shig* was citrus-flavored and kinder to her stomach than caf. "It's just such a shame that all that other data was . . . lost."

It felt too cruel to say *blown to pieces by your crazy brother.*

"Yeah," Mereel said, and squatted down next to her seat. He put his finger to his lips for silence and opened one of his belt pouches. Then he drew out a container, the kind that datachips were stored in, took her hand, and laid it on the little box. "Indeed."

"Mereel . . ."

"Don't you *always* do a backup, Etain? Tut tut . . ."

"Don't joke about this, Mereel." She was starting to get annoyed with him. Skirata had been mortified by it. "Is that what I think it is?"

"We might have behavioral problems, but we're not stupid. It *is*. All intact. Ordo meant what he said, but he didn't use the real set of chips."

Etain's ecstatic relief was instantly slapped down by recalling Skirata's face. "How could you do this to Kal? What if he'd had a seizure or something? He was *devastated*."

Mereel replaced the datachips and stood up. "I know, I know. Ordo and I argued over it, but it was the only way I could get *Kal'buir* to act like it was real. He's usually a great little actor, our *buir,* but he isn't always good at grief. Ko Sai would probably have spotted it."

"Poor man."

"I'll comm Ordo and let him know he can tell *Kal'buir.*"

"Kal's going to be furious. He blames himself."

"Oh, *Ord'ika* can get away with murder. He's the number one son." Mereel went back to the datapad, and smiled again. "And it broke Ko Sai, didn't it?"

It did. But it had very nearly broken Skirata, too, and Etain could see it.

And I just lied and used my unborn son to do a deal that I know won't be honored, so where does that leave me?

They were living in desperate times. Whether it meant that the rules no longer applied, or that the times they lived in were down to ordinary people abandoning those rules to start with, Etain wasn't sure.

16

I don't know why they're keeping me here. They haven't demanded information from me or tried to force me to create an antidote to the nanovirus. I'm bored with no work to do, but nobody ever died of boredom. Sometimes I wonder if the man in the cloak—the one who commissioned my research—has been trying to reach me, but they've taken away my holoreceiver.
—Dr. Ovolot Qail Uthan, bioengineer and geneticist, creator of the Fett-genome-targeted nanovirus FG36, currently held in a Republic maximum-security prison somewhere on Coruscant

Republic Central Medcenter neurology unit, Coruscant, 483 days after Geonosis

"I said *move it,* didn't I? You deaf or something? Clear the corridor! Armed police!"

Boots clattered outside and Besany heard the sound of doors opening and closing, shouts of "Clear!" and the familiar barked orders of a man who'd once entertained her royally in the CSF Staff and Social Club.

Captain Jaller Obrim—former Senate Guard—loved his work on secondment to the ATU so much that he'd stayed. The doors burst open, and she was staring down the barrel of a police-issue blaster with a red targeting laser blinding her. Ordo said the laser was theatrics to scare targets, and no serious sniper would give away his position with one. It certainly scared her. But she wanted to be sure who was taking her surrender before she laid down her blaster.

"Captain Obrim?"

"Agent Wennen, put the blaster down, will you?" He didn't lower his weapon, and it struck her that he thought she might open fire on him. "Come on, it's me. Jaller. Kal called."

She trusted him. If she was wrong—no, she *had* to trust him, and Skirata, too. She lowered the blaster, flicked the safety catch on, and put it in her jacket again.

"That's better," Obrim said. He held his blaster up in the safety position and leaned out of the doorway. "Clear, boys. Stand down. Prepare to transport a detainee. Paramedics—in here."

"I'm sorry about this, Captain." Besany could feel her legs shaking as the adrenaline finished its job. She almost sat down on the edge of Fi's bed to recover, but matters seemed too urgent now. "I had no idea what else to do."

Obrim looked over Fi and gripped his hand tightly. "Fierfek, they want to just finish him off? I've had officers recover from head wounds when they shouldn't have, and ones who died when they shouldn't have, so while I can see him breathing—I want a second opinion. Even a third. As many as it takes." He straightened up. "Where's that gurney?"

"Where are we going to take him?" Besany asked. "I appear to be stealing government property. He can stay in my guest room, but I've got to find someone to—"

"I've got a secure location, don't you worry. And care laid on." The CSF paramedics moved in and began detaching Fi from the sensors and wrapping him in blankets. "If they want to play this game, fine. I can play it bigger."

Obrim was upset and angry. She'd only seen the world-weary side of him, never fazed by anything, but this was very personal for him and it showed. He and Skirata were a matched pair. He might have been the only *aruetyc* friend that Skirata had. They certainly saw the galaxy the same way.

"I'd better call my boss and let him know he's going to have an unpleasant message from Coruscant Health," Besany said. "Need any clerks at CSF? Because I'm going to be fired in the morning."

Obrim moved in to tuck a stray corner of blanket under Fi's body as the gurney was steered away. "Don't worry. He'll never hear about it."

"Kind of hard to ignore, one of his senior investigators storming into a medcenter and holding patients hostage."

"I'll make it go away," Obrim said. "I'm CSF. I can make all kinds of things go away when I need to."

Outside, the medical staff had begun to swarm back, some droid and some organics, and CSF officers cleared a path for the gurney to get to the turbolift. Obrim seemed to have mobilized half a shift to extract Fi from the unit. One med droid, whose identi-tab showed it was the duty administrator, hovered into Obrim's path.

"I insist you return the patient to our care," it said. "Once we've admitted someone, we have to be able to account for them and show they were discharged properly."

"Make up your mind," Obrim said, steering Besany past the droid. "One minute he's a patient and the next he's government property."

"You can't take him. We're responsible for him."

"Until you shoot him full of latheniol, yeah. He discharged himself."

"He's incapable of doing that."

"Okay, I'm ATU. I've arrested him for looking at me funny. Now move it, or I'll book you for obstructing me."

"Then arrest that woman for threatening my staff, too."

"Unless you want *your* rivets felt, tinnie boy, step out of my way."

"This is an outrage. There'll be a formal complaint to your superiors."

Obrim leaned over slightly to make his point to the droid. He had weight and gravitas on his side. "Before you do that," he said quietly, "ask your chief executive about his interest in Twi'lek *artistic pursuits* on every fourth of the month, and if he'd like me to give police surveillance holovids of the visits to the *cultural center* to his lovely wife. Your call."

The droid paused, then backed off and hovered away. "We'll see," it said.

Besany slumped back against the wall of the turbolift, heart pounding again. She would never get her life back, she knew it. She wasn't sure that it mattered. "Where are we going, Captain? Who's going to look after him? I'll do whatever I can."

"First things first, my dear. Let's get him settled. We can worry about the rest later."

"You didn't answer. Where are we going?"

"Home," said Obrim.

He wasn't joking. At the speeder bay, an unmarked CSF transport was waiting with its rear hatch open. The paramedics loaded Fi on board and got in beside him. Obrim followed in his own speeder with Besany.

"It's amazing what you can rent," he said, as if none of the drama had taken place only minutes earlier. "You can rent med droids to look after Granny at home. So I've rented one for Fi. I mean, I'd look after him myself, but I don't know how to get feeding tubes and saline in him."

"What's your wife going to say?"

"I don't know. I just said I was bringing someone home she had to keep quiet about. She's pretty used to some of the irregularities in this job."

"Thanks, Captain. Thank you so much."

"It's Jaller. I think we know each other well enough now, don't we?"

"Yes. I think so."

The first hurdle was cleared. She'd managed to get Fi to safety, thanks largely to the conscience of a bunch of cops who were taking a risk themselves, whatever Obrim said. But the real struggle lay ahead, and it might have no ending for a long, long time.

Fi was still in a deep coma, and as far as medicine was concerned, he was dead.

But he was still breathing. Besany was getting used to seeing the impossible happen. It could happen again.

Arca Barracks, SO Brigade HQ, Coruscant,
483 days after Geonosis

Corr had the air of a guilty man, and Darman remembered that feeling from when he'd first walked into Omega Squad, after the commando brigades took massive losses in the first weeks of the war and squads were re-formed as men died.

But Corr was RC-5108/8843 now, a member of Omega Squad proper, and not just attached to them. He walked into the barracks recreation room in his new armor—Fi's rig, helmet under one arm—but didn't seem comfortable in it.

The whole neat designation system had gone down the tubes with Corr, too. He wasn't just one of the many troopers now cross-trained in commando skills; he was a shiny boy, a real Republic commando, and Skirata insisted that he have the code to match even if his numbers didn't fit.

Darman was determined to make him welcome. " *'Cuy, vod'ika.*" He slapped the seat next to him. "Park your *shebs* there. We'd pour you some of the GAR-issue caf but we like you too much for that. We're waiting for Sergeant Kal."

Corr sat down as ordered, and Niner and Atin leaned across to clasp his arm.

"You can slip into something more comfortable," Niner said, indicating their bodysuits. "That plastoid can crimp the important places after a while."

Corr started removing plates as if they were burning him. "Any news on Fi?" he asked.

"Waiting to hear what happened at the medcenter." Niner passed him a carton of warra nut cookies, which was unconditional acceptance as far as Omega were concerned. Darman noted that Corr wasn't wearing the synthflesh coating on his prosthetic hands, so he had some point he needed to make. "Last we heard, Sergeant Kal had sent in the heavy mob."

"Ordo?"

"Agent Wennen and Captain Obrim."

"Ah."

Darman winced. Corr had been the object of Besany's interest until Ordo took his place—literally. If the former trooper felt that the Null captain had muscled in on his girl, he showed no sign of it. She'd been very *kind* to him while he was recovering on desk duties, he'd said. That was all.

It'd take a lot more than Besany's kindness to put Fi back on his feet.

Corr was uneasy. It was inevitable. "I just wanted to say something before we go any further."

"Get it off your chest, *ner vod*," said Atin.

"I won't be trying to replace Fi." Corr blurted it out as if he'd been thinking about it for a long time and now wanted to get it over with. "I might wear the armor but I'm not the man, and I'm not going to compete with him. When he's fit, I'm out again, okay?"

Maybe he was being diplomatic, or he might not have realized how bad things were. Darman didn't explain.

"It's okay," said Atin. "I was one of Vau's trainees. Joining this bunch was a bit rough."

"Was not," Niner muttered. He'd never been one for a good laugh, but he tried hard—painfully hard—because morale was the squad sergeant's job as far as he was concerned. "It was Daruvvian champagne all the way."

Darman tried to join in the determined jollity, but Corr still had the dent on his chest plate where Fi had had a disagreement with a grenade, and there was no shared joke to be had about it. It was going to be very hard without Fi.

"So you've enjoyed a rich social education with Mereel and Kom'rk, have you?" Darman never felt he could talk about that in front of Fi, because Fi so desperately wanted a *nice girl*, as he put it, and any talk of relationships got to him. Now he'd never get the chance. "I saw Kom'rk once, but he doesn't seem as . . ."

And that was as far as Darman got. Grief ambushed him. He found that all he could do was sit forward with his elbows braced on his knees, both hands to his mouth to stop the searing ache in his throat and eyes from turning into uncontrollable sobbing. He froze, scared to move in case that started him off. Eventually Corr ruffled his hair hard, just like Skirata did, and Darman got his breath under control enough to speak.

"That's what really gets to me," he said. "He didn't get what he really wanted, someone to love him, and now he never will, and I'm angry."

"Okay, Dar." Atin joined in the hair ruffling. "*Udesii.* You can't do anything about it now."

"He's not dead," said Niner quietly.

Darman could feel it hanging over them, the conversation that had seemed fine when they didn't realize how much damage he'd suffered, but now couldn't be spoken aloud because it was too awful. What was not-dead? How did the medics *know* Fi couldn't sense what was going on around him? Brain-dead people sometimes regained consciousness and then reported what they'd heard during the coma, and Darman could think of nothing more awful at that moment than Fi being trapped in some terrible paralysis but feeling *everything.* Dead was better. He wanted a cleaner end than Fi.

"Call Etain," Niner suggested. "She always cheers you up."

But Darman didn't want to call her just to rage about how unfair things were. He settled down with a holozine so nobody would talk to him for a while, and the others played blades, throwing knives into a target board divided into rings and quadrants. When he'd come to terms with this, he'd have something more positive to say to her. They could talk about where they'd go when they got some leave together.

I can't imagine a mission without Fi now.

The doors opened. Skirata wandered in dressed in his civvies—brown bantha leather jacket—with Ordo, Vau, and Mird behind, and simply walked up to each of the squad in turn and hugged them in silence. Then Jusik came in, and everyone turned to stare.

"I thought you were still with Delta when I spoke to you," Skirata said, and it was obvious he hadn't planned to meet him here. "What happened?"

"Delta can handle Dorumaa without me." Jusik didn't

look his old self, either: he was usually the essence of calm good humor however bad things got, but he didn't seem remotely serene or accepting now. His face looked hard rather than thin; he was all rigid determination. "I was only there to slow them down last time. Fi needs me more."

"What d'you mean, Fi needs you more?"

"I'm going to try healing him."

Nobody said a word. Jedi could heal, but they didn't do miracles. Skirata lowered his voice in that way he had when things were going badly wrong and he needed to break the news gently.

"Okay, son," he said. "But Zey's going to skin you alive. He sent you back to do the Dorumaa job again. He won't take kindly to you going off like this."

"With respect, Zey can shove it."

"You sure about that, *Bard'ika*? When the war's over, you'll still be a Jedi, and he'll still be your boss."

"Ah, no, that's where we differ, Kal. We've forgotten what it is to be Jedi. So I'm going to do some real Jedi work now, and help someone in trouble rather than talk big concepts and run errands for politicians. Where's Fi?"

"Jaller's found a safe place for him." Skirata turned to the squad. "You never heard this conversation. Things got a bit hairy at the medcenter, and Besany had to . . . well, blasters were involved. And Jaller. And half the ATU lads."

It was the point at which Fi would have made some witty observation had he been there. The silence was painful.

"Sooner I start, the better chance I have," Jusik said. "Take me there, Kal. Please."

"They'll kick you out of the Order, son. As long as you can face that, fine."

"Look, if you won't take me, I'll find him on my own, because I'm really good at that, aren't I? One of my uses. Scanning by Jedi."

"Okay, okay." Skirata got a look from Vau that Darman could only describe as disappointment. He probably thought that Skirata was being soft on Jusik. "Let's go, then. Ordo, you too."

"I'll wait here," said Vau. "Anything you want me to do to stall Zey if he shows?"

"I don't know. Delta's not going to tell him Jusik's gone AWOL, are they? And they could be gone weeks."

"It'll be a brief conversation, then."

Skirata, Ordo, and Jusik left as quickly as they'd come in. Darman fought not to get his hopes up; he couldn't help thinking that nobody really understood what Jedi could do—least of all Jedi, it seemed—and Skirata might simply have been placating Jusik. The general badly wanted to emulate Skirata, except with the Jedi bits added like some kind of first-aid kit and early-warning system. Avoidance of attachment and anger didn't get a look-in these days.

But that was the challenge, wasn't it? If you had powers like that, standing apart from the messy business of life was just avoiding the hard decisions. Jusik confronted his.

"Fierfek," said Corr, sharpening the throwing knives on the durasteel sections of his fingers, "is it always like that in this squad? And how much transit time do you guys clock up?"

Vau laughed. "Ah, the clarity of the newcomer."

"What did he mean, he was only there to slow Delta down?" Darman asked.

"You know how self-deprecating he is." Vau fed Mird a cookie. "A modest man."

It hadn't sounded like that, but then Darman accepted he wasn't at his most detached today. It was a pity Etain wasn't here: he missed her, as always, but she could also have given Jusik a hand with the healing, as she had when Jinart was shot.

It was no good worrying. Etain would be back when her mission was complete, Jusik would do all that a Jedi could do to help Fi, and his own task was to stay alive long enough to see both things happen. In the end, it was Fi who stayed on his mind today, not Etain, but she'd understand why.

She had such a long time ahead of her. Fi's time had been short to start with, and had ended up far shorter than he could ever have imagined.

Jaller Obrim's residence, Rampart Town, Coruscant,
483 days after Geonosis

"There's something I have to tell you, *Kal'buir*."

Ordo needed to get this off his chest. Dealing with Fi's plight was hard enough, but knowing Skirata was dragged down further by the apparent loss of Ko Sai's research was something he had to deal with sooner rather than later, so he could concentrate on the task at hand.

"What, son?" They waited with Jusik in the impressive security lobby of Obrim's apartment, undergoing automated scans, which showed just how many criminals had scores to settle with the officer.

"I'll understand if you can't forgive me for it."

"Can't be that bad."

"Mereel sent a message—Ko Sai gave Etain some of the gene sequences."

That got his attention. "Etain? Seriously?"

"She's got a knack."

"That's the best news I've heard in a while. Thanks, son." Skirata shut his eyes for a moment. "Is that all the aiwha-bait remembered?"

"It's turned into a negotiating game, but there's more to come."

"That's good. *Very* good."

"And I did something terrible to you, *Buir*. We have her data, all of it. I just did it to shake her down. She's completely devastated by the thought that it's gone, and it's become a lever to get more out of her. You convinced her it was really destroyed."

There. He'd come clean now. Skirata managed a smile of sorts, but he took it quietly. His voice was hoarse. "Yeah, I'm much more convincing when I'm on the verge of a heart attack."

"I'm so sorry. I never thought I'd do anything to hurt you, and yet when it's expedient, that's just what I do."

The security scan seemed satisfied that they weren't Black Sun hit men, and the doors opened. Jusik had a large holdall that clanked when he walked and set off a metal detector inside the hall. Ordo had an idea what it was but wondered what Jusik was going to do with it.

"Big stakes, son," Skirata said at last. "Yes, it was a nasty shock. But it worked."

"Can you ever trust me again?"

"With my life," Skirata said. "And I should be happier about this, but it's hard at the moment, what with Fi and everything."

"I said I'd make it up to you, *Buir*. I will."

Jaller Obrim had a pleasant wife called Telti and two teenage sons who were—in real terms—older than Ordo. The boys greeted them politely and then went to their rooms as if they were drilled to vanish when awkward business was being discussed. Obrim was on duty today, but his wife seemed completely calm about being left with a comatose stranger and a med droid.

"He's through here," Telti said. She led them into a guest suite, where Fi lay looking no more than a man asleep, except for the nasogastric tube and a saline drip feeding into his hand. Besany was sitting beside the bed, her head resting on one hand; the med droid was offline, settled in the corner. "Jaller talks about you a lot. Fi can stay here as long as he needs to."

There were good people everywhere, Ordo thought, just not enough of them. He walked up to Besany and put his hand on her shoulder, and she jerked back as if he'd woken her.

"I nodded off," she said.

"Have you been here all night?"

"Yes. I called in to the office to say I was sick. Then I realized it was the weekend."

"You did a good job. Probably with less damage to property than if we'd extracted him, too."

Jusik placed his holdall in the corner of the room with a loud clunk. "You can stay and watch if you want, but it's boring."

"I saw you heal Jinart," she said.

"I might not achieve the same results," Jusik said, "but it won't be for want of trying."

Ordo wanted to know how he set about doing it: what went through his mind, how he focused, what the energies felt like while it was happening. Right now, though, it was just Jusik sitting on the bed, with one hand on Fi's forehead and his eyes closed, like an act of blessing frozen in time. Ordo watched for an hour, then accepted that he wasn't contributing anything.

"Why don't you take Besany home?" Skirata said. "Come back later. If there's any change I'll call you."

"I feel like I'm abandoning him."

"Okay, but get some rest. When did you last sleep, *Ord'ika*?"

Ordo didn't want to leave Skirata on his own, either, even if the Obrims were there to keep him fed and watered. It had been a grueling couple of weeks; *Kal'buir* wasn't a young man.

"Okay," Ordo said. "I'll shut my eyes for a few minutes."

He thought he had. He took off his *kama* and pauldron and laid them over the back of a chair, then settled back on the sofa by the window. It was the most deeply upholstered thing he'd ever sat on, and he felt he was drowning in it. The next thing he was aware of was waking up to find Besany's head on his shoulder, wondering how she could sleep with a hard plastoid plate pressing against her face, and *Kal'buir* gently tapping the back of his hand. Four hours had gone.

"You need to see this," Skirata whispered. "You really do."

Jusik stood and stretched, joints cracking with alarming pops. "Brain tissue is capable of a great deal of regeneration, even the human type."

Besany stirred. "What is it?"

"Show them, *Bard'ika*," Skirata said.

Jusik ruffled Fi's hair, and he moved. He did it a few more times; the reaction was consistent.

"Don't get too excited," Jusik said. "He's not in such a deep coma now. That's a long way from being conscious, but he's not brain-dead, either."

"You healed that much tissue?"

Jusik shrugged. "Oh, medics misdiagnose brain death all the time. I'm just reluctant to give up. Always was a sore loser."

But Ordo knew when Jusik was pleased with himself. It was the same quiet amusement as when he made some clever gadget. Jusik was good at fixing things, and it seemed he could fix people, too. He basked in the contentment of successful problem solving.

"This is all guesswork, but for once I'll take the mystic Jedi method over the medcenter," Skirata said. "How long do you think you'll have to keep this up?"

"Days. Maybe weeks."

"Zey's going to notice sooner or later. Delta can't stay on Dorumaa indefinitely."

"It's going to take them a week even to start working their way into Ko Sai's facility, unless we want to risk drilling in there with big conspicuous industrial-sized machinery," Jusik said. "I can take a few days away from Fi then and catch up with them. But I wouldn't rely on Zey turning a blind eye to my bending the rules on Fi, and I'd rather be in trouble for not obeying orders on the Ko Sai search than indicate to Zey that I know where Fi is."

"Sooner or later," Skirata said, "he's going to notice he's getting a lot less out of the Nulls, too. Maybe that'll be the time to tell him that Jaing knows where Grievous is."

"Ah, I thought you might . . . ," Jusik said quietly.

"Well, we've all got our little secrets to trade now, haven't we? Yes, Jaing knows, and he thinks it was too easy to be true. Hence my silence on the matter."

"What a dirty galaxy we live in."

Ordo did a few rough calculations. "I think we can count on Delta being stuck on Dorumaa for weeks, and not just because of the cocktails. They're doing the equivalent of excavating with a spoon."

"They're not a cocktail kind of squad," Jusik said, sounding almost regretful. "They won't take advantage of it at all. For some reason, that depresses me."

It was a waiting game now in both the areas that mattered most to them—Fi's recovery and Ko Sai's gradual revelation of what she could do to regulate the aging genes. While Jusik worked on Fi, Skirata used the time to catch up by comlink with every commando in his former training company and each of the deployed Nulls. He had a sense of urgency about him, as if there were things he didn't want to leave unsaid as he had with Fi.

Ordo took Besany back to her apartment and debated whether this was the right time to do as Sergeant Vau had told him.

But she'd already had quite a week when it came to skating on thin legal ice. Spying on classified defense projects and abducting patients at blasterpoint was plenty to be going on with.

He'd wait a few days before he involved her in the murky world of bank raids and stolen shoroni sapphires.

17

Sir, we've managed to get a strip-cam filament into the collapsed chamber using the mechanism from a self-embedding charge. It's going to take weeks to remove enough material to search for organic remains, but one thing the cam has picked up is what looks like a chest plate of Mandalorian armor. I'll leave it up to you to decide if you want to pass that information on to General Zey.
—Sitrep from RC-1138, Boss, to General Jusik

Kyrimorut, Mandalore, 499 days after Geonosis

"**Y**ou said you wanted a laboratory." Mereel was running out of patience, and he'd managed to show a remarkable amount to Ko Sai given that he wanted to kill her. "This *is* a laboratory."

The Kaminoan scientist couldn't quite bring herself to step into the structure. Etain tried to encourage her.

"This is as good as you're going to get for the time being," she said. "And it means you don't have to wait for a conventional lab to be built. This *is* Mandalore, after all."

"It's an agricultural trailer." Ko Sai sounded crushed. Etain was used to all the subtle nuances in her tone now, and the Kaminoan voice wasn't wholly sweetness and serenity any more than their character was. It was just harder for a human being to hear. "This is used for *animals*."

"Don't tempt me to state the obvious," said Mereel. "It's a mobile genetics unit, and I don't see what difference it makes whether it's racing odupiendos or humans that you're assessing. Except the dupies are worth a lot more."

Etain thought Mereel had done well to get hold of it. But Ko Sai had Tipoca standards. Reminding her that she could extract DNA with the pots, pans, and household chemicals in the kitchen wasn't going to help. She lowered her head and walked back into the house.

Mereel shook his head. "Etain, this is what they use at the racetracks. Those guys are as tight on genome identification as any Kaminoan, right along with drug testing. This is just a mini version of what a half-decent university would have."

"I know," she said. He sounded like a husband who'd bought his wife a totally unsuitable gift and was hurt to find she didn't like it. "That's the downside of finding the one thing that motivates her and taking away everything else."

"Okay, we could build a lab like she had on Dorumaa, but that's months away."

"And we don't really intend for her to do any worthwhile Jedi genome research, do we?"

"No, but we certainly want her to design a delivery system for regulating *my* genes."

"I think she's cracking up."

Mereel held up his hands as if he didn't want to hear. "Excuse me while I gag."

"She's no use to us insane."

"If you've got any ideas for soothing her troubled soul, other than calling Kamino or the Arkanians and negotiating a deal, or even doing the same with the Chancellor, then you're doing better than me."

Etain was learning more than she ever wanted to about genetics. Many genes, Ko Sai liked to tell her, controlled aging. Etain didn't just see the enormity of the task facing Mereel; she also saw how many things might go wrong for her unborn child. In both, all she could do was take it a day at a time. She went after Ko Sai and tried to inject a little enthusiasm into her.

"You managed with your lab on Dorumaa," Etain said.

"And that was pretty small, too. You've got all the imaging and analysis stuff. Isn't that a start?"

The Kaminoan sat in the room she had made her sanctuary, a windowless storeroom where she could avoid direct sunlight, and shuffled her datapads into a neat pile. She didn't need locking up any longer. She'd shown no inclination to escape and never left the building unless Mereel made her; it was too bright and dry here for her liking.

"That's the problem, Jedi," she said. "It's a *start.* Not a progression or a continuation. Beginning again is very hard sometimes."

Etain wondered how much difference it would make if she knew her own research still existed, and then imagined Mereel's reaction if she blew one of his main negotiating points. She almost dropped a hint. *Almost.*

"There's always a commercial lab like Arkanian Micro . . ."

"They would never use my methodology. It's too slow for them. They're bulk producers. We all have our niche in the market."

Etain wondered what hatcheries that could churn out a few million clones counted as if not *bulk,* then. But Ko Sai was right: ten years was longer than most customers wanted to wait.

"What would you want, ideally?" Etain asked.

"Better imaging equipment, more computing power, and lab droids."

Etain took a datapad from her robes and slid it in front of the scientist. It was newly published research from an eminent embryologist on expression of some gene whose code number Etain couldn't even memorize, but it was the kind of material that was as exciting to Ko Sai as the latest celebrity gossip holozine would be to most Coruscanti holovid fans. It distracted her. She glanced at the author's name.

"He's mediocre at best," she said sweetly. "I shall savor correcting this."

"Of course—you never published research, did you? Academics didn't even know Kamino was there."

"There were times when that was . . . galling, I admit."

"I'll talk to Mereel. He's doing his best, believe me."

"Perhaps he should have considered his *best* before he and that savage who corrupted him destroyed my life's work." Ko Sai curled her long claw-like hand gently around Etain's arm. "You understand, though. You understand what it is to have so much knowledge and yet have so few outlets for its application."

Etain had that sudden connection with another species, as she had sometimes when looking into Mird's eyes, when she felt she truly knew who was *in there*. Did she understand? She could guess what motivated Ko Sai, imagine what it was to be her, and even think as she thought up to a point. Perhaps she even pitied her, utterly alone and never able to go home, or even mix with her professional peers.

Hang on, this is someone who builds children to design specs, and kills them if they don't meet quality control standards.

It was an ugly thought for any expectant mother. Etain shook off the pity and reminded herself that monsters weren't a separate species, or even wholly different from the rest of their own, and that was what made them monstrous.

"I wouldn't swap lives with you, Chief Scientist," she said. "I just don't understand why you won't concede a small thing to a handful of men who mean nothing to you anyway."

"Skirata would *sell* that knowledge to the highest bidder. Mandalorians are amoral. Look at our clone donor, Fett."

Ko Sai seemed to have no idea just how much of a crusade this was becoming for Skirata. He'd moved rapidly beyond the focus of just saving his boys: he was now repelled by the whole idea of cloning.

"I don't think he would," Etain said. "He's not a paragon of virtue, but I think he'd use it solely on his troops and then destroy it. He'd never sell it."

She hoped that might soften Ko Sai. It happened to be the truth, and sometimes the truth was so unexpected in a dishonest world that it was a shock weapon. Etain left her to chew that over and went back to the mobile gene-tech unit parked outside. Mereel was wiping down the surfaces with sterilizing fluid like a fussy droid.

"I don't think my hearts-and-minds initiative is working with her, *Mer'ika*," she said.

"That's because she's missing one of the essential components in that pair. I'll give you a few nanoseconds to work out which one."

"I think she's finally coming to the end of her tether after being away from Kamino and all her comfort zones for a year. I don't think she thought it through when she bolted."

Mereel stood back to admire his handiwork, visibly subdued. To Etain's lay eye, the lab looked pretty impressive, but then she had no idea what Tipoca City laid on for its scientists. The whole planet relied wholly on cloning exports.

"Like I didn't think through what might happen if we got the research, grabbed the scientist, and then thought we had all the kit for making a solution to the problem," Mereel said at last. "Even Nulls misjudge situations. That's why we're human, and not droids."

"I think," Etain said, "that you grabbed an opportunity because it was senseless to ignore it, and then started to put too much faith in it. As we all do sometimes."

And no woman who conceived a baby as she had could pass judgment on any clone for seizing what he could. Sometimes, things worked out.

The Force made her certain that something positive—she didn't yet know what—would come of all this.

It had to.

Jaller Obrim's residence, Rampart Town,
Coruscant, 499 days after Geonosis

"How's Fi today?" Besany asked. "I brought Dar to see him."

Jaller Obrim stood back to let them in. "See for yourself. And if you can get Bardan to relax for a while, you'll be doing better than me." He clapped Darman on the shoulder. "Good to see you again. How's Corr settling in?"

"Fine, sir. He blew up a gas storage facility on Liul last week, and he was very pleased with himself. Sort of his qualifier for the squad, if he needed one."

"I'm glad to see you boys know how to have fun."

Fi was propped almost upright now, but the tubes were still in place, and the med droid—one that was programmed only to nurse, thankfully—checked the saline drip before leaving them with him. Jusik seemed back to his relaxed self.

"I waited for you," Jusik said. "Time for the next stage."

Darman perched himself on the edge of Fi's bed and took his hand. Everyone did that automatically now. Jusik opened the holdall he'd brought on the first night and began pulling out a set of Mandalorian armor.

"I raided his locker," he said. "You know how much this meant to him."

The Jedi laid out a gray leather *kama* like a tablecloth where Fi could stare straight at it, and placed a red-and-gray helmet and armor plates on top of it.

"See that, Fi?" Jusik sat on the other edge of the bed and tilted Fi's head a little so—if he was conscious of anything at all—he could see the thing he prized most: a set of armor he'd pillaged on Qiilura from a mercenary called Hokan. Besany found it odd that they didn't seem to find killing a Mandalorian unsettling. "You keep looking at that, *ner vod*. Because you're going to be wearing it as soon as you're back on your feet. I promise you. You're a free man now."

Jusik leaned over and looked into Fi's face as if he expected him to answer, but the commando's eye movements seemed random and uncoordinated. Jusik settled at Fi's side again and put one hand on his scalp, pouring every effort into repairing the damaged tissue in his brain.

Besany thought it was time to leave Darman with his brother for a while. Obrim stood at the doorway a long time and eventually surrendered to her tug on his sleeve. She could have sworn there were tears in his eyes; there were certainly tears in hers. They stood in the kitchen and the captain busied himself making caf, missing the cup and scattering grains everywhere.

"He's never going to be back to normal, is he?" Obrim said, voice cracking. "Even if he makes ninety percent of what he was, it'll still be hard on him."

"The clones have a very high definition of *normal,* I've found. They're also incredibly resilient."

"That boy in there . . . that boy saved my men from a grenade during a siege, by *throwing himself on it.* I say that's worth more than a thank-you and a few ales at the CSF Staff Club. He can stay here as long as he needs to. Right?"

Besany had heard that story so many times now from so many CSF officers—most of whom hadn't even been present during the incident—that she was beginning to understand how reputations and legends were made. Obrim was one of life's hard men, and he didn't cry easily. But Fi had somehow become an icon, a symbol to the police, at least, of all those in uniform who did the dirty jobs and got no thanks. He'd become a hero. And, as Ordo mentioned every time she used the phrase, Mandalorians had no word for "hero."

"Right," said Besany. "And I'm glad Kal's got a friend he can turn to."

"Someone his own age to play with, eh?" Obrim rattled cups and said nothing, with the same expression on his face that she'd seen on Skirata's. It was the face of a man working out who he needed to hurt to make things right with the galaxy. "Is this what we elected?"

"What?"

"We both work for government enforcement. We're Coruscant citizens. Is this what we thought we were getting as part of the deal? What's happening to the Republic?"

"I know. I've asked myself the same thing—"

"I did twenty-eight years in the Senate Guard before I transferred to CSF. Did I take my eye off the ball? I wonder if it happened on my watch and I didn't spot it."

"Police can only deal with the law. Not ethics."

"But these decisions are being made by politicians I've known and protected for years. It makes it . . . personal betrayal, I suppose." Obrim seemed to focus on the caf again. "*Technically,* in law, we just stole government property. Like taking old office equipment from a department dumpster, not a living, breathing man with rights. How did we ever let that happen?"

"It didn't happen overnight. It crept up on us."

"But who's going to do anything about it? The Senate's smiling and nodding, and even the Jedi Council—okay, I talk to Jusik too much."

"He's going to rebel, isn't he?"

"He's not happy wearing the robes, I can tell you that. Very moral boy. *Very* moral. None of this seeing stuff *from a certain point of view.* No ambiguity. He calls it as he sees it."

Besany wondered if Skirata knew, and then thought that he probably spotted Jusik's tendencies right from the start. He was good at that. "*Can* they leave? Can Jedi resign?"

"No idea. Maybe they get them to turn in their belt and lightsaber or something."

"We'll find out. Ordo says there'll be a showdown with his boss before too long."

Besany left Darman as long as she could, keeping an eye on the chrono because she was now fitting this into her lunch breaks. Jusik was still sitting there with his hand on Fi's head, doing whatever it was that Jedi did when they healed others, and talking very quietly to him. He glanced up at her, distracted for a moment, and she took Fi's free hand. She found herself with a nervous grip on the tips of his fingers, sensing no reaction, and feeling she was somehow intruding by touching him when he wasn't aware of it, or at least unable to respond to her. With his features slack, eyes half closed and blinking frequently, he looked more of a total stranger now than when he'd been completely unresponsive.

"I'll be back later, Fi," she said. "One of the other Nulls is coming to see you soon. A'den."

Jusik patted her on the hand, not looking up. She had the air taxi drop Darman at the barracks, and then got off a few blocks from her office to take a few minutes to think. Her focus was widening again now, taking in the city around her and the beings streaming past her on foot and in speeders, and she had a moment of frightening clarity.

I pulled a blaster on staff at the medcenter and abducted a patient. Or stole government property. Whatever. I did it. And that's on top of slicing data. They'll fire me, if whoever was watching me doesn't shoot me first.

She was too deeply mired in the situation to lose her nerve now, and damned either way. If she was going to be disgraced, which she was, then it wouldn't make matters any worse if she pulled out all the stops.

I used to be sensible.

Besany sat at her desk and logged into the accounting override system, the rarefied atmosphere where auditors could observe transactions at will. She'd been honest all her life, scrupulously so. It was her job to root out dishonesty among others. But it was time the Republic paid its dues, and it could start with Fi, RC-8015, who didn't exist now, and had never existed in law.

She had the access codes and the ability to cover the audit trail that led to her. It was a relatively straightforward matter to slice into the Grand Army's database and record that RC-8015 had been terminated after receiving injuries from which he was unlikely to recover. Among a few thousand commandos, hidden among a few million men, nobody above his own commander—General Zey—would even bother to check. His place in Omega Squad was already filled, and clones died every day.

She hit the EXECUTE key, and Fi was a free man for the first time in his short and tragic life.

Office of the Director of Special Forces, SO Brigade HQ, Coruscant, 503 days after Geonosis

Skirata never liked to be summoned to anyone's office, but he seemed keen to respond to General Zey today. Ordo accompanied him. He hadn't been summoned, but if Zey wanted to kick him out, he could try.

The Jedi looked like a man under increasing pressure.

"I've cut you a lot of slack, Sergeant," Zey said. "A *galaxy* of slack. A *budget* of slack. Now where is he? And what's Jusik playing at?"

Kal'buir was the last man to be intimidated by anyone, and Zey couldn't even come close to it. Ordo caught Maze's eye, and found they were both tensed to step in to back up their master, like a pair of strills. *Yes, that's exactly what we are. Animals trained to kill, and we can never be trusted not to turn wild again.* Maze and Ordo had an understanding, though. Maybe Maze understood a whole lot better since he'd been educated about his ARC brother Sull.

"Fi's dead, sir," Skirata said. "It says so on the database."

"That is, to use your phrase, a load of *osik.*"

"Really?" Skirata's arms were at his sides, which was never a good sign. "Well, he was in a coma, and medical care was withdrawn. Seeing as the Republic is too nice and civilized to leave a creature that can't feed itself to starve to death, the med droids were ready to . . . what's the euphemism? *Euthanize* him. So one way or the other he's dead, in that the Republic washed its hands of him now that he's no longer useful, and RC-eight-oh-one-five no longer exists. *Sir.*"

Zey looked mortified. He wasn't a callous man. He didn't even trot out all the usual Jedi platitudes. But Ordo still thought less of him for not being like Bardan Jusik.

"Sergeant, I've *seen* the record. I don't know how you did it, but I know you did, and I want to account for his whereabouts."

"Need-to-know, General. And you don't."

"This is *not* your private army, Skirata."

"Except when it suits you."

"Sergeant, you're still a serving member of the Grand Army of the Republic, and we have a chain of command here."

"Is that a threat?"

"I could remove you from your post."

"You could *try,* but even if you kick me out, I'll still be around, and my influence and networks and . . . *abilities to perform* will remain unchanged in all but name. You need me inside the tent, not outside throwing rocks."

Zey probably understood that he'd created the out-of-control Skirata standing in front of him and that there was no putting the man back in his box. Ordo was, as always, proud of his father and inspired by his refusal to be cowed. Zey's only option was to kill Skirata, just like an ARC trooper who no longer toed the line, and Ordo didn't give much for Zey's chances of that. So the fight was on.

"Well, just to keep your records tidy, here's his armor tally." Skirata collected the ID tallies from fallen clone troopers whenever he could, an echo of the Mandalorian habit of keeping a piece of armor as a memorial. *Mando'ade* often didn't have the time, place, or opportunity for graves. "Is there anywhere in particular you'd like me to shove it?"

Zey paused, almost grinding his teeth behind that graying beard, then held out his hand for Skirata to drop the small plastoid tab into his palm. Their eyes locked for a moment, and Ordo willed Zey to look away first. He did. Honor was satisfied. *Kal'buir*—shorter, outranked, no Force powers— was still the alpha male.

"Look, I'm sorry about Fi," Zey said quietly. "I'm sorry about every single clone who loses his life or gets wounded. As Jedi, we endeavor to treat all sentient life with compassion. Don't think we don't agonize about it. I was discussing it with General Kenobi only the—"

"That's the way you talk about *animals,* sir. Not men. If you meant that patronizing twaddle, you'd insist troopers were offered a choice of remaining as volunteers, or leaving." Skirata paused but, judging by the way he swallowed, it wasn't for effect. "And I don't mean with the help of one of your covert ops death squads, either."

Zey stared back at Skirata as if this was news to him. It might well have been: the Jedi generals seemed to be out of the loop as far as the conduct of the war was concerned, in terms of both what the Chancellor told them and how much notice he took of their advice.

"Is there something you want to tell me, Sergeant?"

"Either you know, or you *need* to know, that ARC troopers who get out of line end up executed, and I have *proof* that at least one was targeted by our own covert ops troops."

Zey didn't look too happy. It wasn't the look of a guilty man caught out, though. It was an angry man whose face was illuminated by dawning realization.

"I know nothing of this."

"Then it's about time," Skirata said, "that you Jedi took your heads out of your *shebse,* stopped contemplating your midi-chlorians, and did a reality check. You're going to get a nasty shock one day, General. We *told* you about the vastly inflated claims of enemy droid numbers, and tactics didn't change. We *told* you we should be concentrating forces on a few main theaters, cleaning up before moving on, and not scattering forces so we never quite have the strength to root out the enemy. Again, nothing changed. *None* of this is winning the war. It's just keeping it going. So I wonder how much it's worth risking our necks to find out for you, if that intel isn't used."

Zey snapped. He slapped both hands on his desk, an ordinary man at the limit of his endurance now, not a Jedi. Ordo didn't flinch, but he saw the discomfort on Maze's face.

"Skirata, the Jedi command doesn't run this war!" Zey roared. "The politicians do, and the Chancellor says *this is how we fight.* End of story."

"Doesn't that scare the *osik* out of you?"

"Of course it does. What do you think we are, idiots? But I've learned that's how wars always work—politicians don't listen to the military, everyone lies wildly about their assets, and there are never enough troops to go around. Maybe Mandalorians live in a different reality."

"You've got plenty of assets, actually—"

Ordo had a second of adrenaline-flushed panic that Skirata would mention the Centax clones, but he didn't expand, and Zey was now too angry to stop himself from interrupting him.

"I've fully committed the whole brigade, Skirata, although

I have to ask what your ARCs are actually tasked to do some-times."

"You wanted black ops folk like me to do the dirty work. This is the price of dirty, sir."

Skirata didn't wait to be dismissed, and stalked out almost without limping. Ordo followed. They strode down the corridor, boots echoing, until they reached the parade-ground exit. It was a pleasantly balmy day outside, and they sat on the low perimeter wall to have a *hot wash-up*. It was a lovely phrase for working out what the *shab* had gone wrong, one of those military euphemisms that poor Fi enjoyed so much.

"Zey didn't know about the death squads," Ordo said. "He really didn't."

"He's the head of special forces." Skirata fumbled in the pockets of his leather jacket and pulled out ruik root and some candied fruit, the ruik for him and the candies for Ordo. He chewed savagely, gaze in slight defocus. "He ought to make it his business to know."

"And I think it was wise not to mention the new clone programs. Zey really would go charging in to demand that Windu got answers on that one. I'd prefer the Chancellor's office not to notice us."

"Besany did a fine job there, but I don't want to get her killed." Skirata nudged Ordo in the plates with his elbow. "She's good all around, that one. But put her out of her misery, give her the sapphires, and ask her how she likes the idea of living in the middle of nowhere with a depressed Kaminoan for a house guest. Okay?"

"I'll tell her they're stolen. She's touchy about that kind of thing, being Treasury."

"*Ord'ika,* just take a couple of days out and spend quality time with her. You know what I'm saying."

"Yes, *Kal'buir.*"

Skirata spat the fibrous remains of the ruik into the flowerbed next to the wall. "In a year's time, if we've still got a year, then I want everything in place for an instant *ba'slan shev'la.*"

It meant "strategic disappearance," a *Mando* tactic for

scattering and disappearing from sight, only to coalesce into an army again later. For them, it meant banging out to the bastion on Mandalore and helping any like-minded clones that they could.

They never did get around to talking about Jusik. Zey would realize that and come back for round two with Skirata sooner or later. But unlike Skirata, he didn't have the luxury of *ba'slan shev'la.*

Maybe he needed to think about that. Everyone needed a Plan B—even Jedi.

18

*It took me a long time to understand that winning
a war often has nothing to do with ending it, for
governments at least.*
—General Arligan Zey, Director of Special Forces,
Grand Army of the Republic, on his recent interest in
military history

**Kyrimorut bastion, northern Mandalore, 539 days after
Geonosis**

"I don't want you to get upset," Vau said, "but Fi's not as you
remember him."

Etain nodded gravely as they waited for *Aay'han* to land.
Vau wasn't sure if an emotional shock was a good idea for a
pregnant woman so close to term, but he had Rav Bralor here
if any of that female stuff needed attending to. Mird followed
Etain around, staring fascinated at her belly.

"He's still Fi, and I think I understand post-coma recovery
now," Etain said. "You have no idea how much medical liter-
ature I've read recently. But Mird's *worrying* me."

Bralor flicked her thumbnail against the butt of her blaster,
making Mird whip its head around to stare balefully at her.
"And I can worry Mird. Can't I, my little stinkweed?"

Vau felt the need to defend his comrade. "Strills have very
acute senses, remember. It knows the baby's coming soon."

"As in snack opportunity?"

"As in *parenting,* Rav. Mird is hermaphroditic, remember.

It's capable of being a mother, too, and you know how female animals will mother anything."

"Even you, Walon . . ."

Etain looked up at the first distant throb of a drive decelerating for landing. "I really wish Darman knew right now. I really do."

"Nearly there, kid," Bralor said, squeezing her shoulders. "There'll be a right time. Soon."

But there was probably never a right time for her to see Fi again. *Aay'han* settled on her dampers, ticking and creaking as the drives cooled, and the cargo hatch eased open. Jaing stepped out, steering Fi on a repulsor chair.

"I was just passing through," Jaing said, "but this crazy *Mando'ad* said he'd booked a vacation here."

Etain didn't even pause. She rushed up to Fi, at a respectable speed for a woman laden with cargo, and flung her arms around him. But he didn't quite have the coordination to respond and simply flopped his arm over her shoulder.

He was wearing Ghez Hokan's armor, at least on his upper body. The leg plates probably needed extending; Hokan had been a much shorter man. Jusik understood motivation *very* well.

"We're going to have to feed you up," Etain said. "You're all bone now."

"Fizz," Fi said indistinctly.

"He means physiotherapy," Jaing explained. "You might struggle to understand his speech, but give him a stylus and he can manage to write a lot of what he can't say. He has to point to objects, too—he can't find the right words. Oh, and he forgets a lot. But for a dead man, he's doing great."

Vau found it particularly cruel that Fi—a funny, eloquent lad—had been effectively silenced by the injury. But it was very early days. Bralor went over to fuss over him, too, but Fi had spotted that Etain had filled out rather a lot in the midsection. He pointed.

Etain shrugged. "Your eyesight's fine, then, Fi."

"Neversssss . . ."

"I'll tell you later," she said. "Let's show you the presidential suite and see what the care droid can do."

"It's okay, Fi." Bralor took over. "I'll be around, or else my sister's kid will. Proper *Mando* home cooking. That'll put you right faster than any of that *aruetyc osik*."

But Fi was still looking at Etain's bump, and Vau knew that he had enough recall to draw the very obvious conclusion. Without a major facial movement like a smile, it was hard to gauge his emotional state, but Vau couldn't help thinking that it was a little disapproving, and that he might have been trying to say, *You never said.*

It was too easy to attribute thoughts and words to him. They'd have to take it slowly.

Vau left Jaing and the ladies to fuss over Fi and went to check on Ko Sai. Mird, back in its native environment, looked to him with a hopeful expression that begged permission to do what it enjoyed most: hunting.

"Okay, *Mird'ika*. I have to see Ko Sai anyway." Vau pointed toward the trees. "*Oya! Oya,* Mird!"

The strill shot off at high speed and disappeared into the pocket of woodland to the north, and Vau went on his way. The bastion had started to acquire a routine like a real homestead, and now that Vau, Skirata, or one of the Nulls was around much of the time, Bralor was getting on with overseeing the building work for Skirata. It was definitely feeling *yaim'la,* and was a much bigger complex than Vau had first thought. Land was still free on sparsely populated Mandalore, as long as you didn't want to cram into Keldabe. Up here in the north, a clan could spread out.

But I'm not part of this. I'm just passing through, understood?

The only part of the bastion that didn't have that feeling of busy, wood-smoke-scented warmth was Ko Sai's quarters, where it felt as if she'd created an exclusion zone that was every bit as unwelcoming as Tipoca City without managing to be clinical, white, or shiny.

She seemed to be draped over her desk—Kaminoans, all fluid elegance, didn't *bend.* They *curved.* With her head lowered as she made notes, she looked as if she might droop completely.

"How's it going?" he asked.

"Another day when I lament the lack of data from my last year's work, but if you mean have I recorded more information on regulating the aging genes . . ."

"Let's not insult each other's intelligence. I do."

"Then I have."

"Well, my question's not about that. It's about motive. I still don't understand why you're withholding this information, because you've never made demands."

"Wrong end of the 'scope, possibly. Perhaps it's because I want to stay alive as long as possible, in the hope that something in the circumstances will change, and I can resume my work unmolested."

"Chancellor Palpatine bothered you most, didn't he? That's what made you go into hiding."

"Anyone who creates powerful technology has a responsibility not to hand it to those who'll misuse it."

"I can sense you're not from Rothana, somehow . . ."

"It depends on your definition of *misuse*." Ko Sai never looked quite as imposing as she had on Kamino, and it wasn't just the limited wardrobe now. Exile was eroding her resolve. There might come a time when she simply caved in. "But might I ask why it's so important to you to restore normal aging to these clones? You're not an irrationally emotional man like Skirata. Is it a commercial venture for you?"

"Am I going to rush to Arkania with it and invite bids? No. No commercial value except to those interested in subverting genetic rights management, who tend not to be those best able to pay anyway."

"Curiosity, then, or to prove your interrogation skills?"

"No, it's because it's unfair to deprive them of a full life. Crushing the weak is the hallmark of a small mind."

"The Jedi said Skirata wouldn't sell the data, either, and would probably destroy it after he'd made use of it."

"That's Kal all right," Vau said. "All he wants is to put his boys right."

Vau tried to work out what was going through her mind, but even after years among Kaminoans, and getting to know this one better than he ever imagined he would, he reminded himself that using human motive as a basis for understanding them was probably a mistake. Apart from pride, he couldn't map human concerns onto Kaminoans. The mismatch was probably what made Mereel think they were devious.

"I'll be going then," he said. "See what Mird's dragged back from the woods."

"You will let me know when the Jedi has her child, won't you?"

"Oh, you'll probably hear it all over the bastion . . ."

"She promised me a tissue sample."

No, Vau didn't think that Ko Sai was offering to knit booties. When he got back to the central area, he could see Mird busy at some frantic activity in the field outside. Bralor and Jaing were watching it, transfixed. He had to go and look.

Mird had built a nest. Strills did that. Not only had it built the nest for the mother-to-be, but it had also stocked the larder. A huge, dead, mangled *shatual* lay to one side of the beautifully arranged coils of dry grass.

"It's the thought that counts," Jaing said.

Bralor laughed. "That's the cutest thing I've ever seen," she said. "*Cute* and *strill* in the same sentence . . . well, you learn something new every day."

"How long do they live?" Jaing asked. "I'd heard three or four times as long as a normal human."

"It's true," said Vau. "It worries me, because I don't have a family to pass Mird's care to."

"You're a big softie, Sergeant."

"Would you consider taking Mird if anything happened to me? You never seemed quite as repelled by it as your brothers."

Jaing pulled his I'm-considering-it expression and rocked his head a little. "Yes, I always had sinus trouble. Okay."

"Do I have your word?"

"Yes. You do."

Vau felt a great deal more positive than he had in years, which showed him how much he worried about the animal.

That evening he felt positively benign, joining the others in the main room to speculate on the birth.

Bralor's niece Parja—a mechanic, and making a good living for a youngster—showed up to scrutinize Fi for the first time. "Jaing says you're worth fixing up," she said, squatting down to look him in the eye. "I do believe he's right."

It would have sounded unthinkably callous to anyone but a Mandalorian, but she said it with a smile and she spent the whole evening being wonderfully attentive to him. It looked like a lot more than tact or pity. Etain, watching protectively, gave Vau a totally uncharacteristic wink from across the room. Jedi seemed to have a radar for these things. Contentment could be found in some of the least likely situations, Vau thought.

He slept well that night, with Mird draped across his feet on top of the blankets. It was only the sound of a woman in labor that woke him, and just six hours later, Venku Skirata was born, arguably the most wrinkled and angry looking of babies.

Bralor and Parja studied Venku unsentimentally.

"Kandosii," Bralor said, taking the baby in her arms. "That's a very healthy boy."

Vau reflected on the kind of future Venku might face—or make for himself—and handed Etain his comlink.

"Go on," he said. "You know what you have to do next."

Etain, tearful and exhausted, took the device and fumbled with the controls. He didn't even have to remind her. She keyed in Skirata's code right away, and when he answered, she managed just one word.

"Ba'buir," she said, and burst into tears.

Grandfather.

Kyrimorut bastion, northern Mandalore, 541 days after Geonosis

All the way from Coruscant, Skirata remained convinced that he would take Venku from Etain's arms without a second thought, right until he walked into her room and saw that pitiful look on her face.

"It's okay," she said. "I'm tired and my hormones are all over the place, so if I start crying, just carry on as if nothing's happened. I haven't changed my mind or anything."

Skirata leaned over to look at Venku, then Etain held the kid up for him to take.

"There you go, *Ba'buir.*"

"*Venku's beautiful,*" Skirata said. "He really is." His biological kids must have had their own families by now, and maybe he had great-grandchildren out there somewhere, but this was the first grandson he could actually hold and call his own. "Venku. Yes, that's you, isn't it? Yes it *is,* Venku!" The baby was too young to respond to cooing and tickling. Skirata settled for just holding him like fragile crystal, one hand supporting his tiny head. At least he remembered the drill. "He's *perfect,* Etain. You did well. I'm so proud."

"It's nice to be able to roll over in bed again without getting stuck," she said tearfully.

"You really need some rest, *ad'ika.*"

"This isn't what I thought I'd feel. Any of it."

She sounded just like Ippi. His late wife said it wasn't the way they described it in the family holozines, too. Given the massive upheavals that Etain had been through in the last year, the fact that both mother and child had survived was astonishing. There was a lot to be said for Jedi blood.

Mereel walked in and peered over Skirata's shoulder.

"He's very quiet, isn't he?"

"They sleep a lot at this stage."

"You reckon?" Etain said wearily.

Venku looked like an average baby with nothing remarkable about him except perhaps his head of fine, wispy dark hair, and that ordinariness was the most wonderful thing Skirata could imagine. It was a long time since he'd picked up a newborn and been stunned by it. And it broke his heart that Darman couldn't be doing this instead.

I was wrong. Shab, *was I wrong. I can't keep the lad from his son.*

"You don't have to go through with this," Skirata said. "I know what I said before, but you could raise him here if you leave the Jedi Order. Rav's around, we're all passing through regularly, you could even go to Keldabe and have plenty of neighbors around you . . ."

"But what about Dar?" she asked.

"I need to rethink this."

"I don't want to be sitting here worrying while he's fighting, Kal."

"Women with small kids do that, Etain. It's hard being the rear party to a man at the front, but they do it."

"It's different when I'm serving. I feel like I've got some control over the situation, even if I haven't."

"And who needs you most now?"

Skirata couldn't blame her for dithering and changing her mind. He'd had kids of his own and adopted a lot more, but even he found the world was a different place once the child was there in front of you. It changed *everything*.

And Etain didn't seem like the naïve and well-meaning Jedi who'd enraged him so for thinking it was a good idea to give Darman a son by omitting to tell him she was taking risks. She was a small, thin kid who looked wrung out from the pregnancy, and whose only mistake was to be born with the wrong set of genes in a world that forced a destiny on her from birth. She was just like Darman. He could never blame her now.

"You haven't asked me something," she said.

"Birth weight?"

"Don't you want to know if he's strong in the Force?"

Skirata trod tactfully. He found he was determined not to think of Venku as a Jedi-in-waiting. That could never be allowed to happen. "Is he? It's not a given, is it?"

"No, it's not. But he *will* be a Force-user. It depends on how he's trained to handle it."

She might have been having second thoughts about his future. All she'd ever known before the war broke out was a Jedi clan for a family; stress could make folks default to what they knew best. "And who's going to train him?"

"I will. I might regret taking away his choice to be a Jedi, but I'd rather offer him the wider world."

There were times when she really *looked* like a Jedi, the same way Jusik did, simultaneously both child and ancient sage, swathed in those dull brown and beige robes. Skirata tried to imagine her like a normal young girl of her age, doing mindless fluffy things like worrying about fashion, and felt agonizing guilt for the harsh things he'd said to her when she told him she was pregnant.

He was glad she did it. Darman had a son.

It was going to kill her to stay away from her baby, though, and to cover up the fact that she'd given birth. He'd been so sure it was right for Darman not to know about Venku until he was ready for the news. But now he wasn't so sure.

I took away his chance to name his own son. So where does that leave me?

And Venku was a blend of Force-using Jedi and the perfect soldier, a valuable commodity. Ko Sai's continued cooperation was being bought with a vial of blood and tissue. There was nothing the aiwha-bait could ever do with it, but she wanted it badly. Skirata was going to hand it to her.

"*Et'ika*, let's pick our moment and tell Darman," he said. "Let's see if he's up to it. I'll know."

"But I'm not sure how I'm going to face him after lying to him like that."

"I'll tell him the truth. I made you do it."

"But you were right, Kal. It's already a dangerous situation, whatever I do. There's no way around it." Etain held her hands out to take Venku again, and settled him in the crook of her arm. "Once even a few folks know what his parentage is, the trouble starts. Unless both Dar and I desert, that is, and he won't do that." She wiped the baby's mouth. "I don't think I can, either. I can't play happy families while this war's going on, not like that, anyway."

Skirata saw her point, and wondered how he'd react in the same position. "Fi knows now."

"Yes. But he's not exactly in a position to blurt it out to anyone."

"I'd better talk to him."

"I don't think he understands why I didn't tell Dar."

"Leave it to me. First things first, though—Ko Sai."

Skirata hadn't seen her in a while, and when he and Mereel walked into the mobile laboratory unit that she'd finally deigned to use, she reminded him of someone wasting away who'd managed to muster a little strength to greet a friend. But there was nothing friendly about her. She was just anxious to play with that sample.

But she must know she can't ever make a super-soldier out of it. Imagine being so hungry for knowledge that all you want to do is find out, even if you'll never use it.

Skirata wasn't taking chances. If she escaped from Kamino, then she could try to make a run from here, even now. From the moment she took that sample out of his hands, she was locked in and under surveillance.

"I hear the baby is healthy and well," she said.

"Yeah." Skirata held up the vial. "Now you tell me *how* healthy."

"I don't even have to test for abnormal aging, Sergeant," she said. "Any engineered genes inherited from his father will be designed to be recessive, and those occurring naturally in the Fett genome have been chemically regulated. Apart from any exotica inherited from his Jedi mother, the baby will grow up normally unless he's been *very* unlucky in life's lottery."

"You make it sound so wonderful." Skirata looked at the vial. "And you've had a good rummage around Etain's genome, I take it."

"Yes. *Fascinating.*"

"So this cocktail just tells you how they interact."

"Not *just.* This is the most fascinating part of all."

And Venku didn't need it. Skirata could walk away now, if he believed her. But he had to take her tests on trust, too. He was no geneticist.

Mereel nudged him. "Ko Sai kept her word before, and it's not as if it can do any harm now."

Skirata wasn't sure if Mereel was playing nice-policeman-nasty-policeman with the Kaminoan, but he handed over the sample.

"Have fun," he said, and they left.

The bastion was taking shape. Bralor's droids had built a sheltered circular atrium off the main hub, with a roof that slid back on days when nobody cared what could be spotted from the air; it was ideal for open-air roasts.

"I say we get started on butchering that *shatual* if Rav hasn't already prepared it, *Mer'ika*. Perfect celebratory meal, if we had the whole clan here."

"You said *clan*."

"That's what it is, isn't it?"

"Indeed it is, *Buir*." Mereel smiled. "The war will be over one day."

"It'll be over for *us*," Skirata said. "And the rest of the galaxy can do what it wants. In the meantime, I need to make friends with someone reliable who's worked at Arkanian Micro."

"But not before we roast a little *shatual,* eh?" Mereel smiled. "I'm an uncle now. I have to do things right."

Uncle. *Ba'vodu.*

It was a lovely *family* word. This was where the future all began; these days, Skirata was certain, marked the beginning of hope for his boys—for Mandalore, even.

Yes, Arkanian Micro could wait a few hours longer.

Kyrimorut bastion, northern Mandalore, 545 days after Geonosis

"How do Mandalorian women transport their babies?" Etain asked. "I'm pretty sure they don't travel with this amount of kit just for a few hours' jaunt down the Hydian Way."

She couldn't actually manage the bag of diapers, milk, and changes of clothing. To think she'd once carried an LJ-50 conk rifle into battle: now she was drained to empty by simply lifting a travel bag and forced to resort to a repulsor assist.

Bralor had one last peek at Venku. "Backpack," she said. "But under the circumstances, I'd say cheating is fine. Remember, *Mando'ade* don't *enjoy* pain and hardship—we're just better at putting up with it than the *aruetiise*. Be kind to yourself. This isn't an endurance contest."

"I'll be back as often as I can."

"Any time, *vod'ika*. You certain you want to go through with this? Back in barracks?"

"I can always change my mind."

"Well, trite as it sounds . . . we're here. I just hope Darman's ready for the whole thing." Bralor craned her neck to look through the narrow window slit. "They're wonderful lads, but they can't help being naïve in some areas. Of course, the Nulls got the idea fast, except maybe Ordo . . ."

"What are you looking for?"

"Parja and Fi. She's making him walk today. His balance is shot to *haran* but she's got handrails set up, droids on standby, you name it. That girl never quits on a repair or orphaned nuna chicks."

Etain still saw what Fi had had and then lost: once a perfectly made, supremely fit man, now one who struggled to have a basic conversation, forgot where he was, needed help to eat, and was learning to walk properly again. Parja, never having known that perfect Fi to use as a benchmark, just saw who he was now, and appeared to find that he struck a chord in her. She seemed tireless in her devotion.

I wouldn't cross these people, but if I had to choose who to trust if my life depended on it . . .

But she *had* chosen, and had not been disappointed.

"I'll go say good-bye to Ko Sai," Etain said. It still sounded utterly unbelievable to her, as if this was just a neighbor she had to humor for harmony's sake. It was sobering to think how normal even the most repellent beings could seem if you inured yourself to their ways by spending time with them. Darkness crept up quietly on the unwary. "I wonder what genetic goody I can think up to keep her amused and cooperative."

Bralor resumed her business-as-usual tone again. "You know Kal's going to have to shoot her one day, don't you?"

"I suppose I do."

"Personally, I'd do it now, take the files you have to another clonemaster and trade it with them, because they all know how to age clones fast at some stage. Or just haul the *shabuir* down to Arkania and let them shake it out of her for you." Bralor placed a large floppy parcel in Etain's straining bag. "If she knows anything worth having, that is. That's the *shatual,* by the way, roasted and sliced. Share it with Darman and the boys. Right way to celebrate the birth of a son—even if you can't tell them yet."

Etain walked around the outside of the bastion to Ko Sai's laboratory, Venku held close to her, and caught sight of Parja guiding Fi between two fence rails. Fi fell over; Parja hauled him up with the aid of a droid, and they started over. Fi had once left an impression in the Force of resentment and bewildered loneliness, constantly wondering why he couldn't have the freedom and companionship in life that every other being around him seemed to have. But when Etain reached out in the Force to see what he radiated now, the mix was different— scared, confused, and seeking his old self, but the loneliness had all but vanished.

At last, Fi no longer felt alone. He'd paid a terrible price to reach that state, but he seemed more at peace than he ever had. The Force balanced its books in strange ways.

Holding Venku in her left arm, Etain rapped on the doors. "Ko Sai, it's Etain. Can I come in?"

It was just diplomacy. The locked door was key-coded, and Etain could come and go as she pleased. But there was no point rubbing Ko Sai's nose in it. Seeing Venku might chip away further at her resolve.

"Ko Sai?"

There was no answer. Etain had a sudden cold panic: the Kaminoan had fled with the tissue samples.

Don't be stupid. She can't escape. She's just engrossed in something.

Etain keyed in the code and walked in anyway.

Ko Sai had indeed fled: but she'd escaped to where no-body could follow, taking whatever knowledge she had with her.

She hung lifeless from a noose slung over one of the crossbeams.

Etain put her hand to her mouth, but she didn't scream. She'd seen far too much on the battlefield to react. *I know the drill. I call Kal. Oh no, no, no . . .* She found herself cursing in a sobbing voice under her breath as she summoned Skirata by comlink, and glanced at the note on the datapad that lay still illuminated on the workbench.

Thank you, Etain. It was fascinating.

Once more, Ko Sai, geneticist without equal, had had the last word.

19

Kyrimorut bastion, Mandalore, 545 days after Geonosis

So the aiwha-bait was still jerking his chain, even though she was dead.

Skirata leaned against the door frame and stared at Ko Sai's body, wondering what he had missed. Vau and Mereel checked it over carefully.

"I don't do full postmortems, not even for a hobby," said Vau, "but I can't see how anyone could have come close enough to Ko Sai out here to assassinate her, even if they knew we were holding her."

"She was getting more hacked off with life by the day." Mereel removed the ligature. "She must have known she wasn't going home. But I never had Kaminoans down as suicidal. Excessive self-esteem. It might have been the ultimate act of contempt for us."

Vau prodded the cadaver thoughtfully. "But they're not the most cosmopolitan and well traveled of species. Big deal for them to leave Kamino. Personally, I'm not surprised she went off the rails."

"I'd have taken the pearl-handled blaster and done the decent thing ages ago," Mereel muttered. "But then I'm not an arrogant xenophobic piece of tatsushi."

Skirata could only see a tenuous stream of data that had finally dried up. "I'm glad to see this hasn't traumatized you boys," he said sourly. His shock hadn't taken long to give way to anger. "I was getting worried that it might have scarred you for life."

She'd already done that to Mereel, of course. "She might have run out of information to give us."

"She might," said Skirata, "have been jerking our chain all along."

"Well, I know what I'm going to be doing for the foreseeable future. Collating what we've got and finding another geneticist or three to advise me." Mereel slotted a probe into the computer. "Just checking she hasn't trashed the data . . . no, she thought her work was too sacred even to have so much as a full stop erased. What a gal. Scrub the theory on the ultimate act of contempt, then."

"I still think we should risk it and do a deal with Arkanian Micro," said Vau. "Every cloner has to handle accelerated development. It's what they run on."

"But they're cheap and nasty," Mereel said.

"So? We're not buying from them. We just want them to say, *Hey, those are the genes you need to switch on and off,* and then we get the regulator manufactured by a pharma company."

"I've got that in hand," Skirata said, unable to take his eyes off the dead Kaminoan. He half expected her to be playing dead, not a corpse at all. "First things first."

"Once we know what it is we've got, too," Mereel said. "We're sitting on the cloning equivalent of the Sacred Scroll of Gurrisalia and we can't read the language—not well enough, anyway."

They still had a dead Kaminoan to dispose of, too. Skirata wondered what use he could make of her now. Nobody would ever believe he hadn't killed her—he wasn't sure why he hadn't, in the end—so maybe there was some advantage to be gained here. If she couldn't be useful to him alive, she'd earn her keep dead.

"Delta's still digging away under ActionWorld island, aren't they?"

"Yes, *Kal'buir*."

"I think they need to find what they're looking for. Put the Chancellor's mind at rest. Get him off our areas of interest, so to speak."

"How are we going to plant her there?" Vau asked.

"We're not," Skirata said. "I'm going to have a word with Delta."

Mereel shook his head. "They're not *us*. They stick to the rules. They'll tell Zey."

Vau looked offended. "Don't underestimate how diplomatic they can be, Kal. They didn't tell him about the bank raid, did they?"

"Okay, Walon, I'll get my story straight so we don't dump Jusik in it as the leak on Ko Sai, and I'll provide some forensics for them to slap on Zey's desk."

"Done. Now what about the body?"

"I'm not looking forward to this." Skirata's hatred of Ko Sai and her kind didn't extend to making what he had to do next any easier. "But help me move her into the barn. I'll do my own dirty work."

"I think Jaing and I should do it, actually, *Buir*." Mereel ushered the two older men out of the lab. "Ko Sai and us . . . we go back a long way."

Skirata could always rely on the Nulls. One day they might talk about it, but for the time being he was simply grateful that they volunteered, and wondered if there was now some kind of closure in it for them.

"Are you . . . donating the entire body to Delta?" Vau asked.

"No," Skirata said, suddenly getting a whole new idea, and not liking himself for it. Did she have any family? After all the years he spent on Kamino, he still didn't know. "It wouldn't do Lama Su any harm to think that we got to her in the end. I think I'm going to do the decent thing and send most of her home."

"They'll appreciate that . . . , " Vau said.

"Munit tome'tayl, skotah iisa," Skirata said. Long memory, short fuse: it was the Mandalorian character, they said. "I'd hate Kamino to forget us."

But maybe, one day, they could forget Kamino.

"I'll get Jaing and Ordo." Mereel took out a vibroblade. "This is a job a long time in the planning."

Mereel didn't elaborate, and Skirata didn't ask. He took Vau's elbow and steered him outside.

Ko Sai wasn't the only person Skirata didn't know quite as well as he felt he should.

Besany Wennen's apartment, Coruscant, 547 days after Geonosis

Besany always took her blaster with her when she answered the door these days, and she didn't open it until she'd run all the security scans that Ordo and Mereel had installed for her. But today it was just Kal Skirata who showed up, carrying something in his arms.

"Sorry, Kal," she said. "I always expect you to show up on the landing pad, like Ordo does."

"I didn't want to panic you." He indicated the bundle with a nod. "Not with this little fella on board."

"If I didn't know better, I'd say you were carrying a—oh my, you *are*. It's a *baby* . . ."

Skirata took a deep breath and laid the bundle of blankets— plain pearl gray, very soft—on her sofa, then leaned over it and peeled the layers of fabric away with slow care. "Isn't he beautiful?" His voice was a whisper. "I might need you to look after him. Not all the time, but sometimes."

The baby was a newborn, with a shock of dark silky curls, sound asleep. Besany wasn't sure what to say; she was so fond of Skirata that she'd do pretty well anything for him, but she knew nothing about babies, and she still had a regular job. He took her hand without looking away from the sleeping child, and squeezed it gently as if the two of them were sharing a wonderful joke.

"It's Darman and Etain's son," he said. "Venku."

"Oh. *Oh.*" The information floated on a current of disbelief before sinking in and shocking her. "Oh my."

"This is going to be a little awkward for a while. Darman hasn't a clue he's a father. I'm still deciding if he's ready to find out."

Besany couldn't take her eyes off the baby. He was *real,* a real live baby, lying on her sofa. She still had trouble taking that in. "So that's why Etain's been out of touch for a while. I'd never have guessed."

"She wants to carry on as a general." Venku woke and started fretting, making little ineffectual kicks. Skirata picked him up again with all the ease of a father who'd done this all before, a long time ago. "If the Jedi Council finds out she's involved with Dar, then she gets kicked out. So as far as everyone except you, me, *Bard'ika,* Vau, the Nulls, and a select few on Mandalore is concerned, this is my grandson."

"Which he *is,* really."

"I've got such a tangled domestic past that it won't surprise anyone to find my family dumping a kid on me."

"I suppose having him brought up on Mandalore was out of the question."

"If his father can't raise him," Skirata said, "then the duty falls to me."

Besany still had a lot to absorb about Mandalorian custom. "But you're on active service. You live in the barracks, don't you?"

"Exactly. Now, I rented a place for Laseema by the Kragget restaurant, so I'm going to move in there for the time being and see how we cope between us."

Skirata was a compulsive fixer who could make anything happen through his extensive network of contacts. One day, Besany would ask tactfully about his life before the Grand Army, but she already knew it would give her sleepless nights. "You rented an apartment for her?"

"You think I'd leave her stuck at Qibbu's? You know how Twi'lek girls get exploited in cantinas like that. She's Atin's lady, and that means she's family. I'm a regular at the Kragget and there are plenty of CSF lads using the place, so it's *secure*."

He seemed a little embarrassed. Perhaps he was worried that Besany would feel he'd failed for not settling Laseema in a smart neighborhood like her own.

I'm insane. I really should say no. What do I know about kids? "Okay, just bear in mind my office hours. Have you asked Jaller, too?"

"I've asked a lot of him lately. I'd rather avoid asking again. But it's the best compromise I could think of that still lets Etain see Venku when she's not deployed."

"We'll make it work," she said. It sounded like the most insane promise she'd ever made. But then she'd abducted a comatose commando from the medcenter and done plenty of other ludicrously dangerous things recently; this was just one more act of lunacy on a growing list.

Skirata gave the baby an exaggerated grin and kissed him on the forehead. "It's normal for *Mando* boys to accompany their father on the battlefield from about eight years old, but I think Venku is going to be an early starter."

Besany tried to reconcile Skirata's loathing of the Kaminoans for exposing small boys to live weapons fire with the Mandalorian tradition, but maybe the difference lay in knowing that your father was teaching you to survive, not conditioning you as a product. She wondered if the kids felt the difference. It was a question to ask Ordo.

"So what happens now, Kal?"

"Would you mind if I brought Omega Squad here to . . . well, introduce him? I can't take him into the barracks. Zey might sense him. They can feel each other in the Force, Jedi."

Oh my, yes. His mother's a Jedi. He's . . . a Force-sensitive. Oh boy. We've collected the full set of problems.

"Of course you can." Besany had instant thoughts of what buffet food she might put on the table. She was always ready for guests who never came, and aware that she craved belonging; the pull of Skirata's gang was that she never felt like an outsider there. "Are they back in town?"

"I try to make sure they get the shorter missions, yes." He held up his hands defensively. "I know, I know, I've got the best part of ninety boys from my original batch out in the field, but Omega are special."

"One day, are you going to level with me about *everything*?"

"Even the stuff you're better off not knowing?"

"I've been under surveillance by Republic Intel and I'm digging in files that are awfully close to the Chancellor." A lifetime of knowing what she didn't need to ask and what was best left deniable went straight out the window. "I might as well know the worst."

"Okay."

Skirata picked up Venku and walked around the apartment with the infant cradled against his shoulder, gently patting his back and making doting-grandfather noises. Now wasn't going to be the time she got the explanations, then. Maybe it needed a whole day's debriefing program to cover a long career of removing people and things, or dragging them screaming to a client. She had no illusions. She knew the company Skirata kept.

He came from a dirty world, as did Ordo. But she still felt cleaner in their world than she did in the glossy corridors of the Senate, or even on the street surrounded by citizens who were too preoccupied with the latest holovid to ask what was happening to their society lately.

"Here," she said, holding out her arms to take the baby. "Show me how to hold him. Introduce him to his aunt Besany."

Office of General Arligan Zey, Director of Special Forces,
SO Brigade HQ, Coruscant, 547 days after Geonosis

Etain knew this was going to be bad, despite the informal arrangement of comfortable chairs in the office and the caf on the small table, but she could take it.

There was absolutely nothing that General Zey could say

or do to her that would shift the gauge with her now. Okay, she might get weepy, but that was her postnatal hormonal chaos. She wasn't ashamed.

She had a child, and that changed the way she saw the whole galaxy.

Jusik, also summoned for the *refocusing* conversation, sat with his arms folded across his chest like a little Skirata, exuding silent defiance. His beard was trimmed short, he'd braided his hair tightly into a tail, and suddenly he didn't look quite so much like a Jedi despite the robes and lightsaber. He looked like a man—age unknown—who'd had enough.

Etain gave him a gentle touch in the Force. *It'll be okay.* He turned his head slightly and smiled, and it was clear that it would *not* be.

"I'm *delighted* that you could both make it," Zey said. It was going to be the weapons-grade sarcasm today, then. "Given your very busy schedules." He gave Etain an especially long look. "The Gurlanins thanked me for your excellent work in evacuating Qiilura, General Tur-Mukan, and . . . your *help* in the reconstruction process."

You can't touch me. I have a son. All I fear is for his welfare, and his father's. Not mine. "I did what I could, sir."

"Intelligence reports that some of the displaced farmers have joined the Separatist resistance already."

"It was never going to be a popular decision, and yes, I incurred more non-GAR casualties than I would have liked." *Sew a label on that, Zey.* "Commander Levet deserves a more experienced general."

Zey was still scrutinizing her closely. She felt him reach out in the Force, seeking out what he couldn't detect with his ordinary senses. All he got was her fatigue and sense of accomplishment, but he misread it totally. "I can see it's taken a toll on you."

"It has, sir."

"And you, General Jusik . . . I apologize for dragging you back from Dorumaa, but I've been concerned about you."

"I'm fine, sir."

"And I have no idea where you were for the last few weeks, but I doubt it was all spent on Dorumaa, no matter how loyal Delta are in covering for you."

Jusik didn't answer, but it wasn't a guilty silence. Zey looked from Jusik to Etain and back again, as if looking for a break in the wall of conspiracy, and obviously didn't find one. He defaulted to crashing through the wall in typical Zey style.

"I want you both to listen carefully. We are *very* thinly stretched, and if I had Jedi to spare, I would have pulled both of you out of active service by now. You're both competent, and I don't doubt your good intentions, but you're coming off the rails, both of you." He paused. It was the I'll-let-this-sink-in pause, and for some reason it made Etain bristle. "Now, I understand your comradeship with Skirata. He's an excellent soldier, but *you are Jedi,* and we're fast approaching the point where I can cut you no more slack. Get back on the chart. Start following a few procedures. Skirata is *not* your role model. He's a Mandalorian."

"Yes sir," Etain said.

Zey didn't get a word out of Jusik. "General? Does that make sense to you?"

"I think we disagree on definitions, sir," Jusik said carefully. "Like *Jedi.*"

"Which is?"

"I'm *being* a Jedi, sir. It's something you live in every interaction you have with each living thing, not a philosophy you discuss in abstract terms. And I'm not sure that the kind of Jedi the Council wants us to be is good enough."

"Well, you wouldn't be the first Jedi Knight or Padawan to be rebellious. It's normal. I did it at your age."

"Then why aren't you doing it now, sir?"

"And what would I rebel against? The war?"

"It's a good place to start."

"Jusik, I'm not blind to the concessions we have to make, but I have to answer to the Council and to the Senate, so I don't have the luxury of waging little crusades on the margins."

"But that's we're supposed to do, sir—make a difference as individuals. I'm sorry, but a Jedi's primary duty isn't to keep a government in power. It's to help, to heal, to bring peace, to defend the vulnerable—and when those are just slogans we throw around, and not how we treat individuals, it's worse than meaningless." Jusik didn't seem to have broken a sweat, and he left an impression of a sorrowful calm in the Force. Etain could feel a growing strength emanating from him like a lodestone. "So . . ." He paused and swallowed. "So I'm requesting a transfer, sir. I want to resign my commission and serve as a combat medic."

Zey's shock was palpable. His expression softened, and whatever dressing-down he was getting ready to unload on Jusik seemed to have evaporated. Etain hadn't been expecting this, either. This was a stranger sitting next to her: but the Jusik she had always known was in there somewhere.

"I'm not sure there's a mechanism for that, Jusik," Zey said at last.

"Okay." Jusik nodded a few times, looking down into his lap for a moment. "I've given a lot of thought to the consequences of not leading my men in the field, and whether I'm making their situation worse by doing this, but I can't live with it any longer. We sanction the use of a slave army. It's against every single principle of our belief, and it's a stain on us, and we will pay the price of our hypocrisy one day. This is wrong. Therefore I have to leave the Jedi Order."

And I've just left my baby in the care of others because I want to stay.

Etain was in turmoil. She felt as strongly as Jusik did, but she couldn't bring herself to leave now. Suddenly she couldn't see the roots of her own motives; all the certainty she'd built so carefully—precious certainty, the thing she'd craved from the earliest days when she felt so unsure of her ability to be a good Jedi—crumbled, and she felt both a coward for not standing up like Jusik did, and yet unable to walk away from her troops.

"You're sure about that," Zey said. It wasn't a question.

"I am, sir."

"Then may the Force be with you, Bardan Jusik. And I regret losing you. What will you do now?"

Jusik looked as if a massive burden had been lifted from him. He also looked scared for the first time.

"We always think the choices open to a Force-user are light side or dark side, Jedi or Sith, but I believe there are an infinite number of choices beyond those, and I'm going to make one." He stood up and bowed his head politely. "May I keep my lightsaber, sir?"

"You built it. You keep it."

"Thank you, sir."

The doors opened and then hissed shut behind him. Etain was left in a wasteland. Zey let out a long breath.

"I regret that," he said. "I really do. Very well, General. Dismissed."

Etain walked to the doors and turned around just as they were closing. She caught a glimpse of Zey with his elbows on the desk, head propped on his hands, and knew that it wasn't Jusik's resignation that had deflated him, but that he had asked and answered the question that almost every other Jedi had chosen to ignore.

It was a stain, indeed. And they could all see it.

Besany Wennen's apartment, Coruscant, 548 days after Geonosis

"Aren't you a bit old to look after babies, Sarge?" Niner asked, crunching his way through a plate of crisp moss chips.

Skirata gave him that special *Mando* hand gesture of friendly disagreement, the one he taught his boys never to use in front of polite company. "I raised you lot, didn't I?"

"But we were a bit older, and you had a team of care droids, and you were ten years younger."

Besany topped up the bowl of chips while Darman peered at the baby. With his wispy dark hair, Venku didn't look much like Skirata, but then nobody had seen his kids and they would all have been in their thirties or forties now. He wondered what had happened to make them hand over a tiny child like that to a man fighting a war.

But that was Mandalorians for you. They were compulsive adopters, and if someone was in trouble, they all pitched in. Skirata certainly looked besotted. He wrapped the child in a blanket with the deft hands of a man who knew how to handle babies, and cradled the bundle against his chest with a big grin. Etain and Besany were making a show of keeping the food coming, and Etain looked upset. Well, Jusik had walked out of the Jedi Order. It was a shock for everyone.

Skirata swallowed hard as if he was going to start crying. He was so hard that he didn't care who saw his emotions, and Darman admired that. "His name's Venku."

"That's nice," Atin said. "What would you call a son, Corr?"

"Not Sev, for a start . . ." They guffawed. "I'd go for Jori."

"That's not a *Mando* name."

"I'm still catching up on Mandalorian stuff, guys. Just a white job who's been promoted, okay?"

Darman chewed over the question. "Kad," he said. He was aware of Etain and Skirata looking at him. Maybe he wasn't showing enough interest. "Kad's a nice name."

He moved in a little closer; Etain looked uncomfortable and stared at her boots. Maybe she didn't find babies as fascinating as Skirata did, but then it was his grandchild. It was to be expected.

"Can I hold him?" Darman asked.

He *wanted* to show some enthusiasm, because Skirata was . . . fierfek, this was his own father in as many senses of the word that mattered, the man who raised him. It was rude not to admire his grandson. Darman held out his arms, and Skirata hesitated with an expression on his face that Darman couldn't fathom at all. It looked like sorrow.

"Here you go, son." Skirata laid the baby in Darman's arms, moving them into position. There was a technique to baby holding, apparently. "They don't react much at this age. They basically eat, sleep, and . . . need their diapers changed."

Darman, surprised at how heavy the bundle was, inhaled cautiously. Little Venku just smelled vaguely of powder and skin. But the baby *did* react: he opened his eyes and tried to turn his head, unfocused and totally uncoordinated. His eyes were pale blue-green and glassy.

"He's got your eyes, Sarge," Darman said, lost for anything else to say. What he actually *felt* like blurting out was so inane that he didn't dare: that babies were so tiny, so helpless, that he couldn't imagine ever having been so small. He had a vague memory of babies in glass vats in Tipoca City, but that was different. This was a real live kid in his arms, and he had no idea what to do next.

"Their eyes change color," Skirata said. Yes, there was a definite huskiness about *Kal'buir*'s voice, which usually meant he was emotionally charged about something. "They're all blue at first, pretty well. Might be totally different in a few weeks."

"Right," said Darman. "Do you want him back now?"

"You can hold him as long as you want, son."

"I don't think he's comfortable with me."

"Oh, I don't know. I think he's fine . . ."

Darman felt inexplicably uneasy. The baby seemed to be doing his best to squirm toward him, and for a moment he felt as if Etain was reaching to him in the Force, but that was impossible. She was right there, right next to him, looking toward the doors as if she wanted to get out of the room as fast as she could.

"I'd make a rotten father, wouldn't I?" Darman said.

Skirata looked him straight in the eye, still with that same expression that was somewhere between tears and contentment. "*Dar'ika,* you'll make a great dad, believe me. A *terrific* dad."

"Yeah, maybe, but not yet." It was the first thing that came into Darman's head. The baby scared him, and he wasn't used to fears he couldn't come to terms with or remove. "I need to do some growing up first. Here, take him before I drop him."

Great. What a stupid thing to blurt out. It always upsets him when I talk about getting older.

Skirata just smiled sadly and held out his arms to take Venku. Etain seemed uncomfortable and shot through the door. She was in a hurry to get somewhere, and Skirata jerked his head at Darman to follow her.

"Go and take some time together," he said, easing his hand into his pocket to take something out. "Just go and do normal couple stuff. Plenty of credits on this chip. Here. Go have some fun for a couple of days. We'll eat all the food and talk about you when your back's turned."

Skirata was a touchingly generous man. Darman took the credits and squeezed his shoulder. This was his family—his sergeant, his brothers—and however much he wanted to be with Etain, he needed them, too. So Niner had his answer.

"Thanks, *Kal'buir.*"

Skirata smiled. *"Ni kyr'tayl gai sa'ad."*

Darman understood what that meant. But it didn't really need saying, because Skirata had taken on the responsibility of being the commandos' father a long time ago.

"You know what that means, Dar?"

"You've adopted me. Formally, I mean."

"Yes." He patted Darman's cheek with his free hand. "Time I adopted you all."

"Are you rich, Sarge?" Corr asked. "I always wanted a rich dad."

"Richest man alive," Skirata said, half smiling. "You'll be amazed what I'm going to leave you in my will."

Skirata sometimes had his little jokes, and the commandos didn't always understand them. Darman didn't like to think of his sergeant writing a will. It was all too early for that, but then he was a soldier, and those things had to be dealt with sooner rather than later.

"We'd rather have you, *Kal'buir,*" Niner said. "Though a country estate on Naboo is a reasonable second choice . . ."

They found refuge in laughter again. Darman left Skirata with his grandson and went to look for Etain.

He found her waiting in the lobby, sitting on the fat upholstered arm of one of the sofas, arms folded tight against her chest. She looked upset.

"What's wrong?"

Etain shrugged. "It's just sad, that's all."

"He's happy." Darman showed her the credit chip. "He loves kids. He'll be in his element. Look, he gave me this and said to go off and have some fun. Anywhere you want to go?"

Etain had that same expression that he'd just seen on Skirata's face. He knew he must have said something wrong, but he wasn't sure what. He unfolded her arms with a little gentle pressure and took her hand.

"The baby's upset you somehow, hasn't it?" he said. Of course; being a Jedi, Etain would never have known her parents. "Does it remind you of being taken from your family?"

"No, let's think about where we can go." She threw that switch and turned into the little general again, her wavy brown hair bouncing as she walked briskly ahead of him, hauling him by his hand. "Have you seen the botanical gardens at the Skydome? Amazing plants in there, a nice place where you can eat, all kinds of stuff."

Darman knew all about plants. He had his GAR fieldcraft database of everything he could safely eat if he had to live off the land on a mission, planet by planet. It was a novelty to think of plants as something fascinating to admire. But his mouth felt connected somehow to uncontrolled thoughts that just dug him deeper into this emotional mire. He *had* to say it. He knew what was bothering her now: she wanted him to have a normal life, and she probably thought he wanted a child now that he'd seen Venku, because Mandalorians loved their families and that was how she saw him.

"If it's the baby that's upset you," he said, "you don't even have to think about having one for ages. Not during a war. It's not a good time, is it? Not for either of us."

There. He'd said it, and she would feel better now, let off the hook. There was no point dwelling on his shortened life span. Neither of them knew what was around the corner.

He'd take the pressure off her, because it was the responsible thing to do.

"You're right," she said. "It's not the right time."

The Skydome gardens were just as beautiful and fascinating as Etain had promised. He could tell she was trying to be cheerful and enthusiastic about them, but there was something sad and wounded about her that he didn't know how to make better.

Evacuating Qiilura must have been worse than she'd let on. But she'd tell him in her own good time.

20

Order 65: In the event of either (i) a majority in the Senate declaring the Supreme Commander (Chancellor) to be unfit to issue orders, or (ii) the Security Council declaring him to be unfit to issue orders, and an authenticated order being received by the GAR, commanders shall be authorized to detain the Supreme Commander, with lethal force if necessary, and command of the GAR shall fall to the acting Chancellor until a successor is appointed or alternative authority identified as outlined in Section 6 (iv).

Order 66: In the event of Jedi officers acting against the interests of the Republic, and after receiving specific orders verified as coming directly from the Supreme Commander (Chancellor), GAR commanders will remove those officers by lethal force, and command of the GAR will revert to the Supreme Commander (Chancellor) until a new command structure is established.

—From Contingency Orders for the Grand Army of the Republic: Order Initiation, Orders 1 Through 150, GAR document CO(CL) 56–95

The Kragget all-day restaurant, lower levels, Coruscant, 548 days after Geonosis

"I always said you were a fine officer, *Bard'ika*," Skirata said. "I feel this is my fault."

He slid onto the bench and faced Jusik across the table; the Twi'lek waitress was there in a heartbeat. The Kragget had real live staff, for its regulars at least, and this place was 90 percent regular trade.

"Usual Arterial Blocker, Sergeant Kal?" asked the Twi'lek, whose dancing days were over but who still brightened his day. "Extra egg?"

"Please. And top up the caf for my skinny young friend here, too." Skirata waited for her to walk away. "*Bard'ika*, I'm so sorry it came to this."

"I'm not," Jusik said brightly. It hadn't ruined his appetite, either. If anything, he looked purged. "Okay, it's scary to walk out, but I did it, and I *had* to. The only thing I feel bad about is leaving my command, not that the men need me holding their hands, and not being on the inside for you any longer."

Skirata had long since decided that Jusik was an exemplary man but a potentially lethal officer. He wouldn't see men as resources to be expended in battle to win wars, a price worth paying; he cared too much and stayed too close, and so he would never be an efficient tactician. Skirata both loved him for it and knew he was a liability, and so had made a silent pledge to keep the kid alive—whatever that took.

Jusik had made a stand on pure principle, a man's decision that so few of his superiors seemed to have the *gett'se* to make. That was *mandokarla*.

"Son, I need you now on the outside more than you can ever know. Anyway, you haven't left your boys any more than I have. You'll see plenty of them. You've just . . . well . . . shifted sideways into a self-employed consultancy capacity. Right?"

"I have to get a job and a place to live for the first time in my life. The Jedi Order doesn't set you up for life on the outside. No resettlement package, just like the clones—but at least nobody sends a hit squad after us."

"You've *got* a job to walk into." It was such uncanny timing that Skirata decided not to make any more cracks about the Force, or maybe he was just a five-star opportunist. "And a home, if you don't mind sharing a space with me and Laseema. Oh, and Venku. In fact—"

"Yes. Thank you."

"He's going to need someone around with your *special* skills to help him deal with his own abilities. Etain won't be there often enough."

"I'd love to. I really would. But I can still be useful in the war."

"Oh, I know. Poor old Zey. He thinks that if he confiscates your identichip, you're locked out. He really doesn't get it."

"I think he knows otherwise," said Jusik, "but he doesn't want to be reminded of it." The waitress returned with more hot plates and jugs of caf. "Venku, then."

"I think we might need to call him Kad."

"Why?"

"The lads were talking about names, and Darman said he liked *Kad*. He really ought to choose his son's name, even if he doesn't know it yet."

Jusik chewed, contemplating. "Call him Kad, then. *Kad'ika*. You weren't called Kal when you were taken in by Munin. Doesn't mean he can't be Venku, too, if he wants."

"See? You're a real problem solver. Earning your keep already."

"And I get to take him to *Manda'yaim* when I visit Fi."

"Deal."

They finished their meal in relatively happy silence. There was nothing so bad that it couldn't have something worthwhile wrung from it, and good luck was simply a matter of what you decided to do with the hand you were dealt. Skirata had climbed out of the depths of despair of recent weeks, and was back on the attack, making things happen.

Ko Sai—she definitely hadn't had the last laugh, not by a long shot. *Nu draar.*

He was glad the Kragget never asked its patrons to open their bags for security checks, because that nice Twi'lek waitress probably wouldn't have seen him quite the same way ever again.

"Here's a code key to the apartment, *Bard'ika,*" he said, "but let Laseema know you're coming, because she's still a bit nervous of unexpected visitors. I've got to do Delta a favor."

"They haven't reported to Zey yet. I asked them to hold off until you were ready."

"Good lad."

Jusik's gaze flickered and settled on the bag. "Is it in there?"

"Uh-huh."

"Gross." But Jusik carried on eating. It was an act, but he was probably trying hard not to think Jedi thoughts about compassion. "Anything I can get on with while *Kad'ika*'s asleep?"

"Yes." The boy was a gem, he really was. Skirata was thankful for whatever it was that put fine men—fine sons— in his path. "See what you can dig up on high-security prisons here. There's a certain Sep scientist I'd like to visit, one who knows a lot about Fett clone genomes. Dr. Uthan must be bored out of her skull by now."

"Handy that Omega hauled her back from Qiilura, isn't it?" Jusik winked. "Kind of . . . destiny."

"I promise," said Skirata. "No more Force jokes. This is no time to make new enemies."

Skirata walked out onto a grimy lower-levels walkway, carrying his prize in a cryoseal box in a bag, and found that he was whistling.

No, she wasn't going to have the last laugh at all.

Arca Company Barracks, SO Brigade HQ, Coruscant, 548 days after Geonosis

Delta Squad were still waiting in the TIV on the landing strip when Skirata got there, and Sev wasn't very happy about it.

"This had better be good, Sarge," Scorch said, looking ruffled and in need of a haircut when he took off his helmet. "We haven't eaten in twelve hours."

"Well, thanks for not signing in yet." Skirata put the bag

on the deck of the cramped compartment and pulled out the box. He handed the package to Sev. "Guess who."

Sev looked at the box suspiciously. "This isn't the family-sized pack of spicy warra nuts, is it?"

"No. Definitely not. But if you're going to open it, be careful not to drop it. It'll make a mess."

Sev swallowed. "And why are you giving us this, Sarge?"

"I want you to walk into Zey's office, put that on his desk, and tell him you found her. He can have Tipoca City check the Kaminoan DNA records."

"Her?"

"You know who I mean."

"Ko Sai?"

"No, the Queen Mother of *shabla* Hapes. Who do you think? Of *course* I mean Ko Sai."

"She's dead, then."

"Either that, or she overdid the diet." Skirata rolled his eyes and popped the seal on the cryobox. Sev held on to it, but the smell hit him, and he took the briefest of glances before closing it again. "I've made it look like she had an encounter with incontinent ordnance so it fits your story. And it's a body part she couldn't do without, not something like a finger that any amateur *chakaar* could slice off. It's absolute proof she's dead."

Sev had stopped counting the kills he'd made, and he was no longer sure if tinnies outnumbered wets on the tally. But this shook him, maybe because Ko Sai had been such a figure of authority for most of his short life—and because the Mandalorian knot he'd found anchoring the headless skeleton now made sense.

"*You* killed her, then, Sarge. It was your knot."

"No, son. Neither." Skirata was looking around as if he was expecting company. "She had *Mando* bodyguards, though. And I didn't kill her. We just found the body, I swear. I'd tell you if I had done it, because I don't care any longer, and frankly I'd have enjoyed slicing her up, the sadistic *hut'uun*. But I didn't. And that's all you need to know—for your own good."

Skirata turned to go. Boss caught his arm. "I hear we lost General Jusik."

"You'll see him around . . ."

"And what *did* happen to Fi?"

Skirata looked aside, as if concocting his official line. Sev knew that look now.

"RC-eight-oh-one-five is dead, lads. Call me if you need anything."

They watched him go and closed the hatch behind him.

"The *shab* Fi's dead," said Boss. "I'd love to know what really went on there."

"No, you wouldn't, because we don't *need* to," Fixer said. "Go deliver your present to the old man, then, Sev. Let's call endex on this whole time-wasting exercise."

Sev held the box gingerly in both hands, just in case he had an embarrassing spillage, and made his way down the corridor to Zey's office. He wondered whether to tell Zey what was in the container or just to let him open it and ask him to make a wild guess. Sev would get a few moments of amusement out of his general's reaction, anyway.

We just found the body. I swear. I'd tell you if I had.

"Yeah, sure you did, Kal," Sev muttered. "I believe you."

Sev would have been disappointed if Skirata had done anything less than fulfill all the vows he'd made to slice the Kaminoan into aiwha-bait. It crossed Sev's mind that this also enabled him to look Vau in the eye and not have to feel he'd failed his sergeant.

Yeah, Skirata was a thug, and a thief, and even a little nuts, but he had his sense of honor and decency where the troops were concerned. This was a very generous favor to do for them all.

Sev put down the box, rapped the knuckles of his gauntlet against Zey's doors, and waited, then tucked his helmet under one arm and Ko Sai's neatly packaged head tightly under the other. He jerked his own head at the others in a leave-me-to-it gesture.

The doors slid open. The general was sitting at his desk,

tapping a datapad on the edge of it in distracted annoyance at something other than Sev's interruption.

"Oh-Seven," he said. "You're back."

"Sir."

"I could do with some positive news, if you have any."

Sev placed the box in front of Zey and took a step backward. "Not sure if it's *positive,* General," he said. "But it's certainly *definitive.*"

Zey stared at the package for a while. Then he looked up at Sev. "Oh," he said.

Jedi had that spooky sixth sense. Maybe Zey knew what was in there already. But he looked anyway, and didn't recoil even though his face went distinctly ashen when he lifted the inner seal.

"I think she's dead, sir," said Sev.

Zey closed the box. "You think so? You should take up medicine, my boy."

"You can check the DNA with the Kaminoans. At least the Chancellor has a definite answer, even if it's not the one he was hoping for."

"Would you care to fill in any of the details? Because Palpatine is going to ask me how this . . . *trophy* came into my possession."

"We dug our way into the lab she'd constructed. It had collapsed after an explosion. Messy."

"Ko Sai wasn't the careless type . . ."

"No, but she had a lot of people with short tempers on her tail."

"Dead when you got to her, you say."

"We didn't kill her, sir. You said *alive.* We can do alive . . . when we try hard."

Zey stared into Sev's face, then sighed. "I know you're telling the truth. If you have any information on who got to her first, though, I'm sure that the Chancellor would love to hear it."

Sev rode his apparent honesty a little farther into dangerous deception territory and hoped the omission didn't show up in the Force.

"I don't have any proof who killed her, sir," he said. "But I'd think that the Kaminoans took a dim view of her jumping ship with their trade secrets like that."

"Speaking of which . . ."

"Nothing, sir." It was all true, all of it. Sev could see Zey measuring each word he said, a little frown puckering his brow. "Her computers were totally trashed. No sign of any data."

"And presumably Kaminoans would know what they were looking for."

"We found a few dead Mandalorians, though."

"Ah."

"No ID. Might have been there to protect her, or might have been caught in their own attack. Either way—no Ko Sai, and no data. We did our best, sir."

Zey's shoulders sagged. He was a big man but suddenly he looked smaller than Skirata.

"I know, Oh-Seven. I know. You did well to find her. Take a day's leave, all of you. Dismissed."

Sev wasn't expecting praise. He always felt he was letting someone down—usually Vau—so the comment caught him off guard. He also wasn't sure what to do with a day off, but sleep and excessive eating were the first things that sprang to mind. He saluted, turned smartly for the door, and then stopped.

"I'm very sorry to hear General Jusik has left us, sir."

Zey was still staring at the box on his desk. "So am I. It's always a blow to lose a good man, but it's worse to lose a good Jedi when we need to keep our focus."

Sev didn't have a clue what he meant, but nodded sympathetically. Then he left and put distance between the office and himself as quickly as he could. Boss and the others ambushed him halfway down the corridor.

"Well?" Scorch demanded. "Did he buy it?"

"I think so."

Fixer snorted. "Not much else he can do, is there?"

"We got a day off out of it," Sev said. "Which is better

than a thrashing from Vau, so shut up and make the most of
it."

Delta took a shortcut across the parade ground to get to
their quarters. In the late-afternoon sun, the newly re-formed
Omega Squad—no Darman, but with the new guy from
EOD who could do really dangerous knife tricks with his
prosthetic hands—were playing limmie with Ordo and
Mereel. Skirata had joined in. They played it hard, what Vau
called the *Mando* way, shoulder-charging and tackling one
another with complete disregard for injury, kicking the
spherical ball high into the air. It was about the size of a
man's head—Sev did a double take to be sure it wasn't actually a *real* head—and it cannoned against the wall of the barracks to loud whoops and cries of *"Oya! Ori'mesh'la!"*

None of them, except Skirata, was in armor. They weren't
even in red GAR fatigues, just assorted civilian clothing they
must have picked up on the last mission. There were no team
colors. If Sev hadn't recognized them as his clone brothers, he
would have taken them for Mandalorians whiling away
the time between invasion and pillage rather than fellow
commandos letting off steam.

They suddenly struck him as very foreign, and that surprised him: Vau had taught Delta all the Mandalorian customs and language, just as Skirata had taught his commando
squads, but somehow at that moment Omega and the Nulls
seemed very much more Mandalorian mercs than men of the
Grand Army.

"So," Boss said, as if reading his mind, "if we got in a ruck
with a bunch of real *Mando'ade,* whose side do you reckon
they'd be on?"

Sev shrugged. "Who do you think killed the *Mand'ade* we
found in Ko Sai's hideout?"

"You don't know who did that," Fixer said.

"Yeah, and neither do you."

Scorch put a stop to the speculation. *"Vode an.* Brothers,
all. Okay?"

Delta Squad each managed a casual acknowledgment and
Sev expected Skirata to try to talk them into joining the

game, but he didn't. The six men carried on, oblivious, with the occasional shout or comment in *Mando'a,* and they might as well have been in Keldabe, not Galactic City.

It was . . . unsettling. It was also oddly *tempting* in a way that Sev didn't want to think about.

Commandos were all on the same side. Sev was sure of it. And for the time being, so were the Nulls, although they were a law unto themselves. Whatever eccentricities they had, they were totally loyal, obeying Skirata to the letter.

Skirata paused, trapping the ball under one boot, and seemed to notice Sev for the first time.

"Copaani geroy?" he asked, totally *Mando. Want to play?*

"No thanks," Sev said. "I'll stick to my embroidery. Looks a bit rough. I bruise easy."

Delta Squad walked on, leaving behind a scene that for a few moments could easily have been unfolding on Mandalore, and not in the heart of the Republic.

"Just as well they're on our side," said Boss.

"Yeah," said Sev. "It is."

ODDS

KAREN TRAVISS

*Everyone knows that intel's about as reliable as a Weequay
quay ball. But that doesn't mean it doesn't have its uses.
Sometimes it's the lies and myths that tell you everything
you need to know.*
—Sergeant Kal Skirata, commando instructor, Special
Operations Brigade, Grand Army of the Republic

**Separatist droid factory, Olanet, Siskeen system,
460 days after the Battle of Geonosis
(65 to 67 days after the events of the novel Star Wars:
Republic Commando: Triple Zero)**

Atin liked a big, satisfying explosion as much as the next
man. But there were better ways of putting droids out of action than turning them into shrapnel. He just didn't agree
with the technical details this time.

"Ordo *told* me you were argumentative," said Prudii.

Atin bristled. But coming from Ordo, it might have been a
compliment. "I just want to get it right."

Atin edged along the gantry above the foundry floor, feeling along the rust-crusted metal railing for a sound section
that would take the weight of a rappelling line with a fully
kitted Republic commando on the end. The only illumination

was the red-hot glow from the durasteel sheets feeding into the rollers; droids didn't need light to see. The night-vision filter in his visor had kicked in the moment he and Prudii entered the factory.

It was a high-value target. The factory was said to be one of the largest outside Geonosis. Again, the intel seemed to have lost something in the translation.

Atin found what felt like a solid section of railing and checked the metal's integrity with his gauntlet sensor. Flakes of corroded metal fell to the gantry floor, and he brushed them carefully into a gap to hide signs of entry.

"Five percent extra carvanium does the job." Prudii—Null ARC trooper N-5—pulled out his belt tool kit. "Trust me. I've done a lot of these."

"I know."

"And? Did it work? *It worked.*"

"Okay, I'm not a metallurgist."

Prudii peered over the rail as he checked his rappelling line. "Neither am I, but I knew a man who was."

Atin didn't ask about his use of the past tense. Prudii was both an assassin and a saboteur, and at the top of his game in both fields. Until Atin got to know him as well as he knew his Null brothers, Ordo and Mereel, he would err on the side of caution. Nulls were as mad as a box of Hapan chags. There were only six of them in the army, but it felt like a lot more.

Omega Squad was back at barracks again for a few days. Atin missed the rest of his team, but he'd volunteered for this mission to learn a technique. And learn he would.

I can do this. Argumentative? I just like things to be right.

Prudii dropped down the line, his *kama* spreading on the air as he descended in complete silence—no mean feat for an eighty-five-kilo man in full armor. Atin took a breath and paused before dropping down after him.

If a droid detected them, the mission was over. They'd have to blow the factory—again. And then the Seps would switch production elsewhere—again. If they just churned out millions of substandard tinnies, crippled at the molecular level by a little tweak in the automation, it would save a lot of hunting.

"Nothing personal," Atin muttered, wondering what went on in their self-aware metal heads. "It's you or me, *vode*."

"What?" Prudii's voice filled Atin's helmet.

"Just trying not to be . . . *organicist*."

"Don't give me all that droids-have-rights *osik*."

"Wouldn't dream of it," said Atin.

He landed next to the Null lieutenant, and they skirted the assembly line. On the factory floor, twenty meters below ground level, the rhythm of fully automated production continued uninterrupted. Only labor droids were around during the night shift. Durasteel sheets rumbled between the rollers, were caught by giant claws, and moved to the next assembly line for cutting. At the end of the conveyor belt, a clamshell press shaped the torso cases of battle droids around a form before dragging them through cooling vats with a hiss of steam. The whole place smelled of soot and burning.

A maintenance droid—just a box on wheels with a dozen multifunctional arms—trundled past Atin and Prudii, as blind to the electromagnetic profile of their armor as all his kind were. Atin still held his breath as it passed. But no sound escaped from his sealed helmet. He could yell his head off at Prudii, and nobody else would hear a thing. The deafening noise of the assembly line would have drowned out all sound anyway.

"There it is." Prudii pointed to what looked like a run of oversized lockers on a far wall. Their hinges were as corroded as the gantry. "I *hate* rust. Don't they do any housework around here?"

Atin eased the cover open carefully. No, the Seps didn't inspect the automated settings very often, as long as the stateboard reported that everything was running okay. Inside, racks of data wafers fed template information to the different production lines, dictating wire gauges, alloy proportions, component ratings, and the thousands of other parameters that went into making a battle droid. Atin and

Prudii had just opened up the brain of the entire factory. It was time for a little surgery.

"How many times have you done this?" asked Atin.

Prudii sucked his teeth audibly and rocked his head, counting. "Lots," he said at last.

"And they haven't noticed yet?"

"No. I'd say not." Prudii clipped bypass wires to the bays above and below the slot to isolate it. "Just so I don't trigger the safety cutout." He inspected a substitute data wafer—apparently identical in every way to the Separatist ones—and inserted it into the slot. "This'll make sure the foundry adds too much carvanium to the durasteel, and that the quality control sampling reads it as normal levels. See?" He pointed to the readout on the panel. A cluster of figures read 0003. "Machines believe what you tell 'em. Just like people."

"You *sure* that's enough?"

"Any higher and it'll be too brittle to pass through the rollers. Then they'll spot the problem too soon."

"Okay . . ."

Prudii took a breath. He was remarkably patient for a Null. "Look, when these *chakaare* reach the battlefield, the overpressure from a basic ion shell will crack their cases like Naboo crystal." He removed the bypass clips and attached them to bays flanking a vertical slot farther up the panel. More spiked wafers replaced genuine chips. "And just in case they get lucky and spot *that* little quality control problem, *this* one will reduce the wire gauge just enough so that when it takes a heavy current, it'll short. I like to introduce a different batch of problems for each factory, in case they spot a pattern. How much more of this do I have to debate with you?"

"Just checking, *sir.*"

"Drop the *sir.* I *hate* it."

It was a precise calculation: just enough to render entire production runs of droids so vulnerable on the battlefield that they were almost useless, but not enough to flag the problem when the units were checked before being shipped from the factory—checked by service droids using the same falsified data.

Prudii had to be doing something right. The kill ratio had climbed from twenty to one to fifty to one in a matter of a few months. The tinnies still hadn't overrun the Republic, despite the claims that they could. While Prudii worked, factory droids skimmed past him, oblivious. He stepped out of their way and let them pass.

"Is it true you've tracked down General Grievous?" asked Atin. " 'Cos I know that two of you were tasked to hunt him—"

"Not me. Ask Jaing. Or Kom'rk. Their job, not mine."

Atin hadn't met them yet. "If they've found him, the war's as good as over."

"You reckon? Well, it doesn't look like it's *over* yet."

Atin took the hint and didn't ask about Grievous again. He kept watch, DC-17 rifle ready, anxious not to use it for once. It was odd to be invisible. He wondered why the Grand Army didn't use stealth coating on all trooper armor, seeing as most of their land engagements were against droids.

There was a lot that didn't add up in this war.

"There," said Prudii, closing the panel gently. He stood back to inspect it. "We were never here."

They climbed back up to the gantry on their lines and slipped out the way they'd come. It was pitch-black outside. They had an hour to get to the extraction point and transmit their coordinates to the heavily disguised freighter waiting for them. On Olanet, that meant crossing kilometers of marshaling yards serving the nerf meat industry. Atin could hear the animals lowing, but he'd still never seen a live nerf.

"This place stinks." Prudii settled behind a repulsor truck in a yard full of hundreds of others and squatted in its shadow. The harmless but nauseating stench of manure and animals penetrated his helmet's filters. "Five-Seven, are you receiving?"

"With you in ten, sir. Stand by."

Prudii made no comment about the *sir*. He took the data wafers out of his belt and attached a probe to them, one at a time. He struck Atin as a kindred spirit, a man who wouldn't let any inanimate objects get the better of him, but he was still hard work.

"Shab," Prudii muttered. He held out a wafer. "What do you make of this?"

Atin slotted it into his own wafer reader and relayed the extracted data to his HUD. The readout was just strings of numbers, the kind of data he'd need to analyze carefully. "What am I looking at? I normally blow this stuff up. I've never stopped to read it."

"Look for the code that starts zero-zero-five-alpha, ten from the top row."

"Got it."

"That's the running total of units off the line since the wafer was inserted to start the production run. And the date."

Atin scanned from left to right, counting the line of numbers and inserting imaginary commas. "Nine hundred ninety-six thousand, one hundred and twenty-five. In a year."

"Correct."

"Not exactly smoking." Atin checked that he wasn't missing a row of numbers. "No, just six figures."

"Every factory we hit is producing numbers like that. Judging by the raw material freight we monitor, there're still a lot more factories out there, but I think we're talking about a few hundred million droids."

"That's reassuring. Thanks. I'll sleep well tonight."

"And so you should, *ner vod*." Prudii popped the seal on his collar, lifted off his helmet, and wiped the palm of his gauntlet across his forehead; it came away shiny with sweat in the faint light leaking from the HUD. Somehow he looked older than Mereel and Ordo. "They say they're making *quadrillions* of droids." He paused. "A quadrillion has fifteen zeros. A *thousand million* millions, not a few *hundred*. Are we missing something here?"

Atin took no offense at the explanation. Anything more than three million was bad news in his book; that was how many clone troops were deployed or being raised on Kamino. *"They* say? Who're *they*?"

"Now, that's a good question."

"Anyway, it only takes one to kill you."

"But where *are* they all? I've bimbled around forty-seven planets this last year." Prudii made it sound like sightseeing. Atin had a sudden vision of him admiring the tourist attractions of Sep planets and then fragmenting them. The grip of the Verpine rifle slung across his back was well worn. Atin had no real idea who Prudii hunted, and he was happier that way. "Seen a lot, counted a lot. But *not* quadrillions. They just don't seem to be able to produce anywhere near those numbers."

"But that's why we're fighting, isn't it?" Atin tried not to worry about the HoloNet news and took the political debate as something that didn't matter, because one droid or a septillion, he and his brothers were the ones who would still be in the front line. "Because the Seps are going to overrun us with droid armies if we don't stop them. So why not just reassure the public that the threat isn't that big?"

Prudii looked at him for a moment. Atin got the feeling that he felt sorry for him in some way, and he wasn't sure why. "Because it's only the likes of us that are finding this out every time we crack a Sep facility."

"You report it?"

"Of course I report it. Every time. To General Zey. Mace Windu knows. They *all* know."

"So why is the holonews saying quadrillions? Where did the figure come from?"

"I heard it first from Republic Intelligence."

"Well, then . . ." Intel was notoriously *variable* in quality. "They make it up as they go along."

"Even *they're* not that stupid."

Prudii replaced his helmet and held his hand out to Atin for the wafer. He didn't say much after that.

Millions or quadrillions. So what? Atin, a man who enjoyed numbers, looked at the 1.2 million clone troopers deployed at that moment, added the 2 million men still being raised and trained, and didn't even need to place a decimal point to work out that he didn't like the odds.

But he never did. And it never stopped him from defying them.

"Want me to relay this data to HQ?" he asked.

"No," said Prudii. "Not until *Kal'buir* sees it. *Never* until he sees it."

A good Mandalorian son always obeyed his father. The Null ARCs were no different: they looked to Sergeant Kal Skirata—*Kal'buir,* Papa Kal—for their orders, not to the Republic. A *Mando* father put his sons first, after all, and they trusted him.

Skirata would always outrank everyone—captain, general, and even Supreme Chancellor.

Tipoca City, Kamino, 461 days after Geonosis

Ko Sai was a devious piece of work.

Mereel—ARC trooper N-7—had always thought of Kaminoans as cold, arrogant, xenophobic, and even suitable for barbecuing, but he'd never seen them as *scheming*—not until he began hunting their missing chief scientist, anyway. She hadn't died in the Battle of Kamino, as everyone thought. She'd defected.

Why? What motivates her? Wealth? Not politics, that's for sure.

He knew she was still alive, because she was on the run from her Separatist paymasters now. In the cantinas of Tatooine, he'd heard rumors of a bounty. And when you had only your rare skill in cloning to trade, in a galaxy where nonmilitary cloning was now banned, your attempts to raise credits were hard to hide from those who knew where to look.

The world of Khomm and Arkania had really suffered from that ban. Mereel knew *exactly* where to look.

He stood to attention in the ranks of troopers in the Tipoca training facility, a good, obedient clone as far as the Kaminoans were concerned. A perfect *product*. But their identification systems weren't quite as foolproof as they'd told the Republic. They certainly hadn't spotted his fake ID transponder code. The little chip cycled through randomly generated IDs and, without his distinctive *kama* and blue-trimmed armor, he could disappear right in front of the *kaminiise*. Not even the patrolling KE-8 pilots looking for defective clones could spot him.

You think you're infallible, don't you, aiwha-bait?

One of the Kaminoan technicians walked along the row of troopers and paused in front of him, blinking, gray-skinned, its long fragile neck tempting to a man trained to kill. Mereel, frozen at attention, fantasized: blaster, vibroblade, or garrote? These vile things had wanted to exterminate him as a kid, and he would *never* forget that. He and his five brothers had been a cloning experiment the Kaminoans considered a failure, but Kal Skirata had saved them.

There was time for revenge later. *Kal'buir* had taught him patience.

Patience is a luxury. I'm aging twice as fast as an ordinary man.

He needed to pass through Tipoca City and grab some data without being noticed. The Kaminoan moved on. Mereel savored the knowledge that he knew more about chief scientist Ko Sai's whereabouts than the Kaminoans did, and they'd searched for her very, very hard.

You're going to give us back our lives, gihaal, *me and all my brothers.* Mereel included the Republic commandos, the poor cannon fodder meat cans around him, and even the Alpha ARCs, who'd been ready to kill clone kids to stop the Seps from using them. *An vode. They're all my brothers.* Even the Alphas.

As the troopers fell out, he slipped in at the rear of a line of men to cover his progress toward the administration core of the building. One glanced at him, the slightest head movement betraying what was happening under his helmet. The man was probably well aware Mereel was a stranger from the minute telltale differences in gait or bearing, but he said nothing. No clone could possibly be a security risk.

I'm just borrowing some information, ner vod. *I'm not*

even going to sabotage this cesspit of a city. Take no notice of me.

As the line passed a corridor leading off at ninety degrees, Mereel wheeled left and walked calmly down to the end of the passage. The head-up display in his helmet scrolled floor plans and data before his eyes. He looked both at it and through it to focus on the systems terminal set in the wall. Since the Separatist attack on Tipoca just over a standard year ago, security had been tightened, but that was just for Seps and their droids. *Amateurs and tinnies.* Nobody could keep out a determined Null ARC.

"Mer'ika," said the voice in his helmet. It was quiet and concerned: Skirata rarely raised his voice to them. "Don't push your luck. I want you back in one piece."

"I hear you, *Kal'buir.*" Mereel slipped the docking pin of his forearm plate into one of the terminal's ports. A couple of troopers looked his way from the end of the passage, but he remained unhurried. *I'm just calibrating my suit.* "We might not get another chance to come back here. I'm grabbing everything I can."

Along with the legitimate outgoing code that requested data from the Tipoca mainframe, a second hidden layer hitched a ride to access the root of the entire system undetected. Mereel now had Republic Treasury encryption and de-erasure keys, courtesy of an obliging Treasury agent called Besany Wennen, and they were the most advanced available. Now he could not only read Treasury data but also find encrypted files between Tipoca and the Republic that had been hidden from his previous probes. He might also be able to recover the data that Ko Sai had stolen and deleted.

He wanted her critical research on controlling the aging process in humans. It worked both ways, they said. That meant it was worth a *fortune.* She would try to sell it.

The tree of files appeared in his HUD, a field of flickering amber and blue symbols like a garish fabric. What looked like a plain white wall to humans on Kamino was actually a riot of color beyond their visual range. Only in the

Kaminoans' digital systems did Mereel ever get a glimpse of the way their heptachromatic vision saw the world.

Lots of blue and orange and purple. Tacky. Tasteless.

If he copied just the files he knew he needed, it would take seconds.

You might never get a chance to come back again.

The mainframe held ten petabytes of data. It would take *minutes.*

Boots clattered past him. Mereel concentrated on looking like a regular trooper maintaining his armor's systems, but it was hard to stretch a thirty-second procedure. He could hear his breath rasping in his helmet. So could Skirata and his brother Ordo, waiting in orbit to extract him.

"You okay, son?"

"Fine, *Kal'buir.*"

"No heroics," said Ordo's voice. "Get out now."

Mereel looked at his HUD icon: still amber, still downloading. He was pushing it, all right. But he'd pushed his luck a lot more for the Republic, and a bunch of strangers and *jetiise* didn't mean half as much to him as the welfare of his brothers. The amber icon flashed. More boots clattered past the end of the passage.

Come on . . . Come on . . .

It was taking too long.

His peripheral vision, enhanced by his helmet's systems, saw the Kaminoan pause and turn to walk toward him. *Fierfek. That's all we need.*

It was a crested male. It stood in front of him, feigning concern. Mereel knew it only saw him as a commodity.

"You have been downloading longer than average, trooper."

"Just checking, sir." Mereel heard a faint click on his audio feed: Skirata was edgy. "Slow data response times on my HUD."

"Then please proceed to Procurement and have them run diagnostics."

"Yes sir!" *Don't bank on it, aiwha-bait.* The icon in his HUD changed to green. "*Right away,* sir!"

Mereel withdrew the docking pin and walked back down the passage in the general direction of Procurement. The moment the Kaminoan was out of sight, he dropped back into the ocean of white-armored bodies and worked his way down the wide corridors and walkways to the maze of service passages that led to lesser-known landing platforms.

Mereel knew every meter of the complex. Skirata had encouraged the Nulls to run wild as kids, much to the disgust of the Kaminoans. He looked into the cloud-locked sky, and rain hammered his visor like shrapnel.

"Ready, *Kal'buir*," he said. "Get me out of this *dar'yaim*."

Republic special ops freighter TIV Z766/2, Cato Neimoidia portal, Hydian Way, 461 days after Geonosis

"This wasn't in the op order," said Atin. "We were supposed to sabotage the factory and return to base."

Prudii had ordered the traffic interdiction vessel to Neimoidian space. The pilot didn't seem worried. TIV pilots never did.

"I know," said Prudii. "But this is all about *presentation*."

"Even this TIV can't take on an armored transport."

"You sound scared, *ner vod*. Look at me. No helmet. Would I take a risk without my suit sealed?"

Atin considered showing Prudii where he could dock his character assessment the hard way. "But it's not unreasonable to ask why you're presenting a target to the Seps just to get a few thousand droids that are probably from a spiked batch anyway." He paused for a breath. *"Lieutenant."*

"No need to stand on ceremony with me, *vod'ika*." Prudii shrugged. "We're all brothers. Even those unimaginative Alpha planks, Force bless 'em. Why am I doing this? Emphasis, *ner vod*. Emphasis."

A small, bright spot grew larger in the viewport and resolved into a yellow-and-gray transport with horizontal spars picked out in scarlet. Prudii let it draw a thousand meters behind the TIV.

"Ready torpedoes," he said.

The pilot tapped the console. "Torps ready."

"Steady . . ."

The transport was accelerating slowly toward the jump point.

"On my mark . . ."

He was calculating blast range. Atin could see it.

"Take take take."

"Torps away."

A spread of six proton torpedoes streaked from the concealed tubes in the ship's underslung drive. The TIV shuddered. Atin reminded himself that his Katarn armor and bodysuit were space-tight for twenty minutes, and then realized help would be a lot more than twenty minutes away if anything went wrong. It always was—why did they bother? But Prudii didn't have his helmet on. Either he was confident or he was mad, and being a Null meant he was probably both.

The first and second warheads punched one–two into the transport's starboard flank in a blaze of gold light. Atin didn't see the rest strike because the TIV accelerated from standstill to way-too-fast in a matter of seconds, heading for the jump point. It was definitely emphatic.

Stars stretched and streaked before them as the TIV went to hyperspace and left the stricken transport far behind. Prudii wasn't even waiting to confirm a kill. He smiled as the acceleration leveled out and the TIV settled steady again. The pilot yawned. Atin said nothing.

"You're going to tell me what an *or'dinii* I am for pulling that stunt, aren't you, *ner vod*?" asked Prudii.

"Pointless bravado." If he took offense, Atin was ready to swing at him. "Reckless, even."

"But it's what the GAR would do if it came across a droid transport and didn't know a lot of tinnies were already as good as useless, isn't it?" Prudii sounded as if he regarded the Grand Army as something separate and external. "I didn't bust my *shebs* around half the galaxy this past year so the Seps could work out that their tinnies were already sabotaged. So it's worth the risk to make it all look real. If we

don't take a pop at them whenev
wonder why."

Atin dealt in the measurable and
deconstruct to find out how they w
could build. He was trained in camo
But the world that the Nulls moved in,
was a nebulous haze of bluff and coun
thought he had the hang of it, they'd de
obvious in hindsight but hadn't occurred   e time.

"You think they're that smart?"

"I never underestimate the enemy," said Prudii. "Especially when I'm not sure who the enemy is." He tapped the pilot's shoulder. "Drall RV point, my good man, and make it snappy."

"You Null boys are my favorite fares," said the pilot, and yawned again. "Never a dull moment."

Republic special ops shuttle, uncoded, en route from
Kamino to Drall RV point, Corellian space, 461 days
after Geonosis

Mereel swung through the hatch into the crew bay, and Skirata gave him a playful tap on the ear with the flat of his hand.

"Don't do that again," said Skirata. "If those gray freaks had caught you, they'd have *reconditioned* you."

"They might have *tried.*" Mereel caught Ordo narrowing his eyes in disapproval: *Kal'buir* was *not* to be distressed, ever. "Anyway, this could well be worth it."

Safe from detection even by the Republic, they sat in the crew cabin of the unmarked shuttle and pored over the data from Mereel's haul while they waited for Omega and Prudii to rendezvous. They watched the files play out on Ordo's datapad like the latest holovids while the Treasury software from oh-so-helpful Agent Wennen flagged the most heavily encrypted files and those that had been subject to secure erasure.

almost joking when he keyed in the search pa-
alpatine." It was always worth seeing if there was
out key politicians in any files he sliced, just in case,
he didn't expect to find anything.

But he got it.

"Osik," he cursed.

"Problem?" Ordo nudged him.

"Maybe." Mereel stared at a triple-encrypted file that
yielded to the Treasury software. But it wasn't a message or
a datafile; it was a copy of a holotransmission.

He hit the key. It was a frozen holo of Lama Su. Fierfek, it
was the Kaminoan Prime Minister, and he appeared to be
talking to Chancellor Palpatine.

Skirata swallowed audibly. "Now, this is where life gets a
bit dangerous."

But they watched, transfixed, as the shimmering blue
image of Lama Su sprang to life from the datapad emitter.

*"If you require more clones beyond the current order, then
you must authorize us to begin further production immediately. An initial payment of one billion credits . . ."*

There was a crackling pause: Palpatine's response wasn't
recorded, but it was clear he had interrupted. Lama Su's head
bobbed in annoyance.

*"We must make it clear that the current Kamino contracts
terminate in two years. Apart from the special facilities you
ask us to set up on Coruscant, Chancellor, you will have no
further clone production beyond the current three million
unless you commission more now . . ."*

There was nothing more. It appeared to be all that Lama
Su had filed, probably as some kind of personal insurance. If
the date was correct, the conversation had taken place some
months before.

"Shab," Skirata hissed. "What are they playing at?"

Ordo slowly raised his hand to his mouth. Mereel, who
thought he'd seen it all, revised his grasp of political subterfuge on the spot.

"So is the Republic going bust and not paying its bills?"
asked Ordo. "Or are we seeing something else?"

"Cloning facilities on Coruscant? General Zey never mentioned *that*."

"Maybe he doesn't know. There's a *lot* Zey doesn't know, after all . . . lots about us, for a start."

"How's the Chancellor going to pull *that* off?"

Skirata interrupted. "See what else you can find." He'd started chewing ruik root again, and Mereel gauged his anxiety by the speed of his jaw. He was going like a machine now. "I don't like this at all."

"If this is all the army we've got for the foreseeable future," said Ordo, "then we'll be overrun in two years."

"Unless Prudii's patent droid remover saves the day," said Mereel, stomach churning.

Why didn't I pick this up earlier?

All Nulls were adept spies, used to knowing more about the Republic's inner workings than the Senate itself. Mereel could even find out the smallest and most private details if he needed to, maybe even how many times Palpatine used the refreshers each day. He'd thought that no information escaped him. So being surprised by totally unexpected information left him uneasy and ashamed.

"How did I miss this, *Kal'buir*?" he said, feeling he had let the man down.

"You didn't, son," said Skirata. "You *found* it."

RV point, Drall space, Corellia sector, 462 days after
Geonosis

Prudii obviously hadn't seen Skirata in a long time. Atin watched, fascinated, as he turned instantly from glib cynic to adoring son, hugging Skirata with a clash of armor plates. He stood back, and Skirata patted his cheek, an indulgent grin spreading across his face.

"I have some interesting data for you, *Kal'buir*." The two ships hung linked together by a docking tube, a long way from either Republic or Separatist scrutiny. They gathered in the crew bay of the smaller TIV. It was a tight fit. "We're still not finding droid numbers like Intel claimed. We have to re-assess the nature of the Sep threat."

Atin thought Prudii just meant numbers. It was now obviously that the droid numbers were flawed to say the least. Atin would have been happy to just write that off as Republic Intelligence being *di'kute*—nobody with any sense expected intel to be accurate anyway—but it seemed to bother all three Nulls a great deal. Ordo and Mereel, their helmets stacked side by side on the deck like two decapitated heads, wore matching frowns of concern.

"Come on, this is supposed to be *good* news," said Atin.

Ordo shrugged. "Depends where the original estimate came from."

"But what if it turns out to be right?"

Mereel looked mildly exasperated. "If they had even one quadrillion droids, or a tenth of that, we'd know all about it—because they'd *use* them, and they'd invade Coruscant." He glanced at Skirata, as though waiting for permission to go on. Skirata shook his head. "Anyway, a factory processing more droids than that needs a *lot* of durasteel and parts, and we'd notice the traffic. We're not seeing quadrillion-ton shipments of ore, metal, or components."

"Then it's just Sep propaganda. Everyone talks up their troop strengths."

Atin simply couldn't see why it mattered. They had a better handle on the Sep droid numbers now, and a good strategy, for the time being, for making sure that the millions didn't count for anything like that number on the battlefield. He settled back into an alcove in the port bulkhead and inserted his test probes into the wafer's terminals. He just wanted to see the data for himself, or as much as he understood of it.

"We're fighting small fires all the time, all over the place," said Skirata. "Zey might think these numbers are good news, but it's like saying we're drowning in three meters of water instead of a hundred."

Atin hadn't been raised by Skirata like the rest of Omega Squad, but he knew the man well enough now to read his reactions. He was completely transparent with clones; he didn't seem to be able to deceive them, or even want to. "There's something you're not telling me, Sarge."

Skirata put his comlink on standby. "Yes, son, there is."

"So it *is* Grievous, then? Because if it is . . ."

"It's messy politics." Skirata—a contract killer, an accomplished thief, a man who diverted Republic resources whenever he felt like it—would never lie to his boys. He promised them that. "If you know about it, it might endanger you."

Atin wondered what might be more dangerous than being a Republic commando. It wasn't exactly a steady desk job. But he trusted Skirata completely, even if his curiosity was devouring him. "Okay, Sarge. Orders?"

"Get back to HQ with the TIV pilot and do a bit of skills transfer. Teach the rest of the lads how to make nice crumbly droids."

Ordo cut in. "And thank Besany Wennen for me, will you?"

Atin worked out that Prudii wasn't going back with him. "You're telling me to get lost, aren't you?"

"For your own good," said Skirata.

It had to be Grievous. For a moment Atin wondered if they didn't think he was good enough to go after the Separatist general with them, and then he started worrying for Skirata. Even with a bunch of Nulls, the old *di'kut* would be insane to try to tackle him. And Atin had no intention of walking away if that was on the agenda.

"Straight question, Sarge."

"Don't put me on the spot, *At'ika*."

"Are you going after Grievous? 'Cos if you are, I'm not leaving."

"No, we're *not* going after Grievous."

Atin scrutinized his face. "Okay, Sarge. Be careful, anyway. Whatever it is."

He climbed back through the hatch to rejoin the TIV pilot. Most of the time, he really didn't need or even want to know what the Nulls got up to. Or Skirata, for that matter. He just didn't want to lose any more brothers.

And even if he worked out what was going on, it wouldn't change his job one bit.

RV point, Drall space, 462 days after Geonosis

"Okay, what's your assessment?" Skirata prepped the secure link to General Zey back at headquarters. "What are we going to tell him?"

Ordo shrugged. "Nothing about the holorecording—yet."

"We'd be failing in our duty if we didn't advise him to change tactics, though," said Mereel. "Again."

"You know it's not his decision."

"But it's still our duty."

Skirata frowned and opened the secure link. The Jedi general seemed to have been caught on the hop—the holoimage showed him in his undershirt, hair disheveled.

"Another confirmation of droid production numbers, General," said Skirata. "Same as before. Worst scenario, maybe a few hundred million right now."

"That's better than we thought. I needed some good news. Successfully neutralized?"

"My lads are completely reliable."

"I know."

"We think . . . look, it's pretty clear from what we're seeing that we're facing small-scale conflicts in waves. If we concentrated all our forces on completely overwhelming them a sector at a time, instead of scattering our troops across a thousand fronts, we could break the Seps a lot faster."

Zey chewed his lip. "I hear what you say."

"A big push. Consolidate our forces and hit 'em hard, then move on when they're crushed and hit the next sector. This piecemeal approach is just damping down fires temporarily."

Mereel waited for Zey's reaction. The Jedi looked tired. It was hard to find anyone in the Grand Army who didn't look in need of a week's sleep.

Zey dropped his voice to a near whisper. "I agree, militarily. General Windu reminds the Chancellor of this proposal whenever he can. The answer's always the same. Palpatine thinks it'll be seen as excessive force and might alienate the neutral worlds."

Mereel had no patience with politics. "Tell him we're feeling pretty alienated right now, too."

"I understand your frustration, Lieutenant."

"What does he say about the droid numbers, then?"

Zey shrugged. "He believes that underplaying the threat might be foolhardy."

"Always easier to get the voters to foot the bill for a war if they think the enemy's about to invade, eh? Is that why Republic Intel came up with the quadrillions figure?"

"You're a cynical man, Sergeant."

"Yeah. I was a merc for too long."

"I never said you were wrong."

"Okay, General," said Skirata. He managed to sound irritated. Zey knew the game by now; the two of them conducted a coded conversation, both knowing what the other really felt. Mereel admired their pragmatism. "We haven't found the hub of the Seps' droid production. I assume you'll want us to carry on looking."

Zey sounded older these days. "The Chancellor is most insistent."

"Understood, General."

Skirata closed the link and stared through Mereel for a moment. Then he focused on him again. "Palpatine doesn't want to talk about the real numbers. Clone production on Kamino looks like it might stop dead in a couple of years. I say the objective of this war isn't the one we're being told it is."

"You sound like you expect politicians to tell the truth, *Kal'buir.*"

"Nah, I'm not *that* senile yet." Skirata gestured to Ordo for his datapad, fingers beckoning. "We're bringing the plan forward a little, lads. I'm marking a date on my calendar just under two years from now, and making sure we're ready to take care of our own by then. You understand me?"

"Understood," said Mereel. Skirata had what he called an exit strategy: his plan for the end of the war, not just for himself, but for the Nulls . . . and maybe any clone who found himself out of a job. "Okay, *everybody* looks for Ko Sai now."

"What about Grievous?"

Ordo handed the datapad to Skirata. "Last time Kom'rk got a fix on him, it was leaked information. Someone wants us to find him. Until we work out who and why, we keep a little distance."

"Works for me," said Mereel.

Wars often didn't make sense. He'd read plenty of history, and he'd absorbed *Kal'buir*'s lessons: politicians often made decisions that flew in the face of professional military advice. Whatever the Republic was up to, a long-running war of skirmishes suited Palpatine's purpose.

But it didn't suit Mereel. And it didn't do the mounting numbers of clone casualties any good, either. He felt no guilt whatsoever about using the taxpayers' credit to get the best outcome for himself and his brothers, both those in the field now and those to come.

Three million against . . . how many? Hundreds of millions. They were bad odds, but they weren't impossible, not with the Nulls and a few thousand commandos around. But working out odds meant being clear who the enemy was, and the more Mereel learned, the less certain he became.

"Cheer up," said Prudii. "Average kill rates are going up all the time. I reckon we can shoot for at least two hundred to one." He took a hand-sized slab of metal out of his pack and held it up with a grin. Then he smacked it down hard on the edge of the console. It crazed and broke into pieces. "Those tinnies just can't take the strain like we can."

No, those weren't impossible odds. Bad, maybe; but not impossible. Mereel sat back in the copilot's seat, took out his datapad, and began combing through the hidden data of Kamino's clonemaster. Ko Sai had the whole galaxy in which to hide, but she was hiding from men she had personally engineered to be the very best.

The odds weren't in her favor.

Read on for an excerpt from

DEATH STAR

by Michael Reaves & Steve Perry

Available now from Del Rey Books!

Grand Moff's suite, LQ Flagship *Havelon*

"**S**ir, there has been . . . an incident."

Seated behind his desk next to the panorama of his viewport, which occupied most of the wall to his right, Tarkin stared at the captain. "An incident?"

"Yes, sir. An explosion in the oxygen supply tanker arriving from the planet. It was just off the northeastern quadrisphere's Main Dock when it happened."

"How much damage?"

"Uncertain, sir. There is still a lot of debris flying about. The tanker was destroyed. Fortunately, most of the crew were only droids. A few navy beings and officers—"

"Don't address trivial matters, Captain. How much damage to the *station*?"

"So far, what we know for sure is that the dock portal and bay took the brunt of the explosion. Our security teams can only guess at—"

"Then do so."

The captain looked uneasy. Officers had been sent to the front for lesser offenses than delivering bad news, and he knew it. No doubt this was why the admiral in charge of security had not come to deliver the report himself.

"Sir, both the portal and dock are demolished. The bay is a mass of twisted girders and ruptured plates. Easier to tear it apart and start from scratch than to repair them."

Tarkin would have spoken aloud the curse that rose from his throat had he been alone. But of course, a mere captain could not be privy to such utterances from a Grand Moff. He simply said, "I see."

"Emergency construction teams have arrived and are doing an assessment," the captain continued. "A full report will be tendered as soon as possible."

Tarkin nodded. Outwardly, he was calm, collected. His voice was cool and even as he said, "I want the cause determined, Captain. Without delay." A millimeter below the surface, however, he was seething with rage. How *dared* anyone damage a single bolt, or rivet, or weld of his station!

"Of course, sir," the officer replied.

"If it was a failure due to someone's error, I want to know. If it was sabotage, I will have the entire life history—or histories—of whoever caused it, and the name of the senior officer who slipped up and allowed it to happen."

"Yes, sir."

"You are dismissed, Captain."

"Sir!" The captain saluted, turned, and departed, a lot quicker on his feet than when he'd arrived.

Tarkin stood and stared through the viewport at the infinite blackness, shot with points of light. So cold and empty out there. Well, before too long it would be fuller, by an infinitesimal degree, with the frozen and contorted body, or bodies, of whoever was responsible for this outrage. Retribution would be swift and certain. That was the only way there would be even a remote possibility of making other would-be saboteurs think twice about committing a similar heinous act.

At times like this, he wished Daala were here. Clever, beautiful, and utterly ruthless when the situation demanded it, she could be most diverting—a great relief for a man such as himself, beset on all sides as he was with weighty problems. But the only female admiral in the Imperial Navy was still stationed at the Maw with her four Destroyers, protecting the hidden base where the battle station's plans and weaponry were in ongoing development.

Abruptly, Tarkin made a decision. He waved his hand over the comm on his desk.

"Sir?" came the immediate query from his aide.

"Is my ship prepared?"

"Of course, sir." The aide's tone was polite, but with just a bit of surprise to indicate what an unnecessary question it was.

"Meet me at the flight deck."

"Yes, sir." Cautiously: "Might one ask where we are going?"

"To inspect the damage to the battle station from the explosion. I want to see it for myself."

"Yes, sir."

Tarkin stood, feeling a glow of fierce satisfaction. He had not always been a desk-bound commander. He had spent plenty of time in the field. Now and again it served the rank and file to know that he was still capable of getting his hands dirty—or bloody, depending on the situation.

Grand Moff's lighter, 0.5 kilometer from Death Star

"Look to the forward viewport, sir," the pilot said.

Tarkin, who had been poring over a schematic hologram of the station that showed where the damage was, turned and stared through the port at the real thing.

It was indeed a mess. It appeared as if a giant hand had smashed the dock, then petulantly ripped sections of it loose and flung those into space. Debris of all sizes and shapes whirled and tumbled aimlessly, not having had time yet to settle into any sort of orbit.

Tarkin's expression was pinched tight in anger, but his voice was level as he said, "Bring her around and let's have a closer look."

"Sir." A pause. "There's a lot of debris, sir."

"I can see that. I suggest you avoid running into it."

The pilot swallowed drily. "Yes, sir."

As the pilot began to swing the small cruiser into a wide turn, Tarkin's aide approached.

"Yes, Colonel?"

"The forensic investigation team has a preliminary report, sir."

"Really? This soon?"

"You did indicate a desire for alacrity, sir."

"Indeed." Tarkin offered the colonel a small, tight smile. "Hold off on the flyby," he instructed the pilot. "I'll take the report here."

"Sir." The pilot was visibly relieved at this.

A moment later, the holoprojector lit over the command console at which Tarkin stood, displaying a one-third-sized image of a security force major standing at attention.

"Sir," the major said, giving a military bow.

Tarkin made an impatient gesture. "What do we have, Major?"

The major reached off-image to touch a control, and a second holoimage blossomed next to him. It was that of an Imperial gas tanker. As Tarkin watched, the images grew larger and translucent as the point of view zoomed closer. A flashing red dot appeared toward the rear of the ship, and the POV zoomed in closer still to reveal the interior of the vessel.

"From the dispersal pattern of the ship's interior and hull, which we backtracked by computer reconstruction, the source of the explosion was here—" The officer pointed into the hologram, only his hand and pointing finger becoming visible in the blown-up image before Tarkin's eyes. "—in the aft cargo hold. The precise location was plus or minus a meter of the pressure valve complex on the starboard tank array."

"Go on."

"Given the size of the tanks and the pressure—the oxygen is liquefied, of course—and the estimated explosive potential and expansion, we have calculated that a leak and subsequent accidental ignition of expanding gas in an enclosed compartment is highly unlikely to have produced the level of damage recorded."

Tarkin nodded, almost to himself. "Sabotage, then," he said. "A bomb."

"We believe so, sir." The image zoomed back out to encompass the major again. "We have not yet recovered parts of the device itself, but we will."

Tarkin gritted his teeth, feeling his jaw muscles bunch. He made an effort to relax, giving the major another of his tight smiles. "Congratulate your team on their efforts thus far, Major. I am pleased with your efficiency."

"Thank you, sir." The man smiled.

"But don't pat yourselves on the backs too much just yet. I want to know what kind of bomb it was, who made it, who planted it—everything."

The major stiffened again. "Yes, sir. We will report as soon as we have new information."

"You're already late with it," Tarkin said. "Dismissed."

The holo blinked off, and Tarkin stared into the blank space that was left, as if looking for answers. Sabotage was, of course, to be expected. This wasn't the first time it had happened, and it almost certainly would not be the last. A project this size, no matter how tight the security, was impossible to keep entirely hidden. An astute observer could gather a number of disparate facts from far-flung sources—shipping manifests, troop movements, vessel deployments, and the like—and from those, if he had even the cleverness of a sunstroked Gungan, deduce some general ideas. He might not know exactly what, or precisely where, but he could figure out that something big was being constructed. And with sufficient resources, time, and cunning, this being, and others like him, could discover a trail that led back to this system and this station.

There were shrewd beings among the Rebels; Tarkin had no doubt of that. And there were, more than likely, Rebels among the human detritus down on the prison planet. Perhaps even traitors among the Imperial Navy or troops.

A very tight lid was being kept on this project. Communications had been, and continued to be, squeezed tighter than a durasteel fist. But *somebody* had blown up that cargo ship, and had not done so just because they were bored and had nothing better to do.

Such travesties could not be abided. Nor would they be.

Refreshed from his time in the hyperbaric chamber, Darth Vader once more contemplated his unique fate. He had become accustomed to what he was, for the most part. It was hard, after all these years, to even visualize the face of Anakin Skywalker, Jedi Knight. But that was as it should be. Skywalker was dead. He'd been killed on the bank of one of the lava rivers of Mustafar, and the Sith Lord Darth Vader had risen from his ashes.

He became once again aware of his breathing, and the demand-respirator sped up as he let the dark side take him, let it envelop him in anger and hatred. The power of the Force flowed into him, filling him, fueling his rage. It was, as always, his choice: he could absorb the dark energy, keep it pent within him, a no-longer-quite-human capacitor that could discharge it anytime, directing it toward anyone or anything. Or he could let it flow through him now, be not the vessel but the conduit, and thereby find momentary surcease from the fury that was always so much a part of him.

He decided on the latter.

He left his lightsaber clipped to his belt. Ordinarily he would have used it to practice on the dueling droids that had been specially designed and constructed to test his mettle. Programmed with the knowledge and skills of a dozen different martial artists, and armed with deadly cutting or impact weapons, they were formidable opponents indeed, and had been an intregal part of Sith training since time immemorial. But not everything was about the lightsaber. There were other attributes, other weapons in his arsenal, that needed exercising as well.

Vader inhaled, holding the dry and slightly bitter air for as long as his scarred lungs could manage it. When he allowed the breath to be drawn from him by the respirator, he thrust his right hand toward a nearby mirror.

The aluminized densecris shattered into a thousand pieces, struck by the dark side as if by a metal fist.

Vader was aware of the "unbreakable" substance splintering and falling, tinkling onto the floor, myriad reflections sparkling in the light as they seemed to move in slow motion. At the same time, the Force alerted him to the presence of someone in the doorway behind him.

"Yes?" he said, without turning to look. He knew who it was by the greasy feel of the man's thoughts. Had he been unable to sense those, the mere fact that the intruder had come here to interrupt his exercises would have been enough to reveal his identity. No one else would dare.

"My lord," said Admiral Motti. "Grand Moff Tarkin requests a word with you."

Vader turned, surprised. Why would Tarkin seek an audience now? Yes, the man knew he was on the way to the construction site, but it was bad protocol to break comm silence.

Whatever the ostensible reason, it was a certainty that a hidden agenda lay behind it. Tarkin's deviousness could flummox a roomful of Neimoidian barristers, Vader reflected. Fortunately, the Force was a most useful tool against such intrigue.

Without a word, Vader swept past the admiral and headed for the privacy of his quarters. Motti's mind was not weak, but the emotions roiling beneath the calm exterior made his thoughts easy enough to sense: could he have struck Vader dead in that moment, he would have. The man's mind was a cauldron of seething anger, of hatred and envy, most of which was directed toward Vader. A pity Motti had no connection to the Force, the Dark Lord mused. He could have proved most useful.

"**L**ord Vader," the holo of Tarkin said. The greeting and the slight bow with it were stiff and formal. The image was full-sized, if a bit transparent and fuzzy, occupying the holo plate in Vader's anteroom as if the governor were standing before him.

Vader studied the simulacrum. Whatever the issue was that had prompted Tarkin to call, it wasn't a small one. The man's face was even more dour and saturnine than usual.

"Grand Moff Tarkin," Vader said. He made no effort to disguise an edge of contempt for the title. The military did love its pecking order.

Tarkin wasn't a man to dally with pleasantries; he got straight to the point. "There has been an explosion on the battle station—sabotage. Significant damage."

"And . . . ?"

"We have determined several suspects in its cause."

"And . . . ?"

"Our medical teams have not yet received the first supply shipment of mind-probes."

Vader nodded. "I see. You wish me to examine these suspects."

"Yes. If there are any preparations you need to make, speed is of the essence. It is paramount that we determine who caused this incident, and why, and deal with it force-fully."

"I need no preparations. My ship will arrive in a few hours. I shall speak to the prisoners as soon as I board your vessel. Have them ready. I will determine who among them are responsible."

Tarkin gave him another crisp military nod. "We look forward to your visit, Lord Vader."

Vader gestured for the comm unit to disconnect without responding. *Yes,* he thought. *I'm sure you do.*

This was most interesting news. If the Rebel Alliance was

responsible—and who else could it be?—this action certainly gave the lie to the official image of the dissidents as disorganized rabble posing no real threat. Vader felt a small ember of satisfaction glow within him. He had known for some time that the malcontents were growing both in organization and in power. They had staged guerrilla raids on space stations and supply depots, had managed to obtain military matériel and warcraft from sympathetic industrial and shipyard designers, and had allied themselves with many alien species, playing upon the latters' resentment at being reduced to inferior status in the eyes of the New Order. They were more than just a motley collection of wild-eyed idealists; they now numbered among their ranks former Imperial strategists, programmers, and technicians, and their network of spies was growing more intricate daily. They were scum, true enough, but enough scum could clog any system, even one as complex and pristine as the Empire.

They had to be dealt with, and they would be. This Death Star of Tarkin's could be effective to a degree, but one need not use a proton torpedo to swat a fire gnat.

Vader turned and left his chambers. The dark side would tell him who the miscreants were—tell him, and deal with them as well.

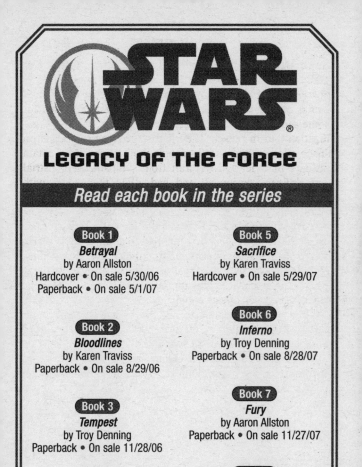

STAR WARS®

LEGACY OF THE FORCE

Read each book in the series

Book 1
Betrayal
by Aaron Allston
Hardcover • On sale 5/30/06
Paperback • On sale 5/1/07

Book 2
Bloodlines
by Karen Traviss
Paperback • On sale 8/29/06

Book 3
Tempest
by Troy Denning
Paperback • On sale 11/28/06

Book 4
Exile
by Aaron Allston
Paperback • On sale 2/27/07

Book 5
Sacrifice
by Karen Traviss
Hardcover • On sale 5/29/07

Book 6
Inferno
by Troy Denning
Paperback • On sale 8/28/07

Book 7
Fury
by Aaron Allston
Paperback • On sale 11/27/07

Book 8
by Karen Traviss
Paperback • On sale 3/04/08

Book 9
by Troy Denning
Hardcover • On sale 6/03/08